THE SLEEPER

Also by J. Robert Janes

The St-Cyr and Kohler Mysteries

Mayhem

Carousel

Kaleidoscope

Salamander

Mannequin

Dollmaker

Stonekiller

Sandman

Gypsy

Madrigal

Beekeeper

Flykiller

Bellringer

Tapestry

Carnival

Clandestine

Non-Fiction

The Great Canadian Outback

Geology and the New Global Tectonics

Earth Science

Rocks, Minerals and Fossils

Airphoto Interpretation and the Canadian Landscape
(with Dr. J.D. Mollard)

Thrillers

The Hunting Ground

The Alice Factor

The Hiding Place

The Third Story

The Watcher

The Toy Shop

And for Children

The Rolly Series

Danger on the River

Spies for Dinner

Murder in the Market

Also: *Theft of Gold*

The Odd-Lot Boys and the Tree-Fort War

THE SLEEPER

J. ROBERT JANES

MYSTERIOUSPRESS.COM

OPEN ROAD

INTEGRATED MEDIA

NEW YORK

Cover design by Madeline Clark

978-1-5040-2218-7

Published in 2015 by MysteriousPress.com/Open Road Integrated Media, Inc.
345 Hudson Street
New York, NY 10014
www.mysteriouspress.com
www.openroadmedia.com

To my memory of Len Cunningham,
who taught at North Toronto Collegiate Institute.
Always immaculately dressed, he would, while having to
monitor a school dance, appear with the most gorgeous
of women. Unlike the rest of the teaching staff who
walked to work, came by bus, or in older model cars,
Len drove a brand-new sports car as immaculate as
himself and invariably with the top down.

Author's Note

The Sleeper is a work of historical fiction. Though actual places and times have been used, these may have been slightly altered. Occasionally the name of a real person appears for historical authenticity, but all are deceased and the story makes of them what is demanded. The few words and phrases in German have very kindly been vetted by Dr. Schutz of Brock University, the bits of French, by Dr. Dennis Essar of Brock, but should there be any errors, they are my own and a sincere apology is extended.

THE SLEEPER

Sleeper: an enemy agent who secretly lies among us until awakened

1

In the eddying dust of the Lower Fifth, time stood still. Grantley's was not one of the 'best' schools, just one of the 'better.' Pale shafts of amber shot among the emerald, ruby and lapis at the tops of tall, leaded windows, and the lingering fluff of the ages mingled with these and became one.

'Please, sir, was it a sabre you used or a rapier?'

'I heard you, Tom. No need to buzz my ear again.'

'Yes, sir. Sorry, sir.'

'Bill, what's a sabre?'

The question, like cannon shot, whistled from the master's lips without a turning of his head. Stricken, Bill stood riveted to his desk. 'A sabre's a . . . a cavalry sword with a long, curved blade, sir.'

Still, Mr. Ashby, the American, the ex-cavalry officer, ex-captain, ex-whatever, didn't look at him or at *any* of them, thought Bill. Just the playing field. It was always that or the Quantock Hills beyond. Peachey, they called him—not to his face, mind, but he knew, they were certain. Peachey or Dan, from *The Man Who Would Be King* by Rudyard Kipling. The argument still raged. It hadn't been settled. Not yet.

'And a rapier, Bill?' asked Mr. Ashby with just the corner twist of a faint, sad smile. All the other masters called them by their surnames. Only Peachey called him Bill or Billy, but was *Goat* ever implied on those latter occasions?

Guilt made Bill's face grow crimson. 'A . . . a rapier's a light, slender sword, sir.' *Rapière*, in the French, some of the older boys insisted, but to seize and carry off by force, they maintained. To rape!

'Used for *what*, Billy?'

Oh no . . . 'For . . . for thrusting, sir. It's . . . it's also called the small sword.'

Captain Ashby uncrooked the stiff leg and turned at last to face them. Peachey *knew* what it was all about, felt Bill, it only increasing the sadness, for Peachey was certain the Germans were going to go on the rampage again, but had he really been there before or was that all a sham as some of the older boys claimed?

Twenty-two pairs of eyes met his own, thought Ashby, knowing this doubt in their minds had gone on far too long. Like boys everywhere, they fed themselves on war and adventure and he had encouraged this because they had then worked for him, and he had known they would. A game.

'I used a sabre,' he said. 'A rapier wouldn't have been suitable, but if you want the truth, I used my revolver far more.'

Revolvers, geezus, crikey, guns blazing as that bloody great black stallion of his had leapt the trenches!

On Saturday, he took seven of them for a hike across the hills, they to lead him to a patch of woods and a dip in the land, a clearing. There was a melon perched atop a sharpened stake, it having all the aspects of a truth vehemently denied and voraciously lampooned.

'Would you show us please, sir?' asked Jackie Peterson, the littlest one, whose father owned a string of hotels and seaside resorts and wore a diamond stickpin in his tie.

Tom—Thomas Barclay Finch—had the sabre. Where he had acquired it and how he had kept it hidden ought to remain secrets for ever, thought Ashby, but said, 'Why do you want me to do this?'

Bill Hamilton took the lead. 'Please, sir. Just to settle the argument.'

'What argument?'

'About how fast you could . . . could kill a man with a sabre.'

'Me, Bill, or anyone?'

They stared at the ground and dug the toes of their scruffy boots into the dew-laden grass. 'You, sir,' came the confession, but from which of them he would never know, for the leaves of the beeches rattled in the early morning breeze. It was 21 May 1938, not even three months since the Wehrmacht had marched into Austria, less than two since 99.73 percent of those people had agreed to Hitler's plebiscite, fudged though that result must surely have been. 'I'm not a hero,' he said. 'You mustn't think that I am. In 1914, even before we went over, I was scared. Most men are. I wanted to piss in the worst way and each time we had to advance, I wished damned hard I could be anywhere else, but wasn't.'

They weren't listening, thought Ashby. Finch still held the sabre, clothed in its scabbard, point down at the ground, hands on the hilt. 'Was your father in the Great War, Tom?'

The eyes that were innocent at evensong wouldn't lift. The lips that could let forth a voice to raise the soul and spirits could barely pry themselves apart. 'N-No, sir. It . . . it was my great-grandfather's.'

'*The Charge of the Light Brigade*,' sighed Ashby.

Excitement leapt into the boy only to fade as Tom said, 'Yes, sir. The Crimea, sir. He never came back. We only got the sword.'

The siege of Sevastopol, the Battle of Balaclava, 1854, Florence Nightingale, England and France joining Turkey against the Russians. He had got them to study that poem of Tennyson's as part of a history lesson.

Taking the sabre from Finch, he raked the sword from its scabbard so hard and fast it sent shock waves through them. Not content, he came to stand before each, and like the man they thought or didn't think he was, he sadly fingered their necks one by one.

'It's swift!' he said to Bill, who leapt in alarm.

'It can't hurt. You wouldn't feel it, not for a millisecond,' he said to Mark Abrahams, whose father owned a chain of ladies' hat-and-hosiery shops.

Trapped in their broken circle, his eyeglasses winking in the sun, he placed that stiff right leg forwards a little, the sabre bringing a startled cry from them as the melon split in half, the halves into quarters, and some of those into slices from which the seeds and juice spattered at them like brains, blood and guts!

'God,' said one; 'Crikey,' another. 'Wait till I tell my old man'; and yet another, 'I'm gonna be sick.'

Ashby swore them all to silence by laying the dampened blade on each of their tousled heads.

The sun was setting now, and Ashby was glad the day was done. Down over the fields and hedgerows, tucked away behind the hills and screened by oaks, Grantley's stood solid enough, a reminder always. There was no sign of the playing field, none of an upper window, for they'd spy on him if they could, whispering, 'He's gone into the hills again.' 'Where . . . where's he go?' 'Don't know. The Benedictine abbey, I think.' 'That abbey, it's . . . it's haunted. He wouldn't go *there*.'

But he might, and they would say, 'He's angry with himself for having shown us that. Now Tics will dress him down and let him go at end of term—he'll have to! Give him the sack, he will.'

'Scared . . . He must really have been scared. It must have been awful.'

How could they know? How could he even hope to make them see the truth? Their Tics wouldn't fire him, not for that. Poor Tics. Anthony had been such a part of it.

As the plum dark folds of the highest Quantocks drew the shadows, Ashby watched the moorland heather on the uppermost flanks and gradually, in the softness of the coming night, the ruined wall beneath his hands grew cold and damp.

After those first few sorties, they hadn't used sabres or revolvers. Most had used Lee-Enfields and had ridden to their new positions in single file, had picked their way through the mud and ever-present fog that had reeked of burnt metal, death and cordite, and only later on, the mustard gas. Up each gentle rise they had gone, never really knowing what was beyond or waiting for them. The wreckage of overturned field guns, gun carriages, shell casings and bomb craters, into which the trenches had collapsed and been filled with mud, dead and timbers, had been everywhere. And now the whole mad, stupid business, not even twenty-five years later, was about to start up all over again and Britain, never mind anywhere else, was tragically ill prepared.

When the boys, still at their windows, heard the engine of his MG start up, the front door of Headmaster House suddenly opened, spilling a pool of light onto the metalled drive as the car shot past and went out through the gates, Bill Hamilton sucking in a ragged breath. 'He's going west again, down into Cornwall. You can bet he is.'

'What's he do down there?' asked Jackie Peterson.

No one knew because Peachey hid that from everyone. A last glimpse revealed the headmaster standing in that doorway looking old and defeated, but they hadn't another thought for him.

'Peachey's on opium,' said Thomas Barclay Finch. 'He eats it like in *The Count of Monte Cristo*.'

'D'you mean, in a jelly?' asked Spider Lawson. 'With a little silver spoon?'

'Right you are, old duffer. Stuff's emerald green, like mint jelly. Tastes sweet and you don't even know there's opium in it.'

'Hashish . . . I think it was hashish, but they called it "hatchis,"' said Bill.

'It's 'cause of his leg,' said someone.

'Opium,' sighed Tanner Biggs.

'And women,' said Finch. 'He's got a woman down there somewhere. You can bet he has.'

The photograph on the mantelpiece in Headmaster House was of Ashby and Anthony, and when the latter had closed the door and come back into the sitting room, Mrs. Ruth Pearce stiffened, her thumb hesitating on the frame. 'Where's he gone this time?' she asked, her voice tight.

'I don't know,' said Anthony. 'If I did, I wouldn't tell you. His private life is his own.'

Tics, the boys all called this *husband* of hers. 'Since when does any of us have a private life?'

Still she wouldn't turn to face him, thought Anthony. Ruth wasn't what one might call pretty—that had gone ten years ago. Of medium height, with straight, shoulder-length, mouse-brown hair, she was cold to some, distant to most, and warm only to the infrequent few who broke down the barriers of what? he wondered. Shyness perhaps. A reserve. . . .

The chunky hips and seat matched the rounded shoulders, and the dark green woollen pullover and tartan skirt went with the brogues. A headmaster's wife, that was all she would ever be, but had she really wanted any of it? Her grandfather had founded Grantley's using the bulk of an estate that, if it had been invested wisely, might have brought a considerable dowry. Her father had seen the school through some good and desperate times only to pop off and put an end to the agony of a carping, backwards vision.

'You ought really to let him go,' said Ruth. 'He can't be tearing off like that every time he gets a notion—what puts those notions into his head?'

Again Anthony didn't answer, she hearing him take up the decanter, hearing its insane rattling against the tumbler, the Scotch neat. 'Why don't you stop avoiding the truth?' she asked. In the photograph they had looked handsome in their uniforms, young, virile and dashing, early September 1914, the Salisbury Plain, the Royal Horse Guards, the Blues. Ypres, then, in late October, and a life she hadn't shared, having only just become engaged to Anthony.

The separate beds had been Mummy's idea. Later, the separate rooms had been his. David Douglas Ashby had been tall and lean and very different, with smashing grey eyes that had made her heart wonder if she shouldn't be loving him instead. His cheeks had been newly shaven and so smooth she had wanted desperately to touch them. The ghost of a tan, though, had made her wonder about his background, skeletons in the closet and all that, not Salisbury and the sun. How wrong she had been, for when Ash smiled, it was still always with his eyes first, and everyone, even herself, instantly would feel that warmth and sincerity, but the *duplicity* too, she reminded herself.

Anthony had brought him home to the school in the late summer of 1934, home like a lost dog, pleased that he had been truant all that time, but saying so little of it, and yes, she had even been pretty then, and he might have been intrigued, but hadn't, and that probably had started her wondering about the two of them.

'Ruth, I can't let him go. Dave's a damned fine linguist in his own right. Picked it up, yes, but then he's had to. Darling, you know as well as I that if war comes Penfield will be called up. Grantley's will miss its first at Oxford, but I'll still have Ash.'

The troops in reserve, but *Darling*. Dear God, she wished he wouldn't call her that. 'His German's good, but it's only an option. You could remove it from the prospectus.'

'His French is excellent.'

'Spoken like a Belgian, not like a real Frenchman.'

'Must you continue to stare at the photograph?'

'Yes.'

'Dave thinks there'll be war.'

'Maybe there should be. Maybe then it would clean up the corruption.'

'I know it hasn't been easy.'

'Oh, do shut up! Set your finals or mark something. Summer's coming.' The end of term, the *end* of it all for another year, and Ash would be off again—out through the gates in that little car of his, *gone* before any of the boys had even left. Like as not his mortarboard and gown would be lying on the floor of his room, though she would never know, had never been in his room, had wished . . . Dear God, how she had.

After Christmas break, he had arrived back in a beastly snow-storm, not a touch of the flu or even a suggestion of a cold. He had been pleased with himself and had gone about the place cheering up the boys and getting them all into shape, and she had wondered what had made him so eager.

Easter break had come and he'd been out through the gates again, and they hadn't even had a card in the post. Then there it was, that frightful motor parked where it oughtn't to be on the green like a flare or a flag or a red badge of courage, and him out there playing rugger with that shattered leg of his and the boys all cheering him on.

There had been a street map of Cologne in the side pocket of the door on the driver's side. A house, an estate—God knows what—had been circled to the south, and not far from Brühl, and the odd thing was, someone had definitely been with him for at least part of the way. A very expensive cologne had been opened and accidentally spilled, drenching the mat. A tart? she wondered. Male or female?

'Ruth, why don't you sit down? If Ash isn't back for a couple of days, I'll see that his classes are covered.'

Still she wouldn't leave that photo, and Pearce knew he would have to get rid of it. Foolish to have kept it, really.

'Why is it you do so much for him?' she asked suddenly.

'I don't. Dave saved my life, that's all, and when I heard he was in Skiathos, I went to fetch him. An opportunity, if you like, and too good to miss. You know how well he gets on with the younger boys.'

They weren't into boys, weren't like that, thought Ruth. They couldn't be, but Ash had been living on next to nothing and wandering from ruin to ruin.

'Ruth, he needed help, and we needed a schoolmaster I could count on.'

In 1914, thought Ruth, David Douglas Ashby had been just a little taller than Anthony, whose jet-black hair had been parted on the left—still was for that matter—while Ash had worn his light-brown hair curly in rebellion. An American and therefore necessary to the cause, oh yes. Orders from the War Office, no doubt, or from the King himself, but a damned fine horseman, they had said. So good, in those times of need, their commanding officer had swallowed regimental pride and let him be.

And now, why now, he still wore his hair that way, it sprouting madly at times of scrum but receding a bit from a brow she had longed to touch. Still, there wasn't any grey and that was a puzzle, for Anthony's hair had been shot through with it when he'd come back ill from that war. Then, of course, it had made him look distinguished, a compromise. Now, well now, it just looked damned seedy.

Both of them were into eyeglasses, Anthony all of fifty and five years senior to his 'Ash,' who was still young at heart, though he looked for all the world in one of his business suits like a Chicago accountant on the run and breezy about it. Like the wind sometimes, the wind in her hair and freedom, damn!

Ash's face was strong, not finely boned and aristocratic like Anthony's. The nose had been broken. The skin . . . She *had* managed to feel it once, had run her fingers lightly along that lower jaw and down the length of that nose. Some silly thing, a comment of Ash's or her own, a dance whose tune she could no longer remember because she *hadn't* really been conscious of it, had been committed to Anthony but had begun to think seriously about Ash.

Was it in the eyes where the truth most lay? she wondered. Anthony had had the bluest of eyes in those early days, but at times, a mask even then and one that the war had only deepened and made more distant, while Ash's look was never masked, never empty, but was it pity that made him look at her the way he did sometimes?

Unbidden, Anthony laid a hand on her right shoulder, she flinching, not drawing away. Instead, she wondered what was happening to her and what had happened between the two of them. 'You were pretty boys in those days,' she said.

The acid all too clear, Pearce didn't quite know what to do or say, and kept his distance.

Some ten miles to the southwest of the school, Ashby waited by the side of the road in darkness. As the car that had been well behind his climbed into the Brendon Hills, the cone of its head-lamps touched the crowns of the trees and he knew for certain he had been followed.

Stepping behind the low stone wall, he watched the car come on to pass by the church, two men in the front, no one in the back, though he couldn't be certain, the car a Bentley four-door sedan, he thought. They would soon turn about, must have been waiting near the school, probably down by the bridge and near the draw-off to Wetherby Cottage.

Set against the cloud-hidden sky, the crenulated bell tower of the little Norman church was clear enough, the smell of the sea always in these hills. He could even hear the surf pounding in Blue Anchor Bay and off Watchet and Minehead, closer in, the crickets, but by heavens, it was lonely.

As though feeling the road ahead, the Bentley crept back, and when it reached the church, it drew to a stop, he hearing the doors open but not closing.

A torch came on, and from among the tombstones he saw their leather trench coats and fedoras as they eased the gate open and started up the walk.

'*Ach, der Amerikaner ist nicht hier, Kurt.* He will have gone back to the coast road.'

A Bavarian, thought Ashby, from Munich probably, a Brown Shirt perhaps, from the early days.

'Maybe yes, maybe no,' said the one called Kurt in *Deutsch*. 'I still think we will have a look round.'

A Prussian, that one. *Touristen*, both of them, they having stopped on the walk but now searching the lawn with that light of theirs. They would see where he had walked.

'Martin, *mein Lieber*,' said the one called Kurt, 'I think I know where that car of his must be.'

Retreating among the tombstones, Ashby tried to recall the layout of the churchyard. He had brought the boys here for a bit of history. Tanner Biggs and Jackie Peterson had made pencil rubbings of some of the inscriptions. A wagon track had wound its way among the canted stones, the ferns and towering oaks and beeches before heading back up to the church and his car. Again and again he watched the beam of that light and tried to remember.

Below the graveyard there had been a fence to keep the cattle out, beyond it, the patchwork fields of the Brendon Hills.

Steps sounded on the gravel. As the two men came together, one lit a cigarette, the other drawing what could only be a Walther P38, the standard issue *Polizeipistole*.

'*Gott im Himmel, Kurt*. Berlin has said no trouble.'

'*Ach*, there won't be any, not when he sees this and feels my hand.'

Together, walking quickly now, they made their way round the far corner, the light soon shining over the MG's bonnet to momentarily blind him, Ashby switching on the ignition, throwing the car into gear and ramming his foot down on the accelerator, scattering the two of them, the fusillade all too clear.

At Grantley's, on Sunday, it was Telford who first noticed the boys drifting off after dinner in twos and threes to some secret gathering ground as the rain came down in buckets, sheeting against the leaded glass of the masters' common room.

'I say, Banfield, old chap, do you think they've got one of the village girls tied to a tree or something? It's a regular circus!'

'Has it escaped your notice that I'm reading the *Times*, Assistant Headmaster?'

'Best go and find out, I suppose,' grumbled Telford, but he didn't. Lowering himself into a chair by the fire, he took up a copy of *Country Life* and began to browse petulantly, his mind still on the boys. Mischief . . . they were always up to mischief. Ashby bred that into them. Men like Ashby.

The fire began to smoke—water again, dripping down the chimney. He could hear each drop as old George Crawley, who taught a smattering of the classics, came in with fresh tea, waving pot and sugar bowl at all comers and saying darkly, 'The boys are up to something.'

Not a head was raised, Telford slapping down his magazine and unfolding himself to suddenly leave.

'Knew he would chase after them,' said Banfield, not lifting his eyes from the print. 'He and Goebbels are past masters at ranting. It seems the Czechs are in for a further mobilization, George. Dr. Goebbels doesn't think it right; Dr. Telford has to horn in on the poor boys' scant pleasures.'

'Tea?'

'Thanks. Don't mind if I do. A spot of whisky?'

'On a day like this?'

The rain poured off the edge of Telford's umbrella. His gumboots would squelch in the sodding grass, the two old friends standing at the windows watching their colleague until he disappeared from view.

In time Telford reached the glade, but all he found was a sharpened stake planted nakedly upright in the rain and a scattering of rinds, the flesh and seeds. Odd that, melons. Definitely out of season. Peterson . . . It would have to have been Peterson in the Lower Fifth. His father owned that beastly hotel in Blackpool where he had stayed last summer thinking he would get a good rate. Overcharged, that's what they had done to him. No sense of loyalty these days. None at all.

Now what the devil had happened here and why were the boys all so interested in it?

Up a rise, huddled amongst the bracken, that wretched boy Hamilton was watching him, and Finch . . . yes, Thomas Barclay Finch was there, too, both with pneumonia in the offing.

There's mischief here, thought Telford, but the heavens opened, the black cloth of his umbrella threatening to burst.

Ashby . . . It had to have had something to do with Ashby's having left the school again like a bolt of lightning.

Late on that Sunday, the car limped over the last of the heights and started down towards the sea. In the distance, Saint Ives clung to the shore, while all along the horizon the turbulent lead-grey clouds still sheeted out of the southwest.

Ashby drew off to the side of the road for a moment. He hadn't slept, hadn't shaved. Though the shops had been closed in Truro, he had, by banging on a back door, managed a pair of silver earrings and a charm bracelet, but those two with the *Polizeipistole* wouldn't stop. If they would wait for him outside the school, they would track him down here. The rocky cliffs and hidden coves of Cornwall had drawn him many times in the past, he automatically thinking of bringing her here, but then, too, Ewen and Monica had been living in Saint Ives and that had been handy. People he could trust to look after her, though they had refused any compensation.

It should have worked. It had every right to have done, but now fear plucked at him. Again he glanced behind. The road was narrow and winding, thrust between low stone walls of slate and turf overgrown with mosses and bordered by windswept fields, the gorse in bloom, the smell of it mingling with that of the sea.

Gulls rode the eddies inland. A cluster of ravens clung to the stunted whin, reminding him of the war, the ravens winging silently through the fog to alight on the tangled skeins of barbed wire that had made their nests before the broken trenches.

All too soon he was among the narrow, climbing streets and lanes, the quaint stone cottages that the artists had taken over as the fishermen had passed away. The years hadn't been kind, and with the decline of the fishing and the loss of the tin mines, Saint Ives had accepted artists and tourists alike as it had accepted poets and writers before them.

Everything, however, overlooked the harbour, where there was a wonderful sandy beach she would have loved. The parish church, Saint Ida's, dated from the fifteenth century. Several shops, a good lending library and a cinema offered diversion. There was even a choice of schools. She would have been happy once she had got used to the place.

He knew it had been too much to expect, yet didn't quite know what he could do about it, especially in the short term.

Monica MacDonald told him where she was, and he started off right away. Alone, Karen was standing at the very end of the quay, watching the tide go out as some of the sailboats and fishing smacks settled themselves on the bottom. The wind played havoc with her fair hair and made the light-blue dress flutter and cling to her slightly parted legs.

She didn't look his way when he called out, wouldn't turn, he saying, *'Liebling, ich bins.'* It's me.

There was no answer. Again using *Deutsch*, he said, 'Look, I know you wanted to be with me, but I couldn't take you to the school. There's only a room. It's not as if they have extra space.'

'They wouldn't understand, would they, *Vati*? They would think I was someone else's daughter.'

'How have things been?' he asked, feeling futile.

'Fine. They are fine.'

'Then why won't you look at me?'

'When I am ready. When you have been punished enough. *Vati*, I *don't* like it here. I *want* to go home.'

'Liebling, you can't. Those people are crazy. You know that as well as I. We discussed it.'

'Die Nazis, Vati? Das Volk?'

The people . . . 'Karen, I need you. I want us to be together.'

She flung herself at him and he held her close. She was only seven, and he knew she was terribly frightened and very confused, for her life had been turned upside down, but when they got back to the house, Ewen MacDonald didn't hesitate. *'Och*, it's na every day a father kidnaps his bairn, David. The lass is rightfully upset and you had best come t' grips wi' it. She needs her mother.'

'Ewen, please don' shout,' urged Monica.

'Kidnapped?' arched Ashby. 'Two years ago Christina and that father of hers stopped me from seeing my own daughter, Ewen. What else was I to have done?'

'Och, I know, Dave, but you canna fight nature,' said Ewen. 'Karen will na forget Christina and neither will that wife of yours forget Karen. You're the sore tooth. At least let her telephone her mother.'

'After what happened to me on the way here? Ewen, she'll *have* to be kept indoors until I can find another place.'

Stubborn, why th' bloody hell did David Ashby have t' be so stubborn? Abruptly MacDonald got up from the kitchen table, Monica turning away to fetch the tea and keep out of things. A drawer was soon slammed in the sitting room. A dozen letters, all in their envelopes and ready for the post, were tossed onto the table.

'We're aching, laddie,' said MacDonald. 'Aching like that wee girl you've caused us t' lie to. *Och*, aye, she's crept inta our hearts and we'd na like t' see her leave, but would will away Creation if it'd help.'

'Sit down, Ewen, please,' said Ashby. 'Monica, what about that tea?'

MacDonald glanced at his wife and saw her nod. Ashby picked up the letters and read the address: 'Fräulein Christina von Hoffmann.' *Fräulein*, not *Frau*, Ashby.

'All right, I'll telephone Christina when I get back to the school, and I'll try to talk some sense into her.'

'The child, David,' said MacDonald. 'Tell th' wee thing you'll take her home. It's what she wants.'

'I can't, Ewen, knowing what I do of what's been going on in the Reich.'

Monica slipped the cosy over the pot and glanced out the window. Karen was ignoring the cat she had so readily befriended and had allowed to sleep on her bed ever since. 'Put the letters away, David,' she said. 'Practice forgery if you must, but somehow answer them.'

The tea helped. There were scones too, and a bit of cheese to tide him over. For several minutes he made no further attempt to tell them what had really happened in the graveyard or why, again, he couldn't take Karen to the Reich. They were trying to understand, but what he'd done had defied everything by which they lived. Both wanted children of their own; both were from Inverness, Ewen, thirty-eight, Monica a year younger. She had been helping out at her father's guesthouse three summers ago when he'd chatted her up and tried to get her to go out. 'Oh, and aye, I would,' she had said, 'but there's someone you'd na want a rumble with.'

Ewen hadn't changed. Unlike Monica, he should have been born three hundred years ago.

'You're quiet,' said Ashby, looking up to see those lovely brown eyes watching him. 'Are you angry with me too?'

The long auburn hair had been braided into a rope that hung forwards over her right shoulder. Fingering the tea cosy, she glanced at Ewen for reassurance, then came to a decision of her own. 'David, she cries herself t' sleep and . . . *Och*, I canna speak the language, can I? Karen needs someone who can . . . someone younger than m'self if she's ever to cope wi' this.'

'Won't the other children play with her?'

Ewen let impatience get the better of him but she stilled him with a glance and said, 'It's her accent, the few words of English she knows. They think she's different, and they hear their parents talking of war. You know what children are like. *Och*, I've told her t' pay them no mind, but it's hard labour when you're young and in a strange place. I was thinking . . . There's a girl comes into town who speaks German. She might . . .'

'Is she German?' demanded Ashby.

Why hadn't he just said, *Damn you*? 'She isn't, and you mustn't hate them.'

'I don't. I just don't want her growing up among them, not now.'

'The girl speaks the language and very well, I think,' said Monica. 'Don' ask me why or how Mrs. Carne down at the post found out. I suspect a tourist came in asking t' mail something, and the girl just happened t' be there t' translate. She's . . .'

It was Ewen who said, 'David, don' be daft. The girl canna be working for th' Boches. They would have taken Karen by now.'

Still the thought wouldn't leave him. 'Where can I find her?'

Instinctively Monica laid a hand over his. She didn't answer for a moment, and Ewen didn't intrude. 'She's up in tha' old stone cottage of Blind William's.'

Ever since she had met the girl, Monica had known she would have to tell him. David and she had gone there once, alone. After Blind William had passed away, the cottage had been left empty. Ewen had been off to the Continent in the trawler, David having come down unexpectedly. Nothing had happened. Nothing, but Ewen still wondered. 'David, the girl shouldna keep t' herself in tha' place. Karen would like her. They'd get on. *Och*, I know they would.'

The cottage, of grey granite, was as Ashby remembered—one room with a flagstone floor, a plain wooden door, but newly painted white, as was the trim. Tucked into a fold in the land, a half mile from the road, it was below the crest of a gentle rise and back of cliffs that fell more than three hundred feet. Sweeping views of the sea were everywhere, while out over the moor, the gusting storm track sent ripples through the grass, the heather and the gorse to the top of a distant hill and the tall, stone chimney and forbidding ruins of an old tin mine.

There was a bicycle leaning against the cottage. Ashby let himself in at the gate in the turf-covered stone wall and, reaching the door at last, knocked quickly, wanting suddenly to get the whole business over.

There was no answer. He knocked again and then again. Going round the side, he gave a timid hello to the barren, weather-beaten privy from which no answer came.

She was down near the base of the cliffs, rooting about in an old boat shed among the overturned pilchard baskets and the forgotten nets. There was a clinker-built lifeboat just beyond her, and he had the idea that she was making her way towards it, but must have heard him, for she swung round and gave a startled gasp as he asked, 'Hilary?'

Warily she said, 'Yes, that's me.'

'My name's Ashby. Can we talk?'

Light from a gap in the floor of the loft above fell on her, but it wasn't much. Still wary, she seemed unable to answer, and he wondered then if she was afraid of being found out, but couldn't put a finger to that either.

Under an open dark-grey suit jacket, she wore a plain white shirt-blouse paired with grey trousers, the dark auburn hair cut short, parted high on the left and feathered back to curl behind the ears in a style reminiscent of the 1920s, and as he came on into the boat shed, she must have seen that she had no reason to fear him, for she said, 'Oh, sorry. I thought you were from . . . Well, it doesn't matter. What can I do for you, Mr. . . . ?'

'Ashby, David.'

Her dark brown eyes gave him the once-over, she waiting for him to tell her more.

'*Sprechen sie Deutsch?*' he asked.

'*Und Französisch*, Herr Ashby, but why do you ask? You're not one of them, are you?'

This last had been said with dismay, as if she had decided to accept him and was now angry with herself for having made too hasty a judgement.

'One of whom?' he asked in *Deutsch*.

'Ach, was zum Teufel wollen Sie?' What the hell do you want? 'The roof obviously needs repair,' she went on. 'The boat's had it—I'm sure it has. There's not a bloody thing worth selling in the place!'

'That boat's as sound as the day it was launched. The nets do need mending. There are lobster traps in the loft, if you'd care to take a look, or did some needy soul borrow them?'

Throwing him a curious look, she said suspiciously, 'You've been here before.'

Ashby found himself looking at her more closely until, at last, he answered simply, 'Yes, as a matter of fact, I have.'

'You're not the one with the little girl, are you?'

'Yes, but how did you . . .'

'There's talk. There always is in a small town like Saint Ives. Since I'm a part of that talk, I listen when I can. She's very pretty but terribly out of place and lonely. Did her mother die?'

He shook his head. 'Karen needs someone to teach her English. The other children are teasing her.'

That hadn't told her very much, thought Hilary, but asked, 'Will you pay?'

Startled, it was his turn to look curiously at her, he laughing at himself as he said, 'Yes, of course. Within reason, you can name your price. It'll only be until the end of term. During the holidays she'll be with me. I might even take her to the States.'

And a long way from here, but an American and a schoolmaster—yes, now that she looked closer, thought Hilary, she could see a bit of Mr. Chips, but the resemblance ended as swiftly as it had come.

Saddened by something she didn't define, she said, 'I work in the mornings until one or two, so anything after that is fine. Why not let her come and have a try, then we can settle on the fee.'

'I have to go back tonight. I only came down to see how she was. Would a fiver a fortnight do until we can talk again?'

Five pounds! 'Six. If you can let me have six, I won't need to sell the boat.'

Late on Monday, the car was there again, thought Ruth, it swung thoughtlessly in beside the playing field, but all banged up and dented, and Ash out there scrumming with the boys.

Anthony was standing on the sidelines watching them with Mr. Telford at his elbow and old George Crawley keeping his distance. The wind, the beastly wind, tugged at their gowns, threatening their mortarboards, they patently ignoring it. Talk was cheap, and talk into the wind, why nothing at all. He'd get off again—scot-free as usual. Ash could do anything he pleased. But had he and Tony ever been lovers? she wondered, as she had before. There had never been a hint of such a thing, of course, not from Ash, but some men *did* go both ways, hiding it from their wives, their mistresses or both.

The game broke up at last, and he came towards them with the gaggle all round him. One of the other boys ran out with a clean towel—Hamilton, it was that Hamilton boy, Bill.

Ruth leaned over the steering wheel and read the milometer—87373.4 and the second time round, or the third. He had driven well over five hundred miles that weekend. There were *two* holes punched as if by a cold chisel in the passenger's door, Telford's voice breaking her thoughts. 'I say, Ashby, old chap. What happened to the motor?'

The towel was wrapped round Ash's neck, he feigning surprise and nudging his eyeglasses back on the bridge of his nose as he said, 'What? Oh, the windscreen, Arthur. Got into a tangle with a hay wagon. Didn't see the blessed thing until it was too late. Went right under it and clear out the other side. Why, hello, Ruth. How are you?'

Wounded, Telford drifted off, muttering to himself and to Crawley probably, thought Ruth. Anthony just stood there looking futile. Ash could even ignore him and get away with it. A hay wagon, but he would have to be told. 'A woman was here asking for you,' she said. 'I told her you had been dismissed, but of course you haven't, have you?'

A woman . . . Christina? he wondered, but said, 'Who? What was her name? Did she . . .'

Stung. That had positively stung him, thought Ruth, the hand with the towel falling uselessly to his side. 'Did she *what?*' she asked, deliberately not sparing him.

He looked to the gates and the road beyond, then back to herself, he asking, 'Did she say what she wanted?'

'You, as I've only just said.'

'Why, then?' he asked, throwing a questioning glance at Anthony, making her wonder if there still wasn't something between them, something dirty.

Her gaze empty, she said, 'Why does any woman want a man?'

It would go on like this, as it always had, thought Ashby, Ruth baiting him if she could, he forced into a defensive position until silenced. 'Look, I don't know what you're implying, but I think I've a right to know who it was.'

'Daisy Belamy, that barmaid down at the Dogs of War, as if *you* didn't know. She's either pregnant or you've forgotten to pay your bill.'

Daisy? wondered Ashby. Why had she come to the school of all places? She didn't know anything of Karen and Christina, nor of the breakup of his marriage, didn't even know he was legally still married.

'Please, sir, what happened to the car?'

Ashby turned to find Bill waiting for his towel, the others now all gone. 'Do you know Bodmin Moor, Bill? Do you know it when the fog comes creeping in and the light of day leaves you wondering?'

'N-No, sir. I-I can't rightly say that I do.'

'Well, it happens to the best of us, Bill. Ended up on the moor. Pitch-dark it was. Couldn't see for piss and splashed my trousers. Then I heard it, crashing at my car and snorting wildly.'

'Wh-What, sir?'

'Some old duffer's prize bull—as for whose, I never did discover or I'd have had the creature shot for assault and battery!'

The horns . . . By crikey, they must have punched clean through the metal, even the gash in the petrol tank that was all bunged up with a rag, a wine cork and some moss. 'Mr. Telford said you had run under a hay wagon.'

Ashby lifted disappointment from the boy's shoulders. 'I did, but that was later. Look, I'd appreciate it if you wouldn't say anything about the moor. The accident was bad enough. You know how it is.'

2

Kapitän Joachim Burghardt heaved a sigh and gritted his teeth. Mondays were never his best and here it was 23 May already. The house on the Böttcherstrasse, in Bremen, was gabled, invoking art nouveau at every turn, the location a well-guarded secret. Some outsiders knew of it, of course, but with the way things were going, it would be best not to tell the world.

Wealth and privilege had always crept under his skin, no more now than in the days of the Kaiser. '*Ach*, I should be flattered by your visit, Fräulein von Hoffmann.' He gave a grimace, indicating the functional bareness of the office. 'But as you can see, you have me at a distinct disadvantage.'

The house had been 'bought' from its Jewish owners. 'AST-X Bremen is *not* to be comfortable, Kapitän. The harder the chairs, the harder you and your people will work.'

Leaning over the desk, he nudged rolled-up sleeves above his elbows, plunking brawny forearms atop the morning's signals and dispatches. 'Then perhaps, *mein liebes Fräulein*, you would be so kind as to tell me why AST-X Bremen, which does not even exist to citizens such as yourself, should undertake to rescue your daughter?'

'Have they not even gone over to England?' she asked.

Burghardt caught the flash of dismay, the toss of that tawny mane, a general's daughter. 'They?' he asked quietly.

The woman brushed the hair back from a temple, then smoothed the pleated off-white skirt over crossed knees. Again she asked if they had *not* gone over and he let her ask it, tempering the relish he felt with the caution of her connections.

'Werner was looking after it,' she said.

The crimson cardigan with gold buttons was just right for this season and the chic shops of the Damm, in Berlin, he noted. The knotted silk scarf—a Hermès from Paris, and perhaps a leftover from that husband of hers—gave the desired air of casualness, the plain gold earrings, that of the demureness of a schoolgirl, something she definitely wasn't, those honey-brown eyes of hers, something else again.

AST-X Bremen ran the Abwehr* agents in the British Isles now that the confusion of past years had all but been eliminated by reorganization under the iron fist of one desk, Bremen and himself.

'Werner Beck, ah yes,' said Burghardt. 'A promising young man, one might have said, "they" being the two Herr Beck took it upon himself, Fräulein, to send after that daughter of yours without, I must add, having consulted his superior officer, myself.'

The windy old bugger! 'I want my daughter back, Kapitän. That "husband" of mine had no right to steal her from me. The Gestapo were inept, the Abwehr also. Both *should* have stopped him at the border last Easter and *never* let him get near her.'

Liebe Zeit, heads were going to roll, was that it? '*Ach, bitte, Fräulein*, a necessary correction. Stolen, I understand, from the house of your father on the outskirts of Brühl while you and Herr Beck were shacked up in the Jardelunder studying each other and the Danish frontier, am I not correct?'

'*Mein Gott*, Berlin will . . .' she began.

Burghardt wagged the stump of a cautioning finger. 'Some coffee, I think. *Kaffee, Frau Dorst!*' he shouted. '*Und* some of that marvellous *Apfelstrudel* of yours for the general's daughter. The *Strudel* won't hurt your figure, Fräulein. It's good to eat a little now and then throughout the day. Besides, you will have missed the day's most important meal, your breakfast.'

His grin was there, she uncrossing her legs to sit straight upright and let that gaze of hers fall directly on him. A sea captain, she'd be thinking, thought Burghardt. Methodical, plodding, a bit of an organizer perhaps, since Admiral Canaris, head of

* The counterintelligence service, that of the Oberkommando der Wehrmacht, the army's High Command

the Abwehr, was often heard to say such a thing. A natural, also, one who knew both how to choose good men and to delegate authority, but she would, of course, have none of it.

An old sailor who looked the part, thought Christina acidly, even to the unkempt, thin grey hair, the wind-burned cheeks and empty dark-brown eyes, they giving him the look he had nurtured all his life, that of the anonymous. 'You spied for the Kaiser,' she said.

'As I was ordered,' he countered.

'And now you spy for the Nazis, but is it, Kapitän, that I must see to your orders?'

Verdammt, she would even threaten him again with that influence of her father's, and of her own, he reminded himself. 'Fräulein von Hoffmann, let us make a little peace. You have your coffee—I assure you it will be to your liking—me, I'll check over what has come in.'

'Just don't forget what I said.'

Ach, how could I? he asked himself, but must loyalty to the party higher-ups always be used? He knew she had taken a shot in the dark by coming here, and when he chanced a glance at her, he saw the light of laughter touch those lovely bedroom eyes and thought Ashby must have been a fool to have let go of her, yet Ashby had had very sound reasons, and still did since she had given him more and more of them.

Burghardt returned to his papers. When he came to the signal he wanted, he found he couldn't suppress an impatient frown. 'Your husband seems to have eluded us, Frau Ashby. Might I suggest you find Herr Beck and have him return to this office.'

Ash had done it again, thought Christina, but arched, 'You can reach Werner yourself.'

'More quickly?' Burghardt shook his head. 'The time necessary will give you both the opportunity to think more clearly. Please see that you do.'

At half past nine that Monday, as light fled out into the night from the Dogs of War, Ashby stood next to the old stone wall that was across the road and not far from the bridge and Wetherby Cottage where those two must have waited for him. Sounds from the pub were mingled with those of the sea and the stream.

There were a few cars parked nearby, and some bicycles, for here the A39, coming from Nether Stowey past the signpost to the Old Coach Road and then that of the school and on to Holford, turned west past the short road to the village of Kilve and skirted the northern fringe of the Quantocks a mile or so from the coast. Beyond the village, a lane led to Daisy's farmhouse, which abutted the ruins of the chantry, and beyond it, Kilve Pill, the stream, soon emptied into the Bristol Channel.

His mind made up, he walked down to the pub to search among the cars, but there wasn't a sign of that Bentley. Just a dusty brown, two-door Rover of rather institutional looks that puzzled. Daisy would be hustling the pints, but it wasn't like her to have come to the school. Had those two been in to question her?

Seen through the tobacco smoke, the chatter and the inevitable custom, the man with the Rover was in hunting tweeds and an open mack, having a pint of bitter and feeding late on steak-and-kidney pie with hash browns. He was over against the far wall with not a flicker of interest from him, just a hasty wiping of a ginger moustache. A big man, in his mid-fifties, from London no doubt, but not on holiday, not that one. An estate agent, then? wondered Ashby, though that didn't fit either, but tough, and definitely he had been in the war. It wasn't just the bearing or the way he gripped his knife and fork or seized the glass. It was in the way he ate with the stolidly mechanical indifference of the trenches, as though to get it all over with before the shells started coming in again.

As the sounds of those round the stranger ebbed and flowed, the man readily accepted his isolation. A couple was playing darts, the girl with flashing eyes and a ready laugh, but he had no time even for her.

Shouldering through to the bar, Ashby gave nods to several, quiet hellos to the parson and the squire. Puzzled, he looked about for Daisy.

'Gone to see her sister in Bristol,' said Martin Dolby, the landlord. 'Said she would be away three days, but it'll be a plain bloody fortnight before she comes back, you mark my words. What'll it be, the usual?' He gave the bar a wipe. 'I'm half run off my feet, what with the wife over in Bridgwater seeing to her mother.'

Still receiving no answer, Dolby drew a pint of half-and-half and set it before the schoolmaster.

'Have you tried to telephone her?' asked Ashby.

'Me? No, come to think on it, I haven't.'

Digging into a trouser pocket, the schoolmaster paid up rather than put the drink on the chit, Dolby giving him a shrewd but questioning look.

'Would you mind if I used your telephone?' asked Ashby.

Right worried he was, thought Dolby, and even sliding far too much across the bar. 'Just tell her to come back,' said Dolby, returning the shilling. 'Sort of warms the old place up, she does. You know what I mean. Tease her.'

Shoulders intruded, the smell of wet tweed as well, Dolby saying rather harshly, 'Well, what'll it be now, sir? Another pint?'

'That and another of your steak-and-kidney pies, Landlord,' said the visitor.

'*Arnold!*' called out Dolby, 'another of them up front! With the hash browns, sir?'

A regimental nod was given.

'The potatoes, Arnold. It's coming up closing, sir.'

Ginger moustache couldn't have cared less, but said, 'And a dollop or two of tomato sauce. That bottle on the table seems to have run dry. You wouldn't have such a thing as a napkin, would you, and a side order of coleslaw?'

His lot had always demanded the world, thought Dolby, the man taking a sip from his pint before collaring the pie and making his way back to that table.

Ashby wasn't long, but the call had apparently unsettled him, though he said not a word of it, simply borrowed a torch and left.

Beyond the village and the church at Kilve, an overgrown path led to an old brick building where oil shales had once been tested. The farmhouse Daisy rented was not that far, but it was in total darkness, and Ashby wondered where she was, as he had ever since her sister had anxiously said, 'But she's not here, Mr. Ashby. She did say she was coming yesterday, that she had to get away for a bit, but I thought she must have put it off until next week.'

Telling her not to worry, he had promised to call her back the moment he heard anything.

Daisy was thirty-six, had been married at the age of seventeen to a man with little money and twice her years. The thick red hair and sea-green eyes of the girl she'd once been were still there, but the husband had driven her to despair with his screams and tears in the night, and ever since she had been chary of military men, yet his own understanding of such had helped, and the two of them had gradually come to know each other.

They had never discussed getting married—the thought had never occurred to either. Daisy wanted her independence, and so did he, but every once in a while they would walk down this lane after closing to pause by the garden gate, those errant hens of hers rebelliously clucking from atop that old stone wall.

Naked, she was beautiful, pleasingly plump, eager yet content, knowing what she wanted, yet not demanding, just letting instinct guide them. The spare key was where it should have been. Letting himself into the house, he shone the light round. In the kitchen, extra food had been left out for the cat, but this hadn't been touched. Upstairs, her bed had been made, but when he pulled the plain brown leather suitcase from the closet, it was packed for that visit.

Her walking shoes weren't in the mudroom. She wasn't in the loft of the barn. She was in the ruined, ivy-covered walls of the chantry, whose remaining monastical buildings had been destroyed by fire in 1848, and when the torchlight found her, he hesitated, for she had been beaten and stripped of her clothing, which lay scattered about, was kneeling with her back towards him, her hands bound behind her with baling wire, the ankles as well, the knees spread widely.

Sickened by what had happened, Ashby was at a loss. Granted he had seen death far too many times. One could never have become accustomed to it even then, or else one would have soon lost one's mind, but this . . . He knew her throat must have been cut, for the knife had slashed both buttocks, and certainly she had been questioned, for the gag her killers had used, being untied at the last, was clinging to her left shoulder, a dirty bit of rope. Hemp, he thought, as the sound of the waves finally broke through to him, he switching off the light to let the darkened silhouette of those crumbling walls close about him, he blurting, 'Daisy, why? Why you, for God's sake? This went too far and makes no sense.'

'We'll just leave this, if you please,' said a voice from out of the darkness. 'There's no good getting your bowels in a knot, Captain Ashby. Let the figs of retribution take their course. It'll all come out in the end.'

'Who the hell are you?'

And still sickened by what he'd come upon. 'Hacker, Captain. Colonel Hacker.'

'Why did they have to kill her? She didn't know anything.'

'And must have convinced them of that. Your motor or mine?'

'Neither, damn you. I have to get Constable Blakey. He'll be checking that the pub has closed.'

Must schoolmasters always be a bind? 'I don't think I would, old cock. I think if I were you, I'd keep mum about it and bugger off back to that school of yours after we've had ourselves a chat, but not here.'

'I've got to return the flashlight—the torch. If I don't, the landlord will only start thinking I must have found something. God, I *loved* her as a friend. We *never* talked about Karen. If I'd known those two would do this, I'd have let them take me.'

'The flashlight,' said Hacker. 'You can return the bloody torch, my man, when we've had our little chat.'

'Not until you tell me who you're working for.'

'Let's just say I'm a friend in need. That little bit of crumpet you've been playing round with has been the victim of a particularly nasty sex attack. I shouldn't want to be involved if I were you, not with a daughter hidden away, and those two wanting to take her home to her mother and your former wife.'

Hacker chose the Rover, forcing Ashby to leave the light on the landlord's doorstep, but when they had reached the little Norman church in the hills, he decided that he had best enlighten the schoolmaster further. 'I was at Mons. Fourth Middlesex under Smith-Dorrien.'

'Second Army Corps and the Mons-Condé Canal, Colonel. Get on with it.'

'Of course. A bloody ditch no more than seven feet at its deepest and sixty-four across, but a bastard to defend, what with the coal mines and the frigging place being built up like that.'

'They didn't have to kill the children, Colonel. Damn them, they should have waited.'

Christ, that from a *captain* and echoing what so many others had cried. 'Sixty of those kiddies, was it, coming along that road at lunchtime? God, the tears, Ashby, the men going soft just like yourself.'

'August 21, 1914, a retreating army, and a little before my time, but this still has no bearing whatsoever on what's happened.'

'Be that as it may, I was right there from the start, and within three days, the Fourth's strength had been reduced to a thousand two hundred seventy-five.'

'And within a few more days, the Battle of Le Cateau had damned near finished you all off, Colonel, but what's it got to do with me and Daisy?'

'Only this. What do you do with old soldiers? You either let them sell insurance or teach school. Since neither—your kind anyway—were to my liking, I found Burma far better.'

Then Hacker had been looking into his background and *was* a policeman, thought Ashby, but not Special Branch. He couldn't be.

'Why not tell me about it, Captain. Begin with this graveyard. To bang three rounds from a Walther P38 into that motor of yours in the pitch of night, you having driven straight at them, suggests more than chance.'

Hacker had been to the school for a look at the car, had been to the church here, too, and round asking questions. 'I think you'd better be the one to tell me.'

'Let's not quibble.'

The schoolmaster tried to lose himself in looking out his side windscreen, still dwelling on his tart of a barmaid. Taking out a cigarette, Hacker lit up but didn't offer one.

'They were following me,' said Ashby at last.

'Skip the incidentals. The evidence is clear enough.'

There was no use in remaining silent, thought Ashby, quickly outlining what had happened, Hacker asking, 'Did they say anything to suggest they might have been sent from Berlin?'

'Yes.'

'Not Bremen?'

'No.'

'Berlin, then. You do impress me, Captain. What's the General Friedrich Otto von Hoffmann like?'

'My daughter would give you an entirely different view of

him. Look, the one called Martin said that Berlin didn't want any trouble.'

'Yet they have most certainly given you plenty, haven't they?'

'You aren't Special Branch. You're MI5, counterintelligence.'

Ashby would think the world of him now, thought Hacker, so best not to mention training regulars in Burma. 'Unfortunately, given our Prime Minister Chamberlain's peace initiatives, the Germans have set this country awash with their bloody agents, Captain. Until recently, every Abwehr and SD* outpost from Hamburg to Bremen, Wilhelmshaven, Münster and Kassel—Dresden even, *and* Stuttgart *and* Kiel—had been developing agents and sending them over here. Now that they've tightened everything under Bremen, things can only get far worse. Some have their bona fides—good cover and good reasons for being here, and we can't do much about them yet—but the point is, old cock, the buggers are picking their bombing targets and we know this. Every aerodrome, railway depot, harbour, dockyard—even the King George and Queen Mary reservoirs and the pumping stations that supply London. Everything, Ashby, including the firefighting capabilities of our major towns and cities. And right in the middle of this, you and your daughter come along to take me away from what I ought to be doing. Where the hell have you got her stashed?'

Hacker was the only one on it, then, thought Ashby. 'I'm not saying.'

'You'd bloody well better. Your two birds will have crossed over to the Continent via Dover, so you can kiss them good-bye. One trussed-up barmaid with her face bashed, her tits carved, buttocks slashed and throat slit, and one more unsolved murder for the Yard, or would you rather I talked to them?'

'Now look . . .'

'You look yourself. You're in trouble up to your arse even if you do let us help you. They'll activate a sleeper, Captain Ashby. Someone they've planted years ago and left to lie dormant. Since that wife of yours has a father who has friends in high places, if I were him and I'd just blown two R-men who should have known better than to disobey Berlin, I'd think twice. Yes, I would. I'd get

---

* The Sicherheitsdienst, the intelligence service of the SS and Nazi Party

that Abwehr of theirs to use someone we hadn't cottoned onto, somebody neither we nor you will ever know about until it's far too bloody late. Where is she?'

'Safe for now. When I think differently, I'll tell you.'

'And have your bloody horse shot out from under you? Have that tom titmouse of a headmaster scream his head off so that the Hun can get a bead on you and shatter that leg of yours when you're out there trying to save him? Use your head, man. If they'll play with that barmaid of yours, they'll play with whomever you've got looking after that child. Let's hope your daughter doesn't have to witness it, because if she does, she'll—'

'That's enough, damn you. I'll warn them myself.'

And stubborn to the last. 'How? By going there? By telephoning or using the post? Do so and those friends of yours will thank you from the other side of the grave.'

Near Flensburg on the Danish border, the Tuesday train was still rushing across the flat farmlands of Schleswig-Holstein. Christina Ashby, née von Hoffmann, couldn't help but feel depressed. Even at midweek there had been no first- or second-class seats available, no chance of a compartment to herself. Had Burghardt known of this? she wondered, clenching a fist at the obvious answer. To him, Werner Beck was still the youngest son of the wealthy importer of cotton who had once given Burghardt hell over spoiled bales in the hold of a rotten freighter.

The railway coach was crammed with sailors of the Kriegsmarine, some so young their drunken mouths had fallen open even before sleep had overcome them, others still grinning at her lustfully, they all stinking of sweat, bad women, cigarette smoke, beer and schnapps, but in amongst them and crowded, too, the peasants stank of onions, herring, hard-boiled eggs, cabbage and farts of their own.

Using a tissue, offended by what she was having to do, she rubbed the window to clear it. The trouble had started with the switch in trains at Hamburg. So few of importance went north, there had only been one first-class carriage and two second-class. Bribery had been of no use. Burghardt again? she wondered. At Easter, Ash *would* use the crowds to get through the Reich's border guards, he to then snatch Karen, but what the hell had gone wrong with those two Werner had sent over? She had been so looking forward to seeing her again.

The wheels rattled over a bog, the bed of the railway sinking under the weight and giving back repeated undulations, the carriage old, high and with those stiff-backed, wooden benches of fifty years ago. They passed a village and she saw a farmer staring dumbly at them from his milk cart.

Werner had been supremely confident, and Burghardt had sent her to deliver the message home that such a degree of self-confidence had not only been reckless but inappropriate. Karen should have been back in the Reich by now. Instead, Werner, having heard nothing of it, would still be waiting, and she knew exactly where he would be, and so would Burghardt.

When she did finally arrive, marsh and bogland depressingly stretched away from her in waving reeds, wind-torn, stunted birch and dwarf willow with endless drainage ditches, ponds, inlets and wider channels that might, at times of high water, become momentary lakes or slow-moving rivers. Sphagnum moss, bilberry, black water and bog mud that stank of rotten eggs were *always* underfoot.

Werner loved the Jardelunder. His family's thatched-roof hunting-and-fishing lodge had been refuge and home, for as the youngest of five brothers, the rest still in the family cotton business, he had had to strike out on his own. Mechanical engineering had proven rather useless in the Great Depression, and he had retreated here to live off the land and take his photographs of nesting birds, drying nets, otters, voles and mink. He had thousands of photographs, had had showings in several well-known, if small, galleries. Sailing, and signing on as a deckhand on a banana boat had helped, but yes, three years of absolute freedom had spoiled him. Then in the spring of 1936, he had found a job with the import-export firm of Donnecker, Luntz and Lammers in Bremen, with supposed warehousing in Bremerhaven, Wilhelmshaven and Hamburg. Everything had come together for him. The Abwehr and running agents into and out of Britain.

He was standing at the very end of a point of land, looking off across the black water towards the Danish border that lay some 300 metres away. He was watching for the Norwegian skiff that would bring Karen to him, still refusing to admit that he had failed.

'Werner, it's me,' she called out. 'Burghardt says you are to return to the office.'

He didn't turn to look at her but remained concentrating on a copse of alders beneath which the reeds were close and hid that very boat.

Would he hate her for telling him? she wondered. 'Darling, they're not coming. Burghardt had a cable—look, I don't know what it said. That bastard wouldn't have told me.'

'What made you go to him?'

Still he hadn't turned. The forage cap, canvas duck coat, oil-skin cape, cords and high boots were those of a hunter or fisher-man. A string bag, the same as the locals used, held two dozen gull eggs, a delicacy much revered when boiled for twelve minutes, yet tasting so strongly of fish she had thrown up immediately and still felt sick at the sight of them.

Again he asked what had made her go to the captain, and she said, 'A telephone call from Ash at 0215. I didn't take it. I couldn't.'

He stiffened. Tall, lean, hard and incredibly handsome, he was thirty-four and only two years older than herself, and yes, she did love him madly because of what he could do to her, and yes, it had been good.

Still without turning, he said, 'Don't lie to me, Christina. Not after breaking our security. Burghardt will have my balls.'

'I hope not.'

'Then don't be foolish! You talked to Ashby and he told you what that cable on the captain's desk contained.'

She wished he would look at her. 'Ash didn't tell me. He sim-ply asked, "Guess what's happened?" and then rang off, but I think he must have been very upset about something those two you sent must have done.'

Beck clenched a fist and said, 'They were told not to cause any trouble, but you . . . What *did* you do? You played right into his hands. Ashby isn't stupid, Christina. He *made* you go to Burghardt. Even after all the years of separation, he could *still* do that to you and you let him, damn you. Even if you *had* used the British courts to get Karen back, he would have kept his silence and gone willingly to jail, knowing war was in the offing and that as a former soldier he would again be useful.'

Liebe Gott, but she had touched a nerve. 'I know Ash isn't stupid, darling. I would never have married him if he had been, and I did love him once.'

'Love, was it, with the mind and heart of a schoolgirl in a defeated nation wanting to sample a little something different! So, what's it to be, eh? Me to England to find out what went wrong, or me to the office as ordered by the Kapitän?'

The firmness of her father came and Christina was grateful for it. 'This isn't the time to disobey orders. Burghardt will know he's up against it himself and is bound to have a little something.'

Beck tossed a dismissive hand. 'He's near retirement and content to rest out his days running the Bremen office.'

Werner hadn't been able to hide his bitterness, a bad sign. *Men*, thought Christina, wanting to shake her head in despair at the sex, but it would be best to be calm yet not avoid the truth and simply tell him. 'Running AST-X Bremen, *Liebling*. Running the British Isles is not so bad, is it? When he retires, as he most certainly will have to when I am done with him, he will have to be replaced.'

How *could* she have said a thing like that, even to himself? wondered Beck, but said, '*Ach*, we should not argue. Now that you are here, we have better things to do.'

Only then did he turn to face her, still angry, thought Christina, and very much concerned with what had actually gone wrong. 'Darling, don't be upset. *Vati* will speak to Canaris and everything will be all right, you'll see.'

Was it at moments like this that he hated her? wondered Beck. 'Burghardt doesn't need another wasp up his ass, Christina. You're enough. There is always the Kriegsmarine for me. War will come. If not this summer, then in the autumn, unless Britain and France are willing to back down over Czechoslovakia and let the Führer march into the Sudetenland without a shot.'

From where he and Colonel Hacker stood among outspreading poplars late on that Tuesday afternoon, Ashby could see them quite clearly. The police were cordoning off the chantry. Extra constables had been brought in from the surrounding villages and towns. Two detectives from Scotland Yard stood looking down at Daisy, one with a black leather notebook, her red hair clashing with the pale, bluish white of her skin. 'Why *can't* they cover her?' he said.

And so near to tears he might just as well have been, thought Hacker, cramming his hands into the pockets of his mack. 'You don't listen, do you, Captain? You were to have gone your way, but oh no, like an errant duck you had to turn righteous!'

'I had no other choice.'

'Good God, man, you're not playing rugger with schoolboys. Those two came straight from Berlin. Not even Abwehr Bremen, Ashby. Berlin, you said. R-men. *Reisagenten, ja?* Travel agents!'

'Have you told our friends from the Yard about them?'

The watchful, green-brown eyes sought him out, the wind teasing the thick thatch of Hacker's eyebrows and moustache as he said, 'You're not that blind, Captain. From now on you'll take your orders from me. The sight of that barmaid frightened you. You panicked, then thought better of it. You were in love—the landlord will swear there was something going on. No, you didn't quarrel. No, you don't own a spring-assisted knife, you're a war hero, a holder of the DSO, the Military Cross, the lot. You had come to see if the two of you could spend your summer holiday in the Lakes District. You're the broken, shattered lover. Try crying as you now all but are, by Christ, and it might just help.'

Turning away to gaze out to sea, Hacker went on. 'Whitehall should be shot for letting the Hun run wild here. Do you know what I took off a chappie last week up at Farnborough? Details, Ashby. Not just of the RAF's experimental station there but the one at Hendon as well. Bugger had a Leica, telephoto lens and all. Frigging tourist on a bicycle, *lederhosen*, no less. A pity the motor hit him, but you know what some of our roads are like. Should have had reflectors on his rear mudguard. Should have. The German Abwehr calls this country the *Golfplatz*, a bloody golf course, a frigging putting green! Well, I won't have it, do you hear? You'll do as I say from now on, my man. Make no mistake about it.'

Finding himself a cigarette and lighting it, Hacker gave the schoolmaster a moment, then asked, 'Does that woman at the school know you've a daughter tucked away?'

'Ruth thinks it's another woman.'

'You're full of surprises. And the boss man, Captain Anthony Pearce of the Blues?'

'Knows Karen is in England, but not where.'

'Good. Now I'm going to give you one more chance before I tell those two from the Yard down there to either leave you out of this or take you in. Here's an address up in London. You will pay it a visit or I will go down there, as I must, and tell them you did it.'

'Karen's safe.'

'But for how long? Believe me, I meant what I said. They'll activate a sleeper for this, *ein Schweigeagent*. An S-man.'

At last, thought Ashby, Daisy was being gently laid on the stretcher, but left as found with hands and ankles still bound, though even from here, as she was being covered, he could see what had happened to her throat and breasts. Her 'tits,' Hacker had called them. 'Before I agree, Colonel, I've got to see my daughter.'

The son of a bitch! 'Don't even think about trying to warn whomever you've got looking after the child. Just let us get this sleeper before he does us any real harm.'

As the last of Tuesday's rain left the moor in mist, it was, thought Hilary, exactly like it must have been back then in Cornwall. The bleak and lonely road made its way across the windswept land where everything seemed bent and torn, and the silent boulders stood like ancient kings.

One felt the past deeply in the darkness of tussock-ringed pools or in the water-filled, bracken-crowded ruts that led to the stark ruins of the old engine house. The story she was writing came so readily at times like this. Pindanter would have stood here as she was now.

The coach from Saint Austell would have been and gone, yet he would listen for its clatter until the wind and the pounding of the sea had finally found him alone.

Zennor lay that way, to the southwest and but two miles from the cottage, while just a little to the northeast of that village, at the tiny hamlet of Tregerthen, the cliffs pitched down to meet the shattering waves, while offshore a piece, the Carracks poked their ragged heads above the sea to tear the bottoms out of ships.

Pindanter was afraid of what he must do that night, afraid that

M'lord Darcy would turn them all in and see them hang from the gallows tree while he drank port with his friends and laughed about it. And wasn't M'lord Darcy the bastard man with eyes that never looked at one for long?

Yes, Pindanter would stand here like this, with the mist beading on his oilskins. He would stare after the coach and he would pray that something unforeseen would come to stop the whole mad business before he had to light the beacon fire and the *Anne of Athlone* would be drawn onto the rocks.

Where poverty and hard times had frayed the cuffs of his oilskins, the mist would gather before seeping over the broad and hairy backs of his hands. It would seep into his sea boots too—cold, it would be like ice, and would send shivers through him.

Gilbert Roope had got him into this, got him in deep, she said to herself. If only he hadn't listened to Gilbert with his scheming ways. If only Blind William's alehouse hadn't been there on that cursed moor, the two roads crossing at a broken signpost and him with a lame whim horse near to death.

' 'Tis a right kettle of fish I be in,' he said and turned away at last, as she did, to stand here still and stare at the lonely stack of the engine house where life had been and life had gone with the crash in the price of tin.

The cottage was well back of him now, hunkered down into a distant furrow and with the slates rattling miserably every time a gale would blow.

Alone, and with time to kill because it had to be killed, he headed well out onto the moor, as she was now heading. The distant engine house drew him as it always had until he was standing lonely by its high stone walls. Through the silence, and in memory, he heard the stamp mill pound and the wheel turn as it hoisted ore and the men climbed down into the depths below, the pumps working nonstop to suck the water out.

'Them was good times,' he said. 'Good work, but damp, mind. The damp was ever fearful. Got t' th' lungs, it did.'

He coughed, and Hilary spat harshly as he would have done, all the bitterness of a man burdened by a wife and two young babes with nought to eat roaring through her mind.

The vessel *must* be wrecked. These were desperate times, and they were desperate people. It had nothing to do with conscience or morals. Nothing to do with God and preachers. All must die. There couldn't be any witnesses. The *Anne of Athlone* must be *smashed* upon the reefs. The passengers must be put into the boats—crowded, terrified, a mother calling out for her child, the rain beating mercilessly down to blind her and drown her cries. Oh God . . .

Frightened by the splashing of her boots, a Montagu's harrier lifted off the tall stone chimney stack to wing its way down into the mist with a cry, Hilary immediately thinking of falcons and of King Arthur riding to the hunt, of ancient Druids, too, and of the kingdom of Dumnonia, but here before those very Celts, another people, and before those yet others.

Cornwall threw up its history. It was always doing this when she least wanted other parts of that history to confuse things, but she should have brought her notebook—why hadn't she? Pindanter would have to kill someone. The night would be wild with the wind shrieking in from the sea. He would have a capstan bar in hand like all the others, would be wading out into the raging surf, fighting to hold on to someone now, *fighting* to maintain a footing.

He would swing that capstan bar, would dash it down hard. A woman, she asked, blood matting her hair to wash away with the rain and the waves? A girl like the daughter of David Douglas Ashby? *No!*

Angry with herself for worrying about such things, Hilary hunched her shoulders against the mist and plodded up the rutted road until she came at last to the ruins. Then she looked up suddenly to the stack that towered some ninety feet above, and wondered why fate had brought them all together.

Fate had a habit of doing things like that. Fate and Cornwall. This place. She was now two miles and some from the cottage, 400 feet above it and another 300 to sea level.

The tin had been in the granite, but near the contact with the slates and schists that were grey-green and laminated, or black, so black down by the sea, they were all mangled and mashed up against the speckled grey of the granite that formed the boss, the naked breasts like this one, in the heartlands of Cornwall.

The ore deposits were said to be zoned, so that in the slates and schists, in the killas, there was little tin, but in the adjacent granite it began to increase with depth and distance until the lode was reached, after which the tin would peter out.

There were rough-hewn blocks of granite in the chimney stack and walls, buff pink, whitish grey and shot through with black flakes of mica. The blocks were set amongst the laminated slabs of slate—not run in individual courses or anything like that, just set here and there, randomly, with ironstone too. The whole had been mortared to stand the test of time, and she thought then that the engine house and its chimney stack would be here long after she had passed away.

Would they bury her here, if she requested it—with a bronze plaque, bolted to the wall of the engine house? *Here lies the body of the Wheal Deep's last owner, one Hilary Bowker-Brown, author of* The Legacy *and other novels.* All of the latter rejected so far.

'They'll chuck me down one of the shafts,' she said aloud and to no one but herself as she picked her way cautiously through the bracken and the arched stone doorway to stand in the hollow of the engine house—stand staring up at the open windows and portals and the gaping, empty cavern where the roof had once been.

The walls were four and five feet thick—beautifully made—with timbers inset for lintels where even larger timbers would once have spanned the gap between the walls.

From there, up so high and open to the sky, to the black and gaping pump shaft just outside the west wall, was only a moment in time. You would think they might have thought to fill the shaft in or at least to cap it over with better timbers and concrete that had since caved, but no, there it was, staring up at the sky, waiting for its votive offerings. The other shaft, the one that hoisted up the ore and that the men climbed down, was over there, not seventy feet away. Larger and just as empty.

Stooping, she picked up a slab of slate. The rain came down.

The letter had stated:

My dear Miss Hilary Bowker-Brown,

It is with regret that I must again remind you of the insurance coverage. As sole owner of the Wheal Deep you are fully responsible and liable should any claims for damages be brought against the mine. It is derelict and extremely dangerous. You may post hazard warnings if you like, but your father and I are in total agreement that these will avail you little in court. Therefore, it is in your best interests to be adequately insured.

Our statement is rendered yet again. You will note that it is now long overdue. Please see that it is attended to immediately, both to save us all any further embarrassment and to save yourself from further concern.

The bailiff

In addition, there was a bill for fifteen pounds, ten shillings, four pence at the provisioner's in Saint Ives. Another for two pounds, two shillings and five pence resided with the stationer—paper, that and ink. Pencils too, rubber bands, erasers and God knows what else.

Yet another bill was for wines and spirituous liquors, namely two bottles of Burgundy and one of brandy for medicinal purposes.

She had had to sell herself—sell a part of her time—to Mr. David Douglas Ashby, who had at first looked so much like one she had imagined from MI6*, only to come further into the boat shed to tell her that he was a schoolmaster. 'I work in the mornings until one or two,' she had said, 'so anything after that is fine.'

Damn! The responsibility would interfere with the writing, indeed as the child already had. To kill her like that, to have Pindanter crush her skull . . .

Disgruntled that things hadn't been working out as well as planned, she pitched the slab of slate into the gaping pump shaft, it to fall forever in silence, before hollowly striking a timber and bouncing to throw up a dreadful racket, only to plunge again as the echoes fled.

Try as she did, she could never hear the stone hit the water below, yet knew the workings must be flooded. There just had to be a bottom to that shaft and to the other one, but no answer ever came back.

Pindanter had tried to continue mining, at first with some of the other lads and then, as they had drifted off, by himself

---

* The British Military Intelligence Service

alone, stubborn to the last, but did he really have to kill? Was it really *that* necessary? A woman? A young girl like Karen Ashby? It would mean the end of him. The very end.

He was desperate. Mary Ellen was with child again. Why were some women so fertile?

When she reached the edge of the cliffs, Hilary gazed off towards the Carracks. Again and again the images of what was to come appeared before her. The wreck, the horror of it, that crucial step over which, once passed, Pindanter must fall.

Far below her, the sea boiled into the cove to wash up on the strand. The apron sands went back and forth, while the grey-green slates were plunged into blackness and the granite boulders mingled with them where the storm beaches had built their ramparts.

The boat shed was higher still, set well off to one side of the cove on a substantial platform of broken waste from the mine. To the east, a good 200 yards from where she stood, a break in the cliffs gave access to the cove, a set of steps having been cut and formed where possible, but still one went down there by degrees, and once at the cove, was suddenly shut off from all else depending entirely on the tide.

There was, or rather there once had been, a ramp of rock over which the boat had been launched, but she didn't think it would ever be possible to do so again. The seas were far too murderous most of the time.

Shivering for no reason, she went back to the cottage, and on the following afternoon while still hard at her writing, Monica MacDonald brought the child. The pleasantries were stilted, Hilary embarrassed and fussing with her papers, only to finally apologize and say, '*The Legacy* is about the tin mines, about what happens to good men when things over which they have no control go wrong.'

Right away, though, Monica caught the drift and said, 'Nothin'' would have been left t' them. Nothin'.'

'Yes . . . Yes, that's it exactly,' said Hilary, giving Karen a hurried glance. 'They were at a loss, you see. All their skills were suddenly of no use and they . . . why, they had to turn to other things, like wrecking.'

Light from one of the two small windows fell across the plain

deal table whose boards had once held each day's catch and had
felt the endless scour of the holystone. Monica wondered how on
earth Miss Bowker-Brown had managed to get the table up from
the boat shed. The manuscript, neatly piled, sat to one side of the
straight-backed chair. The writing pad, fountain pen and bottle of
ink had only just been left. 'Won' teachin' Karen English bother
your work?' she asked.

'*Englisch!*' spat Karen in *Deutsch*. 'I don't *want* to learn *Englisch!*'

'Hush, lass. Miss Bowker-Brown . . .'

'Hilary . . . Please let her call me Hilary, yourself as well.
Bowker-Brown is far too stuffy. I'm thinking of changing it to just
plain Brown anyway. . . . Fräulein von Hoffmann, would you like
to see the *Tordalken*? There are still some eggs.'

The razorbills . . . The switch to German had been so easy,
Monica knew she had done the right thing by bringing the child
here, but Karen wasn't having any of it.

Hilary smiled at the girl and said to her in English, 'Look, if
we're to get on, we'd best get one thing straight. Even if I did
happen to be Jewish, it wouldn't matter. They would still be razorbills and you would still see how they lay their eggs on the rocky
ledges. Just the egg and the rock and a bit of bird poop!'

Confused and taken aback, the child hesitated, Hilary trans-
lating everything she had just said into *Deutsch*, then asking,
'Shall we?'

Reluctantly Karen stomped outside, leaving Monica at a loss
for words, Hilary's gentle chuckle infectious as she said, 'Make us
some tea, will you, and have a read, just a bit? Please, I . . . I have
to know what someone else thinks.'

There were ups and downs for them to negotiate, as well as
bits of bog to avoid. The razorbills occupied the steepest parts
of the cliffs—sheer drops in places—and to see them, both she
and Karen had to lie flat on the rocks and work their way cautiously towards the edge. Only at the last moment did she take
Karen by the wrist. The wind made their eyes water. Pointing
down to the left, she shouted in *Deutsch*, 'Don't be scared. I
won't let you fall.'

'I am not. I am cold!'

'Look, down there. The egg, on that little ledge?'

It was, thought Karen, a very stupid egg and a very stupid-looking waiter-bird with a white front, black frock coat and long, scrawny neck. It stood there looking dumbly up at them, a dunce, and when the wind perilously rocked the egg, what did this *Englisch* bird do but fly away to circle in the air, the waves crashing far below.

'Karen, your father wants me to help you learn English.'

'*Jüdin*, you are *all Juden*! I hate you. I hate . . .'

Shocked, Hilary let go of her wrist. Panicking, Karen threw a glance far below them, then let her gaze come back defiantly as her wrist was taken hold of again, Hilary saying, 'Look, if you don't want to come, I don't want to help you.'

The Jewess let go of her again, and as the waiter-birds croaked and growled and spat like drunken Poles, high above them, the purest white Germanic gulls soared. *Ach*, they were like Messerschmitts *und* Stukas.

Hilary was at a loss as to what to say, but managed, 'Why don't you tell me about your mother? I'll bet you miss her very much. I know I did. I felt as though my life was over.'

Die Jüdin was begging, therefore she would spit at her and say, '*Ein Volk, ja? Ein Reich!*'

'Karen, do you mean you're Aryan, of the highest race?'

'To ask such a thing is to tell me you are just as stupid as those birds!'

'But . . . but you're only seven?' said Hilary.

'*Opa* says I am one of the *Gewälhte*.'

Grandpa . . . the Chosen.

'*Mein Grossvater* is a general. He will *kill* you if he ever finds out you are keeping me a prisoner here!'

Later, alone and indoors with Monica, Hilary didn't hesitate. 'My God, what have they done to her? You didn't tell me she was *ein eingefleischter Nazi*, one of the diehards.'

'*Och*, please don' be too upset. David had t' get her out. He says they're destroyin' a whole generation of young people and that it's very frightening. Thousands and thousands of school-aged children at the rallies, all shoutin' along with the adults, "One people, one Reich, one Leader." '

Ein Volk, ein Reich, ein Führer! thought Hilary in despair, the torches, banners, kettle drums and uniforms, rank upon rank and all rigidly at attention, facing their glorious leader as in

Nuremberg's gigantic stadium where, from 31 August to 3 September 1933, to celebrate Hitler's rise to power, more than half a million were said to have been involved, its grandstand alone having been built overnight to hold 60,000. At last year's rally, he had loudly claimed the Third Reich would continue for a thousand years.

'David had t' get her out,' said Monica. 'He would never have been able t' get across the German border had he na done it at Easter when so many were on the move. *Och*, of course the border guards demanded t' see his papers, but he claimed he was an SS major in mufti and threatened them with dismissal if they didn't let him hurry after someone he was following, the one thing they fear above all others being that of a higher authority and immediate dispatch to Dachau.'

One of three concentration camps that had been set up in 1933, and already infamous in its own right, which was saying something, thought Hilary sadly. 'And Karen's mother, his wife, what exactly did that one want?'

Fingering the manuscript that she had been reading, Monica glanced out the window to see the child waiting by the gate. Nothing, really, could excuse what David had done, and yet she would have to try. '*Och*, if you knew how much he loves the lass, you would understand. He hadn't been allowed into the Reich t' see her, not for a full two years and some, and it was breaking him up.'

She would let a breath escape, thought Hilary. 'So he kidnapped his own daughter.'

Monica knew she would have to tell her. 'He and Christina were torn apart when Karen was three. At first Christina did let him go over t' the Reich t' see Karen every once in a while, just enough, mind, but never for long. A day or two, then a few hours, then . . . why then, when Karen was five, he was refused altogether. *Och*, he's tried the courts, but theirs are na like ours.'

The breakup had been in 1934, thought Hilary, when Hitler had become president and chancellor of the Reich, the visits cut off entirely in 1936, the Reich and its Luftwaffe in particular helping Franco in the Spanish Civil War. 'Getting into the Reich like that was one thing, but exactly how *did* he then get her out?'

'He borrowed a car, but I think he must have stung them

rather hard. *Och*, the lass is a bonnie wee thing. Please don' be turned away by her manner. She'll come round.'

But would the Nazis leave it at that? wondered Hilary, the door swinging open, Karen's voice smashing further thought. 'It is *raining* again! Does it never stop in this shitty place?'

This isn't going to work, thought Hilary, but calmly said in *Deutsch*, 'It will pass. It always does. Go and see if there's sunshine in the west, then come back and tell us.'

They had been *whispering* about her, thought Karen. Jews . . . they were both Jewesses. 'I *don't* have to do what *either* of you tell me!'

'DO IT!'

The child bolted. Karen ran out to the gate in the low stone wall and, once beyond it, to the road and along a piece. Only then did they see her stop to gaze off to the west but neither of them could see into her mind.

Juden! As soon as she escaped, Karen knew she would have to report her father to the Gestapo. Herr Direktor Diels, at the school, had said everyone must do this; so had Fräulein Hauser, her teacher, and Frau Haslinger, *Opa*'s cook, and *Mutti* too.

She would have to tell the Gestapo *everything*. How *Vati* had taken her from the bedroom she always had when staying with *Opa* in his great big house. How they had driven through the night in *Opa*'s great big car with the swastika flags flying from the front fenders and Henke, the Gefreiter* Schellenberg, at the wheel with a revolver to his head, a British Mark VI Webley, a six-shot.

Vati would have shot him, too, but the Gestapo mustn't punish the Gefreiter. It hadn't been his fault that he had had to *crash* through the barriers at Aachen and drive on through into Holland to that darkened lane.

Switching cars, *Vati* had knocked Henke out and they had sped on through the night in their little car. It had been very exciting, very fast. *Vati* had given her a lipstick and a bottle of perfume, had even let her hold the steering wheel and had told her he would teach her how to drive. Like birds they had been. Birds way up in the air, she never thinking what it would really be like, a prison!

It was the one named Hilary who said, 'Karen, Monica's ready to go home. I'll walk partway with you.'

---

* Equivalent to a lance corporal

'Are you really Jewish?'

Quickly shaking her head, she didn't ask if it would matter. Once they reached the road, Monica and the child had at least two miles to cover. They might catch a lift or manage to stop the afternoon bus. Otherwise, the rain-swept moor would simply swallow them up.

At the top of a gentle rise, Monica remembered the manuscript. 'Must Pindanter kill that child and then hide in that derelict old mine of yours? Won't he be terrified? I know I was, and still am, for you made me feel as if it really was happening.'

Until they were gone from sight, Hilary watched them, and then, the rain thinning to a mizzle, she turned and headed out across the moor, the engine house beckoning.

3

On Thursday, 26 May, when Joachim Burghardt heard the couple enter his office, he didn't lower the field glasses or turn to greet them. Instead, he would, he decided, ignore Werner Beck and deal with the general's daughter, since no faster way of discipline existed for a man like Beck. Besides, a superb three-masted schooner had come to anchor in the Weser.

Finally setting the glasses aside, he shoved the fingers of both hands into the waistband of his trousers and hooked his thumbs behind the suspenders. Not turning, he said, 'The Führer has just ordered a further mobilization of our ground and air forces, Frau Ashby. The Kriegsmarine is accepting volunteers into the submarine service.'

The Czech crisis, thought Beck, and knew he was in for it. 'I get the message, Kapitän. I don't yet know what went wrong with the two I sent to that school of Ashby's.'

'Of course he doesn't know, Frau Ashby, but you do see, I was not informed of this little caper. Berlin had to tell me about it and now I have to believe that a naval uniform would look good on him. He'd be a real officer once he had worked his way up in one of those tin sausages.'

'You're enjoying this,' breathed Christina. 'You know very well I use my maiden name.'

'But a maiden you aren't,' he said. 'Did you know, *meine gute Frau*, that before AST-X Bremen was assigned the British desk, our people there were tripping over each other? So many agents, so many who were known only by numbers and whose identities were jealously guarded by those who ran them. Far too much duplication of effort and competition, so . . .' He paused, still not having turned to face either. 'Berlin saw wisdom in consolidation and reorganization under myself. Now why, please, should you and that most current lover of yours think to take it upon yourselves to go back to the old ways?'

He was being an absolute bastard, thought Christina. 'You wouldn't have helped me.'

Burghardt relished the derisive snort he had given. 'In that you are correct. Far too much is at stake for this office to have risked everything on such a trivial matter.'

'My daughter is not trivial!' *Verdammt*, he had pushed the suspenders out and had let them snap back against himself.

'Please learn not to interrupt me, Frau Ashby. Those two that lover of yours sent over thought it would be easy. One little girl and a schoolmaster who had already outfoxed us and set Berlin to tearing the stripes off several border guards and Gestapo they had deemed responsible, but why did those two use a Bentley, if I might ask? It's an expensive car, is it not?'

Beck heard Christina sit down in one of the chairs but didn't glance at her. Burghardt's sarcasm could only mean the old man had had enough of himself and had been on to Berlin about it. 'Kapitän, they needed something fast to match that MG of his.'

'Then why not another roadster?'

'Too noticeable, Kapitän. It was thought a Bentley more appropriate to the parents of the boys at that school.'

'It was *thought*, was it, Herr Beck? Who paid for the car?'

Christina had been right, decided Beck. The Kapitän *was* enjoying himself. Even now he still hadn't turned to face them. 'General von Hoffmann allowed sufficient funds for the purchase of such a car.'

'*Ach*, then he is out of pocket a considerable sum since those two *Dummkopfs* you sent over had to abandon it and make a run for home.'

'But why?' blurted Christina.

Turning to face them now, he leaned back against the windowsill and said, 'Why indeed?' Understandably the general's daughter couldn't hide her uncertainty. Beck was better at it but due entirely to his ignorance of what had happened. 'A barmaid,' said Burghardt, watching the two of them closely. 'Who would have thought it possible?'

'A barmaid, Kapitän. *Bitte*, what is this?' asked Beck.

Struck by the news, the general's daughter had noticeably blanched, but had she still some feelings for Ashby? wondered Burghardt. And if so, could they be used?

As he told them of the murder, the general's daughter took to plucking nervously at her gaily flowered frock until at last her eyes began to moisten. Naked, the schoolmaster would have played with her and she with him, but was her distress over Ashby or over what that barmaid had been forced to endure? 'A murder,' he said, 'which has been emphatically denied, Herr Beck, by the two you sent over.'

'Denied? *Ach*, if they didn't kill her, who did?' asked Beck.

'That we do not yet know,' said Burghardt. 'Perhaps it was simply the act of a former husband. Ashby had, I gather, been keeping rather close company with the woman.'

'With a barmaid?' said Christina incredulously, only to realize that the Kapitän was watching her every reaction.

Lowering that gaze of hers to her hands, Beck's current woman pressed them against her shapely thighs, but was it in anger? wondered Burghardt. Did she consider it an insult that Ashby had been sleeping with such? 'Perhaps it was the act of a sex maniac since whoever did it carved her up before she was silenced.'

'How sure are you of this?' seethed Christina.

Pinching his lower lip in thought, Burghardt waved a dismissive hand and said, '*Ach*, but you see, those two your lover sent over were able to ascertain a very candid opinion before they panicked and ran. Whoever killed her, first gagged her, then methodically used his knife before telling her not to scream as the gag was removed and her answers given. Then, of course, the gag was tightened and the whole process continued, but would Ashby have told this barmaid of his anything useful?'

The hands that now gripped the arms of her chair with whitened knuckles tightened further as she took a moment, then tersely said, 'Ash wouldn't have told anyone where Karen was hidden.'

'Perhaps, but then perhaps not.'

Must Burghardt be such a *Schweinehund*? 'I know him, Kapitän. You can't *ever* know him the way I do.'

And how good of her to have said it, thought Burghardt, Werner at last realizing that everything that had been said so far had been focused on getting this one response from her.

With a sinking feeling, Beck understood that the Kapitän was having the conversation tape-recorded. Lighting one of the small cigars he preferred, Burghardt didn't offer cigarettes or suggest that either of them smoke.

'This morning,' he said, 'I received two telephone calls, two apologies. The first was from Admiral Canaris and the second from your father, Frau Ashby, but I do realize that retirement was offered should I fail in this.'

He blew smoke to one side and spat a shred of tobacco. Sunlight, streaming into the spartan office, made it difficult for them to look at him but easier for himself to spot any slight hesitation or weakness. 'The point is, there will be no more such mistakes. There can't be, because the echelons of the British MI5 still remain almost totally focused on the Communist threat and another revolution like that of the Soviets, while downplaying the threat of the Reich, much to the consternation of but a few in their ranks, and that is something we definitely do not want to change. First we must find out why that woman was murdered and by whom. Was it merely a sex killing—there is still that possibility—or was it done as a means of forcing your husband into cooperating with the British MI5, who have virtually no resources, far too few men in the field, especially those who are decidedly against us, and far too great a need to convince Whitehall and Number Ten Downing Street to increase those resources?'

'You can't mean that!' blurted Christina. 'They wouldn't deliberately kill someone.'

Sickened by the thought, she was afraid for her child, noted Burghardt, whereas Herr Beck now felt a surge of adrenaline, Werner saying, 'Oh, but they would, Christina. The battle has just become a war.'

One ought to let him continue grinning, thought Burghardt. Men like Werner had such a need to prove themselves, especially when in front of women like Christina von Hoffmann.

'Did those two,' she asked, 'talk to this barmaid before she was taken and killed?'

'On four occasions,' said Burghardt. 'Twice at the pub where she worked, once in the village of Kilve on market day—it was then that they asked her for the location of the chantry—and once on that beach itself.'

'By moonlight?' she asked.

Delighting in her acidity, he said, 'Even in late May it is far too cold for bathing in the Bristol Channel. They came upon her in broad daylight, catching a bit of sun while minding a handful of village children. A Sunday-school outing, I believe.'

'Then the two,' said Christina, 'that Werner sent over were being watched by someone from MI5 and yet, Kapitän, they did not realize this?'

Meaning that they had been unsuitable for that task or any such other, though chosen by her lover and employed by the Abwehr, thought Burghardt, again finding himself warming to her suitability. Spoiled, she might well be, pampered and far too used to having her own way, but when faced with such a task and the glory of the Reich would she not come through?

As he studied the end of his cheroot before tapping its ash into a palm, he decided that the time for truth had come and he had best go and stand directly in front of her. 'Is there any feeling left between yourself and your husband?' he asked.

It was, thought Christina, as if Werner no longer existed. 'Why do you ask?'

'Because I must. Because all avenues must be explored.'

The shit! 'Then forget that one. Any regard Ash might have had for me died the day he found me in bed with another man.'

'With two men, Frau Ashby. A party, I believe, and the evening of the 16 May 1934, a Saturday. *Ein Orgie* at the house of a wealthy cousin, Untersturmführer Jaeger. The other man not wearing his uniform or anything else was Obersturmführer Langbehn, but I will spare you the details of which two of your portholes they were using.'

As if she was a ship! But who the hell had told him? 'I was very drunk.'

'*Ach*, I'm sure you were. These things happen, and of course they were SS and of the master race and out to prove themselves, whereas Herr Ashby certainly wasn't.'

What did he really want of her? 'My father will post a reward, Kapitän, of 10,000 Reichsmark for the safe return of my daughter.'

Must she cause him to still question her suitability? 'Your father has already offered far more than an old sea captain such as myself needs to purchase a yacht as fine as that of Herr Beck, Fräulein, and to retire in comfort if and when all this talk of war should cease.'

The depth of her uncertainty was revealed in the look she gave him, she saying, 'Ash won't listen to me.'

'Oh but he will, especially if you were to . . .'

Instinctively she clenched a fist and pressed a foot hard against the floor. 'Ash hates me just as much as I hate him, Kapitän. Werner, tell this dolt—'

Burghardt shook his head and wagged a forefinger. 'Your current lover, though not perhaps as good at performing as those two that husband of yours first found you with, now knows he must only speak when ordered. As of this moment, he has been suspended from active service without pay, which means, of course, that since he is available, the Kriegsmarine can have him if I so choose.'

To give him credit, thought Burghardt, Beck took it like a man, merely snapping to attention and saluting.

Obviously crestfallen, she asked, 'Am I to go over there?'

Again he would tip ash into his palm, thought Burghardt, but he could, he knew, tell her only so much. 'I must, yes, ask that you go over to England to have a talk with that husband of yours. By whatever means possible you must try to make him see reason and let you return with your daughter. You will also, since this office requires the information, find out all you can about the murder of that barmaid and who it is in MI5 that has made contact with Herr Ashby.'

That lovely throat of hers constricted and, obviously thinking of what had happened to that barmaid, she could no longer force herself to look up at him.

'When must I go?'

'When and only when I judge things ready. So, Herr Beck, a means of quietly withdrawing the girl from under their noses. Backup systems, blind avenues that are certain to draw MI5's attention from the one we will actually use. No contact whatsoever with Frau Ashby or any of our existing operatives. We simply can't afford to lose good people at a time like this, not even for a child of the Reich. For this we will have to find someone else, someone so deep the British won't know of him.'

'*Ein Schweigeagent,*' breathed Beck, suppressing the grin of elation he felt.

Dummkopf, thought Burghardt, but allowed a quiet patience to enter his voice. 'A debt that must be repaid, a secret held perhaps. Who knows? An awakening, yes, but let us hope we don't waste that one too, for then heads other than my own will surely roll.'

A sleeper, thought Christina. A homosexual, a former prisoner of war who had turned informant for the Kaiser and betrayed escape attempts, a German woman working as a nanny or housekeeper in a British household—there were plenty of those, as were there Irish nationalists. Really so many possibilities existed, even the payment of a large enough sum, or simply someone who bore a grudge. Ash would never know until it was too late.

As the sounds of London's Friday traffic and the cries of competing news vendors faded from him, Ashby stood outside the entrance to Spurgeon's Bombay Tea and Spice on Carnaby Street in Soho. Mullioned, floor-to-ceiling windows were capped by fanlights, the black, painted oak and gilded letters faded, cracked and lined with soot, the scents of ginger, curry and cinnamon mingling with that of the smog. Across the lower half of both doors were the words PURVEYORS TO HIS MAJESTY, BLENDERS OF THE FINEST TEAS AND SPICES. ESTABLISHED IN 1832. They hadn't even changed it when Victoria had acceded to the throne in 1837.

The teas were to the left, the spices to the right, and the clash of scents came heady on the stillness of the air, for the shop was overly long. There were two counters, backed by ranks of numbered, lettered drawers, and what the drawers didn't contain had spilled over the counters in tall, glass-stoppered bottles with Latin letters for the spices and Chinese porcelains for the teas or lead-lined cases that bore such bold black letters as BULKED: PURE INDIA TEA, CEYLON ORANGE PEKOE, CEYLON PEKOE SOUCHONG and FORMOSA OOLONG.

No one came to ask what he wanted. Indeed, there appeared to be nobody minding the shop. A hammer mill was running behind yet another door and timbered partition at the very back of the dingy warehouse that lay beyond the front shop, the noise deafening: like hail beating mercilessly on a tin roof, now a slug, a sack, a sudden gust that trickled off within minutes to a pebble or two that raced madly round inside the machine dodging the rotating hammer blades.

The dust was everywhere, fine, tan-coloured, and it floated down bringing the pungently sweet aroma of nutmeg. The discharge cone of the hammer mill was sunk into the cellar, while the rest of it rose up through the floor into the dusty timbers above.

'Bloody stuff gets up your nose,' shouted someone in a cloth cap, smock and apron, all of which were liberally covered. 'Here, mate, what're you doin' standin' about like friggin' royalty? This here's out of bounds t' th' likes of you.'

Nutmeg clouded the eyebrows and gnarled face, collecting in the wrinkles that pulled the skin about the antagonistic eyes and grim-set lips.

'Colonel Hacker sent me. I was told to come here,' he shouted as another hundred pounds shot through the machine.

'Hacker,' clucked the little man. 'Hacker . . . Hey, Wilf, you know any Hacker? Christ, th' bloody racket! WILF, CAN'T YOU HEAR ME NONE? SHUT TH' OLD WHORE OFF! Bugger's stone deaf at his age. Perishing terrible ain't it. Hacker?'

The machine died and the dust hung in the air, clinging to everything, and where too much had built up on a nearby timber, it avalanched to the floor, leaving dense little clouds.

The silence was penetrating. Up from the cellar came a shout, 'Bill, for the love of Jesus, what the hell is the matter now? We've got the grind. The blades are set correctly to match the screen. The feed's just fine. Bill, I won't have it—'

A head, shoulders, shirt and tie appeared and then the rest, bald over the crown, big-eared, thick-necked, big-shouldered but stooped and stout.

Bill dragged off his cap. 'Says some'ne called Hacker sent him, Sir John. Don't know no Hacker, does I, nor young Wilf.'

A forearm was gripped in comradeship. 'It's all right, Bill,' said

Sir John. 'Never mind. I'll attend to it, now there's a good chap. The grind's bang on. Why not take your tea break then press ahead, eh what? Champion, Bill. I knew you could do it.'

'That old whore's had it, Sir John. You can't tease life out of th' dead.'

The man from the cellar gave Bill's arm a friendly squeeze. 'You just have, right? Now be a good lad and have your tea.'

He began to roll down his sleeves, to think better of this and to brush himself off. 'Tired,' he said. 'The machine's just tired.' But in the shop, he added, 'If you'll excuse me, Captain Ashby, I shan't be a minute.'

Snatching up a brush, he strode the length of the shop and out to the pavement, the passersby parting, he paying them no mind and brushing himself thoroughly down before straightening his tie.

On the way back, he collected his jacket, then came on to stand in speculative appraisal before him, thought Ashby. Nutmeg still clung to him, the eyes gun-metal blue beneath washed-out brows, the stance tough but not necessarily belligerent, the age about sixty-three. A man, then, who took life as it came.

So this was the schoolmaster. 'Sir John Masterson at your service, Captain. Bunny's sent word. Sorry about there not having been anyone to greet you. I should have known better, but . . . well, duty called. Good of you to find the time.'

'Your Colonel Hacker gave me no choice. I don't know who you are or what you want with me, but I'm not happy about it.'

A flicker of irritation stiffened the stance but it passed into a brief smile, the handshake firm, Masterson almost as tall as himself.

'Bunny's a good man, Captain Ashby. Would have made a splendid detective had the Yard had the sense to hire him. Still, ours is not to complain, *hmm*? We've got him and they haven't.'

'What do you people want with me?'

Stung, Masterson raised his voice. 'We *people*, Captain, can help you, or would you prefer we let the Germans find your daughter? Ah, I thought not. Well, there's a good chap. Knew you'd see things our way. Would you prefer tea or beer? Tea's upstairs in what's left of the tasting room. Beer's any pub you care to choose. The Red Lion in Saint James's, perhaps. Then you'll be near your club and can pop over afterwards. Yes, I think that would suit admirably. Agreed?'

He would choose the tea, thought Ashby, and find out all he could, but again there was that flicker of irritation from Masterson.

The tasting room was almost as long as the shop below. Hundreds of white porcelain bowls stretched in a line atop a counter that ran from end to end, and behind each there was an equally sized white porcelain pot with its strainer. Sample tins of tea were ranked along the shelves. Gas burners stood under waiting kettles, a clock giving the time clearly in quartered minutes, brass spittoons standing sentinel on rollers, but everywhere there was the dust of disuse, the room so obviously having been shut up for years, Ashby had to give Masterson a questioning look.

The rounded shoulders shrugged; the voice, when it came, was somewhat in rebuke. 'Two things, Captain. First, Spurgeon's used to occupy the premises next door as well, and the spice side of things existed hermetically there, so as not to bugger the tea. Second, the tea business has its ups and downs. Taken on the cycle, when the price is right, it can make you a fortune. Taken at the wrong time, it can treat you like a bad woman. I inherited Spurgeon's from my father, to whom the tea trade had just given the clap. Now what'll it be? Some Dum Duma, or would you prefer the Darjeeling? There's no milk by the way, nor is there any sugar. There never was, of course.'

The Dum Duma, from Lakhimpur in Assam, was a 'first-rate self-drinker.' 'The Assams,' said Masterson, 'are the stalwarts of the tea trade in Britain. Marvellous teas, though not so fine as the Darjeeling where the mist rises to hover at about four thousand feet. Here at Spurgeon's we used the shilling when weighing out, same as Brook Bond. In Bombay, and in the hills, I used the four-anna silver piece.'

Selecting a canister, he blew dust out of two of the bowls, shook and banged a kettle to dislodge and get rid of the scale, then filled it and set the water to boil. Using a beam balance and the four-anna piece, he perched himself on one of the stools and indicated that another should be used. 'I met Bunny in Burma, of course, and our paths have more or less crossed ever since, but that's of no consequence, is it?'

'Burma . . . What was he doing there?'

And thank you, thought Masterson. 'Police work. Mainly that and putting down insurrections in the hills and training regulars. Sad, really, to see it all go, the Empire. Giving the buggers quasi-dominion status isn't the answer, but our Prime Minister Chamberlain's got his work cut out for him. This business with Hitler won't stop. Austria and now the Sudetenland and then Danzig, eh? It can't go on, can it? We'll soon be forced into doing something. Poland is my guess. Poland and then, why then, the sky's the limit if we don't stand firm.'

The kettle came to a boil. Masterson glanced at his wristwatch and spoke of oxygen in the water and how essential it was to take the water at exactly the right time. Routine took over, and he made the tea, again keeping an eye on his watch. Five minutes he would allow it to steep. Five and no more.

The clock on the wall had stopped.

'Tell me about General Friedrich von Hoffmann, Captain.'

'Not until you tell me a lot more about why I'm here and what I'm getting into, especially with employees like your Colonel Hacker.'

Oh dear, oh dear, Bunny had really upset him, but must schoolmasters always assume the worst? 'There's not much to tell. MI5 counterintelligence has virtually no budget, as you can well surmise, and few permanent staff. Even now, its main concern is still the threat of international Communism, though I am, thanks to Bunny's efforts and those of others, bringing my associates round to believing the Reich a far greater threat. Myself, I'm what we call a coordinator. I run Bunny and a few others, and they report back to me.'

No budget and few other than Hacker working on the threat from the Reich . . . 'And this place?'

Masterson used a handkerchief to mop nutmeg from his brow. 'Apart from the shop? Oh, a blind, I suppose. Spurgeon's provided the opportunity for a bit of travel, so it's all to the good. We're attached to Section B, counterespionage, but there are other sections: administration, security, military liaison, aliens and overseas control, all of which sounds very grand. B has three main functions: counterintelligence, countersabotage and countersubversion. Major-General Sir Vernon Kell heads it all, as he has for a good many years, and Captain Guy Liddell's director of Section B. There are desks for any number of things in B, enemy wireless, mail, police liaise with the constabulary and the Yard. Have to, you see, because we're under the home secretary and have no powers of search and arrest ourselves. We're part of the civil service, a bind, Bunny would say. He's one of what we call the "Watchers." Moves about the country a good deal, that one. Never stops for long, let me tell you.'

The tea was dark and bitter. 'What, exactly, have you two got in mind for me?'

There was mist on the tea, a good sign, thought Masterson, blowing it away. 'We've had a series of wireless signals come through from AST-X Bremen. Bits of five-letter groupings, is all you need to know, but there's a sleeper somewhere, Captain, and we greatly fear those signals are his wake-up call and that he's to find and take your daughter back. Where have you got her?'

A sleeper . . . Hacker had said the same. 'I'm not saying, Sir John.'

'Oh come now, be sensible. They'll find her, and then what?'

'You can stop them.'

'How? Once they've got her, we might not even know which aerodrome they would use to take her home. Then, too, they might decide to use a trawler and we wouldn't know that until it was far too late. Good God, man, we've not the manpower or the finances to cover the whole of the frigging British Isles.'

They needed something, then, thought Ashby, something like a real coup to convince Whitehall and the prime minister of how necessary MI5 was and how great the threat from the Reich.

'Well?' demanded Masterson, taking a swig of tea to slosh it round and then spit it out.

'I'm still not saying. Right now she's safe.'

'Can you be absolutely certain of that after what those two birds did to that barmaid of yours? I should think not, so you'll tell us where the girl is and let us leak that to our friends in the Abwehr because we want this sleeper, Captain, and everything else he can bring us.'

'And if I don't agree?'

'The Yard will pick you up.'

'I didn't kill Daisy.'

'Good gracious me, of course you didn't, but you don't have an alibi. Not unless you want to tell the court where the girl is and why you've not only taken her from her mother but hidden her away.'

'I still can't understand why they killed Daisy. It makes no sense. That colonel of yours must have known where she was since he came upon me just after I'd found her.'

Oh dear, oh dear. 'Bunny is always on top of things. Has to be, now doesn't he?'

Hesitantly invited into the sitting room of Headmaster House and offered tea, Hacker set the cup and saucer down on the mantelpiece. Neither Anthony James Pearce nor David Douglas Ashby was present or near on this Friday afternoon, the Pearce woman frightened out of her wits about the murder.

Leaving the tea untouched, he said, 'The Yard would be grateful if you would take it upon yourself to let me have a look through Captain Ashby's room.'

'Is he a suspect?' she yelped.

She had even splashed tea on her frock. 'One never knows, does one, madam? Apparently he was intimate with the woman, though I must say it's odd, a man of his calibre having sexual relations with a barmaid. Did you know he was and that he had a wife?'

Ruth blanched. 'A wife? Ash? No. No, I didn't!'

And never mind the barmaid. Beaten by the news of a wife, her head was now bowed, she so near to tears, Hacker knew he had to wonder about her feelings for the schoolmaster, but asked, 'Mrs. Pearce, don't headmasters check out each of the masters before hiring them, or is it that your husband doesn't tell you anything? Come, come, why weren't you a party to Captain Ashby's marital status?'

Defiantly, she looked up at him. 'I wasn't, that's all. My husband and I seldom discuss him. He's a good teacher. Isn't that enough for me to know?'

'Not when there are tears. Were you in love with Captain Ashby? Are you?'

'*Me?*'

'Yes, you, Mrs. Pearce. You're giving every sign of it.'

'I'm not. How could I be?'

'Then you'll let me see through his room.'

Ruth wrung her hands. 'As I've told you, Colonel, my husband's away in Taunton. The boys . . . It will start the school to whispering. Their parents are bound to hear of it and then I . . . I don't know what will happen.'

A scandal, ripe like rotting fish. 'The room, Mrs. Pearce. Your husband's being questioned in Taunton. We thought it might be best to do it there. Out of sight and on the quiet, so to speak.'

'Anthony went to the dentist!'

'Of course he did. And Captain Ashby?'

'Went up to London. He . . . he won't be back until late on Sunday. I . . .'

'We know exactly where he is, Mrs. Pearce. He'll never know I've been in his room. Just a look, eh, to help our investigation along.'

'David didn't kill that woman. How could he have?'

And bleating it out too. 'We're not saying that he did, only wanting to see if there's a connection to those who might have.'

'There's a spare set of keys in my husband's study. David is master of Todd House.' But when they got to the room, he having followed her in full view of everyone who cared to look, Ruth found she couldn't seem to fit the key into the lock.

'Let me,' he said.

The coarseness of Colonel Hacker's thumb and forefinger made her cringe, and as the door closed behind her, Ruth leaned back against it, fighting for composure.

Hacker lost interest in her. The room was plainly furnished: two stuffed armchairs by the fireplace, an end table covered with books, the desk littered with stacks of exercise books to correct and grade, bookcases, a closet, wireless set, bureau and not a hell of a lot else.

When he found the revolver, a British Army Mark VI Webley in a bureau drawer, he said, not turning to look at the woman, 'An old friend, I must say, Mrs. Pearce. Needs one hell of a lot of practice though. Any idea why he would keep it fully loaded in a school for boys?'

'No! I . . . I didn't even know Ash had it.'

Ash . . . And white as a sheet, no doubt, thought Hacker. '*It*, Mrs. Pearce?' he asked.

When she didn't answer, he flicked his wrist, swinging the cyl-inder open further, the brass cartridges spilling onto the carpet. 'Pick those up, would you?'

'I . . . I beg your pardon?'

'I said: Would you pick those up?'

The bell rang in the halls, the sound of trampling shoes soon coming to her, Ruth down on her hands and knees at his feet, fighting for composure while trying to gather the cartridges, knowing the boys would be bound to see her and Colonel Hacker leave Ash's room.

Hacker let a photograph drop, and as it clipped her brow, the woman saw not only a wife—slim, tall, elegant and obviously fair—but a child, a little girl of about three with Ashby's winsome smile, the father and the daughter obviously birds of a feather.

Tears splashed the photograph, the Pearce woman's hand shak-ing so much, the trauma of unrequited love was clear enough.

Looking up at last, she blurted, 'I *didn't* know! No one ever told me, not Anthony and . . . and not Ash.'

A ragged sob was given, Ruth knowing he was looking down at her with contempt.

'Why not tell me about Captain Ashby and your husband, Mrs. Pearce? Sit over there on his bed and let me have the whole of it. What you know of their association, but more than that, what it has suggested to you.'

Everything, then, thought Ruth. Everything.

She might find out that he wasn't from the Yard, felt Hacker, would discover soon enough that her husband hadn't been ques-tioned in Taunton, but by then it would be too late.

There was a recent photograph of Karen Ashby taken with the couple who must be hiding her. A trawler was in the background, and he could just make out the name: the *Bonnie Jean*. Though there were probably any number of such in the registry, it was damned marvellous what one found out some days, pure inspira-tion coming here like this with Ashby up in London as requested.

Now where the hell was that bloody trawler?

On that same Friday afternoon, 27 May, as Hilary waited for them to start eating, Karen fervently bowed her head, and with hands placed together, began to pray: '*Führer, mein Führer*, bequeathed to me by God. Protect and preserve me as long as I live! You have rescued Germany from deep despair. I thank you for my daily bread. Abide long with me. Forsake me not. *Führer, mein Führer*, my faith and my light. *Heil, mein Führer!*"

A spoonful of soup was taken, then thought better of, Karen breaking bread into the bowl and saying, 'They are *not* coming, Fräulein. They are *never* coming back!'

Ewen and Monica had gone to Falmouth in the *Bonnie Jean*. Karen had had her lesson, such as it had been, then a hike across the moors in search of birds' nests, a deliberate avoidance of the mine, and now . . . why now, an early supper. 'Of course they are,' said Hilary. 'They've just been delayed.' But had they, she wondered, or had something terrible happened?

'You *can't* keep me a prisoner in this stinking cottage. I will run away!'

'No you won't. It's far too dangerous, and you know it. Look, if you're really planning to escape, at least have the decency to wait until you're back in Saint Ives. It's bad enough having to put up with someone who doesn't want to learn her English.'

'There will be no need. *Opa* says we will have to fight the British and the French, and that this time we will destroy them and *everyone* will have to speak *Deutsch*!'

The soup, leftover broth made from beef scraps, bacon, leeks, carrots, swedes and cabbage with added onions, potatoes and a little thickening flour, was puddled, the bits of bread drowned as Karen fiercely muttered to herself, *'Juden . . . Sie Sind alle Juden,'* Jews . . . They are all Jews. And then, loudly, 'The Führer will *destroy* you people. He came to *Opa*'s great big house and told me that. He shook my hand, Fräulein Bowker-Brown, and patted me on the head, and I gave him the flowers I had picked, and I kissed his cheek. I did. I *really* did.'

Ach, what had she taken on? wondered Hilary. 'The Führer isn't a god, Karen. You can't believe all that rubbish.'

She would *fling* the spoon at this *Engländerin* and tell her what had happened, thought Karen. She would spit it at her! 'Herr

---

* This prayer was recited before meals by children in Cologne, according to James D. Forman in his book *Nazism*, published by Franklin Watts in New York and London in 1978.

Ewen and Frau Monica are not coming for me, Fräulein. *Opa's* men have found out where they are and have *killed* them!'

'I beg your pardon?'

'*Killed*, Fräulein. *Killed!* Did you think I didn't know why my father was hiding me in this stinky place?'

Neither David Douglas Ashby nor Ewen and Monica had told her everything, thought Hilary. 'It's not stinky. It's really very clean, but Karen, what do you mean by saying that about Ewen and Monica?'

The girl plunged a fist of bread into the muck and shoved it down with her spoon. 'That my grandfather will now come after you. That you will die here, you stupid Jewess. Die, Fräulein. Die!'

As the child raced from the cottage, Hilary paused on the doorstep. Badly shaken, she didn't know what to do. The cottage was far too near the sea, the only road all the access they really had except by foot across the moor.

Going out to her, she said, 'Karen, please don't ever try to run away from me. It's far too dangerous. The cliffs are bad enough, but there are other things you don't know about. The pump shaft for one—it goes down and down into the mine. Then there's the larger shaft the men once used to enter and leave. Neither is safe and you must never go near them. There are also large hills and long, high ridges of waste rock and they, too, aren't safe, especially if you're in a terrible hurry and wanting to escape.'

Out over the moor, the light was sharp, the green and purplish grasses looking as if they, too, with the heather, the gorse and the bracken, had all been forced by the prevailing wind to lean away. Certainly there were people about, not just the local fishermen and farmers. In summer, hikers would cross the moor or skirt the edge of the cliffs, often illegally trespassing. Cyclists and hikers used the road, as did the twice-daily omnibus to Zennor, Land's End and return, and soon there would be the holiday makers, some with their motorcars, who would flock to the seashore at Saint Ives, the curious spilling over into the surrounding countryside, but it *was* lonely even then, and Captain David Douglas Ashby hadn't told her everything, not by a long chalk.

When she saw the van, Hilary wiped her eyes and said, '*Gott sei Dank!* They've not been killed. Come on then, *meine kleine Freundin*. Let's go and have a talk with them.'

'Why were you crying?'

'For a lot of reasons, but please don't worry. I rather felt you and I might have become friends.'

But there wasn't anything for it, was there? she thought. Writing had been a stupid, stupid notion. War was coming, and those who were fluent in *Deutsch und Französisch* would not only be in demand, but obligated to do whatever was needed.

'Amongst other reasons, I came here to get away from some people,' she said, facing Monica and Ewen now, as they stood beside the van. 'They wanted me to join the Secret Intelligence Service and I . . . why, I thought I could hide myself in Cornwall and live my dream. What happened to Captain Ashby when he came down here and you sent him out to see me? Six pounds a fortnight, Monica. Six! And my life on the line, is that it?'

Ewen put an arm about his wife, then confessed, Monica adding, 'They shot at him, but . . . but he got away.'

'Then Karen was right,' said Hilary. 'Her grandfather does have people looking for her and it won't be long until they succeed.'

Pratt's was in Park Place, Saint James's. The club, Ashby knew, had been here since the Duke of Beaufort had taken his friends to the house one evening in 1841, to the kitchen of his steward, Nathaniel Pratt. Going down into the basement, to that same kitchen/ sitting room, he let the warmth and comfort envelop him and tried to ease his concerns over Daisy and what Sir John Masterson had insisted upon. There were several members and their guests, and he spoke briefly to a few. Morocco-covered armchairs and the green baize of the cribbage table complemented the deep red of the walls, the glossy black of the woodwork and the glow from the charcoal under the grill. Blue Delft tiles covered the grill and the stove, both of which were tucked into the fireplace beneath an imitation Roman frieze.

The membership had always been eclectic, a smattering of diplomats and members of Parliament, including that grand warrior, the belligerent Mr. Churchill. Several regiments were represented, the Blues, the Coldstream Guards. There were doctors, barristers, high court judges, writers . . . all came for the comfort and companionship. One didn't have to dress for dinner or put on airs. Anthony had nominated him, and he had always been grateful.

'Hello, George, any messages for me?' he asked. George, like all the stewards here, carried only that name by custom.

'Two, sir. A call from Mr. Anthony. Said it wasn't urgent but would appreciate your ringing him up. He'll be at home, at the school, and said he would wait up if you didn't get in here early.'

Something must have happened at the school, or with the murder investigation. 'And the other call?'

'From Cornwall, sir, from a Mr. Ewen MacDonald in Saint Ives. He said there wasn't any urgency, but that you had best ring the Pilchard Arms before closing. A pub, I believe.'

George looked away, forcing him to ask if there was anything else.

'Well, er . . . yes, there is, sir. You see, there's . . . well, there's your wife. I told her the club was off-limits to women but she wouldn't take no for an answer. She's waiting upstairs, in the billiards room. I've given her coffee—she wouldn't touch tea, whisky or gin. I'm sorry, sir. I know I should have sent her packing but . . . Well, sir, she simply refused to leave.'

Christina, but how had she known he would be in London? wondered Ashby. A sleeper, Masterson had said. A German agent who had lain dormant, but it couldn't have been anyone at the school. It couldn't.

'Sir?'

'It's all right, George. Thanks for looking after her. If I could have a whisky and soda.'

'It's in your hand, sir. I've only just put it there.'

They both forgot themselves for a moment, then George said, 'I've taken the liberty of ringing up the Dorchester over in Park Lane, sir. They've reserved a room for her and I've seen to her cases and things.'

Christina was sitting on the arm of a sofa, all alone and smoking a cigarette, her fourth or fifth no doubt. The long and shapely legs were crossed, one forearm resting on a thigh, the hand with the cigarette dangling over her knee, the dark blue heels, silk stockings and soft, dove-grey woollen dress with dark blue buttons looking well on her, the plain white collar complementing the stunning looks.

A matching cloche was tilted away from him over the right side of her head. She didn't hear him come into the room, remained so lost and staring off into space at the carpet, he had to wonder what she was planning. Finally he said, 'Hello, Christina.'

'Ash!' she brightened, her unexpected smile and delight at seeing him lasting for an instant, but had he been struck by her expression? she wondered. Had it carried him right back to Paris, to that moment when they had first set eyes on one another and had instantly known?

'How did you find out I'd be in London?' he asked.

And wary of her now. 'I didn't. I simply took a chance. When they said you were here, I decided to do a bit of shopping. Otherwise I'd have taken the train to Taunton and then caught a bus out to the school.'

To a place she had never been, and a bus, thought Ashby. It simply didn't wash.

'Aren't you glad to see me?' she asked, giving him a faint and uncertain smile, he saying: 'Why should I be?'

But wondering if she had lied about not knowing he was in London, thought Christina. Impatiently she stubbed out her cigarette and got to her feet. She would use *Deutsch* now, would not let him get away with *Englisch*. '*Ach*, it is as I feared. You're still hating me for something that happened *four* years ago and was really not my fault. Why *must* you continue to take it out on me?'

'There's no use in our discussing it. You can't have Karen, Christina, not with that father of yours wanting to make a die-hard Nazi out of her, and not with the way things are going in the Reich.'

There was only one way to make him yield. '*Vati* told me that you had taken a lover and that the woman had been subjected to torture and then murdered. When I heard the news, I came straight over. I didn't think, Ash. I just knew how upset you would be and I hoped . . . yes, I hoped the two of us could . . . well, could work something out so that no one else would be caught up in what you've done to me.'

'Daisy didn't know where Karen was, Christina. She didn't know I had a daughter or even that I was still legally married. Those two who did that to her would have easily discovered this in the pub and really had no reason to have done what they did.'

In short, it had gone too far and still made no sense to him, but now, as Burghardt had insisted, it was up to herself and she would have to try. 'Please don't let us fight, *mein Liebling*. Let us talk quietly over a meal like two civilized people who were once so very much in love that every waking moment was shared, even though I was often alone with Karen.'

He looked thinner, slightly older than when Karen had been five and they had last seen each other. Distracted by something, and worried not just by her unexpected arrival, he said, when asked what it was, 'Nothing. Just a couple of telephone calls I'll have to answer.'

Two of them, but she would not reach out to him yet, would ask, 'Do the police really know who killed your friend?'

'As I've only just said, those two that father of yours sent over, or didn't he bother to tell you he'd done that?'

But did Ash *not* believe they had murdered the woman? wondered Christina. '*Ach*, I know this must sound false, but could it have been someone else?'

'Who? Hacker said . . .'

'Hacker?' she asked. 'Who is this, please?'

'A policeman. Well, not exactly, but he's the one who first questioned me about Daisy when I found her body.'

She would close the distance between them now, thought Christina. She would reach out to him in kindness, would touch his cheek as she had so often, would touch the dimple in his chin and let her finger linger there a moment, and she would switch to English. 'You're hurting, my darling.'

Ashby felt her arms encircle his neck, felt her pressing herself against him, felt her lips against a cheek, her tears as she said, 'Kurt Meydel and Martin Lund must be the two you want, but please, if you still have any feelings for me, don't let anyone know I told you.'

Trembling, he caught her hands in his and kissed them, said, 'Thanks, and I mean it, Christina. Daisy was my friend.'

But had she been as good in bed? she wanted so much to ask, letting him feel the brush of her lips against his own, knowing he couldn't help but breathe in the soft, warm scent of her, she pulling away suddenly to say, 'Forgive me, please. I . . . I shouldn't have done that. I . . . I had no right.' And when he held her from him, but gazed steadily at her, she said, 'Darling, I know that you're right about what's been happening at home. I've still got my British passport and . . . and I want us to start over, if it's possible for you to forgive that one drunken evening. I've even worn my wedding ring—see? I . . . I won't go back if . . . if that is what you really want.'

Over Bremen, Friday's sun had dipped at last, the sky streaked with orange and grey against which the dark shapes of aircraft were too distant to identify. *Henkels*, thought Burghardt.

Another training flight. Above them, there would be the night fighters. Messerschmitts, most probably, ME-109s.

Lost in thought, he continued to stroll along the quays, the Weser close, the sound of donkey engines ever-present. A child, he said to himself. A sleeper. *Ach du lieber Gott*, hadn't something desperately been needed both to satisfy the General von Hoffmann, who had been making such a pain in the ass of himself, and the Old Man, for Canaris knew only too well of the general's connections and liked nothing better himself than to indulge in intrigue, and didn't one survive in war as in peace by not only protecting one's agents and the whole of AST-X Bremen's British network but by keeping one's superiors happy and never ruffling the feathers of the influential?

Coming to a copse of willows, he thought of what could be made of them, most notably schoolmaster switches.

'Osier,' he said in English. But generals were known to talk indiscreetly, as were admirals when enthused, thus the identity of any such sleeper had to be protected further by using a number beside which that code name would lie in his office safe, should anyone think to open it unannounced.

'*Nummer* 07392,' he said to himself. 'Osier, Frau Ashby, and may God help me if I am wrong.'

Fearing the loss not just of his granddaughter but also his daughter, the general had been far from happy. Snatches of their last telephone conversation came to him. 'No, General, I did not, I repeat *not*, order your daughter to do such a thing. Fräulein von Hoffmann went over to Britain of her own free will. Yes . . . yes, daughters can sometimes be impetuous, General. There is no problem, why should there be? Things will proceed exactly as the admiral has instructed. *Ein Schweigeagent, ja*. Admiral Canaris was most insistent I awaken one who would be both very close to the task at hand and in whom we could place our utmost confidence, while at the same time minimizing any losses should such occur.'

Herr Ashby would be surprised to see his former wife but had there been an element of truth in the general's concerns? Christina von Hoffmann had been twenty-two and crazy about that future husband of hers when the couple had secretly married in 1928, Ashby thirty-five. The general, never happy about the marriage, had tried to have it annulled and had threatened but in vain. That daughter of his had *wanted* Ashby and that had been all there was to it, but now? he had to wonder. Would that old craving come back to her?

When he found the *Thule Sólarsteinn*, the dusk had all but closed in on the superb fifteen-metre yacht Werner Beck poured his love into when not out on the Jardelunder taking eels and other things, including that general's daughter. *Thule* meant 'Iceland' in the early Norse, and *Sólarsteinn* meant 'sunstone,' that translucent cleavage of Iceland spar that polarized the sunlight and had allowed those early seafarers to pinpoint the sun through overcast skies or even, they had claimed, when in dense fog.

Beck's mother had been a Dane, hence the brooding spells that could, at times, be a worry, but her love of the outdoors and individualistic streak had made him a good choice for AST-X Bremen, though he would most certainly have to be taught his lessons.

Beck was in the bilges up to his elbows in grease, repacking the pump. 'Well, at least it's not another woman,' said Burghardt. 'Things have now moved into their next phase, and we must discuss how best for you to pluck that child out of England.'

The spanner was lowered. 'Kapitän, you can't have heard from Christina, not yet.'

The urge to wag a reproving finger was there, but he'd grin instead, thought Burghardt, and tell him, 'She's too busy, I suspect, seducing her schoolmaster.'

Stung by this, Beck angrily went back to work, muttering, 'You're a bastard just like she said.'

One could afford to be affable. After all, that splendid body would be being used by someone else, the enemy, and salt did help jealousy's wounds. 'Bastards always get things done, Werner. Just remember that you've been suspended from active duty pending the safe return of the child.'

At the Dorchester, the dance music came up to them, Ash having managed a balcony table. Using one of the candles to light her cigarette, Christina gazed questioningly at him, for he had noticed her hair, her dress, the jewellery—*everything*—even how the candlelight was caught in her eyes, reminding him of those times they had lain naked in each other's arms in firelight, their shadows thrown large upon the walls and ceiling, but had he weakened?

Briefly giving him a shy and introspective smile, she seductively fingered the stem of her wineglass. 'Karen cried a lot for you, David. There were times when I would find she couldn't stop. Has it been the same over myself?'

She had reached out to touch his left hand, had let their knees rub, hadn't moved her legs, had defied him to move his own, which he hadn't, not yet. 'She did and does miss you, Christina. I can't deny that.'

Tilting up her chin, she blew tobacco smoke towards the ceiling, let him see the fullness of the throat he had loved so much to lightly finger and kiss while saying, *When I'm in you, I feel as if we're one, especially when you're coming,* and she saying, *Deeper, my love. Deeper. Oh yes!* 'Darling, what is it you want to ask? Look, I know you well enough, David. My goodness, that expression! I've seen it a thousand times. It's like we had never parted.'

Wanting to grin, Ashby told himself not to, that old times were old times and not the present. 'Did that father of yours tell you I would be in London?'

Verdammt, he wouldn't leave it. She would have to nod, have to give him that, but first would let him see her indecisively fingering the stem of her glass.

'Who told him, Christina? Look, I have to know, otherwise I can't . . .'

'Can't take me to see Karen?' she asked, abruptly setting her cigarette aside and removing her hands from sight. It had been his turn to strike and he had.

'Just tell me,' he said.

He knowing, she was sure, that she was gripping her thighs

in anger. A deal, was that what he wanted of her? she wondered, but would say, 'Vati has his connections, Ash. He has always had them.'

Admiral Wilhelm Canaris, thought Ashby grimly. The Abwehr. 'Is there someone at Grantley's, Christina? Someone who's been ordered to wake up and keep tabs on me?'

Someone close? wondered Christina, relishing the thought. He had had two telephone calls.

Had one of them been from that school of his? His concern said that it had, but a shrug would be best, for he'd have to notice again those bare shoulders of hers, and perhaps would remember kissing them too, and passionately, while she had stroked his *Schwanz* and gazed steadily at him. 'I wouldn't know about such things,' she said. 'Honestly, I wouldn't. Why should I?'

Yet she *had* known the names of the two who had followed him. 'Could you find out for me?'

David was watching her too closely now. 'Is that the price I must pay?' she asked. 'You know I can't be expected to find out such a thing. I'd only get in trouble. Things have tightened up a lot. Henke . . . *Vati's* driver would have told you that at Easter.'

She was reminding him of what he had done to her, thought Ashby, and when her fingers closed over the magnificent sapphire at her throat, he wondered if she was going to yank it off and throw it at him, but she didn't do that. She removed it and the earrings, all of which he had given her and all of which they had never sold even when down and out, for they'd been left in the safe-deposit box of that father of hers who had refused to release them.

Closing her hand over the jewellery, she said, 'Ash, let's not fight anymore. Darling, I meant what I said. I'll stay here in England with you as a married couple with a daughter we both love, but only if you want me.'

He was, Christina had to admit, still handsome, even with those awful spectacles he had to use, but he was, she also now knew, feeling that he was being watched all the time by someone other than herself, yet he didn't know who that could be. A colleague at his school, a friend, an associate—even someone he chanced only to meet at that pub he used when seeing that slut he'd been fucking.

With a finality that troubled him, she put the sapphires away in her handbag and stubbed out the cigarette she had all but forgotten. He would break, she decided, or he would not break. It was fifty-fifty. 'Well?' she asked, looking steadily at him now as though wanting him.

At last he said, 'Telephone your father and tell him he, and anyone else the Abwehr has got working on it, must leave Karen alone. Those are my conditions.'

And firm about it, but *gut, mein lieber* schoolmaster, *gut.* 'I'll call him from my room, but I must warn you, when you took Karen from his house like that, you embarrassed him terribly. Even Herr Himmler soon learned of it, Goebbels too, but worst of all, Göring.'

Who had, in 1928, been one of the first of the Nazis to be elected to the Reichstag and then, in 1934, had in essence formed the Gestapo and in this year, 1938, been the key figure in the *Anschluss*, but who was also head of the Luftwaffe and a notorious gossip.

Ashby settled their bill. He had already called the school, only to find that Tony had gone out for a stroll, a worry since Tony must have known he would call back as soon as possible. Ruth, however, had been terribly upset about something, and when asked, had burst into tears and rung off. He had then called the pub in Saint Ives only to lose the connection the moment Ewen had come on the line. And, yes, Christina was well aware of the fact that he had made those two calls, but not to whom.

In the lift, neither said a thing. At the door to her room, he waited while she found her key and let them in. Then they stood in the darkness, and he heard her put the lock on, she so close to him, he felt the brush of a bare arm against the back of his right hand.

'Are you still missing me?' she asked.

Ashby felt her fingering his tie and knew he had to get her to call that father of hers. 'A little, yes.'

'Only a little?' she asked, the teasing laughter in her voice. 'To be missed at all is good to know. Every woman should hear such a thing from a man she has once loved and hurt so badly.'

'Christina . . .'

'*Sh!* It is almost like old times, yes? Standing so close, knowing there's a bed on which we can both lose ourselves in each other.'

'The general . . . You were going to telephone your father.'

'He'll have gone to bed. He will only say no, in any case.'

'Try him. Tell him I'm going to take Karen to the States.'

Lieber Gott im Himmel, the States! What the hell did he really want from her? Everything? she wondered, pressing her forehead against his shoulder, forcing his lips to brush against the softness of her hair. If he had *wanted* to hurt her, he couldn't have said anything worse! 'America is so very far. Karen needs me, David—have you not seen that yet? Well, have you not, damn you?'

They still hadn't turned on a light, were now facing each other, he not saying a thing, just *waiting*, thought Christina, she having failed. 'Forgive me,' she said, brushing a hand over his chest. 'Make love to me. Make me feel it as it used to be. Karen needs the two of us.'

Taking off her shoes, she set his glasses on the side table, he feeling her hand grasp the back of his neck, then her lips, the softness of a breath, she kissing him lightly several times, her tongue now lingering. 'Come in me,' she whispered. 'Make me cry out like you used to.'

When she unfastened the halter of her dress, Ashby knew he had to leave. 'Christina . . .' he began, only to hear her give a little laugh and feel her breath against his lips again.

'You were so good,' she said. 'Those two you found me with didn't mean a thing. I know how much you must hate me, but what you don't know is that I cried for days.'

Fumbling, he tried to find those stupid glasses of his, she to want to break them.

'Think about what I really need from you, Christina. Talk to that father of yours. *Ein Schweigeagent, ja?* You can reach me at the school.'

'Wetherby Cottage, George,' said Roger Banfield. 'Close enough to the school and the graveyard. Ideal for a retirement roost if and when, eh? But easily leased in the interim.'

Crawley poured himself a little more of Roger's malt whisky. The rooms in Overton House were comfortable, the fire sufficient.

'Might cause a stir with all this talk of war,' he said. 'Real estate's bound to go down.'

Banfield offered up the fags with a grin. 'Not below five hundred pounds. It's timely and a bargain.'

'Freehold?'

'Of course.'

'Been empty for quite a while, a bad sign,' mused Crawley, taking a sip.

'But near a good stream, with reed beds and willows, George. Spring-fed osier beds all gone to growth, of course. Have to copse them back and prune the orchard. Telford could use the refuse. He's always in need of a new switch.'

Crawley grinned and said, 'Birch is better.'

'Never use it. Like yourself, I have always maintained that the tongue is the ultimate weapon. To err is to sin; to worry is to live in hell.'

'Take a look at it, then, shall we?' asked Crawley.

Banfield tossed off his whisky. 'Let the moon and the stars be our guide, but hand me that torch. We'll take a turn about the school, then go down via the old tote road, which should bring us out into the graveyard at Saint Mary Margaret's.'

Not until they were well away from the school did old George say, 'Something's up, Roger. The Lower Fifth is being awfully close about it. Seems they saw something in Ashby's room, or one of them did, but for the life of me I haven't been able to pry the rest out of that Hamilton boy. Had to do with headmaster's wife, though, of that I'm sure.'

When they came upon Tics, he was in among the blessed osiers, idly fingering the shoots and looking like death.

'We'll need baskets if there's another war,' he said, feeling futile and trying desperately to hide this from them.

'Baskets?' arched Banfield, lowering the light at last.

'Money, for God's sake!' shrilled Pearce, unsettling them. 'The school's accounts are overdrawn again. I really don't know how I can possibly pay you all at end of term.'

And so much for cottages and real estate investments, or of retiring in genteel quietude. Banfield heaved a sigh. A little firmness and common sense were what was needed. 'This crisis will pass, Headmaster, as it has even, if I may say so, before your time.

I have every confidence in our illustrious Board of Governors come Founders' Day.'

'Not this time. Not when they hear how much we are in over-draft.'

Damned chilly that, thought Crawley. Damned odd, though, baskets as a way of paying off the school's arrears. Everyone knew Headmaster was a dud when it came to the finances, but baskets?

It was Roger who said, 'Now come along, Headmaster. Do try not to take it so hard. A spot of whisky is what's called for. Your digs or mine, George?'

'I'm really quite all right,' said Pearce. 'It's just the threat of closing the school.'

And with another war coming on, thought Banfield. Tics hadn't come out of the last one a well man. Fear was a terrible thing, and fear of death under constant fire, perhaps the worst of all.

4

Waves pounded into the cove at the base of the cliffs, the black slates glistening, and where the boat shed had its broken ramp, the sea all but rushed to its door. It was 1300 hours, Sunday, 29 May, and Ashby knew he had to have some answers ready. Monica and Ewen had been adamant. The Bowker-Brown girl had discovered the truth and was refusing to have anything more to do with them. Karen was threatening to run away and had refused to speak to him. He hadn't told her Christina was in London and that he had seen her. Karen wouldn't have understood. It wouldn't have helped.

Turning from the cliffs, he looked towards the grey granite walls and slate of the cottage, which was partly hidden behind a gentle rise. *Bleak* was the word that best described it. Beyond the cottage, the rising slopes of the moor bled the world of everything but the distant narrow, winding track of a furtive road and the towering ruins of that old engine house high on its hill. Somewhere there was a sleeper. Jackie Peterson had known he'd gone to London, and Jackie always received twice-weekly telephone calls from his father, but Jackie's dad couldn't be the one.

When he knocked again on the door to the cottage, there was no answer and, reaching for the knob found that the door opened far too easily. At a glance, he took in the writing table in front of one of the two small windows, the chairs, the hearth, pots and pans, bed with its patchwork quilt and pillows, boots against the wall, clothes hanging from pegs, no bureau, nothing like that.

Knowing that he was invading her privacy, he moved self-consciously about, and when he came to the writing table, ran his gaze quickly over the makeshift shelf of books: *A Londoner's Walk to the Land's End, Rambles Beyond Railways, The Cornish Miner* . . . Nearly all of them had been written in the last century. Pebbles, bits of wave-washed wood, seashells, brittle stars, lobster claws and other 'drift' indicated not only a beachcomber's love of 'wrecking' but an artistic bent.

The flyleaf of her leather-bound journal—the only bit of wealth apparent—held a terse note from her father: *Hi!, this business of earning your way as a writer is a bloody piece of nonsense and you know it!*

An entry read:

> *The shafts to the Wheal Deep must go down more than a thousand feet. I really must get a plan of the workings. Money's such a problem, but I have to know what Pindanter can now expect, for the mine has been closed for several years, and he's going to have to go down there to hide. It's his only escape. What will he find, how will he manage? When one drops a stone, it falls for ever and is really quite frightening, yet I am drawn to the shafts as to the well of my story, and feel so close to things when I stand looking down into either of them, for courage is required, not folly.*

The entry was dated Sunday, 22 May, the day he had first met her. The shafts couldn't be any more than three hundred feet to water, the mine flooded probably in the late 1870s when the price of tin had again crashed and so many of Cornwall's mines had finally closed.

Flipping back through the handwritten manuscript yielded:

> *Haunted by the child's screams, Pindanter ran across the moor, her blood still on his hands. As always, that last wild look of despair under lantern light was with him, he having savagely clubbed her to death, a child of seven with long fair hair and the bluest of eyes.*
>
> *Reaching the mine at last, his pursuers not far behind, he scrambled down the first of the ladders, and pulling it in after himself, hid in the darkness, he still feeling her twisting this way and that and hearing her terrified screams.*

Karen . . . Had she been thinking of Karen when she wrote this?

A marginal note read: *Wouldn't these ladders have been fixed in place by bolts? Must somehow check.*

A single-barrelled, .410 shotgun leaned against the corner into which Hilary Bowker-Brown's bed had been pushed. Taking it up, he checked the breech and found it loaded. A fish knife, razor sharp in its sheath, was hidden beneath the pillows, while a bone-handled skinning knife rested on a shelf before a scattering of books.

He had no right to put her life in danger, should have warned her, should have told her the truth.

When he turned, Ashby saw the girl standing in the doorway, silently watching him, but looking very French and of the Midi.

'Why didn't you tell me you were in trouble?' asked Hilary. 'I might have been able to help. I've friends, people who know of me. I haven't always lived like this.'

'Look, I'm sorry . . .'

'Don't even bother. Just bugger off, Captain. That daughter of yours is a very disturbed and emotionally upset little girl. If I were you, I'd give her back to her mother before she runs off and kills herself. The *Abwehr*,' she said, swinging two dead rabbits she must have trapped up onto the table. 'God Almighty, I might have known, and God forgive me for taking his name in vain. Six bloody pounds a fortnight, right? A fortune, and unsuspecting me goes and lays my life and career on the line and you don't even bother to tell me!' Throwing her beret onto the table, she turned away to pull off the gumboots and canvas duck coat.

'Miss Bowker-Brown . . .' he began.

'So it's to be formal, is it, Captain? I thought I told you to leave. Damn it, don't you dare grin at me!'

'Sorry, it's just . . .' He shrugged and ran a hand through his hair. 'I like the way you stand up for yourself, and I am sorry. It wasn't right of me and I know it, and now I'll leave.'

'Things are never simple,' she said, pulling off a dark, knitted turtleneck. 'I just knew there had to be something wrong with that deal you offered. Too fast, too smooth, too much lolly, and then the child muttering prayers to bloody Adolf Hitler!'

'She is upset, and I do know how unhappy she is.'

'*Eine eingefleischter Nazi, ja?*' she asked, regretting it, for he looked so unhappy himself. Knowing she oughtn't to prolong things, she made her way across the room to the Primus. 'Tea?' she asked, striking the match on the wall. 'It's the least I can do for the condemned. There's no sugar or milk—I'm too poor at the moment—but the tea will be black as ink unless you prefer it weak, as I suppose you might, but did you really manage to get yourself past all those border guards like that and *into* the Third Reich?'

Monica must have told her. 'I did, but I *am* ashamed of myself for not having been straight with you.'

He was grey with fatigue and worry, and must have driven nonstop from London, fearing for the safety not just of his daughter but of his friends, herself included.

'When we first met,' said Ashby, 'I honestly didn't know if I could trust you, fluent in *Deutsch* as I'd been told you were. I was afraid, that I'll admit, and certainly on the run.'

'Aren't you always?'

'Not generally. In the boat shed, you mentioned that I wasn't one of them. Whom did you mean?'

'My "friends,"' she said sadly. 'Their names I can't tell you. If I could, I would, but it's as *hush-hush* as that daughter of yours, and that I *do* find a strange coincidence, but then random chance is often just as much a part of life as anything else.'

Like buying a derelict mine, thought Ashby.

Hilary found two mugs, blowing into each to clear them of possible cobwebs and such, the schoolmaster watching in silence as she filled the teapot and set everything on the table. 'I really can't tell you who they are,' she said. 'Sorry.'

'But they might help if you asked them? Come on, Miss Bowker-Brown, MI5 or MI6? I may be a schoolmaster, but I'm not exactly unaware of things.'

'I didn't think you were.'

'Your German, for one,' he said, sitting down across from her at last. 'Your French. They're MI6, aren't they? What did they want a lovely young woman like yourself to do, probably without even giving you any training? Pose as a foreign student on a visit to the Reich while having a good look at the submarine pens and shipping yards, or was it the airfields, or anything else of interest, even simple things like how well the railways were running and how good was the rolling stock?'

So she was 'young and lovely,' was she?

'They might want you, too, Captain. Did you ever think of that, seeing as you have already talked your way through what *has* to be one of the most closely guarded frontiers and then talked your way right back through it but with a kidnap victim?'

'On the way out we had a little excitement because, though armed, I wasn't driving the car.'

He must have stolen. Dear God, what a gamble, thought Hilary, what a lark, but he wouldn't like what she had best say. 'I've told my "friends" at MI6 that, as a pacifist and the daughter of a suffragette, I want no part of their work.'

And chance had brought them together, thought Ashby, warming to her. 'We think alike,' he said, 'but why, then, did you suggest you might have been able to help?'

Pouring the tea was one thing; telling him the truth another. 'Look, Captain, these "friends" of mine wouldn't care a fig for you and your daughter. Oh, they're nice enough, of the right class—moneyed, some of them, or once of money and still behaving as if they had it—but they wouldn't care about me either, and that's the way it is, because that's how it's always been. They will want their pound of flesh if I ask for their help.'

She tried the tea and made a grimace, was no one's fool, thought Ashby.

'Will there be war, do you think, Captain, because if there is, all this . . .' She indicated the cottage. 'Will have been for nothing. Granted they might even repossess the mine, and that, my dear father would welcome, but you see, I really do speak German and French without the trace of any other accent, even to picking up on some of the dialects if necessary. For much of my life I've been on the Continent at one school or another.'

'And your mother?'

'Died when I was very young. Wars are stupid, aren't they?' she asked, warming her hands by clasping the teapot.

'No glory,' he said, 'only suffering and destruction. Lives lost, and others changed forever.'

'Death,' said Hilary, wanting suddenly to tell him. 'My brother, at Mons. I was four years old, but after that, my father couldn't stand the sight of me. I reminded him far too much of Alex and then of our mother who was always Beth to us, but Bethany to him. Hence France and then the Reich, and yes, I *have* seen and heard it all, and your daughter really does scare the hell out of me in more ways than one.'

Wishing that they had talked like this before, Ashby found himself at a loss for words and tried the tea. Grimacing at it, too, then suddenly smiling, he remembered something and, dragging at a pocket, pulled out a fistful of sugar cubes. 'They're a bit dusty,' he said. 'I took them off one of the boys. *Le travail de Dieu, mais la récompense du diable.*'*

He had watched her as he had said it, the imp, thought Hilary, his expression teasingly one of challenge, and yes, he was waiting for her to continue *en français*, and she would love to but had better not, for that language had its own magic as he, apparently, knew only too well.

The sugar cubes were cast like dice onto the table, she seeing the pocket lint and the hairs, and probably there were sweaty fingermarks as well, for didn't all schoolboys have those? 'Seems like treason to use them,' she said in English, seeing that smile of his come instantly back into what were absolutely smashing grey eyes.

'I took them from Jackie Peterson,' said Ashby. 'Knowing the agony he'd gone through to steal them, I hated to, but then Telford nudged me to action. Our assistant headmaster's got it in for me, Miss Bowker-Brown. I'm . . .'

'Hilary, please. Bowker-Brown is far too stuffy. Besides, I'm a Socialist.'

'And I'm not exactly suitable as a teaching master, but the boys and I seem to get on well.'

I'll bet you do, she thought, but he suddenly withdrew into himself, his expression clouded. 'What is it?' she asked, only to see him shake his head.

'Nothing.' But was it really? he wondered. Jackie could so easily have told his father that dear old Peachey had gone up to London.

---

* An old French saying: God's work, but the devil's reward.

As he explained things, Ashby found himself liking further what he saw in her.

'Spurgeon's Bombay Tea and Spice?' asked Hilary, giving him a frown.

'In Carnaby Street along with all the rest that Soho has to offer these days, the touts, the girls, the gamblers, *les flâneurs* *aussi*. My opinion is that MI5 are desperate for something to come along so that they can get Whitehall to free up the funds and let them staff up. Insofar as I can see, they're totally unprepared for what the Reich might well have in mind. Sir John Masterson runs a few of MI5's Watchers out of that shop, but must report to someone higher. If I could get to that person, I could at least check out his Colonel Hacker, for I don't like what I've seen of him either.'

He would have to tell her, thought Ashby, and come what may. 'Look, if I don't go along with them and let Hacker use Karen and this cottage of yours to set a trap for whomever the Abwehr is using to get Karen, Hacker will . . . Well, he'll see that I'm tied up in a murder investigation and maybe even accused of it.'

'*Murder?*' managed Hilary, blanching as she fingered the edge of the table but forcing herself to look steadily at him. 'Then you had best tell me everything, hadn't you, Captain, especially since I'm invariably all alone and just happen to have a mine whose shafts are uncovered and a cottage whose cliffs are far too close for comfort should anyone I don't know, and never have, take a notion to get rid of me.'

'It won't get to that, I promise.'

'But promises made are often not kept, chance tending to bring on the unexpected at the worst of times.'

As calmly as he could, Ashby outlined what had happened to Daisy, and Hilary saw then that he really did have feelings for the murdered woman and grave doubts about this Colonel Hacker. Nor was he really hoping for a reconciliation with his wife but was trying to be coldly realistic, Christina having become a leader in the *Frauenschaften*** and taken a Nazi lover.

'Christina knew I would be in London, Hilary. Someone high up in the Abwehr gave that news to her father and somehow she

---

* Loafers, strollers, idlers
** The Women's Auxiliary of the Nazi Party

pried it out of him, or he willingly gave it with the hope she would then find out where I was hiding Karen. Granted, I've got to give her the chance she's asked for, but I honestly don't believe her. I can't. You see, it wasn't just those two SS I found her in bed with. It was others. That father of hers kept an eye on her and as often as he could, he would let me know where I could find her and with whom. The *gesunde Erotik*, the *Gruppensex*, even the *Kraft durch Freude* weekends and holidays.'

The healthy eroticism, group sex and Strength through Joy breaks from work. 'And all through it, Karen didn't notice that something was going on?'

'Invariably she stayed with her grandfather. Deliberately he tried to shelter her from it, I'll have to give him that.'

'But drilled it all into her, as they did at school, that she, too, was a Nazi and of the master race.'

'And since Christina still has her British passport, she's free to come and go, and if she can, to take Karen back.'

He had laid his cards on the table and she had lain her own opposite his, but it would have to be said. 'Then that wife of yours has you right where she wants. Not only are you on the run from Scotland Yard, you're stricken with guilt over the murder of a totally innocent woman who just happened to be having an affair with you, and you're fighting your conscience over me and your daughter. Frankly, Captain, I don't envy your position, nor do I envy my own.'

'Could you talk to those friends of yours?'

'*Ah, mon Dieu, Monsieur le capitaine,* do I have any other choice? Not only am I in danger, there are Monica and Ewen. None of us will ever know when this . . . this blessed sleeper comes for Karen. Even if I stop trying to teach her English and have no further contact, he would still think I could well know something useful. Here, you read the damned tea leaves. Maybe you can see something other than what I think they're shouting at me. My God, and dear Lord forgive me for saying your name in vain again, I'm only twenty-eight, Captain, and until you and that daughter of yours came into my life, I was doing just fine. Admittedly broke, but then far too many of us Socialists are.'

She stopped herself, suddenly realizing what she'd just done, thought Ashby. Her French had been beautiful. Absolutely natural. Very rapid, very earnest and expressively emphasized by the hands and eyes, and yet cuttingly to the point, he now knowing he had no other choice. 'I'll let Christina have Karen. I can't do otherwise and be certain of your safety and that of Monica and Ewen.'

Ah bon, her sudden use of French had forced him to say it, said Hilary to herself, but English would be best for now. 'Look, for all I know the person I have to contact could be on the Continent. It won't take long for a letter to reach his secretary. The sleeper can't know Karen's here or he would have made a grab for her by now.'

'Hop in the car and I'll drive you over to Zennor. There's a call box near the church. Give him a ring.'

'Sacrifice myself, is that what you want, Captain?'

'Not at all. I want to set right what I've done, and the only way I can make sure you are safe, even if I do let Christina have Karen back, is for those friends of yours to help us. It wasn't right for anyone to have killed Daisy. It makes no sense unless her killer *wanted* to force me to cooperate.'

Hacker . . . wondered Hilary. Did he think the killer was this Colonel Hacker of MI5, but how could that be?

Zennor and Zennor Head were where Arthur had met the four kings of Cornwall. Having always loved the view, Hilary couldn't help but try to lose herself if but for a moment, for this tiny village lay in a hollow. Beyond the nearby farms with their flattish barns and sheds, the nearby moor with its pastures was a jade-green patchwork divided by crooked hedgerows, while inland, Ice Age boulders lay strewn as if thrown by the gods, the pink of the heather climbing to bare granite tors from which there were other and equally magnificent panoramas of the sea.

The road was narrow, the grey granite cottages huddled closely about Saint Senara, which dated from the twelfth century but had been much altered since. Subjected to the usual stares of occasional passersby, the vicar most frequently, she finally got a line through, and when she came back to the car, Ashby could see from her expression that she knew there would be no point in trying to hide the result. 'They want me to take the train tomorrow and to bring Karen with me. Look, I'm sorry, Captain, but those are their terms. They're . . . they're not saying what, if anything, they can or will do, or even if they'll help us.'

'But they'll have someone watching over the two of you all the way?'

'Probably, but . . . I don't *know*, do I?'

Furious with herself, with them and with him, Hilary threw herself into the bucket seat and slammed the door. 'Drive on, Captain. The noble citizenry of Zennor have seen enough of us to set their tongues to wagging. I don't even know him,' she shouted at the vicar and his dog. 'I'm simply bumming a lift!' But right away she regretted it and added, 'Sorry, Vicar. I'm just not myself. Come for tea whenever you wish. It might even help to have God on our side.'

Thanking her, the Right Reverend Thomas Bottrell touched his hat, gave the MG and its driver another once-over before wolfishly smiling and raising his bushy eyebrows.

At half past midnight the wind rose to a gale, and when a slate came loose, Hilary sat bolt upright in bed. Another and another slid away. She would have to weight them down or else the roof would start leaking again.

Drenched to the skin, even with her oilskins on, she struggled to climb the ladder, and when the first of the lightning came, it revealed a gap in the slates, then the moor and the engine house. Ducking her head to clear the rain from her eyes, she looked again and wondered if there was someone with a lantern standing beside the chimney stack, but then that light went out and the thunder came, yet still she couldn't help but wonder if the sleeper hadn't already found the cottage.

Wedging three spare slates into the gap, she weighted them with a slab of rock. Repeatedly now the lighting threw the ruins into view, casting pale blue shadows over the chimney stack. Pindanter? she wondered. Could it have been her imagination playing tricks with her or had it really been the sleeper?

Joachim Burghardt hadn't been in Cologne in years. A very beautiful city with historic, half-timbered houses and narrow, cobbled streets that echoed the centuries, it was a bitch to get through. Tourists were everywhere even early on this Monday morning, 30 May—English, French, Italian, so many languages, all as if seeming to mock the very threat of war.

When at last his driver headed south towards Brühl, Burghardt heaved a sigh and settled back, the road lined with trees, but the estate wasn't far, and when they got there, he said, 'Wait for me. Generals being what they are, I won't be long.'

Rococo and very baroque, the villa was something else again, for each of the tall French windows rose to an ornate open half-shell, a stone filigree of seaweed and a frowning effigy of Neptune. Impressive it was, but uncomfortable, seeing as General von Hoffmann was waiting. Taking a last drag at the cheroot before grinding it beneath a heel on the newly swept pavement, he glanced up.

Gold lay above everything. Gold and dark blue and red, the coat of arms and family crest set in the middle of the mansard slate roof and right above an ornate clock that was, itself, above a fanlight and the many panes of the entrance doors.

An imposing three hectares of neatly trimmed lawn encompassed both the drive and the long rectangle of a dark blue pond on which several disinterested swans languidly cruised. When he rang the bell, he heard the chimes that must have pleased the granddaughter who had had the run of this fabulous house. 'The child's being spoiled might help us,' he muttered to himself. It was a thought.

The butler looked as if of hammered iron, the entrance hall wide and grand: marble on the floor and walls, columns of it too, cherubs on the ceilings blowing golden horns, a bust of the Kaiser Wilhelm in an alcove, nude goddesses flanking the staircase in green bronze with water jugs balanced on their heads. How many shell casings did they represent?

The staircase divided at its first landing, they taking the right, the carpet so soft no steps could be heard. Foolish, that, said Burghardt to himself, what with Augsburg silver, Flemish tapestries and Old Masters handy.

The butler indicated that he should proceed to the end of the corridor alone. It was into the shit then, and so be it.

The study was dark and lined with books. Crossed swords, stags' heads, suits of armour, a large globe of the world—he caught sight of all of these as he approached a windowed alcove where two in uniform were waiting: the greenish-grey of the Wehrmacht and the dark blue of the Kriegsmarine. General von Hoffmann's legs were crossed, the jackboots gleaming even under the table.

Admiral Canaris had his black patent-leather shoes planted firmly on the floor beneath his knees, but really these gave no hint of what was to come. A round and beautifully inlaid Russian table held their ashtrays, a jewelled, porcelain coffee service, and two cups and saucers. Smoke rose from their cigarettes, both of which lay at the ready in those ashtrays.

'So, Burghardt, a full report, I think,' said Hoffmann.

And no third cup and saucer. 'General, Admiral, *Heil Hitler*.'

'Just give us your report, Kapitän, and be quick about it,' said Hoffmann.

'General, Admiral, my pardons. I have only just come from the aerodrome and have not yet had the benefit of my breakfast or lun—'

It was Canaris, that little and almost frail-looking, white-haired, unmilitary man if ever there was one, who raised a small, thin hand to still the general's ire and quietly said, 'Joachim, things are quickly drawing to a head. Today the Führer has stated that it is his "unqualified decision" to crush the Czechs. Yesterday, he ordered that our ground and air forces be substantially increased and that work on the *Westwalle** be completed. Hence General von Hoffmann is understandably anxious.'

Bringing his heels together, Burghardt nodded curtly and said, 'Yes, of course, Admiral. The sleeper known as Osier has been awakened and is in place. Two telephone calls were made from the Dorchester Hotel by your son-in-law, General.'

Damn the impertinence, thought Hoffmann. 'My *former* son-in-law, Kapitän.'

The iron-grey military haircut suited the massive, blunt head with its large and watery blue eyes, thought Burghardt, but try as he did, he couldn't imagine the grandchild sitting in that lap. 'Herr Ashby, General, made the calls while he was in the company of your daughter.'

Canaris tried to conceal the faintness of a smile. 'Be clearer, Joachim.'

'Yes, please do,' said Hoffmann quietly.

There was a duelling scar on the general's left cheek, just a nick of the foil but a loss that would never have been forgotten.

---

* The West Wall, the Siegfried Line between Germany and France

By concentrating on that one defeat, Burghardt knew he would irritate him, but that he had best not break too many eggs. 'They spent the better part of the evening together, General. Ashby left the woman—'

'My daughter.'

'Your daughter, General. Ashby left her at about twenty-three thirty hours. The calls—'

'Did they have sex, damn it?'

'Unfortunately, that we do not know, General, but it is entirely possible, given that they went up to your daughter's room. The calls were, however, made earlier in the evening and from the hotel's main foyer while your daughter remained at their table. One of the calls was to the headmaster of his school, but it was unsuccessful, the headmaster being out at the time.'

'And the other?' asked Canaris.

Even at the age of fifty-one, and a man of much experience, the admiral could still not hide his boyish enthusiasm for intrigue, but to smile at such an immediate success from Osier simply wouldn't do with either of them, thought Burghardt. 'To a pub, Admiral, in the Cornish town of Saint Ives, the Pilchard Arms. To an Ewen MacDonald. A bad connection, which caused Herr Ashby to break off the call after only a few words.'

Osier had made himself useful by tapping the hotel's switchboard operator, thought Hoffmann, but said, 'Saint Ives . . . When can this sleeper of yours get my granddaughter?'

Must the shit only get deeper? wondered Burghardt. 'Soon, General, but first I need to know everything there is to know about her. Was she happy here? Did she have friends who will not be just missed but longed for?'

'How dare you?'

Canaris knew he had best intercede. 'Friedrich, please. Joachim does know what he's doing.'

'A bumboat captain.'

'*Ach*, not at all. One of my most trusted men.'

Until consigned to retirement or worse, thought Burghardt, but asked, 'How loyal was the girl to the Fatherland, General?'

Angrily Hoffmann started out of his chair. Canaris stood up. The general backed down.

'Karen was very loyal. I made sure of that, but why do you ask?'

'Because Osier may need that loyalty, and almost certainly her help.'

'Doesn't he have people he can call on?' asked Hoffmann, Canaris watching them both.

'A select few if necessary,' said Burghardt warily, 'but it would be best, would it not, to prepare for every eventuality?'

'Talk to the kitchen help. Karen was very fond of Frau Haslinger, my cook.'

'Did they spoil her?' asked Burghardt.

'Of course they did!'

'But was she always obedient, General?'

'Wilhelm, what is this? Must I . . . ? Yes, yes, damn it, the girl was obedient and very loyal to the party, the Fatherland and the Führer.'

'Good. Now what about her feelings towards your daughter, General? Did the child resent Werner Beck's taking her father's place and being her mother's current lover?'

'Must I air the laundry, Wilhelm?'

Diffidently Canaris hesitated, then said, 'Can you not simply answer him, Friedrich?'

'Damn it, how could Karen possibly have known they were lovers?' said Hoffmann. 'The child was always here with me when those two . . . *Ach*, when my daughter and Herr Beck were . . . well, were together.'

Prudery in public still being a Prussian trait, Burghardt felt it best not to smile but quietly said, 'All things are possible, General. If Osier is to safely take the child from wherever Captain Ashby has her, we must be fully aware of Fräulein Karen's feelings towards her father, and since those encompass your daughter and her relationships with other men, it's best we know beforehand exactly how the child views such lovers.'

'My daughter is not a slut, Captain, but why not ask Herr Beck, since he is one of yours?'

'Have you, Joachim?' asked Canaris.

A nod would suffice.

'Then you don't need anything else,' said Hoffmann.

Canaris urged caution. Gruffly Hoffmann said, 'Then yes,

the child deeply resented Herr Beck's infatuation with my daughter.'

Telling himself to take a deep breath, Burghardt said, 'More correctly, General, the child loves her father *and* her mother very dearly. Therefore, she has continually resented Herr Beck's attentions to your daughter and that, General, is why the child came increasingly under your care.'

Did the man know everything? wondered Hoffmann. 'It's a big house. I've a full staff. Of course Karen was spoiled a little, and of course, as her grandfather, I delighted in spoiling her. Can't generals dote upon their granddaughters, Kapitän?'

'As long as it doesn't lead others into trouble, General, and the Reich into losses it cannot afford, but rest assured, when the time comes, Osier will have all the help he needs. I have every confidence that your granddaughter will be returned to you without incident.'

There would be no killing, then, not by our people, thought Hoffmann.

Longing for a cheroot, Burghardt knew there was one more thing that needed saying. 'Ashby mentioned a policeman, a Colonel Hacker.'

'Of MI5,' said Canaris. 'Colonel Buntington Hacker, General, of the Watchers, who fortunately are so strapped for funds there are but few of them and they but poorly paid.'

'The killer of that barmaid, Admiral?' asked Hoffmann.

'Perhaps, but that we really will not know for some time, or ever, will we, Joachim?'

Again it would be best to nod, thought Burghardt, and left it up to the admiral to tell him.

Canaris stubbed out his forgotten cigarette. 'Clearly, Friedrich, your granddaughter will be used by MI5 in an attempt to take Osier and whatever others Agent 07392 may require.'

The news did not go down well, thought Burghardt, Hoffmann searching himself for an out and finally asking somewhat incredulously, 'Has Ashby agreed to such a thing?'

Again Burghardt left it to the admiral. 'Or else, Friedrich, Herr Ashby knows he may even have to face a charge of murdering that barmaid.'

*　　*　　*

Tuesday came and went at Grantley's, felt Ruth, the rain still pissing from the eaves and making rivers out on the Common where the grass was now so very green. Close indoors and bloody damp, life here at the school was killing her. At 10.05 pm she went up to bed, and at 10.21, just as she was dragging the nightgown over her head, she heard the distant sound of Ash's motor on the Old Coach Road. Up and down the hills it went, round the turns, the sound now falling off only to suddenly rise and fill the night, eager yet repulsive, everything in her heaving a sigh only to tense up again. What was she to say to him? How could she even begin to explain what had happened in that room of his last Friday afternoon? That Hamilton boy, Bill, was bound to say something and Ash would learn that long after Colonel Hacker had left her, she had sat on his bed, crying for what might have been. Hacker . . . Dear God, she hated the thought of him. The boy had timidly knocked and then, the others egging him on with urgent whispers from the corridor, had come into the room and after a few moments of utter shock at the sight of her, he having *pissed* himself, had said, 'Mrs. Pearce, I . . . I really don't think you should do that,' and she had felt him taking the gun from her hand and giving her the gentlest of hugs.

As the MG swung in at the gates, she switched off the light. Ash had gotten the car fixed—well, sort of. Even from here she could see that, for the canvas top had been replaced. Taking the shortest way round the Common, he drew up in front of Todd House, switched off the headlamps and ignition, and never mind that no one was to drive a motorcar out there.

Bolting from the car and in under the lamps, he went up the steps, pivoting on that stiff leg. In anger, in fear, she pulled the curtains closed, but remained clinging to them lost in thought. Anthony had been acting strangely. First a call to London on that Friday, his trying to reach Ash with the news of Hacker's visit, then deliberately going out so as not to be in when Ash returned the call. Late . . . he'd been out so late. His shoes and socks had been soaked through, and in the morning, as she had set them before the fire, he hadn't said a word. Where *had* he gone, who *had* he met? A man . . . another man?

Hacker wouldn't tell Ash what she had revealed in that room of his. It would be that Hamilton boy. Withdrawn in class, the boy would soon be noticed, Ash saying, *'Bill, what's been eating you?'*

'Nothing, sir. I . . . I just don't feel well,' for she had very nearly done it, pulled that trigger—killed herself with the gun Ash must have taken from Anthony's room to keep that former comrade-in-arms of his from killing himself, her husband! Dear God, the scandal, though. HEADMASTER'S WIFE COMMITS SUICIDE. The press would have had a field day, her name linked to Ash's and that of Daisy Belamy.

'Ruth . . . ? Ruth, darling, are you all right?'

Cold now, she turned towards the door Anthony had opened *without* having knocked, but had he really met someone when he had been out walking late like that last Friday night and deliberately avoiding Ash's return call? 'Of course I'm all right. I've only just heard him drive in.'

Ruth did have her suspicions, thought Pearce. 'You won't say anything, will you? Ash has enough on his plate.'

And why *shouldn't* she tell Ash about Hacker, wondered Ruth, especially as Anthony had been about to himself but had then dodged the issue and gone out for a walk? Or had it been just a walk? 'I'm going to bed. I don't really know what I shall say to him or do, not that it's any concern of yours.'

As his steps receded, she closed the door, softly putting the lock on, and once in bed, lay staring emptily at the windows where the heavy brocade of the ages shut out the night but, as so often during that Great War, brought her the sound of guns she could not possibly have heard. 'Ash,' she managed. 'Please forgive me. Hacker made me tell him everything and left me nothing for myself. I . . . I didn't even know you had a wife.'

Picking at a floury scone whose Devonshire cream she would leave untouched, Christina added the barest minimum of sugar to her tea, no milk. It was now Wednesday, 1 June. AST-X Bremen would have had her report within five hours of Ash's having left her room Friday night at the Dorchester. It was amazing how fast she had been able to bring the embassy into things. Straight to Croydon and onto Lufthansa Flight 801 by diplomatic pouch, but would Burghardt reveal the sleeper's identity as she had requested and put her in touch with that one's wireless operator? There was much she could tell this Agent 07392, this Osier. They would have to work together, and whether Burghardt liked it or not, that entailed their both having wireless contact with AST-X Bremen, the wireless's location also being a place for them to meet and leave messages for each other.

The tea was lukewarm, the inn, the Rose and Thorn, so old its ceilings were low and stained with fireplace soot and tobacco smoke, the beams wide and dark, the walls crooked, the floors warped. 'Miss . . . miss, come here,' she said. 'This tea . . . You failed to bring the kettle to a full and rolling boil. Surely you must know how to make tea in a place like this?'

Young and impressionable, the girl blushed crimson, curtseyed and said, 'I'm dreadfully sorry, ma'am. I was told to hurry, and . . .' She threw a glance towards the matron, a dour spinster of fifty in black whose rimless glasses did nothing to alleviate the severity.

Reaching out to the girl, Christina said, 'Please, it is all right. Leave it. Ellen, isn't it?'

'Yes, ma'am. Ellen Fairfax.' The German-sounding lady was ever so beautiful, thought Ellen, her clothes absolutely fabulous.

'Ellen, they say there was a murder nearby, in the ruins of a chantry. Is this really true?'

'Oh yes, ma'am. Terrible it was. Now everyone is afraid to go out after dark.'

'But do they know who did it?'

Blanching, the girl hesitated at some thought, Christina saying, 'Please don't be afraid. My husband is British.'

'Oh . . .' Again the girl blushed, then stammered, 'Forgive me, ma'am. It's only talk, mind, but they say it's all being hushed up and that there were two German spies who did it.'

'Two spies?'

'Yes, ma'am. That's what Constable Farr said the Yard had told him. Real put out he was, too. Damned funny, he said, them going after a girl like Daisy, who couldn't have known which end of a gun barrel to point.'

'And what does this constable believe?'

'That he wouldn't say, ma'am,' went on Ellen, throwing Miss Staples, the matron, a wary glance, 'but he did tell me he's been looking for man with a ginger moustache and would like to talk to him.'

'Ellen . . . Ellen Fairfax,' called out the matron, 'attend to your duties and leave Mrs. Talbotte to her tea this instant.'

'She was only asking if everything was satisfactory,' said Christina.

'And is it?' asked Mildred Staples, but thinking, untouched Devonshire, the cloche and dove-grey suit beautifully tailored and very expensive, a German, but a barrister's wife, and down from London for a few days 'rest,' or so the woman had claimed.

'Yes, everything is fine,' said Christina, 'but would you see that the desk is notified I shall be wanting a bath before dinner?'

'That's impossible. You will have to wait until this evening.'

'At about eleven, then?'

'You'll have to be quiet.'

'Of course. Oh, by the way, will they be able to take the stains out of that skirt of mine and mend my shoes?'

Bog water, bracken and peat by the look, thought Mildred. One ruined pair of silk stockings with blood on laddered knees, and one lost heel from a brogue that had been soaking wet, though the tramping about must have been done a day or two ago, and Lord only knows where the woman had been. Certainly *not* in London. Abrasions on the hands as well. 'I shall have to send them to Bridgwater, Mrs. Talbotte. It will take about a week. The hem of that skirt was badly torn.'

And I was out walking in the rain, wasn't I? asked Christina silently. Was it in the pitch of night and a fearful storm in Cornwall, near an old engine house and a cottage too close to the cliffs?

Giving the woman the smile she reserved for servants who didn't mind their own affairs, Christina curtly said, 'That will be all.' But if Kurt Meydel and Martin Lund hadn't killed Ash's barmaid, then had this Colonel Hacker?

'Please, sir, it's me, Bill.'

Ashby wondered if he had missed hearing the knock. The boy looked round the room, frightened by something and still holding on to the doorknob. 'Sorry I didn't hear you, Bill. Head's in a rumble. What's up?'

Bill studied his shoes and searched the floor, someone behind him whispering, 'Crikey, shut the bloody door!'

Finch, thought Ashby. That was Finch. Something had happened while he'd been up in London, and everyone knew about it but himself or thought they did, but no one, least of all Tony, would tell him. Instead, even by this Wednesday, there had still been the whispered confidences, chance looks and quickly averted eyes and the forced jocularity of the masters' common room. 'Did you have your tea, Bill?' he asked.

'N-No, sir.'

The boys had had a meeting, then, a conference. 'Mine's cold but we could warm it up.'

'It's nearly bells, sir.'

'Let 'em ring. Mr. Telford will dress us both down, but I'll stand up for you, Bill.'

'Thank you, sir. That's frightfully good of you.'

The boy was pale, the tears coming readily enough as Ashby crossed the room to gently take him by the shoulder. 'Hey there, what's this? What's happened?'

Out it all came. Hacker had done a job on Ruth and she'd been about to kill herself. Over tea and toast with jam, he got the boy to settle down. 'Love's a funny thing, Bill. There are all kinds of it, but the one thing that's common is that we feel it deeply.'

'She . . . she sat over there, sir, on your bed.'

'Yes, I know, Bill. You've told me. It was good of you boys to have worried about me, good of you to have stopped her. Champion, I'd say. In times of war they'd have pinned a medal on you. Quick thinking, that. Reflexes. Pure instinct. Where do you suppose it came from?'

'I . . . I don't know, sir. I just did it. I . . . I wanted to run. I . . . I peed myself.'

'And here I thought one of you boys was mad at me.'

'We wouldn't do a thing like that, sir. You're the best. Jackie says we should all offer to help. If there's anything we can do, you've only to ask.'

'Good-oh, Bill, that's my soldier. Now tell me about this copper man who said he was from the Yard.'

'He was like death, sir. Finchie swears he must have been a soldier, but Spider Lawson says he must have been a prizefighter.'

'And you, Bill, what do you think?'

'That he was the meanest man I'd ever seen.'

'Shook you up a bit, didn't it, Bill, seeing a woman about to kill herself.'

It wasn't a question. It was more of a statement of fact, of resignation, felt Bill, wiping his eyes again and watching Peachey withdraw into that shell of his as though losing himself in thought and memory.

'Life's pretty bad when a person would do a thing like that, Bill. Try to understand that this copper man drove Mrs. Pearce to it. Not intentionally, mind, but inadvertently.'

Intuitively Bill understood that the interview was over. It was such a relief, like getting Cheops off his back. Peachey was a bloody good duffer. The best!

Rejoining the other boys, he said, 'He's going to talk to us tonight. I know he is. He didn't say so, not actually, but he will.'

'Has he been sleeping with Mrs. Pearce—you know, have they been doing *IT*, for crikey's sake?' asked Jackie.

Bill knew he could ask them to do *anything* so long as he said what they wanted. 'Peachey wouldn't do a thing like that. Tics is his best friend. Besides, Peachey's married and has a daughter.'

A wife and a daughter . . . Peachey!

That evening, when seen from the masters' common room, the heights of the Quantocks were wrapped in purplish-pink and gold, felt Roger Banfield. Daisies and buttercups added an impressionistic touch that tended towards sentimentality but represented merely the benign thoughtlessness of the Benedictine who had felled the woods to scratch a living while they had built their abbey in the hills and said their prayers.

Sipping his tea and whisky, he watched as Mrs. Pearce and Captain David Douglas Ashby of the Blues found the path and disappeared momentarily under the overhanging boughs of a magnificent beech. He knew he ought to tell the others, but ought best to leave the two of them alone. 'George, come here a moment, would you?' he said, nudging the window wide to take in the balmy air. 'The eve of summer is ever pleasant.' He gave a nod towards the hills.

Crawley took up his station and the two old friends all but blocked the view.

'I say,' said Telford, 'isn't that Ashby and Mrs. Pearce going up into the hills?'

Their assistant headmaster never missed a trick. God, how the boys must suffer, felt Crawley, plucking shreds of a roll-your-own from his lower lip. 'It *is*, Telford, but what of it?'

'Well, I only . . .' he hazarded. 'Well, you know. Really, it's most unseemly.'

'Until you know the truth,' said Banfield, fixing him with the look he reserved for the most delinquent of boys.

Flustered, Telford said, 'I . . . I don't know what you're implying. I really wish Headmaster would get this whole business out in the open. I've had to stop the boys from whispering and passing the most dreadful of notes. Their finals are coming. The school's in enough of a . . .'

'A rumble?' snorted old George, exhaling cigarette smoke.

'Yes! If you want to put it that way. I don't like caning boys any more than you do.'

It was Banfield who said, 'Have they been passing notes to the effect that Tics is bent?'

Telford ran an agitated hand over his thinning locks. 'I'm sure I don't know what you mean.'

Crawley boxed him in. 'Oh, for God's sake, Arthur, you know the boys as well as we. Grantley's isn't sainthood. Did the notes claim he was camp?'

'Queer,' shot Banfield. 'A homosexual.'

'There's got to be an end to it,' demanded Telford, furious with them. 'I've enough trouble getting the boys to work as it is, without all this talk of sex and murdered barmaids and *him* out there running about the countryside in that dreadful motor. Ashby should be dismissed.'

'Not Headmaster?' asked Crawley, squeezing the last bit of goodness out of his cigarette, then deciding to bum one of Roger's with but a curt nod to the enemy who stiffly said: 'Headmaster deserves our absolute loyalty and trust!'

'I'm sure,' said Crawley, lighting the cigarette and coughing.

Banfield affected a dry and impatient air, for when all was said and done, it was characters like Ashby that made a school. 'I fear the Great War cost the Lower Fifth's hero a good deal, Telford. One must temper one's judgement with the distillation of history.'

'And *what*, precisely, does that mean?' demanded Telford.

Crawley found comfort in scratching the stubble under his chin. 'That he's been drifting ever since, poor chap. Searching for a reason to it all, I expect.'

'Blaming himself, George,' said Banfield. 'I'm certain of it.'

'You two do talk nonsense!'

'Cock, some would say,' retorted Banfield. 'Cock, Arthur. That shattered leg of his kept our Ashby in and out of hospital and con-valescence for a good two years. Time enough to consider things, I should think, what with all those other poor wounded wretches lying about in the wards for company. Then off to Rotterdam pushing paper for Royal Dutch Shell and trying to get used to the oil business and civilian life. Delayed reaction, like a time fuse and the blessed bomb still buried with the buildings all round and everyone waiting.'

'Six years of it,' mused Crawley with a nod. 'Pity they wanted him to go to America for them—a logical mistake, of course. Ash-by's one of us come hell or high water. The immigrant son from Philadelphia returned to the land of his forefathers.'

These two hadn't been wasting their time, thought Telford, waiting for more.

'Then he packed it in,' said Banfield. 'Lost his chance right there. No more scheduling tankers and messing about with guil-ders. Did a stint of tutoring in Paris—must have been a bit of a comedown being forced to pick up the sou like that. Wandered on the Left Bank, I should think, with periodic rambling off to Greece and the Aegean, to the heart of it all, the searcher.'

'And always with a beautiful girl on his arm, no doubt,' inter-jected Crawley, spitting tobacco flakes to one side and coughing like death.

'And then?' prodded Telford.

'Lloyd's,' snorted Crawley. 'Don't tell me you didn't know our Ashby had been in insurance? It's the languages, Arthur. Those and a smattering of tanker jargon. Lloyd's put him back on his feet and let him take the girls out dancing, the theatre, too, I suspect, and the races of course. Motors *and* horses, Arthur.'

'Then he had to go and get himself married,' sighed Banfield, looking off towards the hills, willing himself to be with them in the woods or up by the ruins. 'A return trip to Paris, Arthur, in 1928, the girl twenty-two, he a thirty-five-year-old repentant cavalry officer wanting to finally settle down, though why, for God's sake, he should have chosen the only daughter of a German general is beyond me. Perhaps that was the trouble, eh, George? His shooting up the Hun, then trying to atone for it by marrying the daughter of such.'

'It can't have gone down well with the father,' said Crawley.

'I should say not, George. The trouble is, Telford, with the new job he had the means to indulge the girl, but then the Crash of '29 came and it all frittered away overnight. No money, no job, and holes in his socks she couldn't even mend.'

'And Paris again,' said Crawley. 'More tutoring but with Daddy hot on his heels to take his daughter back to where things were significantly better, though economically tough, I'm sure.'

'There was, unfortunately, a child,' said Banfield. 'Born 17 January 1931, but the couple separated, you see, Arthur, and our boy was sentenced to live alone and no doubt pine away for that daughter of his.'

'May of '34,' said Crawley. 'Greece again, and tutoring, too, but with very little money and likely wondering if he would ever get back on his feet and get a chance to see his daughter.'

Telford couldn't resist saying, 'Headmaster finding him like that and bringing him back here to the Lower Fifth, but I fail to see that this has *anything* to do with his walking out like that with Mrs. Pearce!'

'Then you must understand,' said Banfield, 'that what happens on the battlefield welds men together like nothing else. Ask any old soldier who's had a taste of it, eh, George? They'll all tell you the same. Hate or love, one or the other, but God help the woman who comes between.'

'Ashby's not a homosexual,' snorted Telford.

Crawley lost patience with him. 'Of course not, you bloody fool. His is the sin of knowing and hers is that of finding out.'

*   *   *

Alone with Ashby, Ruth wondered if he had chosen the ruins to remind her of Daisy Belamy and the chantry at Kilve. He would wait until darkness had fallen, though, and she didn't know if she could wait that long. 'Ash, why not tell me and get it over with?'

'What do you want me to say, Ruth, that I found Tony in a bunker making love to one of the men?'

'Is it the truth?'

How could she understand the utter loneliness, he wondered, the terror of never knowing when one would die, especially since everyone round them had? For all of them the war had long since lost all its illusions. Three years of it had been too much.

'He would have been court-martialled and shot, Ruth. The boy had only just turned nineteen and was killed in action the very next day. I thought . . . Well, Tony pleaded with me not to report the incident, that he had never done anything like that before and never would again.'

'He was desperate, wasn't he, so you let him hide it but exacted a promise—I know you would have, Ash. You gave that future husband of mine a warning, and are as guilty as he is.'

As the last of the sunlight fell, a nightingale called, and from down over the hills came the distant sound of the bell calling the boys to chapel. 'Ruth, please try to understand. It was hell.'

'Oh, don't give me that rubbish about the sound of the guns. Don't tell me that's why he still wakes up in the middle of the night and I can hear him crying like a baby. Don't tell me he was a hero—the VC and the DSO, the 1914 Star with bar and the OBE. Just tell me the truth and why he never talks about it.'

'Because I held him. Because when the shells started coming in that last time, everyone else was dead and he had gone completely to pieces. There wasn't anything left of him.'

The Third Battle of Ypres—Passchendaele—the shattered trunks of the branchless trees in Sanctuary Wood, 23 September 1917, and at the end of it, nearly half a million men had died in that one battle alone.

'God I hate you,' she said.

'Don't. Try to understand. We were both terrified.'

'Why *didn't* you tell me about him? You had plenty of chance.

Instead, you let me think he was a hero charging up that hill, taking that German machine-gun post. Oh, I see, you . . . Well, of course, you thought it was the ideal solution. Let him hide his sickness in marriage. Never mind the damage it would cause. Never mind that I would be forced to live a life of hell wanting desperately for someone to hold me, Ash. *Me!* The very sight of him makes my skin crawl. I *can't* stand it any longer!'

The fireflies had come out amid the darkened ruins reminding her that once they had made her think of tracer shells.

'Ruth, they cut us to ribbons—the men, the horses, what were left of them. They pinned the two of us down and when I held him, he told me that he had always loved me, and when I pushed him from me, he ran up that hill hoping the Germans would kill him.'

The truth at last. 'And you were wounded going after him.'

'Yes.'

Ruth knew she couldn't keep the sarcasm from her voice. 'So you let the King pin medals on him. You were both cowards. Neither of you were due a thing.'

'The hill was there and we took it. I never wanted the medals and I don't think Tony did either.'

'Yet you still didn't tell me about him. You knew I was in love with you, that I would have given anything to have had you change places with him.'

'I couldn't. You were his fiancée. I thought . . . Ruth, I thought it was only the war that had done that to him. I went into hospital. He was captured within a week and put in a prisoner-of-war camp. We lost touch. For me the war was over and I was glad of it, and when I got home I . . . well, I thought he would forget all about it.'

'His desire for other men, yet you didn't come to Grantley's when he first asked you in the autumn of 1920. You were afraid, Ash. You knew only too well the truth of what you had done to me. God only knows what happened to him in that prison camp. The final degradation, I suspect, for homosexuality goes on even more in places like that, and the Boches would have known of it and got him to spy for them. That must be why he never speaks of that time either. But the latest is out, you know. Among all the other nasty little rumours that are floating round the school, just how long do you think it's going to take before they all twig to the fact that the gun Colonel Hacker found in your room was really Anthony's and that you'd taken it from him because you were afraid he might well shoot himself?'

'I didn't take it for that reason. I borrowed it when I went to Germany to get my daughter, and like a damned fool, I kept it loaded in case they came for me. Ruth, Tony needs the school and I think the school needs him.'

'If he can keep his hands off the boys.'

'He's not like that. There's never been any suggestion of it.'

'Little pieces of the puzzle will begin to fit together. The enrollment's bound to drop off. Word gets round. He takes his holidays in Greece each summer but what does he do when he gets there, eh? The least you could have done was to have told me you were married. I could look after your daughter. I could do such a good job of it, even at the school, or I'd buy Wetherby Cottage and move into it. Yes . . . Yes, that would be best. Then maybe . . .'

'Ruth, what *did* you tell Hacker? He took a photograph of Karen and the couple who are looking after her. The trawler they own was in the background.'

Abruptly she turned away to grip the edge of the wall, she bowing her head. 'Everything we've just been saying. That I wished you would love me, that it was all so unfair, and that . . . that when at last you had come here to teach, I had hoped you would see how unhappy I was. That Colonel Hacker of yours humiliated me, Ash. He left that gun in my lap, and though he didn't specifically tell me to, he as much as dared me to kill myself.'

'But why?'

'How should I know? I thought he was a detective.'

Gearing down, Ashby touched the brakes. Dousing the headlamps, he let the car coast through the village before pulling over to the side of the road. Crowcombe's thatched roofs were huddled under a star-filled sky on the western edge of the Quantocks, not all that far from the school. A glimmer of light washed over the road in front of the Carew Arms. Up at the church, two bicycles leaned against the lamp standard, while a third, a woman's, stood bolt upright on its kickstand.

MI5 would have initiated an immediate record search of every port within a 300-mile radius of the school. They would find the *Bonnie Jean* and then find Karen. There would be no need for Hacker to ask again. They would simply leak that information to the Abwehr.

When he got through to the Pilchard Arms, Ewen came on the line and it was good to hear his voice and that Karen was safe. 'Move the *Bonnie Jean*, Ewen. Take her north. Get her out of Saint Ives as quickly as you can and keep clear of any ports for as long as possible.'

'And th' lass, Dave?'

'Hilary knows what has to be done. Just tell her that I'll make it up to her. I will, Ewen. The same to yourself and Monica, and thanks for all you've done.'

Hating himself for not having anticipated Hacker, he rang off. There was just a chance the colonel hadn't found them yet, but why hadn't Tony been at home when he'd returned that call of his from the Dorchester? Knowing what Hacker had done to Ruth would have given them some warning, especially if Ruth had told him the colonel had taken that photo. As to the rest of what Hacker had done, it could only have been to cause a scandal and force himself into revealing where Karen was.

A sleeper . . . Scotland Yard would never be able to apprehend Kurt Meydel and Martin Lund, nor would MI5. Both would have vanished into the Reich to be assigned other duties, but had they really killed Daisy? Everything pointed elsewhere, and that, too, wasn't good, should Hacker succeed in using Hilary and Karen.

Christina would still be in London, at the Dorchester, but when he rang through, he found that she had only stayed Friday night and had left the hotel well before dawn. A taxi had taken her to the German embassy, the doorman said when asked by the receptionist. 'Will you be coming in to pay the lady's bill, sir, or shall I send it over to Pratt's?'

Pratt's would do just fine. Out under the stars, the scent of clover was heavy on the air. 'Christina,' he said, alone and not liking what he'd just discovered, 'where are you?'

At the Rose and Thorn, its occupants long since retired, the wind found every nook and cranny, thought Christina. Apart from Miss Staples, who had seemed to take an inordinate interest in her comings and goings, the inn was perfect. It was just on the outskirts of the tiny village of East Quantoxhead. Reached by a lane off the A39 from Holford and Bridgwater, it was easily accessible to the school, but also to the village of Kilve by a footpath, and if she went out from there to that main road, the Dogs of War.

She had been to the ruins of the chantry, the scene of the murder, and had asked all sorts of questions of the curious, had been to that pub to ask about the man with the ginger moustache, and had seen the farmhouse where Daisy Belamy had once lived.

Ash wouldn't find her until it was too late. It had been so easy to discover where Karen was staying, he so trusting and careless. Foolishly he had made two telephone calls from the Dorchester, one of which had been to Saint Ives. There had been no need for her to have even bribed the hotel's operator for the information. Burghardt would now know, again through her having used the embassy, that she had taken the train to Saint Ives and that last Sunday Ash's little car had been parked outside a small stone cottage in the older part of the town, the home of a Monica and Ewen MacDonald.

He would also know that she had gone out along the road a good two miles to the west, and that Ash had met and talked with a girl named Hilary Bowker-Brown who lived in a small cottage near the cliffs and owned the ruins of an old tin mine, but would Burghardt send Osier to herself as she had pleaded?

And what of this Colonel Hacker? she wondered. Had he stayed in this inn?

It was pitch-dark in the lobby when she came downstairs at near on midnight, but behind the desk, by the telephone, there had been a small lamp. Switching it on, she let her eyes adjust, then quickly scanned the register. There wasn't a listing for a Colonel Hacker but on the night following the murder, and on the preceding two, a Harris Blackburn from Leeds, an insurance salesman, had stayed at the inn.

At 0217 hours, Thursday, 2 June, one of the green lights came on and the first of the encoded five-letter groupings spilled from the wireless transceiver. Burghardt listened attentively. The frequency and manner of transmitting were those of the Bridgwater set, the sending extremely rapid but steady, the wrist action certain but delicate, that of a woman, one might have thought, had one not known better.

The first part of the message came to an end in less than a minute, Bridgwater, he knew, then transmitting at a different frequency, having broken the data down into at least two parcels for added security. Three agents used mail drops to funnel intelligence through Bridgwater. None knew the identity or whereabouts of their wireless operator—Bridgwater had insisted on building a wall round himself. Banks of the latest Telefunken transceivers constantly monitored the British Isles, signals like this one coming in from scattered operatives in Britain, Wales, Scotland and both Northern and Southern Ireland. The small hours were always best, and he did like to be here at least two or three times a week. One kept a finger on the pulse of one's agents, the wireless often the only contact for months.

Replies from himself were then sent by Bridgwater to the respective drops to be picked up by the agents. Having refused to sacrifice himself to carelessness, Bridgwater additionally used two and three drops, a necessary delay that could not have been helped, especially as the British MI5, few though they were, were trying to locate his set.

None of the transcripts had any mention of Osier and Karen Ashby. Indeed, none of those agents, including Bridgwater, knew anything of the matter or of Christina Ashby.

Again he took out the second message she had sent him via the embassy, this one dated last Monday at 1407 hours. Again he reread it, as he had many times:

URGENT OSIER CONTACT ME AT ROSE AND THORN EAST QUANTOXHEAD UNDER NAME MRS. CHRISTINA TALBOTTE. TOGETHER WE CAN MOVE KAREN. SHE IS STAYING WITH AN EWEN AND MONICA MACDONALD IN SAINT IVES, BUT ASHBY IS ALSO USING A HILARY BOWKER-BROWN WHO LIVES TO THE WEST OF THERE IN AN ISOLATED COTTAGE NEAR THE CLIFFS AND WHOSE RUINS OF AN OLD TIN MINE OFFER A PERFECT VANTAGE POINT.

She had been busy, but he couldn't, in all conscience, use Bridgwater to speed up contact with her. Too much would be lost should anything go wrong. Granted, being impulsive, demanding and used to getting her own way, the general's daughter might try to force the embassy to tell her Bridgwater's location, but so far she hadn't, and they had been given strict instructions some time ago not to release it or any other to anyone.

When Werner Beck came in, he read the message she had sent on Monday and knew Karen would have to be taken immediately. Short of himself flying to London and trying to join up with Christina, there seemed only Osier. 'Have you told 07392 to contact her, Kapitän?'

'Not yet, but I'm thinking on it.'

'Then you'd best take a look at this.'

It was a copy of Abwehr Central's dossier on Colonel Buntington Hacker. Burma-filled pages, there were press photographs too. In alarm, Burghardt looked to the wireless transmitter, then to the map of Northern Europe and the British Isles. Though there were no pins, flags or anything else to indicate where Abwehr AST-X's agents were, he couldn't help but think of the losses should Hacker succeed and he not use the only secure avenue that was open.

Satisfied that the Kapitän's balls had been kicked sufficiently, Beck said, 'You can't leave Christina on her own, or even to her taking Karen herself, for she'll be afraid of this Hacker. At least let her team up with Osier and give them the wireless backup they need.'

5

At Charing Cross Station, Hilary watched as people came and went alongside Thursday's train. It was all so normal, so of London's rush hour: bowler hats, black suits, umbrellas and copies of the *Times*, the ordinary always, too, but some of the women far more colourful in light coats over day-dresses or suits, and with silk scarves for gaiety, their cloches or brimmed hats tilted or worn up and back. Monica and Ewen would be well on their way in the *Bonnie Jean*. Ewen had picked Karen and herself up in the van first thing this morning and had driven them to Saint Erth, where they had caught the Cornish Riviera Express on its return from Penzance to London.

But then the trouble had started. There had been two middle-aged men with their wives, all of them speaking *Deutsch*, she still recalling her absolute panic, for Karen's ears had pricked up as meals, beds, rooms and service had been discussed with much laughter or complaint. From Saint Erth to Paddington Station in London had taken a little more than seven hours, but no sooner had they settled in than Karen had asked to go to the loo and hadn't come back.

She had found the girl outside the Germans' compartment, listening to them. Using English she had said, 'Karen, I think you should come back.'

The child had turned swiftly away to face the others and had said loudly in *Deutsch*, 'They can tell *Opa* where I am!'

'Karen, leave it,' she had said in English.

The *Hausfrau* had stopped talking; the *Bürgermeister* had lowered their newspapers. 'What is it, *mein Kind*?' one of the women had asked in *Deutsch*. 'Are you lost? Gunther,' she had said to her husband, 'the child is German.'

'*Ach*, I can see that, Hilde,' he had said, and then, '*Komm her, mein Kind*. Don't be afraid.'

'She's not German,' Hilary recalled saying. 'She's just curious. Karen, I won't have it!'

At Paddington Station, the German tourists had left the train but Karen had stood on the platform looking desperately after them, and unfortunately one of the women had turned and must have said to the others, 'It is that child again, that pretty little blonde-haired girl who tried to speak to us in *Deutsch*.'

They had all paused for a look and then the crowd had swallowed them up, but just how extensive was the German network in Britain? Any one of that four could easily have telephoned the German embassy, who would, of course, have already been notified to be on the alert for Karen and would let this sleeper of theirs know exactly where they were now heading.

The train to Hollingbourne in Kent would take another two and a half hours. With luck they would be home by 10.00 pm, but only if someone was at the house to come and get them.

At last the train began to move. Hunching her shoulders, Karen settled down to sulk, but suddenly the train stopped, the child giving a plaintive cry of '*Opa* . . . ?'

Bolting for the train, a very Mayfairish man was searching for someone, now this compartment, now that, the guard calling out, 'Sir . . . I say, sir, down here.'

Coat open and flying, the man clambered aboard, the train beginning to move again, but they positively *don't* hold trains for just anyone, thought Hilary. Had he been sent by MI6 to watch over them, or would he try to take Karen?

When the man sat opposite her, she felt he had only one interest and that the sleeper was on to them. Never mind that David Ashby might agree to let his wife have Karen back, never mind any of his good intentions or even her own. That school of his was just too far away.

From beyond the ruins of the Benedictine abbey, from up higher in the hills, Christina found a good view of the playing field. Using the binoculars she had bought, she could see, even from such a distance, that Ash, who was calling the play and blowing that whistle of his, just loved being out there, and that the boys all loved having him there. He seemed able to set his troubles aside, and when the soccer ball hurled towards him, he nimbly leapt out of the way. But hadn't he always been like that, hadn't Karen loved him for it, herself as well, but not now, never now.

Though she had sent a message to Bremen last Monday, Burghardt had yet to get an answer to her, and each day, each hour lost only made things worse, since Hacker was bound to find Karen and then, what then?

Burghardt was a fool, too old, too set in his ways and unaware of how things were here in Britain. She shouldn't have to wait, should have been able to go directly to the nearest wireless operator and be in contact when needed.

There had been a rather charming cottage by a stream and some overgrown willow beds. She had passed it on the road. There hadn't been an estate agent's signboard, but the cottage had appeared empty, its garden and small orchard untended. On the pretense of being interested, she could make a few inquiries. Should Osier fail to take Karen, the cottage would bring her within easy distance of the school and Ash would surely come to believe that her intentions were honourable if she bought it.

Glancing at her watch, she knew that Miss Staples of the Rose and Thorn would note again her absence at dinner and continue to question her staying at the inn, yet she didn't want to leave just yet. Ash clearly loved the school, and it was beautiful in its own unobtrusive way.

Reaching the ruins of the abbey, Christina lit a cigarette and, sitting atop a low stone wall, let the closing of the day come to her. This whole business of the murder and Colonel Hacker had unsettled her. Being on her own, she had had to think what was best, but should she continue staying at that inn? Would it really matter where she stayed if this Hacker suddenly took a notion to find and use her to get at Ash?

When a skylark suddenly flew up from a nearby clump of bracken, she quickly stubbed out her cigarette and got down from the wall, only to see a woman standing on the path about 200 metres away. For perhaps ten seconds neither of them did anything other than look at each other from across that distance.

Then the woman came haltingly forwards, Christina quickly putting the binoculars away but wondering why this sudden visitor.

Ash's wife was ravishing, thought Ruth, but why *was* she here, of all places, and why now?

A smile would be best, thought Christina, and an extended hand. 'I'm Mrs. Talbotte, from London and on holiday,' she said. 'The inn where I've been staying will begin to wonder where I am.'

Her eyes were beautiful, thought Ruth, her hair not only perfect but exquisite. 'You can't hide that accent, "Mrs. Talbotte." You're David Ashby's wife, Christina.'

And now you know the false name I've been using, thought Christina, the worried brown eyes and sense of bitterness all suggesting that the woman must view her as a competitor. Had she been in love with Ash? Was she *still* in love with him? 'Do you come here often?'

'*Alone?* Is that why you've just looked beyond me? Well, is it?'

'Not at all. Our skylark has just returned. If we wait, the wren may honour us with its presence. And you are?' she asked.

'Does David know you're here?'

'Please be so kind as to give me your name.'

'Mrs. Ruth Pearce, the . . . the headmaster's wife.'

And not happy about it either. 'Ash still thinks I'm in London but . . .' She would give a shrug, thought Christina, and then tell her what she would definitely *not* want to hear. 'But I had to see the school so as to make up my mind on my own.'

Ruth turned away to hide her discomfort, but couldn't help but blurt, 'Then you've come to take care of your daughter.'

But how—was *this* what the Pearce woman was wondering? 'We've spoken of a reconciliation, yes, but I am still not quite sure my husband meant it.'

'He had a lover—did you know that?'

The Pearce woman was not just bitter about it but fiercely angry, thought Christina. 'A lover . . . ? Please, I . . . I didn't know.'

It would be best to tell her, thought Ruth, and to watch how the news went down.

'A murder . . . ?' managed Christina, her voice barely audible.

'A barmaid,' said Ruth.

'Poor David. He . . . he must have missed me terribly. Is Karen at the school?'

'She's being kept hidden somewhere else. David won't tell me where, but . . . but she has been moved again, today. That's . . . that's all I know.'

Verdammt, he had done it again! 'But . . . but I have to see her. Karen means everything to me.'

The tears came readily enough, thought Ruth, the woman turning away, then letting her see them as she said, 'Mrs. Pearce, you must have some idea where? Please. I've . . . I've come such a long way and I know Karen is very upset and must be missing me terribly. We were always very close. Every day, every evening, we would play cards, or I would read to her or she to me. There are her piano lessons, too. Karen is very talented. Herr Meissner, her piano professor, is convinced.'

Ash's wife had meant every word. 'Look, I won't tell him you were here, but if I can, I'll find out where Karen is and . . . and let you know.'

'How?'

Oh dear, thought Ruth. With such a short, sharp response, those lovely eyes of hers had swiftly narrowed, but she would have to continue. 'Saint Mary Margaret's . . . It's our church and on the road to the school and not far from it. Tomorrow at . . . at four-ish. No, there's a wedding.' She glanced at her watch. 'Let's say the same time as now, at eight. Ash and the rest of them will be in the staff common for an emergency meeting. The school's in arrears and . . . and my husband has found he can no longer hide the truth from them.'

A day, thought Christina. Could she wait that long, and where the hell had Ash sent Karen?

Shoreham, Borough Green, then West Malling and Maidstone, thought Hilary. There would be a few minutes' layover at this last, then it would be on to Bearsted and Hollingbourne Station.

She didn't know what to do, for the man who had joined them still sat opposite her. Karen and she could get off the train early—that might help—but she had the feeling he would be watching for just such a thing.

They could pretend to be going to the loo, could leave their coats and bags, but that wouldn't fool him either, and she couldn't leave her suitcase anyway. The wretched thing weighed a ton—her manuscript and reference books. One of the straps had broken.

As the distance from London had increased, the train had gradually emptied. Now there were only the three of them in the compartment, Karen having fallen asleep. Neither of them had said a word to the man. In all that time, he had sat there, spreading his fleshy thighs as more room had become available, reading his blasted newspaper and studying the racing form or doing the crossword—being utterly bored by it all, or so it had seemed, but not leaving either. Had he the bladder of an elephant?

The blue serge suit was immaculate, the waistcoat a little tight, the jet-black hair thin and carefully trimmed, with brilliantine wavelets on the right. About forty-five, she thought, and still not needing glasses, the eyes of that Nordic blue, the gaze, when he gave it, always bland, the nose big, fleshy and prominent. A man, then, who was at once intense, yet could look at herself and Karen as if all but asleep.

In the dismal half-light of the compartment, his almost child-like fingers had the sheen of dried paste. A nervous condition? she wondered. He had said so little, she had not been able to catch the accent, but he *was* definitely of Mayfair. The shoes, the socks, suit, coat and umbrella, all said that he was.

'Getting off soon, are you?' he suddenly asked, unsmiling.

Flustered, she stammered foolishly, 'Why . . . why, how did you . . . ?'

'Train's late. Unless I'm very lucky, I shall miss my boat!'

The night ferry to Calais, to Dunkerque or Oostende? 'You're going to Dover then?' she managed, but he hadn't any luggage, hadn't even a briefcase.

For some reason he thought her question funny, and when he chuckled, the fleshy thighs tightened as if he was pressing his feet to the floor and getting ready to spring at her.

'Tell me somewhere else this wretched set of wheels is heading,' he said. 'Dover's on this line, is it not?'

His look was piercing. 'Yes . . . yes, it is. Sorry.'

'She's German, isn't she?'

He indicated Karen, Hilary saying, 'Look, I don't see what business it is of . . .'

Abruptly she turned away to gaze emptily into the night, to a lonely farmhouse whose lights seemed lost among fields and hedgerows.

'I only asked,' he said blandly. 'It's of no consequence anyway, but she seemed somewhat unhappy and out of place.'

'Yes . . . Yes, she's German.'

Karen awoke, and Hilary saw her reflection in the window, saw his, too, the three of them, Karen giving a huge yawn and stretching, he setting his paper aside, not smiling now, not anything but looking at Karen as though he would . . .

'What time is it, Hilary?' asked Karen in *Deutsch*.

He would have her own name now, would know all about them anyways. 'Nearly time. Please don't be impatient.'

'Shoreham, ladies and gentlemen. Shoreham,' came the voice of the guard.

One stop down and five to go, thought Hilary, but where was Karen's father now?

The school was all but in darkness, the moon giving ribbon to the slowly drifting clouds. Ashby stood out on the Common, looking up at the sky but thinking of Karen and Hilary who should now be in Kent if all had gone well, but had it? Unfortunately the uneasiness he felt simply wouldn't go away. All day it had been troubling him.

His steps sounding on the gravel of the drive, he went round to the car park. There were four telephones in the school, but all on the same line and each with a button that would light up when in use and he didn't want to use any of them. With twenty-seven masters plus other staff to run through, the task of identifying the sleeper was impossible, and he might not even be with the school. And as for the boys, why, even Jackie Peterson's father looked anything *but* what one would expect of someone working for the Nazis.

When he tried the MG, the engine wouldn't turn over. The rotor was gone. Lowering the bonnet's side screen, he eased the catch closed and did up the leather belt.

Ruth answered his knock in her dressing gown. 'Tony's out for another walk,' she said.

'Where to?' he asked.

'How should I know?'

'Skip it then,' he said. 'I'll come back later if I don't find him.'

Wanting to tell him she had met his wife, Ruth let him walk away, but something must have happened, and she wondered if it had had anything to do with his daughter. Going through to the study, she found the list of telephone calls and ran a finger down over last month's until coming to Anthony's entry for the Dorchester Hotel. It was marked: *Ash re Ruth and Colonel Hacker.* How cold of him.

There were calls that Anthony had made to Taunton and more recently to London. Ash had been back at the school by then but had any of them had to do with him and that daughter of his? Anthony could have been trying to reach some of the parents, for the school was short a good deal. Now more than two thousand pounds. One London number had been called five times.

'Ruth, what are you looking for?' asked Anthony, she stiffening at the sound of his voice.

'Nothing! I . . . I was just feeling lonely. Did Ash find you? He came by. I . . .'

Had she found anything? wondered Pearce, but said, 'I've had to loan him the Austin. He has to make a phone call and doesn't want to make it from the school.'

'Where has he got that daughter of his now?'

'In Kent, at an estate called Clarington Hall. It's near Hollingbourne.'

Ash must have just told him, but why, then, given the constant secrecy, should Anthony have suddenly let her know? 'You look awful,' she said. 'Was there something wrong with Ash's motorcar?'

He would turn away from her now, thought Pearce, would simply not answer.

Ashby switched off the lights and the ignition. He had been heading over the hills to Crowcombe and the call box there, but had suddenly changed his mind and come back down here to the Dogs of War.

Leaving the car, walking up the road to the call box's lamp fanning change over a palm, he knew that whoever had taken the rotor must have been trying to force him into using one of the school's telephones. He had had to tell Tony where Karen had been taken, but if he couldn't trust him, he couldn't trust anyone.

The call to Hilary took a good five minutes to place, and he knew the operator would probably listen in, simply out of curiosity. From where he stood, he could just see a corner of the pub. Old George Crawley and Roger Banfield would be sinking their pints and might have seen something. When a woman's voice came on the line, it was that of the housekeeper, a Mrs. Dorothy Hamble. 'But they've not arrived, sir, nor have they telephoned from the station. Oh my goodness me, sir, it's gone past the time that train should have been in.'

Had it happened? he wondered. 'Could you send someone to check? Please, it's . . . it's important.'

'It most certainly *is*, sir, but the master's away and Miss Hilary not expected. I shall have to ask Albert, I will.'

'Just send someone. It's urgent that you do. I'll ring you back in half an hour.'

Ashby knew that the train could simply have been delayed, but the sinking feeling in the pit of his stomach told him that wasn't so, and when Banfield and Crawley heard about the rotor, it was the latter who said, 'A bad business, that.'

'Surely not one of the senior boys?' asked Banfield. 'We didn't see a thing, did we, George?'

'Just Headmaster out walking,' went on Crawley, sucking on a fag and hunching forwards over the table. 'But, then, our Tics does a lot of that these days. Still fretting over the accounts, I suspect. Did you ask him?'

Ashby nodded.

'And what did he say?' arched Banfield.

'That he had seen no one.'

'Not even us?' asked Crawley, lighting another cigarette and crumbling the one he had just finished. 'A damned uncomfortable business, Roger. A missing rotor. And you're certain Headmaster said he hadn't seen anyone?'

'Perhaps our landlord has,' interjected Banfield. 'A small matter, Mr. Dolby. Any unusual custom these past few days?'

The whole place would have heard him, thought Ashby, but they were all regulars and he could but trust all of them.

'Well, there was someone,' said Dolby. 'A real looker. German, too, and asking about the murder.'

'My wife,' said Peachey.

And looking very lost to the thought, felt Banfield.

'Christina couldn't have taken that rotor,' said Ashby. 'She doesn't know a blessed thing about cars.'

It was Crawley who hazarded, 'Could she have learned in your absence?'

'Well, yes, I suppose, but why would she go and do a thing like that?'

And blind to the woman, thought Banfield. Blind also to Anthony James Pearce, his comrade-in-arms. 'To slow you down, perhaps.'

Everyone at the school had obviously been trying to put two and two together, thought Ashby, but said, 'She doesn't know where our daughter is, but if you want the truth, we did speak briefly about our getting back together.'

Oh my, oh my, thought Banfield, the pleasures of the nuptial bed. 'That couldn't have gone down well with Headmaster's wife, now could it?'

Did they know everything, these two old gossips? 'Ruth would have gotten used to it, but in any case, I didn't tell her.'

But would someone else? wondered Banfield. 'George and I have been thinking of buying Wetherby Cottage. It would suit the couple fine, George. Close to the school, comfortable after a cleaning. Mind, we would have to see that the chimneys were clear, but I think we would gladly let it to you, Ashby.'

'The girl could have her own room,' said Crawley, drifting off into sentiment as he wafted tobacco smoke from himself.

'Time, gentlemen. Time,' called the landlord. Dolby didn't know where Christina was staying or when, exactly, she had last been in, but said, 'I'm keeping out of it until Daisy's settled.'

'I didn't kill her, Mr. Dolby. How could I have? And I don't really know who did, but promise I'll find out.'

'You do that then,' said Dolby. It was damned fishy, all this business of wives claiming to be someone else and asking questions about the murder of the ex-husband's lover. Damned fishy, too, young Arnold finding the woman down at those ruins and then in Daisy's barn. 'If you don't mind my saying so, Captain

Ashby, you want to watch that wife of yours. It isn't seemly, her coming round here like that and you not knowing she's anywhere near.'

'Could I use the telephone?'

Was it that necessary? The look in Ashby's eyes said that it definitely was. 'All right, but mind you pay up and while you're on about it, I'd be pleased if you would settle your account.'

Banfield clasped Peachey by the shoulder and told Dolby not to worry. 'George and I will stand the captain whatever is needed until the impasse is over. Isn't that right, George?'

It was, and they trickled out with the others, Dolby beginning to tidy up. Since the loss of Daisy, he hadn't been able to find a replacement. Either they didn't have her way with the customers, or they were too afraid the same might happen to themselves.

When Ashby had finished making his call, he stood at the bar so lost in thought, Dolby wondered if it had been good news or bad.

'She's safe,' he said at last, though still worried about it, and putting change on the bar, paid for the call and then settled his account with a cheque.

Dolby shook his head. 'Tear it up. I spoke out of turn, Captain. I'm not myself.'

'Nor am I.'

Banfield and old George were hanging round, waiting for news over by Roger's car. God help the two of them if tobacco should ever be rationed. Ashby grinned at the thought. It was good to be with them, good to know he could count them amongst his friends. 'She's safe,' he said.

Dolby caught sight of them and called from the door, 'I say, look, Captain, does this business have anything to do with that soldier fellow with the ginger moustache?'

'Why do you ask?'

'Because, amongst all the rest of it, that wife of yours was making inquiries about him.'

Kneeling before the fire in her room at the Rose and Thorn, Christina warmed her hands, then rubbed her arms and shoulders. Could she sleep, would she sleep? she wondered. She was so keyed up, she didn't know how she could. Everything depended on the Pearce woman, on that chance meeting, but would the woman let it slip that they had met? If so, Ash would be waiting in that churchyard, and if not there, then he would soon know where she was staying. Osier had still not made contact. *Gott im Himmel*, was Burghardt blind to what she could do with such assistance? Werner would have been far more suitable as head of AST-X Bremen. Werner understood her and would know how anxious she was, how driven, no matter the cost.

Having come in late, she had missed seeing the envelope that was leaning against the bedside table's lamp. Powder blue, and of the very best of stationery, it was even scented, but there was no other address than that of *Mrs. Christina Talbotte, care of the Rose and Thorn*. Had Ash found out where she was? Had Osier?

Opening it, and the folded sheet of heavy white bond, she found nothing other than an address. The embassy *had* come through. *Vati* had seen to that, for they would have contacted him first, and he would have told them they had better or else.

Memorizing the address was not difficult, and this she did because she couldn't let it fall into any other hands, especially those of *Mr. Harris Blackburn from Leeds*.

Tomorrow she would go to Bridgwater, but must be very careful to see that no one was following her. She would get Burghardt's wireless operator to send a message *demanding* that he order Osier to make contact immediately.

As the envelope and its contents caught fire, she could hardly contain her excitement. Sleep didn't come. Instead, she kept thinking that if Ash should ever find out where she was, he might then inadvertently lead this Colonel Hacker to herself, and then, what then?

In the morning, she found the shop on a narrow, cobbled street in the heart of Bridgwater. Perhaps two dozen cottontail rabbits hung by their hind legs from meat hooks along the iron rail above the window. Clusters of others hung on either side of the fluted wooden columns that framed the entrance.

In the warmth of that Friday, 3 June, flies buzzed about or settled on glazed eyes, while in the centre of the window, a boar's head stared at passerby. Tufted bows of white paper protruded from its ears. Sugared hams were ranked on either side, the *V* of them expanding into trays of chops, ribs and coils of sausage or blood puddings.

Looking back down the street, searching through the faces of the everyday, Christina still wasn't satisfied she hadn't been followed. Crossing the road, she went into a greengrocer's and bought two pounds of potatoes and some onions while checking the butcher shop a last time. Bunches of cut blue irises in the corners of that window helped to frame the gilded letters of DAVIDSON'S PORK, BEEF AND POULTRY.

'Your change, miss.'

'Oh, sorry. Thanks. I am new to your lovely town. Is that butcher shop reliable?'

Ted Daigles caught the accent right away. 'Run by a countryman of yours, miss. Ernie married into the business after the war. Say, why are you people kicking up such a ruckus over Czechoslovakia? Seems this Hitler fellow really means war.'

Tossing him an innocent look, she smiled and found delight in his shyness as she said, 'But why should those people want war any more than we do? Oh, I see, you have thought . . .'

Taking the proffered hand, he felt its coolness as she said, 'I'm Mrs. Talbotte, Mr. . . . ?'

'Daigles, ma'am. Ted it is.'

'Ted. I will remember that. My husband is a barrister, so you see, I too am . . .' She would give him another smile. 'Married into the business, so to speak.'

Once across the road, the smells of sawdust, blood, and that raw, bone-and-marrow odour of all butcher shops came instantly as the bell above the door announced her arrival.

Standing before the glass cases and the counter, Christina realized that there were only the two of them in the shop, a stroke of luck.

Ernst Reiss laid the knife he had been honing aside and placed his big hands on the chopping block in front of this beauty. Instinctively he knew she was of money and of home, and he had the idea she hadn't come to buy a *verdammt* thing.

Taking in the soft cream frock with its pleated skirt, the plain and open neck with its large and floppy collar, he noted the high, firm breasts and commanding expression, his heart sinking. 'What can I do for you?' he hazarded.

Wary . . . *mein Gott*, but he was. 'Are we alone?'

'Should it matter?'

He was all butcher and about forty-five. The muttonchops were thick and untidy, the hair that shade flax would get when it had ripened too long and the rain had got at it. Small and grey-blue, if faded, the eyes were intent, the nose overly large and florid for a man who must constantly hide himself, the fleshy cheeks, lips and expression sour. Taking all of these in, she found the urge to tell him exactly where things were at almost overpowering, but mustn't let him get her riled. 'Let us just say, Herr Reiss . . .' she began in *Deutsch*.

'Mr. Reiss, madam,' he retorted in guttural if defiant English. 'I left all that behind me the day the British let me out of the prisoner-of-war camp where they had very kindly kept me for more than two years but had allowed me to find useful work on their farms and with one of their butchers. So, what will it be, madam? Some nice back ribs, a few Wiener schnitzel to remind you of home? Some sausage? I can give you . . .'

'Herr Reiss, the embassy was reluctant to divulge your identity, but being the daughter of a high-ranking general who is a close associate of Herr Himmler and others helped.'

'*Ach*, I can't believe that. Me work for those Wehrmacht bastards? They left us stinking in the trenches, Madam General's daughter. Now if you want anything, please, you have only to choose.'

He indicated the display cases, then swung the ham of a hand to the porkers that hung with sides of bacon and ropes of sausage and blood pudding behind him.

'Has Osier contacted you?' she asked.

'Osier? Do you mean this?' he snorted, swiftly reaching for a willow basket. 'Eggs? Was it eggs the madam wants?'

She took two and smashed them on the chopping block. 'Don't be a fool, Herr Reiss. If you don't help me, I'll let the British know that you have a wireless set either here or hidden elsewhere.'

Lieber Christus im Himmel, die Schlampe had flicked egg at him! Tossing her a towel, he silently cursed the day the Nazis had come to him in 1935 with promises of extra cash, a harmless enough activity then, it had seemed.

Reiss drew a tray of chops from one of the display cases and ran a finger up and down the rows, this creature, this slut of a Frau, selecting two. Giving her a grunt she would not like, he tore off some brown paper before flinging the chops onto the weigh scale and said in *Deutsch*, 'Whoever you are, I know nothing of this Osier. *Ach*, they don't tell me, do they? I am given messages that are wisely left only where I want them left, and I then simply send them over and see that any replies are also delivered in the same way. None of them know me, *meine gute Frau*, and I do not *want* any of them knowing me.'

A middle-aged man and woman, both with bicycles, had stopped outside the shop, the woman's with the carrier basket of just such a shop and a string bag of groceries. His wife? wondered Christina, knowing that it must be. 'For how long have you been sending messages only to AST-X Bremen?'

Was he going to have to kill this countrywoman of his? wondered Reiss, but said, 'Long enough.'

'And you honestly don't know if Osier has contacted you to send something over?'

Reiss threw an anxious look towards the street and shook his head. 'I wouldn't. I don't even know any of their names, only their numbers, but you ought to be more careful. It was stupid of the embassy to have given you this address, stupider still for you to have come here. Did you think the British MI5 would respect your being a female, let alone so well connected you could pry such secrets?'

A bit of string was yanked from the overhead spool, the package then being wrapped. 'No, wait,' said Christina. 'Some bacon. Five hundred grams.'

And yet another mistake. 'A pound, I think,' he said, licking sweat from his upper lip, for everything about this beauty raised hackles.

'I need something else, Herr Reiss. A knife.'

She would hear him on the stairs, thought Reiss, would hear him as he crossed the floor above, would hope perhaps that the wife would not come into the shop in his absence.

When he returned, he held it in his hand, and when the blade leapt out at her, she blanched and stumbled back as he said, 'If you want help, ask it of this Osier. Those are the rules.'

Retracted, the blade disappeared inside its stainless steel haft.

'Forget where you got this, or you will find another where you don't want it.'

There was blood on the chops and this made him grin as he laid the knife on top of them before adding the bacon. Out on the street, she paused—another mistake, thought Reiss, silently cursing her.

Pulling off his apron, he tossed it onto the chopping block, reached for his jacket and hurried outside. 'Laura, my love,' he said to his wife, 'I will be back in a few minutes, yes? William, it is good to see you again,' he added to the man. 'Forgive me for rushing off, but that one has forgotten her change.'

Once round the corner and out of sight of the shop, the woman who had said she was a general's daughter went into several shops in succession, making small purchases in each. If she saw him, she didn't let on. Twice she doubled back and that was good, he felt, knowing now, if ever one could be absolutely certain of such things, that she hadn't been followed by anyone other than himself.

When she got into her car six blocks away, she swung those long legs towards him and he had an eyeful and then the ghost of her smile, she drawing him near to say in no uncertain terms, 'AST-X Bremen, *mein Lieber*. Tell them Osier must contact me late this evening at the Rose and Thorn, for I may, by then, have all the information needed.'

Friday was at last coming to a close, felt Ruth. Fog had crept in over the land, bringing the smell of the sea but increasing her nervousness. Saint Mary Margaret's had been built in 1642 and she would wait inside, would wait, as she must, for Ash's wife since she had said she would.

The spare key was where it always was, under the stone nearest the door. As chairperson of the grounds committee, she had the right to enter at any time, but had she the right to tell Ash's wife where her daughter now was?

Leaving the door open, she hooked it to the wall but stepped inside. Would she wait out of the fog, wait until the woman came up the walk . . . and then? she asked.

There were no lights on, but above the altar the last of the daylight filtered in through the stained glass. Walking up the aisle, she hesitated, for everything seemed to be telling her not to say a word about Ash's daughter, that it wasn't right of her, that Anthony had had no right to tell her, but why, *then,* had he?

The smell of beeswax came to her, heavy on that of the mustiness. She and Anthony had been married in this church, but what had it all meant? 'Ash,' she said in a whisper, and only to herself. 'Ash, I really could have helped you.'

Returning to the entrance, to darkness now and the feel of the mizzle against her skin, she found that his wife had still not come, but when she heard someone on the road, she hesitantly said, 'Is that you, Mrs. Ashby?' and knew in her heart of hearts that she should never have used the woman's proper name.

Hacker let her come towards him, he standing on the other side of the gate, and when she got there, caught her by the wrist and said, 'Out having a stroll, are we?'

'Dear God,' wept Ruth.

'Exactly where is Mrs. Christina Ashby, Mrs. Pearce, or is it Mrs. Christina Talbotte she's still calling herself?'

'Please let me go. I . . . I don't know where she is.'

'But she was to have met you here, that right?'

'Yes.'

'Well, I've only just got here myself, so she can't have seen me following you from that school of your husband's. Been down to Saint Ives, I have, Mrs. Pearce, only to find the bird flown. Where's Ashby got her now?'

'I . . . I don't know. He . . . he wouldn't tell *me* a thing like that!'

Then someone else must have. 'They moved the *Bonnie Jean,* Mrs. Pearce. Now that MacDonald couple either took the girl with them or they sent her somewhere else. Which was it, eh? And please don't try my patience. I've been run off my feet, and am not about to take no for an answer.'

Ruth tried to yank her hand away, but he was far too strong. 'I . . . I *don't* know what you're talking about. Karen's certainly *not* at the school.'

'But you've managed to find out the child's name.'

'At last. Now if you'll allow me, Colonel, I really must get home.'

Had the Hoffmann woman heard the two of them? he wondered. Was she that close, this one afraid he would realize it, or had the woman simply been detained and would soon show up? 'Has the door of that church been left open for her?'

'Yes, but I had best close and lock it.'

'And she was to have met you there?'

'Colonel, please let me go. I . . . I don't know anything and I don't *want* to!'

As he touched her tears, the Pearce woman bleated, 'Please don't harm me.'

'I won't, but only if you keep my presence to yourself and leave that damned door open.'

When she reached the sitting room of Headmaster House, Ruth poured herself the stiffest, couldn't help but let her hand shake just like Anthony's always did. Grimacing, she tossed off the Scotch. Hanging up her coat and scarf, she pulled off the kerchief and only then realized that there was a light on in the corridor upstairs.

'Anthony . . .' she called out. 'Anthony, is that you?'

It couldn't be. He and all the others, Ash included, were at the meeting Anthony had called to announce and discuss the accounts' arrears.

Neither Anthony nor herself had ever locked the doors. In all the years she had lived at Grantley's, such a thing had never been felt needed.

Christina Ashby was sitting on her bed, propped up by the pillows and smoking a cigarette. There were grass stains on the coverlet. Bits of grass still clung to her shoes.

'Hacker,' said Christina. 'Did you let him know we were to have met at that church?'

Ruth turned away and started for the door, the woman calmly saying, 'I wouldn't, if I were you.'

'I *didn't* tell him. I didn't! He . . .'

'Made you, didn't he?'

'Yes! but . . . but I didn't tell him I knew where Karen was being taken.'

'And do you?'

There was something metallic in the woman's hand. Backing away, Ruth tried to understand what she had gotten herself into.

Out in the corridor, she reached the stairs, said faintly, 'Please, I'll . . . I'll tell you where.'

'But will you then tell Hacker that you did, or will it be Ash?'

The blade that leapt out of that thing was silvery-grey, double-edged, razor-sharp and a good five inches long.

At 0320 hours on Saturday, Burghardt shook sleep from himself and told his housekeeper to go back to bed. Tearing open the envelope the young Gefreiter from wireless had handed him, he read:

WICHTIG. ATTENTION.
At 0217, Bridgwater sent:
Security breached. Osier not known. Am shutting down.

The *verdammt* embassy must have listened to the general's daughter, or she had got them to contact that father of hers and had then done what she should never have done. Motioning to the boy, he said, 'Come in, *mein Lieber. Komm.* Take off those wet boots and jacket. *Don't* leave puddles or that housekeeper of mine will come back and make you wish you hadn't!'

Going into the kitchen to light the gas ring and set the kettle to boil, he reached for Frau Albrecht's brandy and her tooth glass and said, 'Down that and then have another and another while I write a little something to send in answer. Who would have thought this weather possible, eh? Even my lettuces are complaining.'

Indicating that the boy was to make himself a cup of coffee, he retreated to the office he kept here at home, though few knew he ever used it. Closing the door, he went over to the desk to switch on its lamp and reread the damage that woman had caused. What should he do now that she had not only put Bridgwater at risk but everything else? Had MI5 followed her? Would they wait until she had returned before jumping on that set and shutting it down themselves? *Ach*, why couldn't she have stayed married to that schoolteacher and been a *Hausfrau und Mutter* like she ought to have been?

Knowing that it couldn't be avoided, he would have to send

something, for she would have demanded that Bridgwater tell him to get Osier to make contact with her, would expect himself to send Bridgwater details of when and where such a meeting could be expected, and since a record was kept of all transmissions in and out, Berlin would have access to whatever was sent.

And Bridgwater? he asked himself, wishing he had downed a little of that brandy himself. What would that one do if the general's daughter *did* take it upon herself to make contact again, which she definitely would? Could he gamble and stall for just a little?

Taking up a pencil, he wrote:

At 0217 tonight, send Bridgwater the following: Imperative remain in contact AST-X Bremen. Osier awakened but not yet fully briefed. Take whatever measures necessary to protect security.

Only time would tell how this was going to end, but were MI5 on to her yet?

Saturday morning's early light was definitely unfriendly, the telephone cold. 'Sir John, Bunny here. I drew a blank in Saint Ives. Bastards gave us the slip. Came up here to the school to nose round and spent far too much of the night in a church.'

Masterson chuckled. Bunny never failed to amuse. 'Don't tell me you've decided to take Holy Orders?'

'Piss off!' Hacker let him have the news, then asked, 'Any line yet on that trawler of MacDonald's?'

'Gone north probably to Inverness, old cock. The MacDonald woman's father runs a bed-and-breakfast. Perhaps you should stay over and have a word.'

'Let someone else handle it. I'll work the brush down here and find out who turned that key on me.'

There was a pause on the other end of the line, Sir John not usually one for such. Had there been trouble? wondered Hacker.

'Bunny, it would be most unwise of you to nose round that school. Talk is cheap, and in little places like Kilve and the Dogs of War, it is especially so, but talk there has been. Take the road north. Drive up so as to give them time to settle in. We'll find your key-turner in time, no fear.'

'It wasn't Pearce, nor do I think it that wife of his, but by the way that key was rapped at the door and then dropped on the doorstep to let me know they had got the better of me, I have to believe it a woman.'

'Bunny, let me warn you again. Eggs you may break from time to time, but not until the current nest is tidy.'

6

At just after supper on that Saturday, Hilary borrowed the little Austin-10 that Dotty and Albert used. Even with the side screens rolled down, it was warm and she was glad she had worn a light cotton frock, plain and simple, nothing fancy.

The hops, having been sprayed with Bordeaux mixture to stop the blight, were copper-green under the slanting sun, the light soft and gentle on field and wood. Kent really was incredibly beautiful, and it had been good coming home. Right away Albert and Dotty had taken charge. Already Karen was beginning to feel she might belong.

There hadn't been anything untoward since the man on the train. Perhaps he hadn't been following them, perhaps simply there to watch over them, though you'd think he would have said something of it.

Set among rolling hills and dales, the inn was spacious and sprawling, part hunt, golf and tennis club. Always it had brought rising expectations of good times, though now, as she parked the car, she dreaded what she had to do.

Enclosed porches fronted the main dining room, which over-looked the golf course, while the one that opened off the lounge faced the river and duck pond. There was a grand piano in the bar. Maroon walls and drapes set off lithographs of hunting scenes, while little round tables with Windsor chairs were clustered about the fireplace. Hilary knew they would all crowd in here after the annual dinner. She would have to take a table and wait out the speeches, would then have to speak to each of them, they no doubt saying, *Hilary, luv, where* have *you been*? she answering, *Cornwall*, as if they hadn't already known.

Kay Wynne-Thomas came first, looking radiant in a smashing red dress and heels and saying, 'Hil, darling, why haven't you rung? I've got the most fab news. Gerald and I are engaged.'

Brushing cheeks, they hugged each other. The ring was shown and exclaimed over, Gerald given a hug and a kiss on the cheek, he grinning from ear to ear and asking, 'Care to join us?'

'I can't. Sorry. Maybe later. I'm . . . I'm waiting for someone.'

Eyebrows were raised, of course, and so it went, for suddenly there was talk all round her, and when the singing started, she tried to remain apart, yet not look too out of it, for they were good people and meant well, but they really didn't know a thing about her present circumstances.

Lionel Dandridge took up his post on one of the bar stools, coffee and brandy to hand. Giving her a toss of his head, he indicated the far doorway, and she settled down, for Lionel had answered the telephone when she had called the number she had been given for MI6 to let them know Karen and she had safely arrived.

The tuxedo was just a bit too tight, the shirt and bow tie a little too worn, Dandridge's long legs stretched out as, with affectation, his slim hands set coffee down and drew out cigarettes, offering none to anyone but himself, and *that*, too, was typical. Once handsome perhaps, now jaded, the thick, wide and greying brush of a full moustache went with the roguishly bushy eyebrows, the iron-grey hair and dark eyes that searched, laughed when called upon or were teased by some wayward thought.

She didn't know the men on either side of him but that was nothing new. Estates changed hands and Lionel always thought he might buy one. Never still, he talked as much with his hands as his lips, the heavy gold cufflinks, the last of his father's wealth, catching the light.

Presentable he might once have been, but confidence he simply did not inspire.

'My dear, your dress is most becoming. May I?'

Drawing out a chair, the speaker sat down, she blurting, 'Brigadier, I . . .'

'Yes, yes, I know. You're waiting to meet someone. How's that father of yours? Still not pining after your mother, or was it the brother? I can never remember.'

Smoothing both hands quickly over the back of his balding head, he folded them on the table. 'Cornwall to your liking?' he asked. 'I seem to recall something about a novel. Going well, is it?'

A dark look could not be prevented and this he noted as she said, 'Brigadier, you're *not* the person I asked for and was led to believe I would meet.'

Not trustworthy? he wondered. 'Be that as it may, you've not answered my question.'

Brigadier Charles Edward Gordon, retired, was in his late fifties. Unlike Dandridge, the tuxedo and regimental tie were immaculate. A few wisps of short grey hair still sprouted from the wind-burnished crown of his head. The eyes were the bluest of blue, their expression invariably as if gazing off to the horizon or up into the clouds after one of his hawks, when not breeding hunters or in the boardrooms of the nation discussing how best to put down a crippling labour strike.

That continued gaze of his simply reinforced her opinion of him. 'Look, I'd rather *not* talk to you, and certainly not here where everyone in creation can see us!'

Anger had made her colour rise, she still remembering lost acreage and Clarington's south pasture, thought Gordon, she thinking, no doubt, that it had been stolen from that father of hers, '*swindled*,' as some said; others: '*bought for a song.*'

Catching a passing waiter by the sleeve, he said, 'John, old chap, bring me that bottle and two glasses. This young lady has just had her birthday.'

Damn him! 'Brigadier, don't you dare play games with me. It's nowhere near my birthday. I need help or I wouldn't be here.'

As the singing and the piano grew louder, he leaned closer and said, 'Help you most definitely need. Now please, a little . . . shall we say, trust? It's wisest we be seen among friends. Were I to have driven up to that house of your father's, it would have been quite a different matter, especially as it is being constantly watched.'

'But . . . but I haven't seen *anyone* watching the house and grounds?'

'Surely your assessment of things is far better.'

Was he lying and if so, why? 'Who and how many of them are there?'

'As to whom, that we do not yet know. As to how many, enough.'

Several were singing, laughing and jockeying for space round the piano, Lionel remaining at the bar but having turned to watch herself and the brigadier.

As a bottle and two glasses were set on the table, Hilary noted the label, a Gevrey-Chambertin, Clos de Vigneau, a red Burgundy from the Côte d'Or, the reminder hatefully clear, Gordon asking her to pronounce things, which she wouldn't, he then asking, 'Still keeping in touch with the family, are you? The sister, *hmm*? An old school chum, I gather.'

There was no use fighting him. He would get what he wanted of her. 'I write to Adèle Vigneau at Christmas and Easter, and whenever I feel I should, Brigadier, but whatever happened between that brother of hers and myself is finished, so don't for a moment think I or they would be of any use to MI6 in France.'

'Then enjoy the wine and tell me about your little problem. I've been briefed, of course, by my opposite number, but had best hear it from yourself.'

He had been on to someone in MI5. 'I'd prefer we at least went out to the porch.'

'The patio might be better.'

Gordon found them a table under the willows by the fishpond. Here the sound of the singing was subdued but broken from time to time by bursts of laughter and applause. Others were seated about—the older set and one young couple bent on holding hands, she glancing at them in dismay, perhaps at what she herself was missing.

Letting her talk the Ashby thing out, he found that there was much she still didn't know and that she was very much on the run. Detecting an interest in Ashby, he wondered if it might be useful, so too, a softness towards the child, the mothering instinct perhaps. And when she was done, he said, 'I should tell you, my dear, that I greatly fear the German Abwehr is in earnest. Wireless signals indicate that there definitely is something in the wind. Invariably the small hours are used, but when one of their clandestine sets sends a brief, terse message at 0217 and then, exactly twenty-four hours later, receives a longer, sharper directive, it implies that said wireless agent was standing by for his AST-X Bremen response and that something has definitely caused a stir. Herr Hitler is, I greatly fear, very much in earnest. My other half believes a sleeper has been awakened, and that you may expect an attempt at any time.'

AST-X Bremen and a sleeper . . . but had the brigadier intercepted her request for help and pounced on it for purposes of his own? And who was his 'other half'?

'Sir John Masterson's an able man, Hilary. A bit off the tick in the tea and spice trade at the moment, but you should insist on seeing him. Yes, I think that would be best. Be sure to ask him exactly what they have in mind.'

MI5. 'And this Colonel Hacker?'

And sickened by it too. 'Ah yes, Bunny. Now there's a fellow with a past. Tough, well disciplined, a soldier like myself. A bit too raw when it comes to dealing with subversives. No patience but damned thorough. Oh my, yes. Bunny was rather hard on the gun runners in Burma, but still, a good man when all's said and done.'

She had yet to touch her wine, was far from happy about their meeting, and when she said, 'Does this mean you won't help me?' he caught the note of desperation.

'Not at all, my dear. What it does mean is that I *and* MI6 insist that you go up to London next Friday to have a word with Masterson and that you agree to go along with them.'

'And use Karen?'

'*Sit* down! Don't make a spectacle of yourself.'

He indicated the wine. Hilary shook her head. 'I haven't touched a drop of that since I lost my heart and virtue to a liar.'

Mademoiselle Adèle Vigneau's older brother, and so much for the nuns having taught Miss Bowker-Brown what to look for and expect from a Frenchman. 'My dear, one woman's already been murdered. Neither Sir John nor myself would wish there to be another.'

'Brigadier, you know very well Clarington Hall is on its last legs and that it will all go for taxes when my father dies, and that I will not ask him for anything.'

Hence Cornwall. Gordon took out his wallet and spread fifty pounds in fivers on the table. Glancing round at the others, and shoving the big white bills back at him, she said, 'Don't you *dare* treat me like a prostitute!'

'What a charming thought. Dandridge will be your coordinator. We must try, though, not to ruin your future insofar as the Germans are concerned. This business of Ashby's is a pain but you will stay here in Kent and we will watch what happens, and you will go up to see Sir John.'

'I can't take Karen with me to London, Brigadier, and I *can't* leave her here, not with just Dotty and Albert to guard her. I simply *couldn't*.'

Although her outrage pleased him, and she finally did accept the money, he still said, 'My dear, I can and will tell you only what I feel you should be told and that will have to do, though I must ask one further thing.'

Giving her a moment, he got to his feet. 'Not a word of this meeting to Masterson or to any of them, most especially Bunny Hacker, but also Captain Ashby. It's to be between ourselves and I must insist. Lionel will be careful, never fear, and you will tell Captain Ashby that there is to be absolutely no help from us. Is that understood?'

'But . . . but why?'

'I'm afraid I can't tell you that. Assume it prudent and govern yourself accordingly. There is a sleeper, Hilary, and we must deal with him as I see fit. Perhaps a picnic would be in order. Yes, let's settle on that. Take the child somewhere close and do so on Monday, but let Lionel know of the location. Test the waters, so to speak.'

Let AST-X Bremen make their move. Sickened by the thought, Hilary reached for her wine and downed it, and only then realized that she had broken her word to herself.

This time the messenger came from Berlin and arrived at about 0500 hours, Sunday, 5 June, Burghardt complaining about the lack of sleep. Christina von Hoffmann's daughter had been taken to Clarington Hall, an estate in Kent, near Hollingbourne. Hilary Bowker-Brown, the young woman who had brought the girl there, had met a Brigadier Charles Edward Gordon at a golf and country club.

Again the general's daughter begged him to send Osier to her. *The estate is perfect. Quite isolated and within fifteen kilometres of the sea. Werner could easily take her off once Osier and myself have got her.* She had followed this Bowker-Brown girl to that country club and had not only watched the two meet but had then, Bridgwater having been too far for her to use, driven to the embassy, and had got them to send this to him.

Reaching for the telephone, he said, '*Bitte*, no matter the hour, put me through to Berlin, to the residence of Admiral Wilhelm Canaris. If the admiral is not there, try the Jagdschloss Thiergarten. It may be that he is out riding.'

It took the admiral the better part of an hour to return the call, and by then Frau Albrecht had prepared a suitable breakfast for himself and the messenger, but Canaris was impatient. 'Joachim, what is it?'

'The Ashby problem. Brigadier Charles Edward Gordon.'

And Osier, Agent 07392 . . . 'But . . . but are you sure of this?'

Burghardt told him that he was.

'Then tell Fräulein von Hoffmann to be exceedingly careful of the brigadier, Joachim. This one is very special.'

At the embassy, Christina put her back to the tiled wall of the shower bath, and holding her hands up to the nozzle, let the warmth of the water hammer her face. Every bone in her ached. After driving to Croydon to catch Lufthansa's midnight Ju 52,[*] the embassy had provided a room, but Burghardt's response hadn't come in until 8.10 am. London time. She could sleep for days, but by noon on this Sunday, 5 June, she must be back in Kent, by this afternoon at the latest.

It had all been quite dangerous and exciting. Elation had flooded through her on locking Colonel Hacker in that little church after having had the pleasure of terrifying Ruth Pearce with that knife Herr Reiss had given her, but finding the estate and then watching the Bowker-Brown girl meet someone at that country club had been far more than either, more still when she had looked down the list of members and had found Brigadier Charles Edward Gordon's name and had then been able to send that information to the Kapitän.

---

[*] The Junkers 52, the backbone of air travel in the 1930s and, later, throughout World War II, *Tante Ju* (Auntie Ju) being used for military transport.

Again Burghardt's response, received by the embassy's wireless, ran through her mind.

OSIER TO MAKE CONTACT CHELTON HOTEL, MAIDSTONE. USE EXTREME CAUTION, PROTECT SECURITY. DANISH FREIGHTER *THORSTEIN* STANDING BY IN DOVER. ICELANDIC TRAWLER *EINAR HELGASON* WILL PUT IN TO SOUTHEND-ON-SEA 7 JUNE, 0500 HOURS LONDON TIME.

Next Tuesday. He had finally realized she needed help. She could, she knew, walk right into Clarington Hall and demand the return of her daughter. No one could stop her, but MI5 would only try to take Karen back before she had got her to either of those two ships or the Dover ferry. Now, however, Osier and herself would soon take care of things and Ash would find out exactly how capable and determined was this ex-wife of his!

'Please, sir, it's me, Bill.'

Peachey didn't look up from the motor he was working on, but asked, 'How's the world treating you?'

'Fine, sir. That is, I jolly well think I shall pass the exams this year if all goes well.'

Spanner in hand, he still didn't look up, but called out cheerily, 'And so you shall, Bill. With fortitude, determination and the most amazing machine in the world, the human brain. Top of the lot in maths for you. Granted, as were all of the other masters, I was both gratified and surprised, but that's the way of it.'

Top of the class in MATHS! In spite of all his troubles, and there were many of those, felt Bill, Peachey was grinning.

'I've always had faith in you, Bill, but take a load off your feet and tell me what's bugging you.'

'It's . . . it's not a problem of mine, sir. It's . . .'

An uncaring hand was tossed, Peachey gathering him in to sit on the coach house steps where the roses grew and gave good cover. Finding himself an ice-cold bottle of brown ale from a hidden bucket, he took a swig then passed it over with, 'Just a sip,' the ale crisp and sweet, the moment to be cherished. Kicking off his shoes and pitching his cap and gown into a heap, he loosened that tie of his and said, 'Well, what do you make of it all? Men trying to kidnap my daughter and killing poor Daisy like that, then sabotaging my car so as to ground me when I need it most?'

'Don't let them kill you, sir,' said Bill with utter gravity, Peachey looking away.

'You see,' said Ashby, 'it's like this. My ex-wife came over to tell me we ought really to get back together and that she would willingly stay here, and I thought . . . Well, I really did, Bill, that she wasn't telling me the truth, but felt I had to give her a chance to prove herself, but then I discovered that she wasn't there when I rang up her hotel in London. She'd gone off to God knows where, but I soon found out that she was staying in one of our local inns under an assumed name. News like that kind of cuts a fellow to the quick, now doesn't it?'

'There's the rotor, sir. The sabotage . . .'

'Did she pull the wool over my eyes, Bill? Did she make a damned fool out of me?'

In one long draught, Peachey finished the ale. Sweat from the bottle made him dry his hands on the wiper rag he'd been using. Putting the empty back into the bucket, he discussed the motor, and they both decided that it was a fine-looking automobile and that the Lakes District would suit admirably at this time of year.

'Sir . . .'

'In a moment, Bill. Head's still in a rumble.'

Ashby ran things past himself again. Christina had left the Rose and Thorn, but had she gone down to Cornwall or had she followed Hilary to Kent? Ruth had been giving him the oddest looks at each chance encounter, but did she know something he desperately needed?

Tony had gone up to London to meet with some of the Board of Governors as a preliminary to the annual meeting on Founders' Day, but old George Crawley and Roger Banfield weren't convinced. More than this, they were saying nothing of it, and *that* just wasn't like them.

Hilary might now have met with her friends in MI6, for they wouldn't have delayed, but had they agreed to help? A sleeper . . . Who could it be? Certainly someone who could keep a close eye on him, but somebody at the school? Try as he did, and knowing them all as he did, he simply couldn't think it possible.

'Please, sir, it's about the rotor that I've come.'

'What did you say, Bill?' he asked, his glasses winking in the sun.

'The rotor, sir. Finchie and the rest of the Lower Fifth were having a whip-round for you when Spider Lawson said, "Hadn't we best hunt for it?" That's . . . that's why I've come.'

'You've found it, have you?'

The boys were down behind Wetherby Cottage. A thin column of smoke marked a forbidden fire among the osier beds where the sapling shoots stood tall and close, giving an adequate screen. Crouching in their midst, he picked up the rotor, it already having been cleaned and polished. 'Pitched lightly, sir,' said one of them—had it been Mark Abrahams?

'From the edge of the path behind you, I think, sir,' said Spider Lawson.

'Must have been,' said Thomas Barclay Finch.

'Easy to find?' he asked.

'Why . . . Yes, sir, I guess it was,' said Jackie Peterson, disheartened by the *easy*.

'Who found it?'

'I did, sir,' he said.

'Jackie, what made you chaps think it would be here?'

Quickly, darkly, they looked at one another.

Trust Peachey to go for the jugular, thought Tanner Biggs. 'Tics, sir. Headmaster's been seen coming down here a lot these past few days.'

'Why him? Headmaster's my friend.'

They clammed up, leaving betrayal by Tics all too evident. 'Jackie, I've got to know something,' he said.

'Yes, sir. I understand, sir. We've already discussed it and have taken a vote.'

'Did you tell your dad I'd be in London?'

'No, sir. My dad's been too busy to telephone me. He's . . .'

The boy glanced at the others. Tom Finch said, 'His dad's a ham in his spare time, sir. Like others round the country, he *listens* in to German spies!'

'To their cricket talk,' said Bill, 'but like the others, he's not spying *for* the Germans, sir. None of them would do a thing like that. It's only a hobby but they *all* report everything that they hear coming in from Germany.* They know it's from there because, if three ham sets at different locations here are used, they can, by each drawing a line to the set, pin down the source within a very small triangle. They then tell . . .'

'The Secret Service, sir. MI5,' said Jackie. 'When I telephoned him this morning, my dad said there's been steady traffic coming from our area. Well, as near as sticks to it. Bridgwater, sir, and in the small hours, but he thinks that something must have happened because the last message he heard was short and final, but Bremen's answer was . . . Well, a little bit longer.'

'Will he be down for Founders' Day?'

'Yes, sir. I expect so. At least, I . . . I certainly hope so.'

Swearing them all to secrecy, he said, 'I may need your help again.'

As he walked away, he didn't bother about the willows, but let the switches hit him or not. Peachey or Dan . . . There was now no longer any question of it.

'In the Great War, he saved Tics's life,' said Tanner Biggs.

'And Peachey knows Tics is bent and trying desperately to hide it from everyone, even that wife of his and especially the Board of Governors,' said Spider, who *did* know more about such things, an uncle of his having been reportedly that way.

'Headmaster's wife is certainly under a cloud,' said Bill, shaking his head at such things. 'Seems to me like she *wants* to tell Peachey something he needs to know, yet can't find the courage.'

'Or the grace,' said Tanner. 'Grace is sometimes far too high a price to pay when you've been wronged like she has.'

When they returned to the school, they could see that Peachey had just knocked at the door to Headmaster House and that Mrs. Pearce had come to open it, and they wished they could hear what was being said but knew they couldn't, that it wasn't for their ears anyway.

'Ruth, I have to know. The gun's not in my room where I locked it up after Hacker's visit.'

Was there panic in his eyes, she wondered, but said, 'I really

---

* This network of licenced amateur wireless operators soon became of inestimable value.

wouldn't know, would I, beyond what that bastard tried to make me do with it.'

'Yes, I know, and I'm sorry, but Tony might have thought it best to take the gun back and lock it up himself.'

Then why *did* Anthony wait? she wondered, wanting so much to ask it but saying, 'He might have done, but why didn't he simply ask you to return it?'

'Ruth, please.'

Stepping aside, she held the door open, and when he paused on the threshold to look steadily at her, she wanted so much to say, Do you know how I feel about myself, having been married for years to a man who could never love me as a husband should? But she held her tongue.

'Is Tony coming back from London tonight?' he asked.

Was he that desperate to know? she wondered, wanting now to tell him she had met his wife and that the woman had scared her to death, but instead, she somehow found the will to angrily say, 'How should I know what he does? Perhaps he's staying over. Telford would be the one to tell you, not me. Perhaps Anthony's found someone up in London. He's certainly made enough calls from that study of his.'

'I'll just take a look in there, then.'

'You do that,' she said, closing the door on the world out there, shutting the two of them in, she *wanting* to tell him everything about that wife of his, yet wanting to hold it back. 'Tea?' she asked. 'The keys to his desk and things are in that clay pot he brought back from Greece, the one with the paintings of centaurs and warriors, circa 560 BC, but a fake, if you ask me, and at one hell of a cost we could ill afford.'

Hating what he had to do, Ashby knew Tony couldn't be the sleeper. Even if he did find the gun, it could mean nothing more than that Tony had felt he had every right to take it back, and being too embarrassed and afraid of any further fuss, had decided it best not to say a thing of it, but London . . . Why had he really gone up to the city? To meet with Christina? Had she telephoned him, he to then ring her back several times? He did know where Karen was now staying, and removing the rotor from the MG would have been child's play to him.

There were the customary stacks of exercise books and half-set examination papers in folders marked 'confidential.' When he opened the centre drawer, the usual sorts of things appeared, but then, too, a photograph of himself, young and in Blues' uniform.

Slamming the drawer shut, he went through the rest of the desk in a hurry, completely ignoring the list of telephone numbers, thought Ruth, he now pausing to look in anguish through the leaded glass windows at the boys out there playing cricket. He wouldn't know that she had met his wife and had told her where their daughter was staying, nor could she even say, Beautiful though she is, that wife of yours is very frightening, Ash. As I retreated from her, I nearly fell down the stairs, she grabbing me by the wrist but holding the point of that knife against my stomach, my saving myself only by blurting, 'Is one murder not enough? Kill me and you will never get your daughter back.'

'Tea's on,' she said, startling him.

'How long have you known about that photograph?' he asked.

His distress at having found it was all too clear. 'Long enough. It wasn't always kept in his desk. Until quite recently it was upstairs in his bureau.'

'And the gun?'

'It's not here. I've . . . I've already looked.'

He went upstairs anyway and she heard him rooting round futilely. Then he was at the telephone in Anthony's study, taking chances with it. 'Hollingbourne,' she heard him saying. 'Yes, Operator. Clarington Hall. A Miss Hilary Bowker-Brown. Please hurry. It . . . it may be urgent.'

For all of five agonizing minutes he waited, Ruth then hearing him say, 'Hilary, it's Ashby. Did you manage to speak to those friends of yours?'

To the girl's answer, whatever that was, he gave no response but warned her that company might be on its way, describing Anthony for her and then that wife of his, but added, 'I don't honestly know about either's intentions, but Christina was staying near here and didn't bother to tell me.'

When he came back, they had their tea in silence, not in the house, but outside under the magnolias until at last Ash said, 'Ruth, the friends of the girl who's looking after my daughter won't help me, nor am I to go anywhere near her.'

'And Karen?'

'Is still finding everything difficult but liking it a little more. To get her out of herself, Hilary said they were going on a picnic. When I told her it was far too dangerous, she replied that she really had to do everything she possibly could to get Karen to believe her a friend.'

A picnic . . . 'What will you do if your wife decides to come back to you?'

'Bring Karen out of hiding. Stop the hurting. Try to make up for everything. It's . . . it's what Karen really wants. She's a wonderful little girl, Ruth, and I have to do everything I can.'

'Wetherby Cottage would suit,' she said curtly. Reaching for the teapot, she changed her mind, for her hand was shaking far too much.

'Has Hacker been back here?' he asked.

'Hacker?' Her cup rattled. 'No . . . No, of course not. Why do you ask?'

'Because, as I told you before, if he ever finds out where Karen is, he'll leak that information to the Germans. He won't even bother to ask my permission. He'll just do it.'

From the side of the hill, the patchwork fields were grey-green in summer haze, the hedgerows and oak woods alive with the distant calls of birds. Slowly Hilary let her gaze travel over the land but there was no sign of Brigadier Gordon or of anyone else, although Lionel Dandridge *had* said MI6 would be watching for the least sign of trouble.

Down over the hills and dales, the distant ragstone tower of the Church of Saint Nicholas tolled its carillon. All of her friends were either married or planning to be, all with no thoughts of the war to come, none either of doing anything out of the ordinary.

Near the church, a straggle of houses crept uphill, some of them solid Georgian places. Others were of that red brick common to Kent, but there were cottages, too, with either slate or thatched roofs and white, plastered walls, and of course there were the oast houses that tipped their canted conelike roofs above the crowns of the trees.

Karen had spread the tablecloth in the shade. The pony flicked its tail. The roan, a gelding and a fine hunter, tossed its head and snorted at something, Hilary saying, 'It's all right, Chancellor. It's only one of the farmers burning branches or refuse.' But there was no smoke in sight, just the softest of breezes bringing the warm scent of the land, of plowed earth, crops, clover and bees, she decided.

On her best behaviour, Karen had opened the picnic hamper and had begun to set things out, but would she bolt and run should this sleeper come at them, wondered Hilary, and would Dandridge and the men with him not be able to get here in time?

With the sounds of cutlery came the flash of an uncertain smile, Karen then setting the napkins precisely in place.

Indicating the pony, Hilary said in *Deutsch*, 'Meg hasn't been ridden in such a long time, but see how contented she now is. I think you've found a friend.'

'You will not give her to me. Herr Albert was just saying that to please me.'

'Then let's shake on it, shall we?'

Getting up, Karen came to her. 'Why should you do such a thing for me?'

'Because I, too, would like to be your friend, and because I think we both need this.'

'You don't really want this picnic. You're afraid my grandfather's men will come and take me away.'

'I do want the picnic, perhaps more than anything, Karen. Like yourself, I want so much to be at peace, but yes, I *am* afraid—why shouldn't I be? But Meg really is yours, for keeps, or for as long as you are here.'

The site was far too exposed, felt Hilary, Dandridge having insisted on it. Several roads crossed through the area, any one of which could be used and not all of which could be closely watched without a lot of men.

Again the roan tossed its head. 'Chancellor, what is it?' she asked, but could find no answer. Sliced ham with homemade piccalilli relish, devilled eggs and buttered bread were being set out by Karen, egg-salad sandwiches, too, that the girl had helped Dotty make. Radishes came next, and she would be remembering how she had gathered them under Albert's careful guidance, then washed, trimmed and diligently split them into fans under

Dotty's patient eye, but would she run to Dandridge when told to, or would she do only what the sleeper wanted?

'Hilary, the picnic, it is ready.'

Riding boots, breeches and jacket that had once meant so much to herself and had been carefully put away by Dotty had fitted almost perfectly.

'Please come,' said Karen. 'Please let us not worry so much we can't enjoy something so lovely.'

There was still no sign of smoke, yet Chancellor remained uneasy. A line of beeches followed the road at the foot of the hill. Next to it was a low stone wall, the brush thick with honey-suckle, hawthorn, wild plum and pin cherry all in blossom. Forcing herself to search each dip and hollow, Hilary found nothing untoward. Tidying Chancellor's forelock, she hugged him and whispered, 'What is it, a cigarette?'

The rattling, metallic call of a chaffinch was startling, the day just far too quiet and far too still. Unseen before this, a motorcar was parked on that road in a hollow and well to the south of them, the hedgerows thinning as the road crested the next gentle rise. Although she could only catch a glimpse of its roof, she felt it a small, dark green sedan, the colour all but melding with that of the leaves.

'Hilary . . .'

She had moved along to the saddle. 'I'm coming. Sorry. You must be starved.'

The butt of the gun was cold. The owner of the sedan was probably just out walking his dog. Shoving the revolver back down into the saddlebag, Hilary rewrapped it in its towel, and indicating the latter as she drew the two out, said, 'My pillow. Bet you didn't think to bring one. Eat that lot and you'll soon want a nap.'

There were strawberries, too, and Devonshire cream, and still more sandwiches. The revolver had been kept through all those years since the Great War but had been taken out and fired when her father had been away and Albert, bless him, had judged it prudent and known it would remind her of the brother she had hardly known. If someone was about to come for Karen, they would work their way round the hill and come at them from over its crest, flushing them quickly downhill towards that motorcar.

At a point perhaps a thousand yards from the hill, the spreading arms of a magnificent beech rose above the far edge of a pasture, and where its shade hid the sun, the cattle lolled. Using binoculars, Christina surveyed the hill, the location perfect. Karen was eating a sandwich, the Bowker-Brown girl saying something, but why hadn't Osier made contact with herself at the Chelton Hotel in Maidstone as Burghardt's message had stated he would? Had Osier others with him, others he hadn't wanted her to know of?

The Hilary girl sat facing the brow of the hill, which was steep and rising towards the sun that was now all but behind Karen. She had taken a folded towel and had placed it beside herself, but did she suspect something? Was this why she sat not facing the view but the crest of that hill?

'Hilary, do you like my father?'

'I hardly know him.'

'But would you *like* to know him?'

'Yes . . . Yes, of course.'

Karen had nodded at something the girl had said, thought Christina. Choosing another sandwich, Karen took a radish and then passed the bowl to the girl, who never for an instant let her gaze stray from that crest. Cleverly she was using Karen's eyes as a mirror to the downslope behind herself, and when Karen again looked towards the pony, the girl simply kept herself focused on the perceived threat.

Again they were talking.

'Hilary, my mother doesn't love my father and hasn't for a long, long time. He's not a Nazi; she is, and thinks the Führer is not only right but that he will conquer the world.'

'But does your father still love her, Karen?'

'I think he would *like* to forgive all her mistakes and that he would like us to be together, but Herr Beck, he is *Mutti*'s latest.'

It was infuriating, felt Christina, not to know what they were saying.

'Do you like Herr Beck?' asked Hilary.

'They have been together for some time.'

'That's not what I asked.'

'*Opa* says he is a good German, a true Nazi, and that in time he will prove himself, but that *Mutti* could do better if she wanted. She doesn't, and . . . and I think Grandpa is willing to accept this, myself . . .' She shrugged. 'He *is* very handsome, and he *does* have a nice sailboat he keeps in Bremen and a hunting lodge in the Jardelunder. It is near Flensburg, I think.'

And in Schleswig-Holstein on the Danish border, thought Hilary, not liking the thought.

'*Mutti* hates going there. She says she always gets her feet wet and her backside bitten by the flies, which are horrible, the clouds of them so thick.'

The Bowker-Brown girl laughed at something Karen had just said, but was it a sign that her vigilance had lessened? wondered Christina. Again she, herself, thought the place perfect for an attempt and wondered not only where Osier was but why he hadn't moved in on them. Had he been waiting for the girl to relax? Was he letting her get so used to the picnic, she would forget to watch the crest of that hill?

Perhaps a half hour went by, the girl still not having changed her position but now peering into Karen's teacup to read the leaves as Karen leaned forwards. A moment, then, when the brow of that hill wasn't being watched, the two of them avidly discussing things.

'The leaves tell me that someone tall and with lovely grey eyes and a super smile has come into your life,' said Hilary.

'That is my father,' said Karen. 'You are only teasing me. I want what the leaves say.'

'Of course. Do you see that one, and the way the others are pointing at it? That means he really does love you very much, Karen Ashby, and that there is, yes, a *third* person in your life.'

'My mother. Will *Opa*'s men come for me today, Hilary?'

'Not now, not here. At least I don't think they will. They wouldn't have waited this long, not them.'

'Then why is it I feel someone is watching us?'

Dropping the cup, the Bowker-Brown girl leapt to turn and look downslope towards the road and the beech tree. Hunting the pastures and the surrounding woods, she remained ready to grab Karen and make a run for that roan of hers.

Unseen from the picnic, the Hoffmann woman left the tree to pick her way among the cattle, Brigadier Charles Edward Gordon watching her with consuming interest, for she was an extremely attractive woman. Rough trousers, the hair tied out of the way, she had even chosen white tennis shoes and had darkened them with earth.

Having left her sedan in that hollow had, of course, been a mistake. 'But is she working alone, Lionel?' he asked.

'By rights, she should have walked up that hill by now and demanded her daughter,' said Dandridge.

'But looks as if expecting company,' said Gordon. 'Though we can't be entirely sure, it appears that MI5 haven't yet cottoned onto her, nor to the presence of those two on that hill.'

There had been no sign of Bunny Hacker, Sir John Masterson or anyone else of their incompetent ilk, thought Dandridge, and when the brigadier handed him the binoculars, he saw a honey buzzard fly up from the broken trunk of a dead elm near the Hoffmann woman. 'She's using that hedgerow as a screen, Brigadier. There's something in her right hand, but her fist is too tightly closed for me to see what it is.'

'Look for wasps.'

'What?'

'Please don't yelp at me, Dandridge. We wouldn't want her to get stung. Honey buzzards eat insects, especially wasps and bees.'

When she stopped suddenly, Dandridge saw her backing cautiously away and then saw the swarm.

'Can you deal with her, Lionel? Have others follow but not too close. Bunny's no fool and will soon be on to her. It really is a puzzle, his not being here. Too busy, perhaps, chasing elsewhere for the child.'

Taking the binoculars, Gordon trained them on the schoolteacher's former wife, she now heading back to the beech tree.

Up at the picnic, thought Gordon, Hilary and the child were still unaware of the woman's presence, or that of Dandridge and himself. Perhaps an hour went by. At seven years of age, playing cards was obviously a serious business. Hilary was sitting cross-legged, facing the child but now with her back to the crown of the hill, a mistake if ever there was one, the afternoon decidedly hot. Even the sound of birds had retreated, that of a distant cowbell muted, the roan tossing its head.

Shuffling cards had never been easy at that age, he told himself, and when some of them shot out onto the tablecloth, the child must have given an exasperated cry before flicking her gaze anxiously up.

'Karen, what is it?' asked Hilary.

Swiftly the child looked to the right and left, Hilary Bowker-Brown fighting lethargy as she scrambled up, knowing only too well, thought Gordon, that she couldn't move fast enough, for two men were now on the crest of that hill, set against the heat-hazed sky and sun, the one carrying a Schmeisser, the other a Luger.

Fanning out, they started downhill towards the child.

'Karen, run!' cried Hilary, snatching up the towel and trying to get the gun free of it. 'Karen, *please*! They'll hit you!'

Hilary fired at them, the sound startling the horses, the man to her right dropping his weapon to clutch at a left shoulder and angrily yell something to the other, as again and again she fired, sending another shot at the one she had hit and two at the other.

Retreating back over the hill at a staggered run, having snatched up the Schmeisser, they were soon gone, the sound of the Hoffmann woman's car now starting up, Gordon laying the binoculars on the sedan until it had disappeared from sight.

'Well, well, well,' he said. 'I gather it's time for us to leave, Dandridge. Were you told our Hilary would be bringing a weapon?'

'No, sir. She stupidly didn't forewarn.'

'But stupid she definitely is not. She even held back two cartridges in case needed.'

Having wrapped her arms about the child, she was obviously telling Karen Ashby that everything was all right.

'Karen, they've gone. Please don't cry. Your grandfather wouldn't have wanted them to kill me.'

But of course the child had known it would be otherwise had she run and not stood still.

On Tuesday, 7 June, Hacker swung the Rover in at the gates. Seen in the distance, the manor house was stately. Plane trees lined the drive, the house looking perhaps Italianate, but in red brick and with fluted limestone columns and upturned cornices: three storeys, twenty-six equally spaced and arched windows, and my God the money, but the longer he looked at the house, the more uneasy he felt. This was class, but what Christly business did Ashby's nanny have in coming to a place like this, and why, of course, had AST-X Bremen not simply taken the child? Few if any staff, acres of wood and field, and any number of access routes, including simply walking away across field and stream, and never mind at that picnic. No, it wasn't right. Having been called back by Sir John, who had received word of it from MI6, no doubt, he had had to leave off tracking the *Bonnie Jean* to hurry here.

The Bowker-Brown girl was in the rose garden, taking the shade and the peace and quiet of a latticed summerhouse beneath apple boughs in blossom and sitting in a chaise longue with pillow in her lap and looking like death warmed over and as wary as a crippled finch.

Sad and quick, those dark brown eyes watched him as he approached, she sizing up the retreats available—two routes of escape for her, latticed archways in between and nice, yes, it was very nice if one liked that sort of thing.

A gardener, an ancient retainer, could be seen through an arched doorway in the brick wall upon which the roses climbed and made their tangle. She could retreat at a pinch, could probably call up the reserves, that old codger with the spade no doubt having a bloody Lee-Enfield stashed nearby. Taking no chances, she had figured it all out ahead of time, a natural, and that, too, he'd best not forget.

Letting his gaze linger on her, he took in the sleeveless cotton frock, the tight, small chest and stiffened shoulders, the newly polished, well-used brogues. Down to her underwear, she had thought of everything. 'Miss Hilary Bowker-Brown?'

David Douglas Ashby had been right, thought Hilary. Although this one had the voice and stature of a detective, the deliberate undressing she had just received had told her all she needed to know. 'Yes, that's me, and yourself?'

He gave his name but also Special Branch, a lie, of course, but she would challenge him lightly. 'They said they would be sending someone this afternoon at three, Colonel. Why, then, have you not carried on as you should have?'

Good Christ Almighty, who the hell did she mean? he wondered, and she could see this, too, damn her. 'Better early than late, eh?' he said, managing a smile and indicating one of the cane chairs she had positioned so that wherever he sat, she would always be facing him with her back to that brick wall and its retainer.

But no matter. Pulling out a black notepad and flipping it open before himself, he sat directly opposite her, the armchair sighing as he filled it.

'About those two men on that hill, miss. Why not start right from the beginning by telling me what on earth made an innocent like yourself take along a weapon? No need to rush. I've told that cook of yours we won't be needing tea.'

She winced at this and frowned, and he knew then that she wasn't so much of a natural she could hide her feelings, that she had told the cook to definitely bring the tea so as to keep an eye on them.

'Look, you're not from the Yard, Colonel, so why not put that notepad away? You're from MI5's Watchers.'

Aware of him, was she, and encounters with Ruth Pearce or even with Ashby himself and the corpse of that one's barmaid? Letting his eyes narrow, Hacker noted the shudder she gave. 'Then let's just start at the beginning, shall we?'

Her head was shaken. 'Chief Constable Whitfield, in Maidstone, knows everything about what happened, Colonel. Should any harm come to me, or to any of my father's staff, or to Karen Ashby, I have thought it best to advise him. You see, I *can* identify the man I hit, and certainly that one must know that if he ever comes back, I most certainly won't miss but will kill him.'

Goddamn it, how on earth had Ashby found her? 'Was it the schoolmaster's sleeper?'

That had cut it all to the quick, thought Hilary. Never for a moment had she taken her eyes off him. 'That I simply wouldn't know, would I? But I can tell you he was the same that followed Karen and myself on the train down from London.'

'But not from Saint Erth?'

Again this little bird of Ashby's shook that head of hers, hands still under the pillow on her lap, eyes never having left himself for a second. 'Then perhaps you had best tell me about him, hadn't you?'

'Look, there's no need for your getting short with me, Colonel. I wouldn't have told the constabulary anything had my friends in MI6 come through, but they weren't there when I desperately needed them, and now they won't even reply to my repeated calls.'

Christ! 'Just what the devil have you to do with Military Intelligence abroad?'

And MI5's arch rivals, but to give him credit, Colonel Hacker *did* listen, thought Hilary, and when he asked what Brigadier Gordon was like, he knowing she would think he ought rightly to know himself, she said, 'Very sophisticated, very shrewd. A hawker who raises falcons and hunts with them.'

'Honest in his dealings with others, is he?'

Had he known it a sore point? 'He did filch sixty of my father's acres, but that was some years ago.'

'And yet you trusted him?'

'I had to. I had no other choice.'

'You did, and you do, Miss Bowker-Brown. Ashby ought to know on whom he had best depend, but for now, simply tell me about the one who followed and then let you wing him. Strip him to the buff if you can. Tell me if he was married, the lot, and be quick about it for I've got to ring London.'

And know well enough of Brigadier Gordon to have to tell someone else in MI5, thought Hilary. As she described the man, she noted Hacker's reactions, even to her mention of the paunch, the blue serge suit, waistcoat and gold hunter whose crystal fob had been about the size of a musket ball. 'Victorian or Edwardian,' she said of this last. 'The hunter I'm not too sure of because, for a man in such a hurry to catch the ferry, he didn't take it out all that much.'

Did she fuck as well as she sized things up? 'And he didn't catch it either.'

'No he didn't, did he?'

'Where'd you hit him?'

This she told him, adding, 'He was startled—taken aback, Colonel, in shock perhaps, and dropped his gun, which the other one then recovered.'

'What sort of weapon? Come, come, surely a thing like you ought to have some idea?'

'Ought I, Colonel? Why, please?'

'Just tell me. Don't piss about.'

'A machine pistol, a Schmeisser.'

'How the devil could a thing like you be certain of that?'

'Because I'm not a "thing," Colonel, and because I've seen several close-up before, in the Reich. It's what made me shoot at him first, that and his having followed us down from London.'

Two men, fast over the crown of that hill, she making a dive for the revolver she now had hidden under that pillow in her lap. 'And the other one?' he asked.

'Younger. The one with the Luger was in his late twenties or early thirties. Fair-haired, tall and thin. Look, everything happened so quickly. There really wasn't time to think.'

Instinct had led her, she knowing her guns as well. 'But they shouted to each other?'

'The one with the Schmeisser yelled something at the other.'

'In *Deutsch* or in English? Good God, girl, surely you can recall that much?'

And you can forget it, Colonel, until I know more of yourself, thought Hilary. 'I'm afraid I simply don't know. Words *were* spoken but . . .' She would give him a defenceless feminine shrug. 'But I have no knowledge of them. Sorry.'

'And the child? Has she?'

'Karen remembers only the sound of the shots.'

Ashby's nanny was just like her kind, holding things back in hopes of touching base with bloody Brigadier Charles Edward Gordon. 'I don't like it when people hold out on me, Miss Bowker-Brown. Especially when I'm to be responsible for them should anything untoward happen. We've already had one young woman stripped naked, cut up and her throat slit. Should we have another?'

Why the emphasis on the *young* and the *naked*, never mind the *cut up* and *stripped*? wondered Hilary. And had poor Daisy Belamy really been that young?

Drawing out the Webley, she let him see how it was not only pointed at him but with steadfast determination and a clear understanding of how to use it. 'If I knew anything more, Colonel, rest assured I would tell you. I simply want out of this mess. It's none of my doing yet seemingly all of my responsibility.'

Fuck MI6 and Brigadier Gordon, thought Hacker. He wouldn't smile, would simply tell the cunt how it was going to be. 'Your responsibility, oh my, yes. You will now draw Abwehr AST-X Bremen to yourself and that girl, Miss Bowker-Brown. You will let this sleeper they've awakened get so close to you, his breath will dampen that slender throat of yours until we nail him and all who are with him.'

Of wealth and connections, thought Hacker, she still couldn't hold back the tears that trickled down those fair and Cornish wind-burned cheeks. 'On Friday you will go up to London and have a chat with Sir John Masterson of MI5. Then and only then, you will buzz off back to that cottage of yours and leave it up to us to let Jerry know.'

Brigadier Gordon had *also* insisted she meet Masterson on Friday and had stated that she was to go along with MI5 . . . 'But . . . but there are the mine and the cliffs? It's . . . it's by far the most rugged and dangerous part of Cornwall's coast and definitely not always safe even at the best of times. Karen . . .'

'Had best do exactly as you tell her.'

As he got up to leave, Hacker tapped the gun. 'Where did a thing like you learn to shoot like that?'

How dare he treat her, or anyone, like this? 'Albert taught me. Albert Long. He was in the Boer War and badly wounded, so Father brought him home here to Clarington. He's a very dear friend.'

'He the one with the Lee-Enfield that's been pointing at me ever since you drew that thing?'

'Yes.'

'Make sure you bring the Webley, and when they come for you, use it. Us or them, right? So let's get on with it.'

The room in darkness now, Hilary looked down over the drive. Moonlight was everywhere. After Colonel Hacker had left, Karen's father had come by train, angry with himself and very upset by what had happened. Desperately wanting to do the right thing, he was adamant about leaving early in the morning with Karen. They would go to Dover and be in Oostende by noon or a little later. By nightfall, they'd be at the estate near Brühl, Karen back with her grandfather.

Leaving Karen's room, he came along the corridor to the one he was to occupy for the night, would see her by the window and know she hadn't wanted to turn on a light.

'Hacker won't let you and Karen leave for the Reich,' she said. 'I lied to him, Captain. I said I'd not heard what those two shouted to each other on that hill, but I did.'

'You were hoping your friends in MI6 would still come through.'

She wouldn't turn to face him, not yet, thought Hilary, but said, 'Something must have come up for them not to have intervened. Brigadier Gordon wasn't the person I expected to meet—not by a long chalk for he's too dishonest, if you want the truth. Major-General Sir Stewart Menzies is head of MI6 and has known me since I was a child. Ever since I came back from France he's had his eye on me and would, I know, have welcomed my request for help.'

Hence what she'd said at the cottage, thought Ashby. Now very close to her, she still hadn't turned to face him but would have to be asked. 'Could the brigadier have intercepted your request and used it for his own purposes?'

They had thought alike, felt Hilary, and hadn't avoided its implication, but . . . 'I simply don't know, Captain. MI6's leaving Karen and me to face that alone tells me something's very wrong.'

When his hand came to rest on her right shoulder, she stiffened. 'What did they shout at each other?' he asked.

Dear God, why couldn't he simply hold her? 'Do you want it in English or in badly spoken *Deutsch*, except for the last two words?'

Reaching out to her, Ashby drew her round and held her, and when he felt the tears, said, 'Everything's going to be all right. I'll take it from here on in, even if I have to sit in that cottage of yours and wait for them with Karen.'

And he would, too. 'The one yelled, "Christ, she's hit me. Oh damn and blast it!" and the other, "Go back!" I could have killed the first one. Don't you see, I almost did? I didn't think about it, I just fired as Albert had told me to. You don't bring the revolver up to eye level and take aim when pressed. You spread your feet, bend your knees, shoot from waist level and always bang two rounds at whomever you're trying to hit, but . . . but they didn't know I'd have a gun, didn't think it possible.'

Putting her arms about his neck, Hilary felt the nearness of him. It had been such a long, long time since she'd been held like this by anyone, and he did make her want to be held.

When he let go of her, she said, 'Thanks. I guess I just needed that. Now I must go. It's late.'

'And Karen's got her heart set on my taking care of you,' said Ashby. 'She . . .'

Hilary placed a forefinger against his lips. 'I know what she said, Captain. Something happened to the two of us on that hill. Instead of hated enemies, Karen and I became the best of friends. Comrades, I think, and it's for that reason among others that I shan't want to let her down.'

'Me neither, but the both of you.'

He had taken her hand in his, wasn't yet going to let her leave. Giving him a brief and introspective smile, she said, 'Too much moonlight, I think. I really mustn't, Captain. I can't become involved with anyone, not anymore.' And reaching out, touched his lips and ran her fingers lightly down over the line of his face until, leaning closer still, she quickly kissed him. 'There, now you can tell Karen that at least we did that.'

Hurriedly she gave him everything she could about those two on the hill, he to say he had no recollection of there having been anyone like that connected with the school, and when she had turned away again to look out the window, she said, 'I used to love it on clear nights like this when I'd come home for a short visit. Then everything was magic and I felt as if this old house really was mine.'

Though he hated to ask, Ashby knew he'd best. 'Could the sleeper be Brigadier Gordon?'

'That . . . that I wouldn't know but . . . but can't think it possible.'

'Yet are sickened by the thought?'

'Yes. Yes, of course.'

'Describe him for me.'

This she did and when done, said, 'Lie with me, please. Look, I . . . I don't want you making love to me, Captain. I simply want to be with someone I can trust and I do need to sleep if I'm ever to be awake enough to deal with whatever comes.'

Hilary knew she wanted it to happen. Suddenly nothing else mattered, not even that she'd known him only a very short time, but when he draped that arm of his about her waist, she settled down, was suddenly content and gave that sigh of knowing she'd been right about him all along. But what of Brigadier Charles Edward Gordon and this sleeper, she wondered, what of AST-X Bremen and his former wife?

Joachim Burghardt fiddled with the bone-handled pocketknife that had served him all his life. It was now Wednesday, 8 June, and having listened to what had happened in Kent, he had then had to listen to Christina von Hoffmann's blistering anger and charges of incompetence being matched word for word by the savage scorn of that father of hers. Clearly Abwehr AST-X Bremen had been caught by surprise with this kidnap attempt and he had best proceed with caution.

'General, I greatly fear the British MI5 *and* 6 are spinning a web for us with that granddaughter of yours.'

'By now the whole thing should have been over, Karen here with me and you . . . you . . .'

'General, your daughter has stated very clearly that the Bowker-Brown girl was all too prepared for what was to happen. Previously, as your daughter wisely advised this office, that girl met with Brigadier Charles Edward Gordon of MI6, not MI5 whom we already know are attempting to use your granddaughter to trap Osier. Brigadier Gordon is section head for Belgium and northeastern France and no one's fool.'

'Then what, precisely, has he in mind?'

'*Ach*, that I do not yet know, but be advised this office has a particular interest in him.'

Offering cigarettes that were coldly declined, he watched as the daughter took out one of her own and, lighting it, let the scathing anger of her gaze rake over him. 'What have you really to offer us now that you have failed?' she asked.

What was yet uncertain, felt Burghardt, had best be kept to himself, but had MI6 made that attempt for purposes of their own, and if so, why had that girl been armed? Gordon wouldn't have told her to shoot at them, so if he *had* set it up, then he, too, must have been taken aback by the result.

'*Verdammt*, why can't you answer me?' said Christina.

'Fräulein, please. It will do none of us any good, that daughter of yours especially, if we continue to remain at each other's throats.'

Snorting at this, she crossed her legs, brushed a tidying hand over a thigh and coldly said, 'Then what has happened to Osier? Did he get away or was he even there?'

Liebe Zeit, her sarcasm had allowed her to put a finger on it. Quickly Burghardt again ran things past himself. There had been no sign of anyone else other than those two who had come over the hill at the picnickers but obviously, if he had set it up, Gordon would have been watching, or would have delegated someone, and of course they would have seen this general's daughter and would have followed her afterwards. But letting her believe it *had* been Osier could do no harm and might prove useful, especially if it were to bring her closer to the brigadier.

'Tell me something, Fräulein, have you been taught how to use a pistol?'

'Of course, but you will already be aware of this, so why, please, do you ask?'

'*Ach*, forgive an old sea captain. I just wanted to hear it from yourself.' And yes, anger did make the general's daughter even more exquisite. Having tasted success in Britain by using and confronting Ruth Pearce, then countering Colonel Hacker and thereby getting the better of him, and by watching Brigadier Gordon meet with that girl, she had found espionage all to her liking, though now failure had exposed her to the ridicule of a domineering father who would privately blame her for not having walked up that hill and taken her daughter as she rightly could have.

But compliments would only lessen the need to prove herself. 'Fräulein, after you succeeded in getting away yourself, what, please, did you do?'

'I . . . Why, I caught the ferry at Dover and went to see Father, then we came here.'

'Determined to tear a strip off my back, but tell me something, did you inadvertently lead MI6 to my very door and to Herr Beck, whom I had intended to use to take your daughter off when Osier had freed her?'

'Why you . . . How dare you?'

'Fräulein, I dare because I must. Far too many others depend on me. General, you and this daughter of yours have already made far too many serious errors in what is a very dangerous game.'

'Has this Osier crossed over himself and returned to the Reich?' demanded Hoffmann.

'General, although Agent 07392 is very close to this office, surely you are aware that I could not possibly reveal his whereabouts or identity.'

'You're incompetent and will be relieved of your duties.'

'By whose order? That of the admiral? Far too much is at stake. MI5, having been slow to awaken to the threat, will soon be turning their full attention to smashing our networks in the British Isles; many, but fortunately not all, in MI6 here on the Continent are already intent, but neither you nor this daughter of yours seem to have realized those two organizations compete with each other, each privately thinking the other incompetent and undeserving of additional funding they themselves are desperately in need of. Fortunately Osier, though highly positioned, has not yet been identified and is still useful to us. A setback, yes, but now there is much more to be gained because of MI6's interest, and as a result, the taking of your granddaughter has just been given a Priority One.'

Irritably Christina stubbed out her cigarette. 'And what am I to do, Kapitän?'

How good of her. 'Apart from calming yourself, for that, I am sure you know, will be necessary, you are to return as quickly and unobtrusively as possible. Ingratiate yourself with that former husband of yours. No doubt you will be followed by agents of MI6 and those of MI5, and no doubt, if needed, we will pick them off your back.'

'And the fly in this web of yours?' she asked, *Vati* having given her a nod.

'Will be taken by the spider they have yet to know and never will.'

'Then why won't Osier meet with me? It's not right, this . . . this secrecy of his. We could have succeeded had he made himself known to me.'

Gut, she was now coming back to believing it *had* been Osier, but was still feeling that deep sense of loss and betrayal, still smarting from the knowledge that she could well have led MI6 to this very door. 'Believe me, please, Fräulein, when the right time comes, Osier, in whom I have nothing but the greatest trust, will make contact. Remember, though, that you are dealing with someone who, unknown to the British, has lain dormant for years. He could, you must understand, lose everything, for the British do hang spies, so mistakes just can't be made, can they? Caution is the nature of this business; vigilance its very watchword. Also, please, Herr Beck will definitely be involved, so keep that in mind and if you should see or meet him there, guard his presence as you would that of Osier.'

Through the open windows of the flat, a breeze stirred the curtains, bringing the sounds of Bremen's commerce. It was midafternoon and warm. Christina spread her fingers, and rising up on her knees a little, pressed her hands flatly down on Werner's stomach. He would see how her eyes quickened at some wicked thought, but quite suddenly the pressure from her hands would cease. Idly she would tease his pubic hairs and settle back on her haunches, would drive him deeply into her now. 'So, I don't know when we shall see each other again,' she said.

'You've missed me.'

Her nipples brushed against his chest as she kissed him, she hungrily, he less so, and when he turned aside, she heard him ask, 'How was it, then, you and Ashby?'

And jealous, so good, yes good, thought Christina, leaning back to playfully touch the tip of his nose. 'Pleasant when one is the doer, *mein Liebling. Ach*, I had to seduce him, and that took time, I must admit, but when he came, he revealed how much he had missed me, but . . . but does the news upset you?'

'Why should it?' he said, his expression grim.

'Werner, *mein Schatz*, it meant nothing! It was necessary and . . . and I did it because I had to.'

My treasure.

'Admit that you enjoyed having him in you. A triumph.'

He was really angry about it. Even his *Schwanz* had gone limp and would have to be reawakened, but when she kissed him, he bit her on the lips and she slapped his face hard.

Stunned, he lay pinned beneath her straddling knees. Gingerly exploring her lips for blood, she sucked in a breath, her breasts rising, he looking at them now, she at last clasping herself by the buttocks.

'You bitch,' he said, and meant it too. 'You *were* followed, you unthinking *Schlampe*. Right to the house of that father of yours and then to headquarters here and also, I suspect, to this flat. Two men, Christina, both all the way from Dover.'

'Who were they?'

He would infuriate her more because she needed that, would shrug and say, 'I don't know. Burghardt does.'

'That bastard! Why didn't he say so and have done with it?'

Another shrug would help. 'I wasn't told of the meeting today with you and your father, nor anything of the attempt to take Karen from that girl.'

'But has Osier made contact since?'

Anger tightened her skin, flushing the nipples and flattening her middle.

'*Well?*' she demanded.

He could take her now and get the better of her, or he could tell her how it really was. 'Not by wireless, not that I know of. The Kapitän's keeping things far too close. I can't do much. *Ach*, I saw to directing those two vessels to Britain that he let you know of and have a call on whatever I need to get Karen when you and Osier have finally freed her. The *Thule Sólarsteinn* is ready to sail, but I must wait until he gives me the order.'

They were dependent on Burghardt. 'Could you find out who Osier is and where I can get in touch with him?'

She had lost all interest in having sex. Running his eyes over her did no good, Christina simply gazing off towards the windows, until he said what she wanted, 'The Kapitän will have that in the safe.'

'Then we must get it.'

And fiercely said at that. '*Liebling*, for me to do what you ask, I must break all the rules and am in enough trouble as it is.'

'A coward I do not need.'

Beck grabbed her as she bounced off the bed, but she pulled her arm free and, backhanding him, turned away to stand calming herself, spoiled, rich, still quivering with rage yet beautiful and, he asked himself, dangerous?

When she reached for her step-ins, he said, 'All right, you win. Now come back to bed and let us settle this business that husband of yours has placed between us.'

Still she refused to face him, her shoulders squared, her back straight, the cheeks of her ass taut.

'Karen saved the life of that girl, Werner. She *didn't* run when they came over the top of that hill and that . . . that meant that they couldn't shoot the bitch and now . . . now I *don't* even know if one of those two really *was* Osier.'

'*Ach*, come and forget it for a while. The girl will soon be taken care of and I'll bring Karen back to you, I promise.'

Mechanically her hands went out to him and she took his cock and began to put a little life into it, was still far too distracted.

'Karen is beginning to like the girl, Werner. This could be a problem even Burghardt hasn't realized.'

Beck sat up to clasp her breasts. They kissed but she drew away and said, 'I *want* Karen, Werner. *Mein Gott*, that attempt was such a futile effort. Osier, if it really was him, had *everything* yet failed.'

Tenderly kissing her lips, she resisting still, he brushed his own across each eyelid. 'But was it really Osier, Christina?'

'I . . . I think one of them must have been. Why else would the girl have fired at them? I thought they would keep coming at her, but Karen . . . Karen *ruined* the attempt and when they fled, Karen held her tightly, Werner. Tightly.'

Running his hands over her hips, Beck kissed each breast and then her throat. 'Could there have been anyone else watching that hill?'

She pulled away to look searchingly at him. 'I didn't see anyone. I would have known.'

Maybe yes, and maybe no, thought Beck, but he had best not remind her that she'd been followed on return. When he asked about the Bowker-Brown girl, whatever interest Christina might have had in their having sex vanished.

'It's not just that she's pretty, Werner. She's very French-looking, very alluring when seen sitting in the dark at a table beside a fishpond and facing Brigadier Charles Edward Gordon who was secretly, I am sure, captivated by her, though he would have been with any beautiful woman.'

Herself? wondered Beck, letting his eyes drift over her naked-
ness but thinking, A failed attempt and then herself being *followed* back to the Reich. Had Gordon set the whole thing up?
'He's a falconer, *mein Schatz*,' said Beck. 'His first love is the mer-
lin. Though he prefers to hunt the Yorkshire moors, he also has
an estate in Kent near that girl's Clarington Hall. Be good to him.
Get as close as possible. *Ach*, I think that is what the Kapitän must
now want you to do.'

'And the Bridgwater wireless? Am I to use that butcher, Ernst
Reiss, at Davidson's Pork, Beef and Poultry in spite of Herr Reiss's
objections?'

She must have gone there and would have broken their secu-
rity by so doing, yet the Kapitän hadn't said a thing of it, thought
Beck, which could only mean he had best go carefully. '*Liebling*,
I'll try to find out.'

'You had better.'

Later, although AST-X Bremen never slept, the house on the
Böttcherstrasse was all but deserted. While Christina watched the
street below, Beck knelt in the darkness, the safe set into the wall
below the shelves on which the Kapitän kept the AST-X Bremen
logbooks.

Never one to leave anything to chance when in a hurry over
important matters, Burghardt had written the combination on a
slip he always inserted into the first of the logbooks but *Scheisse*,
the dial was already set at the last number, a zero, the door opening so easily he had to wonder if the Kapitän hadn't left it that
way on purpose.

There were rolls of microfilm, code books, forged passports
and travel documents, four bundles of used English one- and five-
pound notes, assorted bundles of other currencies and a Danish
M1910/21 pistol with a box of 9mm cartridges. A heavy gun, with
six-, eight- and ten-round magazines.

The pistol had been placed on top of the banknotes and Beck
knew then that not only had Burghardt left the safe all but open
for him, but that this subordinate of his must now say absolutely
nothing of his having done so to Christina von Hoffmann.

Dossiers, passed back to her, gave details of Colonel Buntington Hacker, an earlier photo showing him in uniform with cap,

Sam Browne belt and swagger stick, but even then, thought Christina, he had worn a moustache, just as had his Mr. Harris Blackburn of the Rose and Thorn in East Quantoxhead.

A circled news item concerned the young Chinese wife of a gunrunner. Not only had her wrists been bound behind her back and her ankles, too, she had been stripped, tortured, violated and then had her throat cut.

The dossier on Brigadier Gordon yielded only loose snapshots recently taken of two men, and when Christina saw them, she sucked in a breath and bit the knuckles of her right hand. 'That one,' she said, not liking it at all, 'tried to take Karen and failed when the girl shot him.'

'And the other?' asked Werner. '*Bitte, mein Liebling*, you had best tell me.'

'The younger one was with him on that hill.'

Others having followed her here, Gordon having got what he wanted, thought Beck. 'Keep the photos. Memorize their faces, then destroy them. The Kapitän has several duplicates and won't have counted them.'

But would he have? wondered Christina, sickened by the thought of never knowing *exactly* what was going on, but hadn't the Kapitän said Osier was highly positioned, that he had nothing but the greatest trust in him, and that he was very close to this office, to AST-X Bremen, Karen's escape having now been assigned a Priority One? And hadn't that file on Gordon, for obvious reasons of security, been deliberately emptied of all but those photos? It would be just like Burghardt to have done a thing like that! 'Now the file on Osier, Werner. Please hand it to me.'

There was nothing but a single sheet of paper and on it nothing but the number *07392*.

'Would he have the identity elsewhere?' she asked.

'Not likely.'

Uneasy about what they had just discovered, Christina retreated to the windows to watch the street and try to think what best to do, and when Werner, having closed the safe, came to stand behind her, she leaned back against him and he put his arms about her.

Later, they walked along the quays in silence. There were ships in the harbour, lights from them, yet still she had no answers, only questions. But the order of the things in that safe had to have meaning. 'Seeing as that file on Osier must have been under his dossier, Werner, is Brigadier Gordon Burghardt's 07392?'

It was now or never, thought Beck, and he had to tell her what the Kapitän must have wanted him to say. 'I think so, but all I really know is that Canaris thinks him very special.'

7

It was raining when Hilary got up to London on Friday, 10 June, and where the water guttered over the faded gilding at Spurgeon's, it made her think of fortunes lost. Soft on the pungent air, her uncertain 'I'm looking for Sir John Masterson' fled to the far end of the shop where a young man on a stepladder was taking stock. 'Sir John?' she said. 'He's expecting me. I rang him and we *did* agree that today, at just before noon, would suit.'

'Give me half a mo', miss. I won't be a tick.'

Climbing down from the ladder, he disappeared through a door at the back, Hilary turning to look out at the street. People hurried by, motorcars honked, lorries made deliveries, it all seemed so day-to-day. She had tried her best not to be followed, had hoped the man she had wounded was all right and that the younger one was not out there on the street. Colonel Hacker had offered absolutely no protection, nor indeed anything else, even to where he would be or how she might get in touch, but with her father's visit, Karen and she had come a lot closer. When she had awakened in the morning to find herself still beside Ashby, he had asked how she had slept and she had seen the warmth, the concern, the interest in those smashing grey eyes of his and had said, 'Too well, I think,' and known their relationship had also changed.

'Miss?' called out the stock boy. 'He says you're to meet him upstairs in the tasting room.'

Letting herself in, Hilary pulled off her mackintosh and thought to drape it over one of the stools, then thought better of this and hung it from a nail. She had split a seam in her left shoe, fashion being something the months without high heels in Cornwall had made painful, and she *would* get dressed up! Carefully removing the shoes, muttering to herself as she drained each, she said, 'These people will be useless to us, worse still a danger.'

Masterson saw her open the leather handbag and take out, not a compact to touch up the lipstick and rouge, but the Webley service revolver she had brought along for company. Deliberately the girl checked the safety, then as an added precaution, the empty chamber she had let the hammer rest on. She had a good figure, the well-tailored linen suit having a nutmeg shade to complement the colour of her eyes and hair, and when she straightened a stocking, he saw that she had nice legs, but more than this, that she was intuitively French in every gesture.

There were no bracelets, only the watch she continually glanced at with growing irritation, and when she went over to the windows at the far end of the room, she scanned the street below with a care that impressed, for she stood all but to one side and not boldly out.

Hurrying along the corridor and in the door, he said, 'Don't pay the shop much mind, Miss Bowker-Brown. It's merely a front. If war comes, which I daresay it will, Göring's Luftwaffe will no doubt put paid to it and the legacy my dear pater left me.'

'What's in the van?'

'Tea, spice, and two wireless sets and other listening gear. When I'm not here, I'm in the field trying to nail clandestine transmitters, so . . .'

Glad we've got that out of the way, are we? he wondered, taking in the big brown eyes that were still giving him the once-over.

'You're not exactly what I expected,' she said.

'But you look as though you could do with a good feed. Come along then. My treat. It's . . .why, I guess it's on the house. Why, yes, it is.'

Struggling to get into her shoes, and nearly falling off balance, she said, 'This one leaks.'

'Know just the place,' he said cheerily. 'We'll stop by on the way.'

And they did. A positively super job was done by a little man in Kingly Street who even gave the seams several wipes with waterproofing compound. 'A shameful rain, miss,' said the man.

'I shouldn't want to catch a cold if I were you. Spoils the fun, now doesn't it, a runny nose?'

'He's *not* my lover.'

'Now I didn't say that he was, did I?' he asked.

Masterson held the door for her and beamed at the compliment. 'Our Thomas is given to overstatement, Miss Bowker-Brown. Not to mind, eh? Bunny been in lately to have those brogues of his reshod?' he asked the shoemaker.

They were out the door before an answer could be given. Crossing over, ducking between two lorries and in under the awnings, Sir John paused to give the street his perusal.

Satisfied, he again held a door open for her, and when they had found a table and had settled in, he said, 'They do a nice set of chops here,' she demurely swinging her knees away from his and placing her hands before her, he continuing with, 'The fish and chips are rather good, but so, too, is the Welsh rarebit. They've nothing like Cornish pasties, though, or likky pie, but will, if you wish it, offer a rather pleasant shenagrum.'

Beer, nutmeg, brown sugar, lemon and rum. 'The leek pie is a favourite, Sir John, but let's just get this meeting over.'

'Of course, but glad to have you aboard. Bunny sends his compliments and praises, and let me tell you those are very rare indeed. I gather you shoot extremely well and that your reaction time suggests you let instinct govern when pressed.'

Just *what* were they expecting, that she *work* with Colonel Hacker and back him up? 'I did wound one of them. Have you checked the hospitals and doctors?'

Looking up at a waiter, Masterson ordered two pints of half-and-half. 'And give the lady the lobster tails, Arthur, the Salisbury steak, medium rare, one baked potato and a side order of coleslaw. I'll have the usual. That suit?' he asked her.

Pleased that he had ordered but wondering why he had avoided answering, Hilary nodded, but he didn't give her a chance to ask. Hunching forwards, elbows on the table, he said, 'When will you be going down to Cornwall?'

'On . . . on Sunday, I guess.'

'Make it tomorrow early. Bunny will look after you, not to worry. I've given him a free hand with this, Miss Bowker-Brown.

Just go about whatever you do down there. Give the girl her lessons, go for walks—be seen in Saint Ives and out on that moor. Rest assured we will let the opposition know when and only when we judge it appropriate.'

The Abwehr. 'Won't this sleeper suspect a trap?'

And ever cautious. 'It all depends, now doesn't it?'

'I . . . I'm afraid I don't understand?'

Reaching for his pint, indicating that she should also, he said, 'Exactly how certain are you that those two you met on that hill were really from the Abwehr?'

'I . . . I wouldn't be here if I . . .'

'If what?'

'If I didn't believe they would try again. I saw them, Sir John. I *hit* one of them and I gave that Colonel Hacker of yours a very detailed description of him. Did you not even bother to check the hospitals and doctors?'

'My dear, there are simply far too many, and others who are not even registered, but please, these two chaps of yours shouted to each other.'

'Yes, but . . . but I didn't hear what they said.'

With a finality she would fail to appreciate, Masterson drained his glass and ordered another. Bunny had said the little vixen was hiding something and by God, she still was. 'Look, Miss Bowker-Brown, your friends in MI6 have left you cold, so why not cooperate and let us get on with the job?'

Taking a sip to give herself a chance to think, Hilary knew he would have fed queries up through the chain of command and had a look at Brigadier Gordon in particular. 'All right, I had best tell you, hadn't I? The one I hit didn't know German very well, if at all. The fair-haired younger one might have, but everything happened so quickly, I can't say he said anything more than, "Go back," and that was given in perfect *Deutsch*.'

'And the one you hit was the one who had followed you and the girl on the train?'

A nod was all she would give, thought Hilary, but hadn't Karen's father *asked* if the sleeper could be Brigadier Gordon?

'It's odd that MI6 should have buggered off and left you like that,' said Masterson. 'Could they have run that little show, not to see if you were on your toes, but to snatch the child for later use in a trade-off, the mother giving them whatever info they wanted in exchange for her daughter?'

'I beg your pardon?'

Had the thought not occurred to her, or had she suddenly remembered something and decided to keep mum about it? 'Let me put it this way. Could they have staged that attempt for purposes of their own?'

Brigadier Gordon *had* insisted she take Karen on a picnic, thought Hilary, and . . . Oh damn, she *had* forgotten to tell that to her father. 'I could have killed one of them, Sir John. As it is, heaven only knows how badly he was hit.'

Their lunches came, Masterson marshalling his bangers and mash and asking, 'But did Brigadier Gordon know you would be armed?'

Oh dear . . . 'I . . . I kept that to myself.'

He reached for his pint. 'Then they could have set it up and have suffered accordingly.'

'But . . . but they would surely have forewarned me,' insisted Hilary. 'They . . . they wouldn't have kept that from me, lest I take the matter to Major-General Sir Stewart Menzies.'

Dear God, was she that well connected? 'Then I'd best tell you, Ashby's wife has come over again. Bunny thinks she might have been here earlier. Have a look at this and tell me if you've seen her.'

Having hardly had a chance to eat, Hilary set her knife and fork aside. The woman was incredibly beautiful, the felt cloche and woollen suit fitting perfectly, and yes, earlier when trying to warn her by phone, Ash *had* described her perfectly. 'No . . . No, I've not seen her.'

When she handed the photograph back, Masterson resisted the impulse to smile but said, 'I do believe I've spoiled your lunch. Don't tell me you and the schoolteacher are having it on.'

'We're not. It's . . . it's just that, having seen that photo, I can't understand why Karen's mother should hate her father the way she must. Surely the couple could have come to some agreement, if for no other reason than Karen's well-being?'

'You're not in love with him, are you?'

'Is that different from "having it on"?'

Oh my, oh my. 'We just can't have him interfering, that's all. Let us take care of this sleeper and all he'll bring us, and then you and the captain can do as you please. I take it you and the child are getting along all right?'

Again Hilary set her knife and fork down. 'Much better, yes, but would that really matter?'

Letting a breath escape, he told her that she might need the child to come to her when called, and that their getting along could well make all the difference. 'But never forget, please, that Ashby was quite attached to that barmaid of his and will be worrying about yourself. We simply can't have him anywhere near that cottage of yours, Miss Bowker-Brown. Now eat up. That steak of yours is getting cold.'

She began to tell him of the mine, the cottage and the terrain, he ordering tea for her and another pint for himself and asking details of her, she soon gaining more and more confidence in him.

He was most curious about the boat shed and when told, said, 'It sounds as if it was once used by smugglers.'

'That whole coastline was and is, and right round it,' she said and grinned, only to think of the possible dangers and, glancing at her watch, to say abstractedly, 'I must try to get a look at the plans of the mine while I'm here.'

'You do that,' he replied, mopping his plate with a last bit of bread. 'Let Bunny know if there's any bother. Leave a note for him in that outhouse of yours. He'll not come to you and knock on the door. In fact you won't likely see him until the end.'

Had they already consulted the plans? she wondered, and when he asked how well she knew Brigadier Gordon, she bleated, 'Why do you ask?'

'Because, my dear, he's tricky. Has to be, now doesn't he?'

Dropping her gaze to her plate, seeing the brief sampling here and there, she said, 'Like every other ordinary citizen, I really know very little about MI6 and certainly didn't know that he was involved. Indeed, if you want the truth, I would never have thought it possible.'

'But it is odd Gordon should have dealt with you himself. You see, it puts things on another level and makes him vulnerable, and that is something he would never do unless absolutely necessary. Dandridge there, I gather, at the club?'

Shoving her plate aside, she nodded and reached for her tea.

'Well, not to matter,' said Masterson. 'It'll all come out in the wash. Lionel's no fool, but then Gordon wouldn't use him if he was. Oh my, no, but you do see, I trust, that even with Dandridge, your brigadier might not tell him everything.'

'Those two on the hill . . .' she said, aghast at the thought that Gordon might well have had something to do with it.

But had Ashby suggested the same? wondered Masterson. 'Now tell me what you know of the headmaster at that school of the captain's.'

Putting far too much sugar into her teacup, Hilary tried to give herself time to think, for he wouldn't have asked unless there had been a good reason. 'I'm afraid I've never met him, Sir John, nor has Karen's father told me anything.'

So be it. 'Pearce was once a prisoner of war. There's evidence, never proven I must add, that he might have been an informant. There's never been an inquiry, and it may simply have been a rumour.'

'Have you told Ash?'

Ah, now at last a very definite interest in the schoolmaster. 'Certainly not, nor will you. Is that understood?'

'Betray myself, betray my friends, betray my lover, if that's what he might one day become, Sir John?'

How sharp of her. 'Just leave it until we get what we have to. Then you can have him *and* the daughter, if you wish, and I will give you both my blessing.'

Out on the street, they parted with a handshake, he watching as she walked away, a pleasant enough little piece. Yes, she would do nicely, and when it was all over he would draft her into MI5 if for no other reason than to keep her from MI6.

The man was there when Hilary turned onto Old Compton Street and went along it to catch an omnibus at Charing Cross Road. He was there when she walked through the now-empty Covent Garden whose predawn markets would have rung with shouts and the trundle of barrows. And he was there when she got to the Public Records Office in Chancery Lane, and there, when empty-handed, she had returned to the door to search the street for him.

About her age, he was tall, good-looking, with straight flaxen hair, no hat, a newish grey mack, grey flannels, brown Oxfords, both hands in the pockets of his coat, the collar up.

Remembering the picnic, the warmth of the day, the smell of clover and Chancellor's nervousness, she recalled the Luger in his hand, the panic of that moment, and again felt quite ill, for if he could walk round London like this, how safe would Karen and she be in Cornwall?

When a taxi came along to let someone off, she was out the door like a shot and into the back. 'The Geological Museum, Exhibition Road, South Kensington and hurry, please! I don't want to miss my train.'

'Right you are, luv.' By the look, she had money, and who was he to question a fare like that? 'You're not being followed, are you?'

'Yes, as a matter of fact I am.'

'The bloke in the mack?'

'Yes! He's my ex. Could you . . .'

She flashed those big brown eyes in the mirror, and when, finally, they had gone along the Cromwell Road and had turned that last corner, added, 'Thanks, I knew you could do it.'

First in the library and reading room, then three clerks later, she was standing in the cellars between towering shelves of file boxes while a little man in a blue smock teetered on a stepladder. 'It only takes a bit of looking, miss,' he said. 'I know it's here. Oh dear, oh dear, it's been red-flagged. The entry's missing.'

Government regulations being what they were, it took time getting the use of a telephone but at last the line was through. 'Sir John, it's me, Hilary. Someone's taken the only set of drawings to the underground workings of my mine.'

'When?'

'At noon today while . . . while we were at lunch.'

'The name given? Damn it, girl, to get that file they must have had to sign for it.'

'Mine, so it has to have been a woman and she must know of me. There's . . . there's something else. After I left you, I was followed but lost him. It was the younger of the two from the hill, the German, I think, though he could have been as British as myself.'

And there on orders from Brigadier Charles Edward Gordon?

wondered Masterson, cursing the thought since MI6 hadn't wasted a moment. 'Don't for God's sake tell Ashby. Simply let Bunny know.'

'But without the plans, and with them knowing the layout, surely you don't expect me to go back there with Karen?'

'I do, my dear, and you must.' It could be that MI6 had the plans, thought Masterson, and it could be that Abwehr AST-X Bremen had them.

All along the Landwehrkanal in Berlin, which here followed the Turpitzufer, the leaves of the lindens drooped and the sooty smoke from the barges hung in the damp air. It was Saturday, 11 June, and as Burghardt got out of the Mercedes that had collected them at the aerodrome, Werner Beck came round to stand beside him, and they both looked up at the row of four-storeyed, once-fashionable houses that had held the Naval High Command and the headquarters of the Abwehr for far too long.

Dwarfed by the window behind which he stood, Canaris didn't wave, and Burghardt wondered if the general had been at him again and if the admiral had had second thoughts.

'So, my young friend,' he said to Beck, 'here we are, but please do not be too ambitious. Leave most of the talking to me.'

'Does this mean I'm to be reinstated?'

'Not at all. It means that for reasons of his own, the admiral requested that I should bring you along to carry my briefcase.'

They went up the steps into naval headquarters, and from there, once past the sentries and the Leutnant on duty, the elevator being out of order, found their way through the warren of renovated rooms, narrow corridors and staircases. The buildings were totally unsuitable, yet both Canaris and the Oberkommando der Kriegsmarine had stubbornly refused to move.

An outer office and two secretaries barred their way but the admiral, somewhat shy and self-effacing, came to welcome them.

'Joachim, it's good of you to come on such short notice. Herr Beck . . . Gentlemen, my humble abode.'

The office on the third floor was always, thought Burghardt, a shock to those who didn't know Canaris. Of modest size, a former maid's room perhaps, it held an iron cot, a few filing cabinets, a handful of plain chairs, an old leather couch and that same unas-suming desk the admiral had had for years. Beyond a large map of the world, there were portrait photographs of former Abwehr chiefs and even one of the Spanish dictator, Francisco Franco, but only an etching of Canaris as a young man. This last hung next to that of a Japanese demon, while on the other side of the etching were two photos of the admiral's wire-haired dachshunds, Seppel and Sabine.

For some reason, the dogs weren't present, though the carpet indicated they most certainly had been, and recently.

'You're not impressed, Herr Beck,' said Canaris quietly.

Caught off guard, Beck stood to attention. 'It's not my busi-ness to form judgements of my superiors, Admiral.'

'Good. Then let this be a lesson. The simpler, the better. Now, please, gentlemen, there is time for coffee and a small chat. What have you brought for me?'

That was nice, thought Burghardt. The admiral had put the onus on them, while saving the rest for later.

Beck hung their coats on the stand. One of the secretaries had the coffee on a tray and he stepped into the outer office to offer Frau Schonenburg a little help. Not so old that she couldn't appre-ciate a good-looking young man, she smiled but shook her head. 'It is all right, Herr Beck. He is just a little preoccupied today and has missed his usual rest, but you mustn't mind.'

Unfolding the ordnance map of Cornwall, the admiral ran his eyes along the north coast until he found the encircled cliffs and cottage. 'Saint Ives is too close,' he said.

'But the location so isolated, it is all but remote,' offered Burghardt.

'And the ruins of that mine?' asked Canaris.

Using a pencil, Burghardt pointed things out on the map and then on the latest of the drawings, those dating from 1875. 'The pumping shaft is here just outside the western wall of the ruins, the entrance shaft to the mine, a little to the south and larger.'

'There is another entrance here, Kapitän,' said Beck. 'An adit breaks through the face of the cliff, Admiral. It would have been used for draining the workings at and above that level, and for moving some of the waste rock out.'

So this was the young man who would, if required, accomplish what Osier had as yet been unable to do, thought Canaris. 'And in the mine itself?' he asked.

Burghardt gave his subordinate a nod, Herr Beck saying, 'Flooded below a depth of fifty fathoms, Admiral. A small area of ancient workings lies nearest the surface, about 1500 metres to the south of the engine house and downslope from it. Below these ancient workings . . .' Canaris held up a forefinger. '*Bitte, Herr Beck*. Define ancient for me.'

'Nothing has been noted, Admiral, beyond a few words, but I would assume they are probably late medieval.'

'And below these "ancient" workings?'

'And below ground everywhere else are the far later workings, and not just those of the Wheal Deep. Breakthrough into other workings in 1868 allowed expansion into the Wheal Garrett, about a mile and a half to the south, but as with it, so too, the Wheal Deep. In any underground mine, it is down with the sinking of the shafts, out with the driving of the crosscuts or levels and adits, then up with the winzes or raises to extract the ore via the stopes, the ore often being dropped down to a lower level or half-level to be moved out to the shafts and hoisted to the surface. Waste rock is then used wherever possible to fill the mined-out stopes, but when the price of tin fell, the Wheal Deep ceased. Crosscuts and stopes were all abandoned, but these should still be accessible and fully timbered where necessary, especially since, in the levels above flooding, the water will have been drained via the adit to the cliffs.'

The explanation of mining had been succinct, and certainly the Führer would think highly of such confidence, but . . . 'What about caving?' asked Canaris.

It was now really only between himself and the admiral, thought Beck. 'Some, no doubt, but you see, there are many passages.' Spreading the plans of the mine, the admiral noting the age and mustiness of the drawings, especially those of the earliest, Beck quickly pointed things out.

'And the number of levels?' asked Canaris.

'Twenty-five main levels to the flooding. The levels are at two-fathom intervals or close to it, but there are also the half-or intermediate levels, steps if you like, as the ore was followed and taken, with the winzes, the steeply inclined shafts or chutes between, and even occasional ventilation tunnels, and further underground shafts as well. It's a warren, Admiral. It will offer endless possibilities.'

All well and good perhaps, felt Canaris, yet . . . 'How is it, then, that you propose to get the child out through the mine, but only if necessary?'

Everyone knew that the admiral not only liked possibilities where the imagination could run, but better still preferred clear and decisive solutions. Quickly Beck searched for and found a much earlier set of drawings. 'Through these ancient workings, Admiral, for they will have been long forgotten. Indeed they were doubtless not even known of when the mine itself was opened. It was only as this level was driven under them that a breakthrough must have occurred and this note, dated 4 July 1827, was made on the drawings. Since the tin, however, increased with depth, they were soon forgotten as the mine got deeper and deeper. Handheld drill steel and black powder were used for most of its life, with always the hand-pulled or pushed haulage trams and wheelbarrows, never pit ponies. For the later, more recent history, it was essentially the same, though not always with the intent of going deeper, for by then they were using the new dynamite and, at times, bringing down much larger volumes of ore and waste rock. Old workings would have been reopened and what lower-grade tin ore was left, scavenged. But still, and as always, the miners had to chase the veins wherever they ran, so there are tunnels and tunnels, openings and openings. It's perfect, Admiral. Even if the British think they have us, I can still find another way through to those very early workings, and I will have the plans in my pocket and know of them—they won't.'

The image of each level's tunnels and openings was projected onto the next above, so that when viewed in plan, the hen scratching and ruled lines tended to overlap, but such confidence, thought Canaris, must be tempered. 'I've been in many mines, Herr Beck. Tin, yes, and silver in South America. None were pleasant or "easy." Most had men at work and long accustomed to the perils, while all of the abandoned ones presented an absolute torment of uncertainty and outright danger. You have no guarantee that needle in a haystack, those "ancient workings," will offer the escape you think. Also that child will be terrified and you have no guarantee she will remain quiet should you have to take her down there.'

There was no sense in avoiding it, thought Beck. 'I have two alternate routes, Admiral: the main shaft and the adit. Both will, no doubt, be watched, and of the two, the adit offers the better route if needed. Karen will, I agree, most certainly be afraid. Sounds will echo and be confusing but not just to ourselves, also to any who might pursue us.'

But had Herr Beck ever been in such a mine or even in an operating one? wondered Canaris, and how would he react himself? 'What mines have you been in?'

'Iron in Lorraine, Admiral, coal in the Ruhr, and potash to the north of Mulhouse.'

That last in Alsace. Herr Beck had obviously expected the question and had been prepared, so *gut. Ja, gut.* 'What makes you think MI5 won't suspect you of using the mine, if necessary?'

'*Ach*, the flooding and the danger,' said Beck, 'but you see, Admiral, I really have found an exit route. This early haulageway that extends right to below where the stamp mill and washing tables used to crush the ore and separate the cassiterite, continues on towards the adjoining Wheal Garrett. To get to it from below, there are any number of possibilities. Once there, we can not only reach the surface through those ancient workings, but will also be well to the south and downslope of the engine house and its main haulage and pump shafts, things the British will most likely be intently watching. The Luftwaffe's photo reconnaissance was able to provide these aerial photos. Long moundlike ridges of waste rock lie between the ancient workings and the remains of that engine house, and on this early set of drawings, Admiral, whoever noted the ancient workings also noted "surface fissures." That means that the horizontal sheeting planes and vertical joints that naturally cut such igneous rocks as granite into blocks, offered those very early miners a way of gaining entry. Bracken and surface rubble now hide those entrances, as they must have, no doubt, for centuries.'

For millennia? wondered Canaris. Herr Beck had, however, looked quite deeply into things but that early haulageway's timbering could well be highly questionable, subsequent rockfalls no doubt apparent. Certainly General von Hoffmann had set them a task, and since he was on the best of terms with Reichsführer Himmler, failure was not an option. But the child would not be taken into the mine unless absolutely necessary. 'What about that county road that runs past the cottage and but a kilometre from it?'

Beck acknowledged it would be closely watched by MI5 and that this had forced him to concentrate on a final exit as far to the south of it as possible. So intense had their discussion been, they had completely forgotten their coffee.

'Joachim, what do you think?' asked Canaris.

'That I am grateful it is not to be myself, Admiral.'

'And the other business?' asked Canaris.

That of MI6 and MI5 competing against each other instead of working together. 'Progressing, Admiral. Brigadier Charles Edward Gordon will soon have to make a move. Osier, of course, will be aware of this.'

Agent 07392. 'And the general's daughter?' asked the admiral.

'Prepared also.'

Joachim was no fool, the woman could be very useful. 'Her father wishes me to convey to you that should you fail, he will, indeed, hold you responsible, as will the Reichsführer. Now, please, a little coffee and for you, Herr Beck, a photograph of Hilary Bowker-Brown taken yesterday, I believe, in the rain and in London as she discovered someone had stolen those plans to that mine of hers. But it is interesting, is it not, that a girl should have wanted to buy a derelict mine and live like a hermit, especially one who can, apparently, use a revolver?'

No more than twenty-eight, she was of medium height, the hair most probably dark brown, the style not new but deliberately cut short and swept back on both sides so as to keep it out of the way when needed. 'She's very French-looking, but does she also *think* like a Frenchwoman?' asked Beck.

'A good question for which, alas, we do not yet have an adequate answer, saving only that she spent much of her school years going from school to school and fighting far too often with the nuns over topics they felt she had no business thinking. The evils of war and the rights of the common people who become victims of such senseless killing and destruction, none of whom receive any posthumous remembrance nor even a mention in history books other than as casualties; the banks and their hold over personal finances, for another; the need for social well-being, too; and Karl Marx, Communism, Socialism and, if I may quote a reference, "the rights of the poor that God himself *and* his only son *demanded* they have." A problem, I think, Herr Beck, should you have to settle her, even in that mine. Major-General Sir Stewart Menzies of MI6 would not have had the slightest interest in her, including his setting aside her socialistic convictions, were she not extremely capable.'

The Abwehr had been busy. There were dossiers on the girl, but others on Captain Anthony James Pearce, Captain David Douglas Ashby, a Roger Banfield and one on Sir John Masterson. Leaving Beck to look through them, Canaris drew the Kapitän out onto the tiny balcony that overlooked the canal. 'Joachim, how certain are you that this will succeed?'

Far too many in Berlin must now be watching the outcome. 'I'm never certain, Admiral. My whole intent is to minimize risk and maximize return.'

'Colonel Buntington Hacker could be confronted with the murder of Ashby's barmaid.'

'A fact he would most definitely deny, Admiral, unless . . .'

Canaris gave him a faint smile. 'Unless we had indisputable proof.'

Taking the envelope from him, Burghardt couldn't help but see the return address of New Scotland Yard.

'It is the summation, Joachim, of their investigation. Use it if necessary.'

'The Abwehr never ceases to amaze me, Admiral.' Quite obviously it had come from a source within the British upper echelons, but had it been deliberately leaked by Brigadier Charles Edward Gordon?

'Sir John Masterson must be stopped,' said Canaris. 'If AST-X Bremen is ever to succeed in England, Wales, Scotland and even in Ireland, both North and South, he and his Watchers, who are the only ones in MI5 that currently see the Reich as a threat, must be dealt with. All the others, such as they are, seem far more concerned with the Soviets and Britain's Communists. That . . .' He indicated the envelope. 'Will stop him, at least for a time. Masterson may well believe that Hacker, being overzealous and knowing they had to have a success against our threat that Whitehall would notice, killed the barmaid. But, Joachim, Masterson will also know that he, himself, will be called to account if ever the truth comes out. All that is necessary, then, is that we release that document to the British press.'

'And Brigadier Gordon?'

'Still has much to tell us.'

The hawk, noted Christina, was hooded and on the heavy leather gauntlet of his left forearm, and when he removed the hood and untethered the flying jesses, he gave that arm a short lift and the bird sprang into the air. Taking a coiled thong with a feathered lure, he began to let it out, and as he swung it round and round, the hawk circled with it, calling sharply. It was Saturday, 11 June, and early, she having come up here as she had before, to survey the school from a distance. Not expecting to have met anyone, she was hesitant yet terribly excited for she had recognized him at once, and hadn't both Werner and herself decided who he really was.

As the length of the thong increased, the lure came low to the ground, then went higher and higher before dropping towards the ground again. Round and round it went, the mist grey on the pinkish-shouldered moors of the Quantocks.

He wore no hat, this brigadier, this Osier, the dark blue canvas duck coat buttoned but open at the throat to reveal the soft grey collar of a plain Viyella shirt. Whipcord trousers and gumboots completed the attire. Swift-winged, the hawk rose and fell, the lure never far from it until Gordon suddenly thrust the arm that held the thong above his head, the hawk hitting the lure so hard feathers flew, its cries those of elation and hunger.

Giving it a moment before coiling in, he walked easily towards the hawk, his voice but a gentle admonition. 'My dear, dear lady, don't be so greedy. Your time will come.'

The bird was refusing to give up the lure, felt Christina. It couldn't understand the lack of blood and warm flesh, was tearing the thing to pieces, but had the brigadier *known* she would come here? Had he had someone follow her?

Giving the hawk a bloodied tidbit, he coaxed it onto the

gauntlet, calming it by stroking the back of its head and lightly preening the feathers.

'It's not your land, is it, dear lady?' he asked, finally taking notice of her.

Pulling off her kerchief, she shook out her hair. 'No, of course not. I only came up here to see the ruins and listen to the song-birds.'

Introducing himself, he said, 'Please don't be afraid of Morgan, Mrs. . . . ?'

There was no sense in her lying about her identity, she giving it and taking a firm hand in her own to feel its coldness and see those bluest of eyes give her the once-over, then expectantly take her in with appreciation. 'My husband is one of the teaching masters at Grantley's,' she said. 'Do you come here often?'

He held the arm with the gauntlet out to her. 'Morgan, stay,' he gently said. 'Stay, my pretty. Stay.'

The hawk hunched its shoulders and she thought it would spring at her, but he tethered the jesses, causing her to wonder if the assumed threat had been intended, he wanting to see if she could bring herself to relax with him in control.

Again she asked if he came here often. When he shook his head, she found her cigarettes and began to open the case only to feel the quiet rebuke of, 'Please don't. The smoke will only upset her.'

Wrapped in mist, the school lay well below them, beyond the moor and then the oak woods on the lower slopes.

'Is it a good school?' he asked, noting that she had plunged both hands into the pockets of the flecked tweed jacket of her suit.

'The school?' she said. 'I'm afraid I wouldn't really know, Brigadier. I've only just come over.'

That wasn't quite true, thought Gordon, but decided to leave it just as she would, no doubt, her disappointment at the failed attempt to take her daughter. 'Found a place to stay, have you?' he asked.

'A cottage,' she said. 'Wetherby. It's just down the road, near the bridge. I've not moved in but hope to. My husband and I have been separated for some time. I'm hoping to bring the two of us back together, not just for my own sake but for that of our daughter.'

But how much, then, did she really know of himself? he wondered. She seemed as though excited by their meeting, and he had to wonder if Joachim Burghardt hadn't told her to arrange just such a thing.

As Gordon stroked the hawk's head, Christina noticed a gentleness she hadn't thought possible. As if at one with the creature, it responded totally. 'She's very beautiful,' she said, wondering not only how much this Osier really knew of herself, but why he had chosen to meet her here.

When she said she must leave, that she had an appointment with an estate agent to see over Wetherby Cottage, he thought that AST-X Bremen must have warned her to be careful, but that she would, quite possibly, be amenable to further contact. 'We shall be at Llynwood, the home of my cousins, for a short time,' he said. 'It's not far and just to the west of us a mile or two. Do come for a drink. It's a lovely house and well worth seeing.'

'I will. Yes . . . yes, if I can get away, I will.'

Watching as she strode downhill, he waited, and when a young cottontail darted out from some bracken nearby, he loosed the jesses and lifted Morgan into the air, the hawk, a harrier, coming far too close for comfort and causing the schoolteacher's wife to shield her face.

As the rabbit's shrieks pierced the early morning silence, it began to kick and squirm as rabbits will, and Christina Ashby, née von Hoffmann, half-lowered her arm. Still terrified, she looked uncertainly back at him from perhaps one hundred yards of moor.

'Sorry about that, Mrs. Ashby,' he called out as he approached. 'Natural of her and a fine kill, but I mustn't let her consume the rabbit, not if I'm ever to hunt with her.'

Crouching to free the rabbit, he broke its neck and pocketed it before taking the hawk back onto his forearm and calming it, his time with the hood and then the tethering, his tone of voice again betraying a gentleness the Ashby woman found both difficult to understand in one such as himself and disconcerting. 'Let's walk down together,' he said. 'The invitation to Llynwood was genuine, Mrs. Ashby, though now I feel I owe you a profound apology and perhaps even a supper should you so choose.'

Wetherby Cottage had been empty for some time, but where sunlight streamed in through the bay windows of the sitting room, it shone across a herringbone floor Karen would be sure to notice was crisscrossed by the diamond shadows of the leading.

Alone, Christina stood with the sunlight warming her silk-stockinged feet. Some time ago she had kicked off her shoes and removed the woollen socks she had worn up on the moor.

The estate agent, Mr. Horris Lamb of Taunton, had gone away to see to the papers, she having agreed to purchase the cottage and having put down a deposit of fifty pounds. But would it be enough to convince Brigadier Gordon that they could work together and that she wasn't a threat to him? And would Ash believe what she was now going to claim?

The meeting with Osier still excited her, but would the brigadier again try to take Karen without her help, even as MI5 were trying, or would he do something to stop them?

There were benches beneath the widows, storage places that were lined with cedar. Karen would love it here. Ash would see this clearly and might accept that she hadn't stayed in London at the Dorchester as he must have expected. He'd have telephoned to find out and she would have to lie, couldn't tell him she had been back to the Reich and had only just arrived again. But had Ruth Pearce told him she had threatened her? Had Colonel Hacker told him she had locked him in that church?

When he came up the walk to find her shoes and socks, and know she was in the cottage, he called out and she heard him clearly. Hesitantly he came on through, went into the kitchen, the pantry, found no sign of her and called out again.

As he climbed the stairs, Christina heard him pause. Hesitant still, he came on, her heart hammering now, for he would see the lie of it all and spoil everything, and she had to get Karen away from him.

Noticing the cigarette she had left to smoulder on a windowsill in one of the bedrooms, he waited, she to finally say, 'Hello, Ash.'

As he turned towards her, she stepped in on him so fast, he was caught off guard and felt the urgency of her embrace, her lips, her body, the sweet smell of her, the softness of her hair against a cheek.

Grabbing his hands, she said, 'Darling, this place is perfect. Karen will love it and you can come home to us every day.'

'Christina, what are you up to?'

A faint and nervous smile would suit best, her lips trembling with uncertainty. 'That sounds as if you do not want me back. I thought . . . Well, after you had left my room at the Dorchester, we would . . . Well, you did say that if I came to the school, I could tell you what I had decided to do. But . . . but where is Karen? Isn't she with you? She would love this house, would be so happy. It's what I've come to realize we must do, darling.'

Freeing his hands, he awkwardly straightened his glasses, was obviously quite disconcerted by her coming here like this.

'Just where have you been since the Dorchester?' he asked. 'I tried to call you.'

Since that, too, had been anticipated by herself, her smile could now be a little braver. 'Why, I came to see the school, of course. I wanted to make up my mind, Ash, but unfortunately, not knowing of it, stayed at an inn near where that . . . that poor woman . . . That lover of yours had been murdered. Naturally I wanted to find out all I could about her.'

'But used a different name, a Mrs. Talbotte from London.'

'Of course. I couldn't involve you, could I, until I knew what I had to do?'

Having removed her suit jacket, she had hung it over a door-knob.

'They tried to take Karen, Christina. They would have killed Hilary had she not shot at them.'

So it was *Hilary* now, was it? She would turn away, would walk towards the window where she'd left her cigarette, would let him see her reach for it. 'I didn't know. My God, how could I have? Is Karen all right? She'll have been terrified, poor thing.'

'She's fine.'

Sitting down on one of the benches, she would let him see how the sunlight brought out the amber in her hair. 'Is it that you think I must have had something to do with that attempt? Well, is it?' she asked.

He didn't answer, only remained standing in the centre of the room, still not knowing exactly what to think, the fool. 'All right, I did go back to the Reich. I went to see my father's friends, and yes, I did come to know what they had tried to do and that this girl, this . . . this nanny you've got looking after our Karen really did shoot at them. We argued. I told him that Karen could well have been killed or seriously wounded had those idiots returned fire. One of them, I gather, told the wounded one not to do so, but to leave because Karen was standing far too close to that girl. Hearing all of this, I . . . I came over at once, and . . . and now am waiting for you to decide. You.'

Was it all a lie? wondered Ashby.

'I packed and left,' said Christina. 'I told Father I wasn't coming back.'

Waiting, seeing that he was not yet going to respond, she gave him another faint smile and said, 'So it has all been for nothing, has it? Having bought this cottage for Karen, am I now to sell it, Ash, or is there not some way I can convince you I meant what I said?'

When he came to her, he placed a hand on her shoulder and she knew she had won.

'They'll probably intern you, Christina, if there's another war.'

There was sadness to him, that sense of loss and yes, still a little doubt, but no longer so much. 'Where's Karen?' she asked, looking up at him.

The deliberately opened buttons of her blouse were one thing, thought Ashby, the lying yet another. 'Why did it have to happen to us?' he asked. 'You weren't a Nazi when we married.'

Verdammt! 'Karen, David. I've been so lonely I . . . I no longer know myself.'

She had tried to lean into him, he backing away. 'Karen's being moved. I can't say where to, not until we sort things out, but I'll bring her to the school just as soon as we do.'

'It's this girl you've got looking after her, isn't it? Karen's let her take my place.'

'No one can or ever will, and you know that. Karen still wants to see you and even that father of yours.'

'But not to be *with* me, Ash?' Stubbing out her cigarette, she left it lying on the bench. 'Have I failed? Have I lost everything? Can you not forgive me?' Catching him by the hands, she stood up and kissed him hard, his rush of breath soft against her tears as she pulled him closer and wrapped her arms about his neck. 'Take me, Ash. Take me like you used to. Do it now!'

Ruth Pearce saw them from the garden. They were just a blur

behind the leaded glass, but was it that same blurring that made their passion appear all the more ardent and was it jealousy that made her own cheeks hot, or anger at his having been deceived by that wife of his who would have killed her had she not told her she would never get her daughter back if there was another murder?

'He's being a bloody fool, Anthony!' she said. 'The next thing you know, they'll be having sex on the floor!'

Ruth burst into tears, Pearce putting a rare arm about her as she buried her face against his chest. Later, she watched the boys at cricket and tried not to think of Ash lying in the arms of that wife of his. Dave stood like some brave old Christian forced to face the lions. Finch wound up, the boy's form good for the Lower Fifth, the crack of bat and ball like a pistol shot, the cries, as Ash ran, like those of the Romans in the Colosseum.

She had so wanted to tell him everything that had happened, still did, though it would hurt him, the truth about that wife of his, but would he ever forgive her for having told the woman where that daughter of his could be found in Kent?

Finch wound up. Ash swung. *Crack!* and he was off again.

'Marvellous, that,' said someone. 'Not bad for an American. Takes me back a while, let me tell you. Mrs. Pearce, isn't it? Ah, I thought so. Masterson, Mrs. Pearce. Sir John.'

Though he didn't quite look it, Ruth wondered if he was a parent. 'If it's my husband you want, you'll find him in his study going over the accounts with Mr. Telford, our assistant headmaster.'

How stiff of her. 'No, I rather thought I might have a word with Captain Ashby. They tell me he's rather good with languages but is forced to teach mathematics, history and other things as well.'

The lie of his wanting to poach Ash for another school was all too evident and it made her angry. 'What, exactly, is it that you want?' she asked.

'A word, that's all. How well do you know Captain Ashby, Mrs. Pearce?'

'Are you from the police?'

'Good God, no, madam. I'm just a friend.'

'It's about Karen, then, isn't it?'

'It might be.'

Finch bowled again. Ash let that one go by, then spotted a hit to keep the boys on their toes, that Hamilton boy catching it, Ruth knowing then that Ash had put it right to him.

'He's quite a soldier, isn't he, Mrs. Pearce?' said Masterson.

'I . . . I don't know what you mean?'

Then try this on for starters, thought Masterson. 'Colonel Hacker asked if I'd pop in to see the captain.'

Hacker! In tears, Ruth turned away only to turn back and ask, 'Has something happened to Karen?'

The cross the Pearce woman bore was clear enough, thought Masterson, but he would coldly say, 'Not yet, but we would take it kindly if he didn't interfere. He hasn't any plans to, has he?'

'I . . . I wouldn't know. His private life is his own.'

And her bleating it like that. 'Met his wife, have you?'

'No. No, I haven't. Why . . . why would I have?'

Yielding up the bat to loud objections, Ashby gave the troops a few pointers while polishing his glasses as he left the field to stride towards them.

'Vespasian couldn't have done it better, Mrs. Pearce,' mused Masterson, startling the woman and causing her to flee as he called out, 'Down in your neck of the woods, Ashby. Thought I'd pop in to see how you were holding up.'

Irritation flickered, the schoolmaster gazing after the headmaster's wife while saying, 'What is it that you really want, Sir John?'

'The child's now safely in Cornwall with that nanny you hired, but you're not to interfere. You're to stay right out of it and I wouldn't have come all this way to warn you, had I not felt it necessary.'

'And if I don't?'

Lord save us, must he be so stubborn? 'Then pay the price. Bunny needs a clear field and can't be worrying about loose threads. That Pearce woman was hungering to tell you something. Any idea what it was? She seemed put out that I'd come along to interrupt.'

'Ask your Colonel Hacker. Ask him why he did that to her. She might have killed herself.'

'But didn't. Care to tell me about it—your side, that is? Do so while you walk me to my motor.'

The light was lovely over Grantley's, thought Masterson. 'Reminds me of my old school, Ashby. Never wanted to see the place again, but must be getting on. Come, come now, what did she want to tell you?'

'Probably that she's leaving her husband at end of term. It was a marriage that could never have worked.'

And the schoolmaster still not certain that was the reason. 'Perhaps it's all for the best. Staying with a relative, I suppose? These things are never easy, are they? Well, cheerio, then, Ashby. With luck it'll soon be over.'

8

Cornwall was simply not being its most pleasant, felt Hilary, but of course that wasn't the problem. It was the loneliness, the very thing she had always welcomed. After endless games of cards and double cups of cocoa, Karen had finally fallen asleep in the bed they would have to share. At 10.00 pm a steady mizzle had settled in, bringing with its dampness, the incessant pounding of the waves.

Irritably Hilary ran her fingers though her hair. It hadn't been an easy trip. Colonel Hacker, though he had passed by their compartment a few times, hadn't even nodded to indicate that things were all right, nor had she been able to identify anyone else as having been with him. At Saint Erth, she and Karen had had to stand waiting like refugees on the platform, no sight of him or of anyone else come to meet them. Finding someone to drive them here hadn't been easy or inexpensive, and maybe he had wanted this so that the sleeper would be certain to see them.

Again the sound of the waves came. Usually April, May and June were the best of months insofar as storms went, but now . . .

Seeing herself reflected in the window glass with the mizzle beading on it made her think of Pindanter. Did he really have to kill, and once hidden in the mine, what would he encounter? Certainly bad ground, probably water breakthrough, obviously old memories of near-disasters and disasters. Hadn't the infrequent hand-powered fans, turned by sleepy boys, merely circulated the oxygen-depleted air and toxic fumes from the newer dynamite or older black powder? Hadn't the night core at the Wendron Mines, a good two miles to the north of Helston, not come to grass in

1875, the men having died of asphyxiation? Hadn't three men been killed in the Carn Brea not far to the southwest of Redruth in June 1882, the detonators and dynamite having been kept far too close to lighted candles?

But what about the killing of that child? she asked, and finding the place in the manuscript, readily saw that the writing had been much altered, the death of that girl having come and gone at least a dozen times. A murder then, a murder now? she asked herself, the child screaming and trying to get away as Pindanter caught her by an arm, the others yelling, *'Kill her, Pin. Bash brains in an' leave t' sea.'*

Tangled in kelp, her body would have been endlessly rolled back and forth, the girl now dead, then alive, then dead again, yet looking so like Karen Ashby that she had to ask, How *could* you have written such a thing?

Printing HACKER on the back of the opposite page in bold black letters, she wrote DAISY under it and added a question mark simply because he *had* threatened Ash, had said he would as much as see him accused of the murder if he didn't go along with MI5 and stay away.

Rivulets like tears ran down each windowpane. Ash wouldn't be here to help them if help should be needed. Karen would, she thought, do the right thing and come to her if called, but if she didn't, what then?

When a sudden rockfall was heard from directly beneath the cottage, she leapt, looked to Karen and tried to still the panic, the sound trailing away to distant rumbling that grew fainter and fainter. Certainly there had been sounds like this before, and at any time of day or night, the workings yielding to built-up stresses as timbers rotted and gave way. There had always been the creaking of those timber posts somewhere in the abandoned workings. Pindanter would have heard them snapping, too, the sudden fall of rocks and then . . . why, then, the utter silence that would, he hoped, signify an end to the current 'run' but mightn't.

'The knackers,' Mrs. Carne at the post had said of the sounds. *'Now you're not to worry, miss. It's only the little people who still work that old mine of yours.'*

Cornwall was full of such nonsense. Even so, she wished the knackers wouldn't do it, not tonight, not with the Abwehr out there somewhere and her not knowing when they would come for Karen nor if Colonel Hacker could even stop them.

When a scraping came, she stealthily lay down on the floor in front of the hearth to press an ear to the flagstones. Never loud, the sound seemed near enough. Pauses made her gaze into the fire. First had come the rockfall and then the scraping.

Hearing it faintly, she listened hard. It was of iron on rock, as if someone were dragging a cold chisel along a seam. In time, though, the sound stopped, she to lie here still but gazing into the embers for answers.

Sometimes the 'runs' broke right through to grass, taking whole cottages and other buildings. And yes, one could find such hollows, some quite deep, but each emphatically stating that all was not well underground.

When hours later, and unknown to her, Hacker saw her through the mizzle and the window, she was lost to thought but standing before a fire she'd built up, and was looking curiously down at its hearthstone. There was a tumbler in one hand, a brandy bottle nearby, she taking a sip, he sucking at bloodied knuckles and gingerly flexing his left fingers. Bastard rocks had all but got the better of him. Bastard mine, the little slut had chosen. Damned dangerous, but still she didn't know he was watching her.

Crouching, she ran a finger along the edge of the hearthstone, was getting far too curious for her own good. Another sip was needed, and another, she taking a knife to run it round the stone.

Hilary knew it fitted perfectly, for there wasn't even space for the blade of the knife, the slab of stone rectangular and shoulder wide. Fossil corals were set in its grey limestone, giving delicate filigrees of silica. Strange creatures, Pindanter would have thought. And Blind William? she asked. What would *he* have thought of them before the loss of his sight, he having used the new dynamite for 'shooting the rocks,' but having also used, while fossicking the old workings, a hand-made fuse as in the old days instead of a Bickford safety so as to save on the 'expenses'?

Shutting her eyes, groping, she felt the stone and when, by accident, the glass of brandy toppled over, Hacker knew she was being too smart for her own good, for he had read what she had printed on the back of that page, had seen the question mark she had placed beside the name of Daisy Belamy.

The brandy caught fire, the girl watching the flames, and when those were done, she began to get ready for bed, was still lost to that slab of stone and no doubt thinking of smugglers.

Pulling off the bulky cable-knit pullover and still puzzled, she laid it over the back of a chair. Shirt and brassiere came next, she running hands over the marks this last had left, then slipping them over her tits while still wondering about Ashby's barmaid, was she, or still thinking about that hearthstone?

Unlike the barmaid, her tits were small, firm and well rounded, the nipples stiff from the damp and cold, and when she raised her arms to shrug into a nightgown, they lifted and tightened. One sleeve became caught, the nightgown still hiding her head, smothering her, blinding her, trapping her just as, when fully clothed, Daisy Belamy's arms had been trapped, the slut trying to cry out for help when held down and asked again and again where Ashby had hidden that daughter of his.

When the nightgown was pulled on, the girl dropped her trousers and step-ins and he had a glimpse of the rest of her, a nice little bit and tight probably, but things had gone too far with Ashby's barmaid, who hadn't known a blessed thing. A pity, that. The Abwehr would just have to take the rap but then this one had had to get bloody Brigadier Charles Edward Gordon involved and that one was playing games of his own, or was he? That was the rub. Sir John simply hadn't been able to find out.

Letting his gaze move slowly over her, Hacker felt the urge to have her under him. Once fucked, the neck would snap, the girl going limp. The Abwehr again, if necessary, and no problem.

Returning to the hearthstone, the little bitch shut her eyes again and, down on all fours, felt for and found what she was looking for—the clay-filled holes, near each side, that when emptied would accept the ringbolts that were used to lift the stone out of the way.

Getting to her feet, obviously excited by what she had discovered, she went over to a shelf, and cautiously reaching across the sleeping child, found the bolts and, having screwed them in, braced her feet apart and moved the stone, lifted it right out and stood there staring down into the darkness.

Unknown to her, dead sheep, badgers, voles, mice and rats, their bloated bodies floating in the black and putrid water of the workings below the main shaft, had made the stench all but unbearable. And everywhere there had been the fuzz of decay, the timbers much broken, but there hadn't been any bats and he had wondered at this. Hydrogen sulphide and methane could well have discouraged them. A nasty thing, old mines. He would have to destroy that scribbling of hers, but first the child and AST-X Bremen's sleeper and all those Brigadier Charles Edward Gordon might or might not be using.

As the last of the brigadier's dinner guests left the house called Llynwood on that same Saturday night, Christina heard Gordon say a quiet word to the butler who would now leave the two of them alone.

Drawing the crocheted shawl the brigadier had found for her more closely about her shoulders, she waited. The other guests, neighbouring landowners, had thought her his mistress, but had tried their best not to let on while he, in turn, had silently been amused by her predicament.

Rejoining her, he said, 'My dear, the gun room is far more comfortable. This place always leaves me a trifle cold. These dark, panelled walls seem fit only to hang the portraits of the lesser beings Cromwell should, by rights, have beheaded.'

'But were they not relations of yours?' she asked, he having taken her by the arm.

'Oh I daresay this side of the family wisely sided with the Lord Protector, intrigue and spying being both sup and soul to them and to himself.'

'And your own branch of the family?' she asked with laughter in her eyes.

'Decidedly with the monarchy and forced to fend for themselves in foreign parts.'

'But survivors,' she said, and saw him grin and nod.

Done in maroon morocco, with scattered leopard, lion and impala hides on the floor, their mounted heads looking on, the gun room was definitely a man's room, and as his fingers touched her own, Christina paused as she took the glass he had poured. Holding a sip on the back of her tongue, she let him see what he wanted in her gaze, then swallowed and said, 'Schloss Reinhartshausen. My compliments, Brigadier. Your cousins keep an admirable cellar.'

'I'll show it to you, if you like.'

'Later, perhaps.' And sitting on the arm of one of the club chairs, she crossed her legs. 'A cigarette, I think. Would you?' she asked.

'Tobacco will only spoil that Riesling. Surely a wine lover such as yourself must know this.'

Even so, he lit it and, feeling her hand close over his own, brought the flame closer to her, she blowing smoke aside but still holding onto him. 'You are right, of course, Brigadier, but at such times, a cigarette is, I think, more necessary than the taste of a wine I could never forget.'

'You're not nervous, are you?'

'Is there some reason why I should be?'

Sitting opposite her on one of the sofas, he raised his glass to her and said, 'How did it go with that cottage you were looking into? Wetherby, wasn't it?'

'I've yet to sign the papers.'

'No other competing offers?'

'None that I'm aware of.'

'Then, if I were you, I wouldn't place all my faith in these West Country estate agents. Your Horris Lamb could well be entertaining another offer.'

'But . . . but I have agreed to purchase the cottage and have given him a deposit.'

The thought of such a betrayal *had* unsettled her. 'Trust is such a fragile thing.'

'Has someone made a counteroffer?'

She was a woman, then, who did not take kindly to her plans being interfered with. 'A Roger Banfield and a George Crawley. Both are masters at that school of your husband's.'

Quite obviously the brigadier had been having her followed just as he had done in Kent and on the Continent, and just as obviously he now wanted her to know this, but was he really Osier?

'My dear, let us not fence with each other. You will never get that daughter of yours out of this country without my help.'

The high colour that raced into her cheeks only made her all the more alluring, she saying, 'Am I to understand that you will help me and if so, Brigadier, what in turn are you asking?'

'Nothing but a little cooperation. What could be simpler?'

Setting her glass aside, Christina got up. 'I really must go. It's getting rather late.'

'Of course.' Reaching to put out her cigarette, he said, 'One always has to be careful of fire in these old houses, but why not wait until we've had a talk? MI5 has people watching that daughter of yours and hoping AST-X Bremen's sleeper will fall into their net along with anyone else he might have with him, but they still, I must emphasize, do not know who this sleeper really is.'

Getting up, he went over to a cabinet to open a drawer, now had a pistol in hand, a Mauser. Not knowing quite what to do, she waited, he then handing her the weapon and saying, 'It's fully loaded. Keep it with you if you wish, but please do listen to what I have to say. We've much in common and are, I believe, after exactly the same thing. That husband of yours might take it upon himself to intervene, and I do know MI5 fears that he might, but we two can and will solve everything, though I must ask, could he have followed you here?'

'Ash? I . . . I don't know. We . . . we did meet at the cottage, but . . .'

Was the husband waiting outside? wondered Gordon.

It was now, felt Ashby, nearly an hour since the last of the other guests had left. Fog had drifted in to shroud the house called Llynwood and make more distant what lights were still on, but why had Christina chosen to come here in the first place and why had she stayed? Granted the sleeper had to be someone close to the school, but someone from here? Try as he might, no name came forth, and when the front door opened and a man came out wearing a dark blue duck coat and gumboots, the beam of the torch shone on the stone steps and metalled drive.

Following him at a distance through park and woodland, Ashby soon came to a paddock and stables. Four hunters were in box stalls, and as the man passed them, he checked on each before taking the ladder and climbing to the loft, Ashby then hearing him talking to someone.

'Morgan, my pretty, don't be so eager. She has come to us and will stay the night.'

There was a pause, and then, 'What is it? Has she followed me here or has someone else?'

The light was extinguished. The horses fidgeted. Perhaps five minutes passed, perhaps a little more, Gordon now certain someone had followed him, Morgan telegraphing this by her nervousness.

Christina Ashby had been shown the fog and had quite willingly agreed to stay the night, but had she inadvertently led that husband of hers to him?

Feeling for the perch, he put the hawk back on its roost. Drawing off the gauntlet, he pocketed the torch and climbed silently down the ladder. If Ashby *were* here, he couldn't be interfering in Cornwall, and perhaps that was all to the good, but only if the schoolmaster didn't take a notion to make a blessed nuisance of himself and spoil everything.

Reaching the ground at last, he switched on the torch, a man of sixty perhaps, felt Ashby. Again the man looked into the stalls, even said a few quiet words to each of the hunters, seemed prepared to let himself be watched, though not knowing really by whom or from where, and certainly he was Hilary's Brigadier Charles Edward Gordon, but could he be the sleeper? Christina's having come here implied that he was, her staying the night only reinforcing it.

Taking the pins from her hair, Christina could see the brigadier's reflection in the dressing table's mirror. Insisting that he build up the fire before he went off to bed himself, she hadn't dared ask if he was Osier, nor had he said it in so many words, but every time she went over things in her mind, it all made sense. Agent 07392. Someone, then, who was exceedingly well placed: Brigadier Charles Edward Gordon of MI6.

He had even given her the gun, which now lay on the dressing table. He had gone out to have a look round, but had come back satisfied, and as he came towards her now, she hesitated, her hands still touching the back of her head, he putting his own on her shoulders and saying, 'You might like a little company, but if not, please simply say so and I'll leave.'

When he held her breasts and trapped her arms up like that, he smelled nicely, was gentle but slightly withdrawn, as though he always had to keep a little of himself back.

Laughing softly, looking steadily at him in the mirror, she said, 'Undress me.'

This he did with surprisingly sensual patience, he fingering each garment while running that gaze of his appreciatively over her, touching her here, touching her there, making her lift her arms up straight above her head, he turning her and touching her again and again.

He had a good body, tangled grey hairs on the chest and groin, the maleness of him extended but not yet fully erect and, *Gott sei Dank*, he hadn't been circumcised. The scar of a bullet wound drew her lingering gaze, so, too, that of the shrapnel that must have torn across the left side of his rib cage and up under that arm. Gently leading her over to the fire, he held her by the hands, looked steadily at and into her, let her feel the warmth on her backside, and said, 'I meant it, my dear. I will get that daughter of yours out of this country and safely home, but of course you must help me a little.'

Lieber Christus im Himmel, what the hell did he want? she wondered, but he kissed her again and again. Brushing her hair up and out of the way, he found the curve of a shoulder and gently bit the skin, his *Schwanz* now stiffly erect and hard against her seat, she closing her eyes as he slid his arms under hers and lifted her up, placing both hands firmly against the back of her neck. 'Do it,' she said. 'Take me here on the floor.'

Gently chiding her, Gordon ran a hand down over her breasts and the flat firmness of her stomach, and only when he touched her mons to part the lips, did she arch her back, his other hand now caressing that softest of bottoms. Dear God, but she was a beautiful thing.

Throwing a last glance towards the dressing table where she had left the Mauser, Christina felt herself letting go. Turning to face him, she sucked and bit a stiffening nipple, he sliding fingers into her, her clitoris now so stiff she tried to hold on, tried not to come, but did.

As she climaxed, she threw her head back, the whole of her quivering, she to kneel on the floor now, to demand, for suddenly everything inside her was going crazy and he was making it happen. Giving a broken cry, she tilted back her head, he to hold her by the breasts and pull himself deeply into her again and again until he, too, had climaxed.

Stroking her as they lay together, he whispered, 'No doubts about me now, my pretty? If there are, you will find all the proof you need at the embassy, for I arranged for a little something to be sent over to the admiral that Joachim will now have and will then send back to you to cement our relationship.'

Alarmed, scrambling to get up, she had to be held down by force, he whispering into her ear, 'Dearest, the *Thule Sólarsteinn* of Herr Beck hasn't yet arrived off our coast, but no attempt will be made to take your daughter until it does, so please be patient.'

'Are you Osier?' she asked.

If ever a woman could kill, this one could, he felt, but smiling at her, said, 'Osier, of course, but you had best not tell anyone, had you?'

Still far from satisfied, feeling as if she had just given herself to the enemy, he could see that she was desperately hunting for a way out but was held too tightly, her arms now pinned to the hearth rug, he all but on top of her.

'Your code number,' she asked.

'My dear, why would I have been told a code number that has been routinely assigned to me by AST-X Bremen? All of my contacts with them, and there have been only a few, have been through the use of Osier.'

But hadn't that butcher, Herr Reiss, said that he only knew the *numbers* of those for whom he sent messages? 'I still want it.'

Her breath was coming too quickly, her chest rising and falling, the anger clear enough. 'Would that I could give it to you, but I can't. Hadn't we best simply trust each other, seeing as you want your daughter but without my help, are unlikely to succeed? After all, isn't that why Burghardt had to awaken me?'

Reiss might not yet have been given Osier's number. Mollified somewhat, she lay there, his hold gradually lessening until kisses and then encircling arms were hesitantly accepted, he entering her again. But long after he had gone to his own room, still having left the pistol with her, Christina lay next to the fire, wondering about him—wanting, she knew, to believe he really *was* Osier.

Touching those places he had touched, she found her throat still dry. He had sent something to Canaris. What could it have been?

The coffee was Dutch, the rolls German, the butter Danish. It being Sunday, Bremen had yet to awaken. Thumbing through the document Canaris had given him a week ago yesterday in Berlin, Burghardt again read through the summation of New Scotland Yard on the murder of Daisy Belamy, yet still he couldn't make up his mind. The thing seemed too good to be true. A scandal for MI5, what there was of Britain's counterintelligence service suddenly awakening to the guilt of one of them. A major coup for AST-X Bremen. Gold on a platter.

More coffee didn't help, nor did another roll with Frau Albrecht's gooseberry jam. Was there not something wrong with the document? Though yet to be formally charged and arrested, Colonel Buntington Hacker had most probably killed Ashby's barmaid in an excess of zeal, but could this source of the admiral's have been deliberately fed the document? And if so, why, please, would anyone other than an Abwehr agent do such a thing, knowing the disaster it would cause MI5 when released to the British press?

Certainly the document was genuine. He had had all the routine tests conducted, the paper, the type, even an analysis of the wording. It was from New Scotland Yard, and someone very high up in things had had it stolen.

There wouldn't be any other copies on file. Given circumstance and time, Hacker could well go free, AST-X Bremen and the Abwehr being accorded the blame.

Again he read through it, yet still his hesitation refused to leave. Reluctantly folding it, he slid the document back into the envelope Canaris had provided. Four bundles of British one- and five-pound notes lay beneath the pistol he, himself, had chosen. The courier would come at 0600 hours. By noon the diplomatic pouch would be in London and at the embassy.

Before she had left for England, Beck and the general's daughter had been into the office safe, and he had to smile at the irony, for the two had wanted Osier's identity, and now here was himself desperately wanting that of the admiral's source.

Another Osier? he wondered. Another agent known only by

number? Internal politics being what they were, he couldn't have asked or questioned the admiral's judgement. And, yes, there were still those infernal holdovers from the times before the reorganization. The chaos of those early years of espionage in Britain had left a legacy of agents, some still known only by their numbers, they jealously guarded not only by the agents but by those who had put them there.

At just over a kilo, the Danish M1910/21 pistol was heavy. Sturdy and eminently reliable, its weight and length had gone against its adoption and very few of them existed. Not as sleek as the Luger, it was blocky like the Mauser. Danish, of course, because the man to whom Christina Ashby would take it was Danish, or so his false papers would state.

Fortunately the general's daughter had had the good sense to tell the embassy where she might be contacted, the Rose and Thorn in East Quantoxhead under the name of Mrs. Talbotte. And fortunately, given his instructions to him, she had yet to trouble Bridgwater again. She would deliver the money, the document and the gun when the *Thule Sólarsteinn* docked in Weymouth, and would lead whomever would follow her right to that yacht, they and herself believing Werner Beck would be there.

Beck wouldn't be, of course, for he had taken that yacht of his down the estuary and had let MI6 see him do this, they concluding he was on his way to Cornwall, but once at sea, Beck had transferred to the *Reisende*,* an armed merchantman that would take him to Cherbourg where he would then board the *Hálfdan Ragnar*, a yacht supposedly out of Copenhagen, the sails chalk red with age, the leftovers from a coastal lugger. Beck wouldn't be putting in to Weymouth at all, someone else would. Instead, he was sailing as a Danish ex-bumboat captain, a drunk but attempting to dry himself out and travelling under the name of Harald Jensen, having lost wife and sons to a desperate need for alcohol.

The child would be taken, the general content, the admiral pleased and none of them the wiser.

On Sunday afternoon, 12 June, a young couple came to the cottage to do some sketching. In better times Hilary knew she would

---

* Tourist, traveller or voyager

have shown them round and tried to make friends. Both were British, the girl with gorgeous, soft red hair and lovely sea-green eyes, he tall and dark, and with honest sky-blue eyes and tousled black hair.

He called her Ginger, she called him Biff, and the two were a pair of larks, loving every minute of their day, sketching the cliffs, the sea and moor, even hunting for birds' nests. Of course they wanted to study the ruins, and of course she told them it was far too dangerous, but at 4.00 pm, wanting to get a closer look at them and all but certain they could mean no harm, though keeping the Webley close, she called out, asking if they would like tea.

Biff answered that tea was out, 'But will you accept this?' he asked. 'Ginger thinks you might like to have it.'

The sketch was beautiful, the distant engine house bleak, a relic of its times and superb, if available, as a jacket illustration for a novel yet to be completed.

'Don't smudge it with your fingers,' he said, and he had the nicest of smiles and a lot like Karen's father, for it lit up his eyes and spread nothing but an aura of sincerest warmth.

'Thanks. It's . . . it's awfully decent of you, Mr. . . . ?'

The wind pulled at his hair. 'Just call me Biff. Ginger does.'

Was he Welsh? she wondered, that accent suppressed, his wife not saying anything much but standing out there distant on the road, waiting and waving, the wind tugging at the collar of her blouse and blowing that lovely hair about.

'Are you sure you can't stay for tea? It's nothing fancy. You wouldn't be putting us out, and both Karen and I would love a bit of company.'

'Ginger has to do her letters home, but thanks. Perhaps another time.'

'The sketch is perfect. Tell your wife I'll hang it on the wall next to my desk.'

'You're the writer, aren't you? Yesterday the woman at the post told us you wouldn't mind a couple of amateur artists tramping about the place.'

'Please feel free to come again. It was kind of Mrs. Carne to have sent you.' How *could* she be so trusting? wondered Hilary. Had the loneliness got to her?

Late that night a rockfall, somewhere in the mine, sent its

echoes up through the cottage, she sitting bolt upright again in panic, moonlight everywhere. Out over the sea there would be a sheen of silver; out over the moor, the Wheal Deep would throw its shadow.

Holding the painting at an angle to the moonlight, she realized that Biff and Ginger had signed it with their initials: *BG*, Brigadier Gordon.

'Ash,' she softly said, though he was nowhere near. 'Ash, in spite of my doubts about him, the brigadier did send help, but I still wish you were with us.'

Late on that Sunday, as Gordon scanned the summation of New Scotland Yard's investigation into the murder of Ashby's barmaid, the schoolmaster's wife watched him closely. She had been out and about, was still flushed and breathless. The woollen skirt had caught some burs, as had the ankles of her silk stockings. Grass and mud clung to her shoes.

'Were you followed?' he asked, tossing the document onto the table where the banknotes, a thousand pounds' worth, lay with the Danish M1910/21 Burghardt had sent the woman.

'Ash did try, but I lost him this time.'

Gordon noted how the excitement of the chase still pinched her nostrils and made her eyes even more alive and alluring. 'My people were in contact this afternoon, my dear. Hilary Bowker-Brown had no fear of them, but is being watched round the clock by MI5. Apparently your daughter, though wary of them as visitors, now feels comfortable in the presence of the girl, even to holding her by the hand when Hilary invited my people to tea. They are ardent Welsh nationalists, Christina. Young, in tiptop shape and exceedingly cool-headed, but they must, I fear, know absolutely what Joachim has in mind. Did he not put a note to that effect in that diplomatic pouch he used?'

Osier had obviously *not* been in wireless contact with the Kapitän, thought Christina. Perhaps he hadn't yet been told of the Bridgwater set, perhaps he felt she herself would be looking after such things and he had no need to risk his own security, but still she would have to test him further. 'Will your people bring Karen here to Llynwood, or take her to the yacht?'

'Neither. The yacht won't be safe once the hue and cry has

been raised unless, of course, Joachim has had her name and registry changed.'

Christina wouldn't yet let him see the note Burghardt had sent, but asked, 'What, then, do you intend to do?'

'My people have a cottage in the mountains of northern Wales. Once they've got Karen safely away, and MI5 are looking elsewhere, I thought you might join them and give the matter of that document a little time before you release it to destroy Colonel Buntington Hacker and those who employ him.'

'And yourself?' she asked. 'Will you not be joining us?'

'Most certainly, but I must be careful. I can't be seen to have been involved, can I, but later, if you were to hand that document to that husband of yours, he would, I'm sure, take care of the rest.'

'And Karen?'

'Will by then be home and safe.'

And she would, thought Christina, have the pleasure of seeing Ash's face as he read it, knowing Karen had been taken from him. 'Burghardt's note said only that the *Thule Sólarsteinn* would be putting in to Weymouth tomorrow.'

Which would allow a day or so to make the run down to Cornwall. 'And is it definitely Werner Beck whom Joachim is sending?' he asked.

The champagne she had held off sampling trickled down her throat, making her feel, thought Christina, as though naked with him beneath a mountain waterfall. Enjoying the moment, she smiled and said, 'My lover, yes, though every part of me now wants yourself and we were, I think, made for each other.'

Beck reached for the binoculars. The house was on a hillside above this tiny finger of the Helford Estuary, and from it, a steep flagstone path led down to the shore and to a 5.5-metre yacht that looked as though it had never been used. No other houses seemed near, just thickly wooded hills and a road.

He hadn't put in to Falmouth Harbour. Only at the last had he decided on making for the river. Wanting every possible out, including a little of his own, he had looked for a place to leave the *Hálfdan Ragnar* but appear as if with someone. It was now Tuesday the fourteenth.

A car was parked a short distance from the house, but there

were no signs of electrical or telephone wires. Old, of white stucco with dark trim and leaded casement windows, the house was perfect. A rockery, awash with colour, tumbled from the drive in which the car was parked, the rhododendron superb.

Satisfied that the household would not awaken for a bit, he climbed down into the cabin and set to work, was shaving the last of the drunkard's whiskers away when he saw a fair-haired woman with two children come out of the house. A dog was with them, a cocker spaniel, the three soon on the lawn and gazing down at him, the children held by the hands. None of them knew quite what to make of the visitor.

Hurriedly wiping his face on the towel and reaching for his seaman's cap, he went on deck to grin and cheerily wave a good morning. His clean but faded blue denim shirt and trousers would have to do. There was still no sign of the husband and father, and as the woman and her children came down the path, she hushed the spaniel, it heeling obediently.

Cupping his hands, Beck shouted, 'A seized-up fuel injector, and I am lost, I think. Yes . . . yes, that must be so.' Giving her the name of the yacht, he told her he was on holiday.

They got all sorts of people in summer, thought Mary Anne Livingston. Several ventured much farther up the Helford. 'Have you registered with Customs?' she called, her uncertainty all too clear, she felt.

Holding up a fistful of papers, he answered, 'At Falmouth, *ja*. I was heading down the coast to Land's End.'

'Then you had best come in.'

She must have said something to her son, for the boy began to object. Repeating her request, he dejectedly turned away and began to climb the path, Beck realizing that there was someone else up there after all, and cursing his luck.

The dog began to move about, the woman and her daughter remaining next to the shore. Leaning over the side, he put his rucksack into the dingy. Mist still rose off the water, a heron labouring along the far bank, the woman again calling softly to the dog.

'I'm Mary Anne Livingston,' she said as the boat nudged the sand, 'and this is Anna, whose brother, Derek, has gone to tell his father we've company.'

But why had the father not come himself? Taking her hand in his, he felt the cool firmness of it. 'Harald Jensen of Copenhagen, at your service, madam.' She was in her mid- to late thirties, with soft blue eyes and shoulder-length, pale blonde hair.

'I expect you would like a cup of tea,' she said, again with a touch of uncertainty that puzzled. 'We don't get many visitors, I'm afraid. You'll be something special.'

The daughter was the image of the mother, Beck tousling the child's head. Grinning, he asked if she would like a ride on his shoulders. 'It's a long hike up to the house, is it not?' he asked, making friends with the spaniel and glancing at the mother for permission.

'Please,' he said, handing the woman the rucksack. 'If I can leave the boat here, I can find a place to fix or replace the fuel injector. Maybe today, maybe tomorrow.'

'Yes, of course, it will be all right,' said Mary Anne, hesitating yet again. 'My . . . my husband is quite ill, Mr. Jensen. He does so love it when someone pays a visit. I'm sure he will know exactly where you can go for help.'

Ill and *Gott sei Dank*, his luck had just returned. Hoisting the girl onto his shoulders, he reached for the rucksack only to hear the woman say, 'You had better let me take that. You'll soon find that Anna is enough.'

And uncertain of him again, felt Beck, she wondering how a fuel injector could be so heavy, the rucksack crammed with ropes, a grappling iron, two flashlights, his gun, the Wheal Deep's drawings and other things, all of which could well be needed.

The dog came when called and they started up, the woman going first, Beck thinking that he must be out of Cornwall in three days at most, less if possible, and that this anchorage would simply have to do. From here it wasn't all that far to Saint Ives, but had he a need to go there at all and what would he find when he got to that cottage?

From Blind William's cottage to the edge of the cliffs, it was perhaps two hundred yards, and from there along the same to the east, and then down to the boat shed by degrees, though vertically one hundred. Standing in the tiny cove on that same Tuesday, 14 June, her satchel holding revolver and torch, Hilary looked up at the cliff whose all but sheer face towered uncomfortably above. In plan view, the tunnel, the adit that had led to the building of the boat ramp must lead to another tunnel that gave access to the area below the cottage, Blind William's hearthstone completing the way in and the way out when smuggling. Yet there was no further evidence of the adit's breakthrough to the cliff face, not that she could see, and there wasn't another cove nearby.

Each time a wave came in, the water would rush into the cove to spread the apron sands and rattle the shingle. Forgetting her troubles for the moment, Karen had found wrecking to be an all-consuming task of great interest. Gathering firewood was one thing, distastefully disentangling the strands of kelp another, but old bits of netting might have possible use. Cork floats, colourful pebbles, seashells and a dark-green bottle were added to the collection that now nearly filled one-half of the orange crate that had been rescued from the surf. The driftwood basket was full.

Crouching, Hilary sketched the outline of the cove in the sand. The rampart the boat shed rested on was to the west of her, the path to the top of the cliffs, directly in front. Hence the cottage would also be off to the west but not so far, and from there to the shafts, in a south-southeasterly direction, it would be at least two miles across the moor.

Two miles of tunnels and workings. Could it be as much? she wondered. The pump shaft was just outside the western wall of the engine house, and from there to the main shaft, going in a southwesterly direction, it was about seventy feet.

The miners had used a winding engine. Eventually wire rope had replaced its hemp, the headframe holding a large pulley wheel at the top to raise and lower the iron kibble that would have brought the ore to the surface and sometimes taken the men down, a dangerous practice, for they were to use the 'ladder roads' to climb into and out of the mine. All of this headframe apparatus was long gone and now there was only the gaping hole of the shaft, some twelve by eight feet.

Drawing a line from the main shaft to the pump shaft, she marked in the latter's size at almost eight feet in diameter, before sketching in the ruins, the road, cottage and cliff face.

The adit had to be behind the boat shed.

Going over to the shed, she soon found, as she had so often

before, that there was little granite among the broken killas of grey-green schist and slate. 'Karen, come and help me. Let's have a look in the shed for the entrance to the tunnel.'

The lifeboat really was as good as Ash had said when they'd first met. All down the length of the floor there were still items of one kind or another, nets, flats, pilchard baskets, cutting tables like the one she had rescued, overturned barrels, but at the back and hiding the cliff face was a solid wall of heavily tarred timbers. Only by listening closely could she and Karen hear that water was still draining out of the workings.

Up in the loft there were, among other things, the lobster traps that, as Ash had said, were really quite all right, and through gaps in the roof, light did seep and she could see at once that repairs would be needed.

Again, heavy timbers blocked off the cliff face, she straining on tiptoes to run her hands over them. 'I know it's here, Karen. It has to be. It's just the right distance from the cottage. Blind William must once have been a smuggler. The cove's perfect for it.'

Together, they picked their way back along to the loft door and struggled to open it, light immediately flooding in with a view of the cove and the waves. More nets clung to pegs in the rafters, the open wickerwork of the lobster traps making them appear as cages.

Air was rushing into the wall through seams between the timbers. 'It's got to be behind this,' she said. 'Please don't be afraid. Just help me find it.'

Pushing first on one and then another of the timbers, Hilary tried each but all were far too solidly in place. Standing back, they both looked at the wall. Upright posts stood against the timbers which lay piled horizontally, one on top of another. The posts in the middle of the wall were only as wide apart as Karen could stretch her arms. 'These two posts are very heavy,' she said, 'but why is this, please?'

'To hold the roof.'

'But this they do not do?'

A cross timber ran above them, from one side wall to the other, tying those together. Above this cross timber, the rafters slanted upwards until they came together to form the crown of the roof. Tarred wooden pegs in those two middle uprights, a peg nearest the cross timber and another next the floor, could not be found in any of the other posts.

Prying on one of the pegs, it soon came out, and when the post was moved, Hilary realized they had found the entrance and together they opened it. Taking the torch out of the satchel, she checked to see that it was working, inadvertently shining it on the floor of the tunnel where a litter of broken rocks lay amid pools of water. A ladder led down. Ash wouldn't want her to go in there, not with Karen, but at least she could have a look.

Grantley's, on this Tuesday, the fourteenth, was all but ready for Founders' Day tomorrow, thought Ruth. Out on the Common, the wind wafted the canvas tents and marquees and stirred the school's banner with its coat of arms and ridiculous Latin motto, which translated into 'a clean heart and a cheerful spirit,' and God, the hypocrisy of it! One could have wished for knights in armour instead of laurel leaves in battleship grey and blue with the quartered shield bearing chevron ermine arms. Her grandfather had found it somewhere and had modified it, and tomorrow the boys would all be cheering it, after which would come the annual regimen, a tour of the buildings, meetings with the masters, quiet little consultations and then the luncheon at twelve sharp and laid on with style, she not having had to take even the simplest part in its planning. Useless, that was what she was and had become. A nothing, but forced to listen to the driest of speeches and to act out the lovingly attentive wife of the headmaster!

Cricket, rugger, soccer came in the afternoon, then tea at half past five and closing, and God, she couldn't go through with it, not anymore, not with herself not having spoken up and told Ash the truth about that wife of his.

'Ruth? Darling, may I come in?' asked Anthony, her back to him, she still gazing out through the leaded panes.

How defensive his voice was, how pitiful and pitying. 'You're in, so what's the difference?'

'Only that I asked.'

Why *did* he have to do it to her? she wondered. Feeling him near, she stiffened.

'Ruth, there's something I must tell you.'

'What have you done? Told them where that daughter of his now is? The last time she was moved, you told *me* she had been taken to Kent, Anthony. You didn't think that I might then meet that wife of his and that she would make me tell her.'

'And did you?' he softly asked.

'Damn you, yes! She . . . she forced me to. She had a knife and would have killed me had I not told her she would then never get her daughter back.'

A knife . . . 'Ruth, I . . . I didn't know you would meet her. How could I have? I thought you would like to know where the girl was and that if I told you, it would make you feel as though you'd been brought into things.'

'And now?' she asked.

Pearce wanted to reach out to her. He almost did, but knew she would only turn on him. 'Darling, Ash needs our help. There's still time to undo what's been done.'

'I don't believe you. I don't even want to hear it. I wish to hell I'd never married you.'

'Ruth, Dave knows who the sleeper is.'

'Is that why he came looking for that gun of yours you'd taken back from his room?'

'Darling . . .'

'You bastard! Get out of my room before I scream!'

Choking suddenly, she went all to pieces, and as she rushed past him, he tried to tell her that it hadn't been himself who had taken Ash's rotor and that the gun was still in his room and that Dave could have it if needed. 'I've told him where it is, Ruth. Dave knows who this sleeper is. It's a Brigadier Charles Edward Gordon of MI6. He found his wife staying the night with Gordon at a country house near here. Ash mustn't leave because of tomorrow, but he desperately needs someone to go to Cornwall and tell this girl he's got looking after his daughter who the sleeper is.'

'Who took the rotor from his car, Anthony?'

'It was Banfield. Thinking I was the culprit, Roger took it upon himself to warn Dave that the sleeper must be someone at the school and very close to him.'

'He chose an odd way to do it.'

'Not really, not knowing that the boys would find it soon enough and show Ash where it was among the osiers I'd been looking at far too many times. Now will you go? Banfield was the one to suggest it. Roger . . . Well, Roger felt it might help you to get over things.'

'And Ash?' asked Ruth, seeing Anthony's eyelids flicker and that cheek muscle of his twitch.

'There's a train at eleven that should get you to Saint Ives by mid- to late afternoon. I've drawn you a map of how to get to the cottage.'

How could he possibly have done that, having never been there? 'And Ash, Anthony? Surely, given such a serious matter, even Founders' Day can do without him, or is it that you know Colonel Hacker will be there at that cottage and that I will most certainly have to confront him with the truth as well?'

'Ruth, please just go and take care of it. When . . . when I was in that prisoner-of-war camp, the Germans did try to get me to inform on the others but I refused. I had to because . . . Well, because one of the men who was involved in an escape attempt was rather dear to me.'

'A hero, are you?' she asked, and turning from him, went downstairs and out along the cobbled path that led from building to building.

As he watched, she disappeared into Milton Hall, would now be walking down the corridor to the room in which Dave was teaching.

Five minutes later, Ash was at that car of his and handing Ruth his mortarboard and gown, for she had told him what she had done and about that wife of his, and had known that only he should bring the warning. Ash held her tightly, Ruth kissing him on both cheeks, then standing there looking after him as he drove off.

She had known this husband of hers hadn't wanted Ash to risk his life, but had known Ash would have to, that there could be no peace for him otherwise.

9

Beck couldn't believe his luck. Mary Anne Livingston's husband, Alfred, was nearly twice her age and dying of emphysema. At 0800 hours the nanny had come to take the children off her hands and the son to school, the day nurse soon afterwards.

It had been the husband who had suggested Helston for the repairs and had told them to make a day of it. Penzance and now Land's End and she driving.

'I've never been down here,' she said. 'It must seem odd, really, but my husband's business interests were always elsewhere. There seemed no need until . . . Well, until.'

They were driving across moorland that often rose to bald, grey granite outcrops on the heights, the sea always present, one huge and breathtaking expanse. Scattered, isolated farmsteads stood among green fields on distant slopes that were more gentle. Old mines seemed everywhere. Stone hedgerows, crooked and overgrown, the buckthorn dark and windblown, bordered most of the fields, while across the moorland, the gorse was golden, the heather pinkish, neither yet in full bloom, bracken clustering about the wettest areas.

Laying a brief hand on her forearm, Beck said, 'Try not to think of your troubles. Let's just take the day as it comes, Mrs. Livingston.'

'Oh how right you are, but I hate myself, don't you see? It's selfish of me to want to enjoy a day. It's been ages since I have.' And he was nice, this handsome Danish sea captain who had unexpectedly sailed into her life and would soon be gone. The fuel injector had been no problem. They would pick it up in Helston tomorrow morning. By noon at the latest, he would be out of her life, but would he think of her and of what she had been through these past twelve months? Would he know that all her friends had gradually found it increasingly uncomfortable to visit or write, as if the presence of death were too near and the fabric of what her life had once been in the London house had suddenly ceased?

Alfred had asked that she bring the children and come with him to Cornwall, to the house of his boyhood. At first the children had been very unhappy, but gradually they had adjusted. Children were like that, given half a chance.

'Why not stop the car, Mrs. Livingston?' said Beck. 'Please, it is good to feel the wind as you walk across the moor.'

Pulling the car off to the side of the road as best she could, she found her hands wouldn't leave the wheel, Beck reaching to switch off the ignition, the wind coming in through the side windows. 'Please,' he said. 'Just let yourself go for once.'

Her smile was brief and hesitant. 'That sounds like a proposition, Mr. Jensen, and that is definitely something I don't want to hear.'

'Then rest easy. I've spent lots of time out on the moors. They are almost a second home to me.'

'I thought you said you were a sea captain?'

'Of course, but even we have boyhoods to which we must return, just like your husband. Mine was spent on the Jardelunder.'

Wasn't that mostly of bogs and marshes? she wondered, but said, 'Look, I'm sorry. It's just that I . . . Well, I've not been alone with another man, and a stranger at that, in ages. People might think . . .'

Beck grinned. 'Let's let them think what they will.' Getting out, he went round to open the door for her. 'I do believe there will not be many, unless they are hiding in the rabbit burrows.'

She had to laugh, for he had swept off his hat and bowed, before swinging an arm round to indicate the emptiness. Some farms were off-limits, others didn't mind so long as care was taken, the stiles used when crossing over, and the cattle gates being always closed after use, but at once he was striding away from her, stooping here and there to call out the names of the various plants he recognized as old friends and stopping near a bog where sphagnum moss, cotton grass, bog asphodel and bilberry grew. There were two other motorcars on the road—tourists probably—they some distance from them. Taking off her hat, she turned to face the wind and the sea. 'Why have you really come to Cornwall?' she asked. 'I know you've said you're on holiday and all that, and that you've got to get the engine fixed, but is there some other reason?'

The car seemed so far away now, thought Mary Anne, and there might just as well have been no one else but themselves.

Beck motioned to her to follow, and when she hesitated, he started off, she soon catching up, and together they walked towards the rocky, broken crest of a tor. 'I once had a wife and two children,' he said. 'Because of things I will not discuss—losses, yes?—I began to drink. So . . .' He stopped and grinned at her. 'Now you know I was a drunkard and am trying my best to stay away from it. Three months, Mrs. Livingston, and not a drop but I still want it, I'm afraid.'

They began to walk again. 'And this wife of yours?' she asked. Had there been something dishonest in his eyes? she wondered.

'Doesn't want to see me, and I can't blame her,' he said.

'Don't your children miss you? I know mine would.'

Beck searched the terrain ahead of them for a hollow, some sheltered place, for he would have to kill her. 'Yes, of course they do. I've a friend in Saint Ives who might be able to help. He used to know my wife's father in the old days.'

'Then your journey has a purpose. I knew it must have. I could feel it.'

They reached the top of the tor where lichen encrusted the granite, she lifting that face of hers up to the sun and shutting her eyes, he to settle on some wind-bent elm alongside the nearest hedge.

'Let me drive you to Saint Ives,' she said. 'Why not see this friend who knew your father-in-law? I can pick you up tomorrow.'

Luck again, wondered Beck, or caution on her part? 'All right. Yes . . . yes, that would be perfect but let me out at Saint Just. I can then catch a bus to Saint Ives.'

What *was* there about him? wondered Mary Anne. 'We're almost halfway round the peninsula. It's just as easy for me to drive you. There's no sense in my doubling back, now is there?

Besides, it'll give us more time together and I want to see all of Land's End.'

The light had gone from his eyes, causing her to wonder what he was really up to.

'Zennor, then,' he said, 'but let me walk from there. It can't be any more than three or four miles by road.'

Everywhere the mine gave evidence of its past, thought Hilary. Sometimes there would be a heap of broken rock that had to be negotiated, it having fallen from the tunnel's roof between the sets of pillars, each with its cross-ceiling timber. Sometimes there would be only a few rocks, but here a ringbolt jammed so hard into the wall, the eye of it had been all but flattened, here a broken powder box covered with a hair of rusty filaments in a shallow pool through which a current slowly moved, here a broken barrow that had been shoved aside. And always now if one looked ahead, that intense feeling of being shut in and closed off from all else.

Karen, for obvious reasons, was far from happy and crowded closely, whispering, 'Let's go back. I *don't* like it here.'

'*Sh*, it's all right. We won't go much farther.' But why were they whispering? There couldn't be anyone else. The timbers across the entrance had been securely in place and the only way to have put them there was to have done it from the loft of the boat shed. They were not very far from the entrance, perhaps a hundred feet. When approached, light from the loft door would still be filtering in, offering its hope and release.

The tunnel wasn't absolutely straight. In some places a ragged wall jutted out. Protruding from a crevice, there was a rusty pick, its handle broken. An iron bar that had been used for scaling the walls and roof had been left as if the miner had but walked off the job, and when the slablike black slate and grey-green foliated schist, folded, smeared over and into each other, ceased at a mass of speckled grey granite, the whole of it was pitch-dark beyond the cone of light coming from her torch.

As if leaping out at one, veinlets of white quartz intruded the granite. Some were as nets, others fingers, others like lightning bolts, and when Hilary shone the light over them, there were isolated grains of pyrite, the brassy-coloured fool's gold, not yet the cassiterite, the adamantine-lustered granular masses, prisms and dipyramids of the oxide of tin, the 'black tin' that had been hunted for so diligently, but dear God, if one let it overcome one, it was a creepy place. Everything was wet and clammy. Water didn't just drip constantly from the roof, many of whose rocks looked anything but secure. Each source made its own noise, the water also seeping down the scaled, still-jagged walls, and the timbers, oozing into a yellowish-brown slime from which tiny stalactites hung, and always there was this musty, acrid, fetid smell.

Ragged, emptied slots and gashes, all of them questionable and some no more than the width of a man's shoulders, began when well into the granite. These openings, these stopes or working areas, cut up into the rocks on either side of the tunnel and into its roof, defying the beam of the light, it being swallowed up as in a ghostly haze. And always now there were the rust-encrusted 'steels,' the short, two-foot drill rods, each of about an inch and a quarter in diameter and taking three hours or more to drill a mere twenty inches, each bit lasting but twenty minutes. Sharpening had had to be done on the surface, in the smithy's shop, the rods heated, the bit hammered sharp, and then ground sharper.

'Karen, these openings are where the miners followed the tin-bearing veins. They had to drill the holes by hitting these rods with a heavy sledge. Sometimes the miner would have done it himself but far more often one of them would hold the steel while another hit it, and heaven help the hands of his partner if he missed. Once drilled to a depth of about twenty inches, they would load the holes with black powder and fuse, clear the area, and blast the ore out, after which they would come back to scale it down with pick, bar and shovel. Candles . . . they would have used candles for light. Only years later were they able to find carbide lamps that would last a whole core, a shift of eight hours. Six if in a very deep mine where the temperature would have been nearly a hundred degrees Fahrenheit.'

'Can't we go now?'

'In a moment,' said Hilary, noting how hollow was the sound of their voices.

Sometimes a bit of rough, heavily planked staging, still with its ladder roads, had been left to show where the miners had stood and worked or crouched and done the same, but distances were very hard to judge, and not always was there room to stand straight up, and what timbered support pillars there now were often appeared as if far too shaky to touch. One post had a split right down its centre; another was sagging; the top of another pushed out in a mass of splinters. Rock dust and grit were everywhere.

When some 150 feet into the mine, the adit came to a crosscut, timbered tunnels leading off to the right and left while it continued on ahead and at a slightly greater tilt so as to better carry the seepage out to the cliffs.

Hesitant now, Hilary knew she had no business bringing Karen into a place like this, none herself as well, but she couldn't have asked the child to wait at the entrance, and it was *exactly* as she had imagined. Absolutely dark when the light was switched off; silent as a tomb, except for the constant dripping and occasionally sudden, distant sounds of something sighing or popping—timbers, those? she wondered. And always now there was the thought that once beyond a certain point there could be no retreat because they had come too far. 'Karen, please don't be afraid. Please don't cry.'

Setting the torch down to give her a hug, she said, 'We'll go back now, shall we?'

A rock fell and they heard the sound of it somewhere. A rush of rubble followed but that, too, was distant. The main shaft, she knew, must still be almost two miles away so the sound couldn't possibly have come from there or from the pump shaft. When perhaps 200 feet from the entrance, she felt the floor of the adit must have risen yet again, giving still more slope to the drainage, but now they were truly in the mine and entirely alone and certainly there could be no escape, should the sleeper come after them.

Wetting a finger, she felt the soft, cool air coming in from the entrance to eventually rise up the shafts. It must have lessened the smell of the other, and as for Colonel Hacker and whomever he had with him, he would be up there on the surface, watching the cottage, not knowing where they really were. Not unless he had seen them go along the cliffs only to drop out of sight as they had gone down to the cove.

*   *   *

Rough moorland stretched away from the small stone cottage to touch the edge of the cliffs, noted Mary Anne Livingston. Between the cottage and the road where they had left the car, there was more of it, and then far more to where they were now standing. Having driven Mr. Jensen to Zennor, he must have seen someone, for he had told her in no uncertain terms to drive on and to hurry about it, and when they had stopped near the cottage to inquire, no one had been at home, but quite obviously he had known whom to expect. Refusing to leave and head for Saint Ives, he had taken her by the hand and had forced her to walk the mile and a half from the car up to these ruins, the wind making her eyes water, he probing about and knowing she would wait because she couldn't outrun him. But was he thinking she had asked far too many questions about him? He would need to have the car, would need to go back to the house and that sailboat of his, but did he feel the latter no longer possible?

Off to the west, a small brown sedan was parked on the crest of a low hill, facing their way. The late sunlight glinted from its roof, the car seeming to be watching them, the ruins perhaps two miles to the south-southeast of it, but distances were so very hard to gauge, the light, incredibly clear. No one seemed near the motorcar, nor indeed anywhere else, but then, and slowly too, the twice-daily omnibus to and from Land's End came towards the cottage and she thought to run down to it, thought to be quit of this place. Picking her way along the rutted road, past ferns and sedges, gorse and blackthorn, she started out, he saying, 'Don't!' That was all.

'Please let me go, Mr. Jensen. I meant you no harm, only kindness. My husband needs me as never before, and so do my children.'

When she came to the chimney stack, it was huge and towered over her, the thing of stone and nearly fifteen feet across and perhaps eighty or ninety feet high. Inside the ruins, she looked up at open portals and broken walls, the wind echoing as it gusted, he watching her now and not ten feet from her, but not beckoning, not anything like that.

The engine must once have rested on a raised bed of concrete and stone. Down the middle of this bed there was a water-filled slot. An oily iridescence covered the water. He made no sound, said nothing further, just looked at her as though she didn't exist, and when he went through a doorway diagonally across the ruins from her, he vanished from sight.

'Please don't do this to me,' she said.

A rock fell and sometime later she heard it clatter but then the sound of it ceased as if he had snatched it up.

The blue denim shirt and trousers were faded, the knees now blackened by peaty mud, as were his forearms.

Beck told her not to worry. 'It's the pump shaft they must have used to remove water from the mine. The sound of it would have been constant comfort to those working below unless, that is, it had suddenly stopped.'

Again a stone clattered into space and she listened as it fell. Perhaps five feet of rubble lay between her and that . . . that hole, she sickened now for he had taken her purse and keys to the motorcar from her, had taken her by the shoulders.

Deep in the mine, the sound of that terrified scream and the echoes it had brought were now but a memory. Having panicked, Hilary had dropped the torch, Karen shrieking in terror and flinging herself at her.

Now the light shone from beneath a pool and the child couldn't stop sobbing.

'Karen, *please*,' said Hilary. 'We have to go back and bring help.'

There could be no hope for whomever had fallen, and she knew this, for that scream had been suddenly cut off by a solid bump and a rush of rubble and timber. With Karen clinging to her, Hilary strained to recover the light, the water ice cold and deep.

'*Liebling*, listen to me. You must stand here and hold my clothes. Karen, I have to go down there and get that torch.'

Drunkenly the rescued light fled over the mined-out stope, illuminating long-left candle stubs on bits of ledges high above them, finally touching the lowest of the ladders Blind William must once have used to reach the floor of the cottage.

Shivering, she got dressed in a hurry. Having pushed herself and Karen to come this far, she knew they had taken one of the crosscuts, but that she had lost all sense of time and only by chance had found their way upslope and into the stope. Here the mined-out vein had narrowed and gone this way and that as it had intruded the granite above, the beam of the light finally being lost in the darkness up there.

Four ledges, thought Hilary, now drying the torch but still shivering. Four benches and four rough wooden ladders, then the floor of the cottage, and only a bit of this, a ragged opening that must lead up to the hearthstone, but she couldn't possibly do that with Karen. They were perhaps six hundred feet in from the entrance to the adit at the boat shed, and another two hundred or so to the east of it at a right angle. The first crosscut had ended in a winze, it rising steeply for about twelve feet, or two fathoms. Using the ropes and ladders that had still been in place—all no doubt left by fossickers and smugglers—they had then climbed from level to level until they had reached a point, she thought, perhaps some 120 feet below the cottage.

Giving Karen another hug, she brushed a hand fondly over the child's hair and dried the tears. Responsibility would be best. 'Here, you hold the light. I'll take you by the hand.'

In *Deutsch*, Karen blurted, 'Why did she fall?'

There was another rush of tears. 'I . . . I don't know,' said Hilary. 'Karen, I feel awful too.'

'Was it *Mutti*?'

'How could it have been? Your mother's . . . No, it couldn't have been her, but we have to hurry. Every minute counts, so please try to be brave.'

'I want my mother, Hilary.'

'Yes, I know how you must feel. It's all right. I understand.'

'She was good to me, Hilary. She is very beautiful.'

'Did she play cards with you the way I do?'

'*Opa* does. *Opa* lives in a great big house. It . . . it is big like Clarington, only better, I think.'

'Don't tell Dotty that, or Albert. They would both be upset.'

'Will they keep Meg for me?'

'Yes . . . Yes, of course they'll keep the pony for you.'

'We're never going to get out of here, Hilary.'

'Please don't say that. This tunnel will take us to a lower level.

Once there, we must retrace our steps until we reach the adit from the boat shed. Here, watch out! Be careful. It's steep.'

Lowering her down the slope, Hilary sat on the floor and stretched out her legs. Karen waited for her with the light. All round them there were loose rocks, the child flicking the beam over them until settling it on a lonely, dirty white candle stub that had stood fastened by its wax for years as if waiting for the miner to relight it.

Partly under the wax, there was a small tin box of matches, Hilary prying off the wax only to see on its lid the grim-faced, spike-helmeted countenance of Kaiser Wilhelm II, with huge muttonchops and handlebar moustache, the matches having been manufactured and sold in England by Bryant and May of London, but dear God, was that portrait some sort of sign? There were six of the matches left, and each was little more than two inches long and with a good half-inch head that was a dark cocoa brown. They couldn't be of any use, not now, not after such a long time, and certainly they had been left after 1859, maybe 1865 or 1870 and not that long before the mine had been closed for good.

Pocketing the box and the candle stub, she again took Karen by the hand. 'Feeling better now?' she asked.

'A little, yes.'

When they finally reached the adit, they turned off towards the right. 'Soon we'll be able to see the entrance,' said Hilary. 'As soon as we can, we'll go and get help.'

'My mother would have come after me, Hilary. She doesn't love my father anymore.'

'Yes, I know. It's not very nice when that happens, is it?'

'She loves Herr Beck. He makes her happy. For a long time before she met him she didn't smile the way she would when with him, but *Opa* still thinks there is something wrong with him and that if only she would let her heart listen to his advice, all would be perfect. More grandchildren for him, a brother and sister for me to help look after.'

'Karen, *sh*!'

The daylight had all but gone, but still there was enough to see that someone with a rucksack was standing in the entrance to the tunnel. Tugging at Karen, Hilary pulled her into darkness and whispered, 'Let me have the torch.' And then, 'Karen, give it to me, please!'

They had to find that winze again, had to reach that stope and climb those ladders, had to get to the cottage before he caught up with them.

'I've got a gun!' she yelled. 'I'll kill you if you come after us!'

But where was the gun, where the satchel? She must have left them in the stope when that scream had come and she had knelt to comfort Karen and the torch had fallen into that pool.

'Karen, listen to me. That wasn't your father. He would have called out to us.'

The MG's engine was overheating; the rad had sprung a leak. Two flat tyres had slowed Ashby down, then a tour bus that had broken its rear axle on the narrowest of roads, then a farm lorry pulling a wagon, and now this! He knew he was somewhere between Five Lanes and Bolventor, but still east of the Fowey and well out on Bodmin Moor. Letting the ghost of a smile come, as did the irony amid clouds of steam and fading light, he thought of Bill and the damage Kurt Meydel and Martin Lund had done to the car in that graveyard. He thought of Daisy, too, and of Hacker, then of Christina and Brigadier Charles Edward Gordon, and always of Hilary and Karen. Even though she hadn't liked or trusted the brigadier, Hilary would still think him MI6 and trust anyone he sent.

Alone in all that emptiness, with its crags and tors, its moors and bogs, Ashby could see no one else. Some three miles to the north-northwest were Brown Willy, Rough Tor and Hawks Tor, and to the southeast maybe five miles, Kilmar Tor. Cattle grazed, but they were distant, beyond them, two shire horses and a few ponies, the wind bringing the smell of moor grass, peat, farm animals and bog water.

'I have to,' he said aloud as he started out on foot. 'I haven't any other choice. If Christina links up with Brigadier Gordon, Karen will come to her and that will leave Hilary to deal with them all on her own.'

Right round Weymouth Bay, Christina could see that there were lights. They lit up the long row of Georgian houses that had been turned into hotels, shops and bed-and-breakfasts to line the promenade, lights glimmering also from the dark water across which came snatches of music from a pavilion. Werner would be waiting for her, as would Osier, Brigadier Charles Edward Gordon.

Taking the elevator at the Gloucester Hotel, she went up to the seventh floor. Burghardt had had the embassy forward a pouch for Werner, just as Osier had said the Kapitän would. All the cash he would need and a Danish pistol, the M1910/21 that must have been in the safe Werner had opened, and with six- and eight-shot magazines that held 9mm cartridges. A heavy gun, it was even longer than a Mauser and would not be easy for him to hide, a puzzle, Burghardt having chosen it.

All along the corridor there were darkly stained side and end tables, the heavy cream brocade of the walls setting off cut-glass vases of flowers and cabinets of china. Longing for a cigarette, excited and wanting to calm herself, she tried not to hurry. The Dolphin Suite the brigadier had taken must be at the far end of the corridor next to that staircase. Gilded wall brackets held gooseneck lamps with pleated linen shades that threw a dusky yellow light over oils in heavy frames: scenes of the seacoast and nearby farms, things painted years ago. One was of a farm girl feeding chickens, her straw-coloured hair exactly like Karen's.

Reaching the suite at last, wanting still to be certain she hadn't been followed, she glanced apprehensively down the length of the corridor to the lifts and beyond.

Mein Gott, it was quiet. Everyone else must still be at dinner.

There were no lights on in the suite and that was odd, so too, the lack of welcome. Softly closing the door, she took out the gun, thumbing its safety off and waiting. Had MI5 arrested Werner and the brigadier? Would they now arrest herself?

'My dear woman,' said Gordon, 'do come in. There are things we must discuss.'

Still she couldn't see him. Everything told her to leave while she could, that this wasn't right. 'Osier,' she said, he answering:

'I assure you we are quite alone. Keep that gun of Burghardt's in hand if it makes you feel more comfortable. I merely want to talk. If at the end of our discussion you wish to leave, then please rest assured we will give you every opportunity since we do not want a scene.'

'*We?*' she managed. Was he *not* Osier?

'A few associates, that is all,' he answered, and when still she hesitated, 'Have I not made myself clear?'

'Where is Werner?'

This was not going to please her. 'Not on that yacht.'

'You're lying!'

'My dear, I wish I was, but Joachim Burghardt has outfoxed us and sent a Dane who claims he knows absolutely nothing. Herr Beck is no doubt already in Cornwall while I, fool that I've been, thought him here and called off my people there. In short, Christina, it will be up to Herr Beck to wrest your daughter from MI5's Colonel Hacker.'

Turning, she put the lock on and then the bolt, would shut the two of them in, decided Christina, until she had got everything straight.

'Why not come into the other room,' he said. 'There's a lovely view overlooking the bay and the pier. You can even see the ferry terminus to Cherbourg, should you wish to change your mind and take it.'

He *wasn't* Osier. He *couldn't* be. 'Have you a cigarette?'

'Certainly, and I've a damned fine brandy if you wish, or champagne.'

'And?' she asked, seeing him more clearly now in silhouette against the windows.

'And an offer, my dear, that I do not think you can possibly refuse if ever you wish to take that daughter of yours home.'

For some time now Karen and the girl had made no sound. Beck hesitated, the darkness of the mine absolute. They had taken the first crosscut and had stumbled, fallen and hurried up this towards the left, the girl often dragging the child to her feet.

As he had shone his light at them, they had turned away, the girl pushing Karen in front of herself, the timbered crosscut continuing on and then up, they going from level to level until finally into what must once have been a stope, a working room and face from which the ore had been extracted, he having caught the girl by an ankle and dragged her back, only to have her suddenly kick him.

She had scrambled away, and after a minute or so he had heard her ragged breathing, then had heard her fall several times as though injured, only to get up and carry on.

Now it was as if they were no longer here.

Water lay beneath Hilary's broken left hand. Easing herself into a sitting position, she slid the hand below the surface, trying to still the pain.

Beck knew he was close to them, but was there something else? he wondered. This last bit of tunnel must have led them to a point below the cottage, and above them there must be a connection between the two; why else would she have come this way?

Pocketing the light, he removed the rucksack, took out his knife and began stealthily to pull himself up into the stope and make a circuit of its floor.

Hilary heard him but only once. Easing herself upright a little more, she tried to find a rock with which to defend herself, but all were far too big to lift with one hand.

High above, and unknown to them, Hacker waited just below the floor of the cottage. From Zennor, he had followed the one AST-X Bremen had sent and a woman, the car then having been moved well away from the cottage, the woman no longer present, she having been pushed, no doubt, into one of the shafts, the man then climbing down to a boat shed and going into the mine, himself deciding on a very different entrance.

Rung by rung, on the first of what could well be a sequence of ladders, he began to ease himself down below the cottage and when he came to a bench on which the miners had once stood and worked, felt his way across it through the rubble, was still well above the others.

To Beck, aprons of broken rock skirted the walls of the mined-out stope. Each time he stretched out a hand, he felt the rough surfaces, but not the clothing of that girl. Had she found the gun she had mentioned?

Hilary knew he was getting closer, but as yet, not from which direction. She and Karen could get up at the last moment and try to make it back through the maze of tunnels that had led them here. She wished she could have found the satchel with Alex's revolver. Their torch was now somewhere else.

When Karen stiffened in alarm, Hilary knew he had found them.

The child began to whimper, Beck saying in *Deutsch*, 'So, that is enough, I think, Fräulein. Now you will come with me.'

Rung by rung and still above them, Hacker stealthily lowered himself down the next ladder. The bench he came to was wider than the one he had left, though not by much, but it was clearer of rubble insofar as he could tell, though he must go easily. He had to get down there before they left the area, but when the Bowker-Brown girl tried to scramble away, the child shrieked and filled the workings with her cries, until the Boche cursed the child and shook her hard, then switched on a torch.

Blinking, shielding her eyes from the painful glare, the Bowker-Brown girl had trapped herself in a far corner. Warily she thought to go to the left and then to the right, never once taking her gaze from that Boche. Hurt badly, she had undone the buttons on her shirt, making a sling of it for her left hand.

Releasing the child, the Boche watched as Ashby's daughter scrambled across the floor towards the girl. Falling twice, getting more scrapes and bruises and torn clothes, she finally reached Bowker-Brown, who held her tightly and said, 'Don't try to talk. It's all right.'

Hilary could see that the satchel was lying on a large rock to her left and near the pool where they had first lost their torch, but that the man had not yet caught sight of it. She could also see beyond him and above, and well back of the ledges, a faint shaft of light that must be coming in from the cottage.

'Please, my name is Werner Beck and I mean you no harm. Let me just take Karen and go. She will be quite safe, I assure you, and happy once she has been returned to her mother and grandfather.'

He was lying, of course, thought Hilary. There was no way he could leave her here. 'Doesn't her father have a say in things?'

'Ach, that is simply not possible. It never was.'

Brushing Karen's tears away and chucking her under the chin, she managed a smile. 'Help me up then, Herr Beck. I seem to have hurt my hand rather badly.' Hacker . . . was Colonel Hacker now in the mine?

Beck didn't move, for somewhere above them in the darkness, a revolver had been cocked. The stope, he knew, would go up behind him to ledges, each about a fathom or two in height but often only a yard or so wide. At each of these ledges, the face of the mined-out stope would be quite irregular, the hanging wall steeply inclined above the working face and with, no doubt, loose rocks that had probably never been scaled away.

Sensing that Herr Beck must have finally seen that the hearth-stone had been moved, Hilary reached for Karen's hand, he switching off his light and throwing himself to one side as a stab of flame, a brief flash lit up the stope, the bullet ricocheting, she cringing to shield Karen and shrieking, 'Don't fire! Please don't!'

Hacker scrambled down the next ladder, Beck rolling over onto his back and firing at him, one rock falling and then another.

Dragging Karen after her, Hilary started towards the tunnel. She had to find it, had to get them out of here, but when the 'run' came, the sudden rockfall filled the stope with noise and dust. Choking, trying desperately to breathe, she huddled over Karen until the sound of the rocks had finally trailed away to a silence broken only by that of themselves.

As a torch came on, the beam of it searched for them through the dust until at last it had picked them out.

Beck coughed several times and then said, 'Karen, your mother is waiting. She's here in England and not far, and with a little luck, we will soon be together.'

Christina crossed her legs and, resting the hand with the pistol on her knees, sat looking at the brigadier. He was handsome, and he had been a gratifying lover.

'What you wish is just not possible,' she said. 'My father would never agree to come over.'

'And Werner Beck will never get that daughter of yours out of Cornwall.'

She tossed her head. 'You're forgetting that you told your people Werner was to have arrived here in Weymouth, Brigadier.'

'They'll have gone back to the mine. They'll be there now.'

'And Colonel Hacker?' she asked.

'Will not have their help. My dear, having wanted a tidy end to things, he has no one else, but you see, he really must be stopped and you must give the Yard's summation of the murder of Ashby's barmaid to your former husband as Burghardt intended.'

Hacker, if successful, thought Christina, would be arrested, Ash getting everything he wanted. 'Werner won't fail.'

Somehow he had to make her put that damned gun down.

'Perhaps you are right, but its possibility is something you had best consider. General von Hoffmann can tell us much, Christina. In exchange for what the Reich and its Oberkommando der Wehrmacht intend, including army and divisional strengths, weaponry, codes and Luftwaffe support, I will let you and your daughter leave England.'

'You forget, Brigadier, that I am the one holding the gun.' He had turned on the lamp behind himself, was sitting on the couch opposite her.

Even with the light shining in her eyes, felt Gordon, it was doubtful she would miss, but was she really intent? 'Your father need not give himself away, my dear. We could agree to meet in Switzerland.'

'Berlin would only learn of it. The SS and the Gestapo keep tabs on everyone, generals especially.'

Those shapely legs of hers uncrossed themselves, she getting to her feet, he wondering if she had ever killed before. 'My dear, did I not say all exits here were being watched?'

'Osier. And here I thought you were the one Burghardt had awakened and I willingly let you fuck me.'

Not taking her gaze from him, she reached for a pillow, he saying, 'Why not wait until we hear how things have gone in Cornwall?'

'That could take hours.'

The telephone rang, she flicking an uncertain glance towards it, the cushion now covering the muzzle of that gun.

'My dear, they will only rush the room if I do not answer.'

Motioning with the gun, she said, 'Tell them we are still negotiating and that we are both hungry. Some coffee, I think. A few rolls and some Brie perhaps. I haven't eaten in hours.'

When he had rung off, Gordon felt the cushion against his back and said, 'I wouldn't, if I were you.'

'Then go into the bedroom and I will tell you what you will and won't do.'

Had there ever been an Osier, he wondered, and if so, why then had Burghardt failed to inform her of how to make contact and then identify the sleeper as he should have?

Motioning with the pistol, she told him to draw the curtains and then to sit on the edge of the bed, facing her. Closing the door behind herself, she came to stand over him, her grip on the pistol tightening.

Still smiling, Christina shoved the cushion and the muzzle of the gun against him and said, 'Ash and that girl he's got looking after my daughter will soon be joining you.'

Another loose rock fell from the roof of the stope and then another, Hilary cringing, as did Karen. Hugging the child, she huddled against a wall, dust continuing to fill the air, and when a trail of loose rubble slid away, she was blinded by the light from his torch and brought her injured hand up to her lips in panic.

Beck knew she was terrified and not just of himself, for the roof could cave again at any moment. 'Please, you have no other choice but to follow me,' he said.

'But to . . . to go through the mine . . .' she stammered.

'Whoever fired at me will have others with him, and they will have heard the rockfall. I can't chance going back to the boat shed. We must find another way out.'

'Someone fell down one of the shafts,' said Hilary, Karen burying her face more deeply against her.

Lowering the light, Beck said, 'An accident. A woman I was with who had given me a lift and wanted to see the ruins.'

'You . . . you *pushed* her!' cried Hilary, turning suddenly from him, and when he made her turn back, she blurted, 'Karen needs me.'

'Then listen. Whoever fired that shot must be dead.' Touching the child's grimy cheeks, Beck ran a thumb over the tears. 'So,' he said, patting her, 'your mother wants you to come home, Karen, as does your grandfather.'

Karen tried to tell him that her *Opa* would punish him if he hurt Hilary, but the words just wouldn't come, Beck realizing that her loyalties to the *Vaterland* were gone. 'Make no mistake, *Liebling*. I will kill your friend unless you do exactly what I tell you.'

'Karen, he means it. We'd . . . we'd best go with him.'

When they left the stope, Hacker sat up and brushed the dust from himself. Bastard Kraut still had his gun, unlike himself. A pity, that, but it couldn't be helped. Finding his torch, he cupped a hand over it, letting a sliver of light protrude. By a stroke of luck, the next ladder down hadn't been knocked away. Straightening it, he started down only to cringe as another rockfall came, and then another and another, their sudden rush repeatedly filling the stope with sound until all had trickled away to silence. But the rockfalls would definitely have put Herr Beck off his guard, and he had the child to thank for the name of AST-X Bremen's agent. Worked properly, the child could prove useful again so long as the schoolmaster didn't decide to join them.

It was now nearly 11.00 pm on that Tuesday. Frantic, Ashby laid a hand on the Rover's bonnet. Unfortunately the engine must have cooled some time ago. From where he stood at the side of the road, he could see that there were no lights on in the cottage. No one else was about. From out on Bodmin Moor, and two miles to the east of Bolventor, he had managed a lift to Bodmin, and from there to here in another farm lorry. Having just told the farmer to bring the constables from Saint Ives, he had to wonder if they would get here in time, for he too had heard the rockfalls.

Having borrowed a torch, he hurried into the cottage to see at once that rock dust covered everything. 'Hilary,' he managed. 'Hilary, are you still alive?'

The hearthstone had been lifted with two ringbolts and set aside. Shining the light down into the dust, he found a rough-hewn ladder that had been made years ago from wreck. With difficulty, he climbed down into the dust-laden air and when he came to the ledge on which the ladder rested, began to search for another, but there wasn't one.

No sound came up to him other than that of loose rocks sliding against others as adjustments were made. Thinking to call out, he stopped himself, for there had been a different and much better sedan parked at the side of the road some distance from the cottage and much closer to Saint Ives. Had those who had come in it walked back to the cottage? Had it been Brigadier Charles Edward Gordon and Christina?

The road was dark and unfamiliar, Christina cursing it, for she was having to drive on what in the Reich would be the wrong side. Reading the map while at the wheel was all but impossible. She *had* to get to Bridgwater, had to get Ernst Reiss to transmit a message to Burghardt. She had killed the brigadier, and then the man who had pushed the food trolley into the suite, he having accompanied her to the car.

No one had followed her, or so it had seemed. No one had yet been warned to watch for her either, for she had even driven right past a police constable who had been standing under a street lamp in the market town of Yeovil and he hadn't tried to stop her. But why *did* there have to be so many little towns and villages, so many bends and turns, the signposts having to be scanned under flashlight?

To get to Werner and Karen had simply not been possible. Bridgwater was far enough and still another thirty or forty miles, but once there, and the message sent, Burghardt could then notify the embassy to send a diplomatic car that would take her to Croydon and a Lufthansa flight.

Finding a cigarette caused endless trouble, getting it lit even more, but was Werner with Karen now?

There it was again, thought Hilary, the sound like that of a badger worrying rocks. They had managed to reach the adit that would lead to the boat shed but had gone in the opposite direction, gone deeply into the mine, and only then taken another crosscut into yet another stope, Herr Beck forcing them farther and farther from the crosscut, the grey of the timbers and the granite giving anything but a sense of security. Never wide, now no more than shoulder width at most, the mined-out stope had pinched, jigged and climbed erratically, causing her at last to lose all sense of direction. Now repeated feelings of despair all but overwhelmed, worse still, claustrophobia and the thought of being left to never see the light of day again.

As a constant, forceful spray of water hit her, Beck switched on his light but allowed so little she couldn't avoid the sour and icy stream, it catching her fully in the face.

Beyond the spray, the stope began to pinch out, and when she could go no further, Hilary wedged herself aside so that he could see she wasn't lying.

Shining the light fully up into the remaining gap, Herr Beck silently cursed, and she could see that the lines of fear were there in his cheeks but made more gaunt by the water, for he must have known what it meant. Hadn't twenty been killed a half mile to the north of Saint Just, in the Wheal Owles, in 1893 when they had broken through into flooded old workings, their bodies never to have been recovered? Wouldn't the rock behind this spray be already weak enough and just ready to burst?

Seeing her looking at him, he immediately switched off the light and pushed himself away, Karen giving a yelp, for he had inadvertently stepped on her foot, Beck grabbing the child and covering her mouth before angrily shaking her.

'So, now we must wait,' he whispered. 'Don't try anything.'

Pulling Karen against herself, Hilary began to rub the child's back. They were both filthy, both soaked right through, exhausted, terrified, and always, as now, with thoughts of being left alone, of being snuffed out like a candle, unable to breathe because the panic was too great and there was no more oxygen.

Biting her lower lip to still the claustrophobia, she kept up the rubbing, but all too soon, though standing, Karen dropped off, her limpness frightening. 'She's asleep,' she whispered, he feeling for her own lips and pressing a hand against her mouth.

They must, thought Hilary, be more than a mile and a half from the cliffs. There had been crosscuts, but he had chosen not to go up any of them until that last one. There had been winzes, places in the roof of the crosscut where short bits of tunnel had given sloped access to other levels or had once been chutes down which to pass both waste rock and then the ore. Ladders, pipes, access ropes, mine cars and rails had often been left in places, reminders of them elsewhere, and broken timbers, lots and lots of those, rooms and rooms, chambers, areas where 'bad chokes' had clogged a tunnel, forcing the miners to cut a 'side-lye' to go round the run. Places, too, where the men, most of whom would probably have had *nothing* for breakfast but a fried slice of turnip, had once eaten their lunch of larded bread sprinkled with salt and a dusting of black pepper, seldom the much-revered pasties, unless filled with cooked, chopped turnip, leeks and potatoes. But how *could* she have even thought of Pindanter hiding himself away in this hell?

When she could no longer hear Beck's breathing, Hilary eased Karen to the floor and, wedging herself upwards, stepped over the child to blindly feel her way back.

Now it was as if the badger made no sound, but that constant forceful spray of water continued and soon the sludge of grit and finer dust that would normally have covered the rocks was absent and she could touch the spray.

Ahead, and unaware of her, Beck strained to listen beyond the sound of the water. He was now perhaps at a point halfway out of the stope. Whoever had been following them had sensed that they had heard him. Probing with his left foot, he felt the floor ahead, the heavy tread of the climbing boot telegraphing the differences not only between loose rubble and solid rock, but where the loose was packed hard enough to step.

By clinging to the walls of the stope, by wedging himself against them, he climbed above the floor and soon heard the Bowker-Brown girl pass stealthily below him.

The *Schlampe* would take the brunt of things.

Climbing down, leaving Karen behind, as she had done, he began silently to follow, but the girl made so little sound, he was forced repeatedly to pause.

When she reached the crosscut, he heard her give a sigh of relief, for now she knew she and the child could walk out to the adit and from there escape.

Unknown to him, Hacker lightly ran a hand up over her chest and when he caught the open collar of her shirt, let his fingers close about the base of her throat. Touching her lips, he dropped a hand to a breast and Beck heard the stifled rush of breath and knew the man had found her.

Again Beck began to climb, wedging himself against the walls. When a loose rock fell, and then another, he held on, clinging to a ledge until again his left boot had found purchase.

Knotting Hilary's hair into a fist, Hacker pulled her against himself and wrapped an arm about her waist. Like this, they waited in pitch-darkness until Karen, in a quavering voice, called out in *Deutsch*, 'Hilary . . . ? Hilary, where are you?'

A rock fell and they heard the child's stifled gasp, heard her say in *Deutsch*, 'I must not cry.'

At once Karen began to find her way back down the length of the stope. Now and then she stopped. Accidentally banging a knee, she gave another gasp, Hilary stiffening and trying to move, but Hacker wouldn't let go, and when Karen again cried out, 'Hilary, where are you?' the echoes trailed away to rebound from far-distant walls.

Beck eased himself down to the floor of the stope, silently cursing the child for having awakened, and when Karen bumped into him, he tried to clamp a hand over her mouth, but she bit him, and as she struggled to get free, her screams filled the air, he flinging her behind himself.

Hacker waited. Arching as he lifted her up, the Bowker-Brown girl tried to get free, and when the Kraut flicked on a torch, Hacker rushed her at him, Beck's gun going off, Hilary shrieking as she stumbled into the German, they rolling over, Beck firing again and again, the stench of cordite everywhere, she waiting now—waiting while he clung to her until, at last, he had let her get off him.

When he had recovered his light, Beck shone it fully at her. Blinded, she saw bright spots long after the beam had left. Getting uncertainly to her feet, she pulled Karen to her and waited.

Distant from her, Herr Beck was standing in the crosscut, looking down at something. '*Komm her,*' he said. 'There is blood.'

Stumbling, she went out to him only to be knocked to the floor, to lie stunned and bleeding at the mouth, Karen anxiously rushing to hug her and stammer, 'Hilary . . . Hilary, are you all right?'

Beck dragged the bitch up and hit her again. Pitching her from himself, he left her lying there, Karen crying out and being told to follow.

Though distant, the echoes making it all the harder to pin down exactly where their voices were coming from, Ashby knew he daren't call out. He was now well along what must be the adit from the boat shed, hadn't yet taken any of the crosscuts since reaching it, had steadily picked his way deeper and deeper into the mine using the light from his torch but sparingly.

Hacker must have entered the mine via the cottage—of this he was certain—and whomever the Germans had sent had come in through the boat shed, but was Hacker now dead?

Faintly, and by echo only, he heard Karen crying, 'Hilary . . . Hilary, where are you?' And then, '*Mutti,* I . . . I want *meine Mutti.*'

Some three miles to the southeast of Bridgwater, and hopelessly lost, Christina waited at the side of the road. Having found a call box, she had, she knew, done the unpardonable. Awakened in the dead of night, Ernst Reiss had told her to stay where she was and that he would come to her. 'There are marshes nearby. It is a very famous little piece of our history," he had said, perhaps for the benefit of his wife.

Moonlight bathed the farmlands across what must be a plain. From the hill she was on, she could see that hedgerows cut the land into pastoral quietude, and when an owl flew suddenly out of a nearby tree, she watched its dark shape. A dog barked somewhere, the sound of it carrying on a night like this. Clutching her shoulders, she knew the silk dress she wore was far from adequate. Longing for that shawl she'd been given, she realized that she had left it in the brigadier's suite. Burghardt would have to send help; that was all there was to it. And Ash, she wondered. Would Ash ever know that Colonel Buntington Hacker had killed his barmaid?

The stope was like a maze. Dusty grey timber posts, streaked with a slime of sulphurous mud, stood sentinel, some so overstressed they resounded when struck, others shaky and teetering at the slightest touch, others all but fallen over.

Beck swung the beam of the light round the workings, concluding that it was an area of bad ground but that it would have to do. Taking the child by the hand, he walked her well into it, advancing in among the pillars until he found what he was looking for. 'Sit,' he whispered in *Deutsch*. 'Stay here. This . . .' He tapped a pillar. 'Should hold.'

'Hilary won't come. She'll . . . she'll know she shouldn't.'

'Then you must make her come to you, because I must deal with the one who is following her.'

He went away and Karen watched as his light passed among the forest, its trunks grey and sometimes splintered, each throwing a shadow well ahead of him.

When the light went out, she realized Herr Beck would wait for Hilary to lead the man to him. Hesitating, for her knees were bleeding again, she knew it would hurt to crawl, but she *had* to find Hilary, *had* to tell her where Herr Beck was hiding.

---

* Sedgemoor, site of the defeat, in 1685, of the Duke of Monmouth

The post was strong, and when she stood up, she wrapped her arms about it. Blindly groping for the next, her hand finally touched it but . . .

Hilary heard the stifled cry as Karen stumbled and fell, but the child got up and carried on and when she heard her name being tremulously called, she answered, 'Darling, stay where you are. I'm coming.'

'No, you mustn't! Herr Beck, he is . . .' Karen shut her eyes and gagged. Choking, she tried to catch a breath, tried to swallow.

Hacker hit her on the back and let her suck in a breath.

Having heard her, Beck made a circuit of the stope by feeling from post to post, but when he came up behind where he thought Karen must be, there was no one. Using his light, he shone it ahead, and finding Hilary, grit-covered and staring myopically out of the darkness, he heard the man yank the child against himself and shout, 'All right, that's enough. I've got the child and I'll kill her if you don't give up.'

Letting the light find them, Beck soon saw that blood soaked the left leg of the Englishman's trousers and that he had been badly hit. '*Liebling*, you did not do as I told you.'

'Sod it, Beck,' said Hacker. 'You haven't a chance. I've men covering every exit.'

'*Ach*, I must now conclude that if there were any more than the two of us, I would be very surprised.'

The ginger hair was matted over the broad, pale brow, the moustache streaked with blood, as were the chin and cheeks and the backs of the hands.

Karen squirmed, the Englishman pulling the child tightly against himself, Beck taking aim anyway as a post sighed, but then a voice in *Deutsch* came calmly through, though distant from them still, '*Liebe Zeit, mein Herren*. All exits are now covered. Let my daughter go. Give us time to get out with the Fräulein Hilary and then the two of you can take care of each other.'

Vati . . . Was it really *Vati*? wondered Karen.

'Ash,' cried Hilary. 'Oh thank God, you've come,' but another post sighed, another toppled, Beck firing as he swung the light at Hacker, she shrieking now and running, knocking into another post and another, they letting the roof shed more and more loose rocks, which—when she stopped to desperately try to get her bearings—were heard to trickle down among those posts that still held.

'DON'T ANYONE MOVE!' cried Ashby in English. Beck leapt. Hacker snatched Karen back and kicked out hard only to have his wounded leg collapse and Karen dart away, the beam of the one light catching her and then that of the other.

'KAREN, OVER HERE!' cried Hilary. 'HURRY!'

'KAREN, GO TO HILARY!' cried Ashby as the roof began to fall.

A pillar snapped, others breaking in rapid sequence, Beck firing repeatedly at Hacker, who tried to get up and escape as a wall of dust rushed ahead into the crosscut, and tons and tons of rock fell.

Choking, gasping, Hilary crouched over Karen, sheltering the child against herself and trying to cover her own head as rubble raced to lap against them until a trickle of rock fell, and then others but in sequence, each threatening another run, the timber posts tightening so much she could hear the wood creaking and popping as the stress was taken up.

Cautiously getting to her feet, she called out in English, 'Ash, can you hear me?' And when no answer came, cried, 'Ash, Karen's safe with me.'

It did no good, for when Beck found them, he shone his light into her eyes and nudged her chin with the still-warm muzzle of his pistol. 'Come,' he said in *Deutsch*, 'the two of you, and not another false move, Karen, or I will kill her.'

His glasses gone, his light also, and with rock dust still smarting his eyes, Ashby could but follow, stopping when they stopped, blindly groping forwards when they continued, not calling out, only letting them believe he had died in the cave-in. He should, he knew, have let Christina have Karen, but constables or no constables from Saint Ives, was she with Brigadier Gordon and now outside, waiting for Beck to bring Karen to them? If so, then neither Hilary nor himself stood a chance.

Longing for yet another cigarette, Christina knew she had none. As she waited in the car in darkness at the side of the road, she fingered the pistol, had taken it out and inserted the spare clip.

Uneasy about waiting like this, she wondered what was taking the butcher so long.

Rolling down her side window, she listened to the night. It was now almost 0400 hours. The dawn would come at 0515 or thereabouts, but had Reiss not thought of this, and what, please, was she to do if he didn't come?

Soon, however, a bicycle approached, its lamp flickering through the darkness, and she heard the patient squeaking of its sprocket. He hadn't thought to bring a farm lorry as she had felt he would. Perhaps that wife of his would have asked far too many questions, but a bicycle . . . Where did that leave her?

Leaning the delivery bike against the car, Reiss softly said, 'So, *mein liebes Fräu*, what is the meaning of this?'

'You've got to help me.'

He didn't argue. Instead, he simply asked, 'What have you done?' and when she told him, and said that she needed to contact AST-X Bremen, he immediately said, 'Wait, then, while I tuck the bicycle out of the way.'

They would drive to wherever he kept the wireless, thought Christina. She would stand over him until he had sent Burghardt her message and then they would have to wait for a reply, and he would have to leave her with the wireless, put the car out of sight, and keep it all from his wife.

'*Liebes Fräu* . . .'

The startled gasp she gave, felt Reiss, was indication enough that she feared not just the British but himself. 'Frau whatever-your-name-is, my son and his wife and children live on the farm I lease. The wireless is in the smokehouse, it being the one place no one other than myself goes. Unfortunately AST-X Bremen cannot be contacted now, for the British have listening sets nearby and are trying their best to pin down that set of mine, but I will do so tonight and we will have the answer you need, I assure you.'

Not until tonight . . . A smokehouse . . . Weren't such far too hot for a wireless, and why would nighttime be any safer? Wouldn't the British hunt for that set of his at night as well?

'Please, *meine gute Frau*, your unexpectedly coming to the shop, as you did on the third of June, alerted the British. Twice now I have seen people watching it. Once I was even forced to serve a customer who, like yourself, was not really a customer.'

'And now?' she said.

'For now you must drive back along this road until we come to the bridge. There's a lane that runs alongside the river and leads to a disused barn where you can leave the car and wait until I come back tonight.'

The bridge wasn't far, the lane axle-deep in mud and under overhanging branches, and when they reached the barn, the headlamps shining on it, he said, 'I will open the doors. As soon as you are in, switch off the headlamps and engine. The fewer who know we are here, the better.'

'Just remember that I've killed and will do so again if necessary.'

Ach, how good of her. 'Of course.'

This beautiful creature, who had asked of an Osier he knew nothing of, did as instructed, he closing the doors only to find her switching the engine and headlamps back on.

Returning to that open side window of hers, he said, 'Osier has contacted me twice since we first met. Unfortunately I don't know where he stays and have only a drop box for him, so he, too, will have to wait, but I can see that a message is left for him as well. Anything you like, but keep it brief, as it will be in pencil on a scrap of paper since the two of us have yet to work out a code.'

What was it that Burghardt had said of this butcher? wondered Christina. That Herr Reiss would always put step after step between himself and those who funnelled messages to him for transmission and return. 'Then give me that flashlight of yours,' she said.

'Certainly.'

As he handed it over, he watched as she reached for the ignition key and had to juggle the pistol as well. 'Don't try anything,' she said. 'Keep away from the car.'

'Of course.'

Getting out of the car, Christina backed him up against the wall in front of it, and taking aim, waited as he stammered objections before falling to his knees, having pissed himself at the thought of dying like this.

Closing the gap between them, she said, 'Now do you understand how it is with me?'

Tugging at a pocket handkerchief, he dragged it out to mop

his face. Mouldy straw littered the floor round and beneath his knees. Pigs had once been kept here and the stench of them had remained to mingle with that of his urine.

Yanking at her ankles, she falling back, he scrambled on top of her, the gun still in her hand but now also in his own, a finger jammed behind the trigger so that she couldn't fire.

Angrily Christina spat at him and tried to get free, but he was too heavy, too strong, and when he pressed a forearm against her throat, it was as if she couldn't breathe.

Passing out, she lay limply under him, he saying softly, 'Well, Frau whoever-you-are, what shall we do with you seeing as AST-X Bremen has ordered me to do everything possible to protect the wireless?'

Unconscious, she was even more beautiful, and certainly she would be a glorious fuck, right from the *Vaterland*, but he had no time for that. Finding the spring-assisted knife he had given her in her handbag, he again straddled her to gently slap her cheeks, she awakening to distantly blurt, 'Ash . . . ?'

The woman's body hung upside down, impaled on a splintered timber that had jammed itself into the pump shaft. Sickened— horrified by the sight—Hilary grabbed Karen and held her. The dress had been torn right off the woman, her skin a ghostly pallor where not marred by mud, abrasions and massive bruises, the eyes wide and staring, the mouth open in the scream that had been silenced. She wasn't young, wasn't old. Having hit the timbers and the walls of the shaft so many times, her legs and arms were broken and twisted at odd angles.

Karen was sobbing, and Hilary wanted to comfort her but couldn't.

Lowering the beam of the light, Beck let it play over the putrid flotsam of bloated small animals and debris that bobbed up and down among the broken timbers with each oscillation of the sea. To their right and left, Hilary could see that openings gave access to the shaft but as yet there had been no sign of Ash and he must have died in the cave-in. Voices did come, however. Shouts, but these were far distant from them.

'They believe we all must have been killed,' said Beck. Coiling the rope that now tightly bound Hilary's wrists, he tugged at it, nearly pulling her off her feet, and taking Karen by the hand, started out, the beam of his light passing quickly over the walls to give a last glimpse of the body.

'Who was she?' blurted Hilary.

He didn't answer, for voices came again—Ash must have earlier got a message to the police. They were calling down the main shaft, but when Beck and Karen and herself finally reached it and had turned into that haulageway, the sounds had ceased. Yanking on the rope, he reminded her to hurry. Time, distance and orientation soon became entirely lost as they picked their way through the workings, always striking farther and farther from the main shaft and climbing from level to half-level to level. Exhausted, wanting desperately to stop, Hilary knew they must be closer to the surface, but were they really? Karen hadn't said a thing since they had left Colonel Hacker and her father. Doing exactly as Herr Beck told her, poor, frightened Karen plodded stolidly ahead, dutifully waiting when he paused to consult the plans of the workings. Always he appeared to be searching for something, the broken, sagging timbers failing to dissuade him.

Then there it was, and Hilary felt her heart sink, for a ragged, gaping hole at shoulder height lay to one side of the tunnel, having been intersected years and years ago. No more than two feet in diameter, it appeared dark and uninviting.

'Ancient workings,' he said, and folding the plans, tucked them away before gathering some pieces of the granite for them to stand on. All too soon he had climbed up into that hole, he and his light vanishing, the rope that bound her to him tightening.

But then the rope slackened, and he came back.

'There *aren't* any ancient underground workings,' seethed Hilary. 'There *can't* be. The Celts and others right up until the Middle Ages, and even now, concentrated the tin on the surface by streaming, by placer mining.'

He paid no attention. Forcing Karen into the hole, he told her to crawl up it. 'There is a cave, *Liebling*. When you get there, don't be afraid of anything you might feel. Just lie down and wait.'

If still alive, Ash would never find them, thought Hilary, but said, 'Her knees are hurting her. Can't you at least wrap them in something?'

Beck threw her a silencing glance and told Karen to go. 'For the *Vaterland, ja*? And when the Führer pins a medal to your tunic, your mother and grandfather will be proud of you, yourself as well.'

In despair, Hilary watched the child disappear. Beck would kill her now, and with one broken hand and both wrists tied like this, was there nothing she could do?

But he said, 'Now yourself, Fräulein.'

'Then untie my hands.'

He shook his head. 'Use your elbows. The tunnel angles. It goes along, then up, then along and finally up.'

Still she hesitated, was looking into the darkness behind him, Beck wondering if she had seen Ashby, but that couldn't be, and when he smiled at the ruse, she turned and did as told. Even so, he unwound the rope from his left hand and went back along the crosscut some distance. Listening closely, he waited. Surely Ashby would have tried something by now, even if badly injured?

In silence, Hilary waited with Karen, for the cave was absolutely dark. Not a glimmer of daylight came through from above, but when the German had rejoined them, light from his torch revealed charred granite walls where fire had been used to mine the rock. Wicker panniers, much broken and decayed, had spilled their lumps of ore. Iron Age adzes, though badly rusted, had short handles of hardwood so smooth from use, Hilary noted they were as if polished. Bunches of eight to ten straight, thin lengths of wood were tied together with strips of now-curled, much-decayed leather. The sticks, having been dipped in pine resin or animal fat, were the torches that had been used. Terra-cotta vessels, also broken, would have, she thought, carried the water these Celtic miners had once dashed on the fire-heated rock to shatter it. Sharp-edged spalls of granite littered the floor. Though far smaller, and of an indeterminate depth below surface, the cavern made her think of the salt mines at Hallstatt, in the mountains of Upper Austria, though there the miners hadn't had to use fire except to get at the salt. Terrified, yet amazed by what they had accidentally stumbled upon, she knew that there had to be a date for this. The mines at Hallstatt had begun about 1,000 years before Christ, the most recent of them from 700 to 500 BC, though all three of those mines had tragically ended soon after this last due to a terrible avalanche that had not only buried them and everything else, but had filled in some of the shafts and underground workings with trees and glacial rubble. But here the date must be the latter: from 700 to 500 BC perhaps. Joint cracks and the horizontal sheeting planes in the granite, those same elements that had led naturally to the tors and crags so common in Cornwall, had been used to good effect.

As Herr Beck continued to search the roof for a way out, Hilary continued looking at what they had found, for stone hammers showed where samples of the ore had been pulverized, the rudimentary assays done by washing the dust in shallow, reddish pottery bowls whose triangular designs were as dark as the charcoal. If only she could pick up a hammer . . .

Another iron adze lay next to a flint chopper, the beam of the light passing quickly over them, and always there was this damp smell, as if of a burrow, and always now the roof above them became lower and lower as they moved towards the far wall.

Crouching, she felt the floor and, quickly picking something up, surreptitiously slid it away in a pocket. A rubbish of bones lay about, some charred. Insofar as she could tell, they weren't human, but of an exit there seemed no sign. Again and again Herr Beck shone the light at the ceiling, but at each blackened fissure where the smoke from the fires must eventually have issued, there was only hard-packed, angular broken granite, a rubble that had been jammed into them.

It was something he hadn't calculated on, and obviously he hadn't thought of Hallstatt and what had put an end to it.

Disheartened by the lack of an exit, Hilary told him, 'Those fissures must have been filled in long ago either by nature or to hide the tin-bearing veins.'

'Then we must find the one that is easiest for us to clear,' said Beck, but since it was almost 0600 hours, they had plenty of time, for he and Karen couldn't have left in daylight anyway. The girl would be useful in keeping Karen quiet, but once night came, he would have to kill her and then try for Bridgwater, and once there, get Ernst Reiss, of Davidson's Pork, Beef and Poultry, to help Karen and himself.

Reaching the shop at last, Reiss put the bicycle on its kickstand and went to unlock the door. It was still far too early to open up, and he didn't want any undue attention. Leaving the CLOSED sign in the window, he went into the back and put the kettle on. Laura, he knew, would be wondering where he had gone and why anyone should have telephoned like that, forcing him to go out in the small hours of the night, but he had often gone to the farm and come back before dawn, so she would not worry about it too much. And as for MI5's having watched the shop, as he had told Frau Ashby, he hadn't seen anyone since her one and only visit.

But her handbag had held some interesting things. Photos of a child, her own no doubt, a membership card in the Frauen-schaft, implying *Kinder, Kirche und Küche*—children, church and kitchen—an old saying adopted by the Nazis who believed firmly that a woman's place was in the home, yet someone had given her New Scotland Yard's report of the murder of Daisy Belamy in the ruins of that chantry near Kilve, a murder everyone hereabouts knew of from gossip and the newspapers or radio. Apparently a Colonel Hacker of MI5 was the prime suspect and must have killed the woman in a moment of unbridled zeal, for Hacker's job was to apprehend people like himself.

There were one- and five-pound notes, perhaps 1,000 pounds in all, and nice to have. The perfume, lipstick, nail file, compact and all other personal effects he would have to dispose of. Since the gas ring was already burning, he held the woman's papers and passports to it and then, when those had crumbled to dust, the Yard's summation on the murder of this barmaid the woman's schoolteacher husband had been seeing.

After having said the name of the husband, she had known what he was going to do to her and had said in *Deutsch*, 'Please don't. I can and will make it worth your while.'

Turning over onto her stomach, lying there in the straw, she had even hiked that dress of hers up above her ass and had spread her legs, had waited, he letting her squirm until he had broken her neck. With no ID, and left just as that barmaid of the hus-band's had been left, she and the car would eventually be found, but would it matter to the schoolmaster?

As their voices became louder, Ashby realized that he must have climbed to a level nearer to them, but in pitch-darkness, had he any hope of saving Hilary and getting her and Karen safely away?

Feeling forwards, he came at last to where their voices were, only to realize they must be above him. Beck knew English but, like many Germans, probably little if any French. Karen, however, had once spoken a little, but of recent years none at all that he knew of, yet could he chance it so as to alert Hilary to its use? '*Chérie, je t'aime, toujours je t'aime,*' he called out.

'*Vati? Bist du es wirklich?*' she cried. Papa? Is it really you?

In a burst of rapid French, Hilary said, 'Ash, *nous sommes dans une caverne que les Celtes anciens exploitaient pour l'étain. Il a son pistolet et son canif, mais je pense que celui-là est vide.*'

'That's enough!' shrieked Beck in *Deutsch.* 'Come up here at once.'

An ancient cavern worked for tin, thought Ashby. A pistol that she thought was empty, a knife . . .

Yanking on the rope, Beck spilled her onto her back, she yelling, '*Je lui suis attachée par une corde.*'

'*Verdammter Engländerin,*' yelled Beck, yanking on the cord and putting a boot down hard on her chest.

'Don't! Please don't!' shrieked Karen, running at him only to be swatted out of the way, but as the ground rumbled deep below them, each paused in doubt and fear, then glanced uncertainly at the others.

Torchlight soon shone down through the tunnel, Ashby having also felt the ground shifting. Setting the drill steel aside, he quickly wormed his way into the tunnel and was soon with them. Beck, Hilary and Karen were at the far end of the cave, the light and pistol pointing at him, the ceiling not far above them.

'There's no time to lose,' said Ashby. 'You'll never manage it, *mein Lieber.* Police constables are watching every possible exit.'

'But not above us,' retorted Beck. 'By my reckoning we must be a good fifteen hundred metres to the south of the engine house and much lower on the slopes of that hill. There'll be bracken and a litter of loose rocks hiding the entrance while mounds of waste rock lie between us and the engine house.'

'Then let's hope none of that waste has been piled above,' said Ashby, wondering how much time they actually had and cursing the loss of his specs, for he couldn't see them clearly.

'Start emptying this fissure above me,' said Beck, and pulling on the rope that bound him to Hilary, made her get to her feet and stand much closer to himself.

'Karen, come here,' said Ashby, hugging her tightly and kissing her on both cheeks before saying *en français*, '*Souhaite-moi bonne chance, ma petite.*' Wish me luck.

'No more French,' said Beck. 'Just move the rocks.'

Hilary wouldn't know that she was just a blur to him, thought Ashby. Karen, however, would. '*Liebling*,' he said, 'are the rocks up there tightly jammed together? If so, we are going to need a pry bar.'

Beck shone the light up above them, Ashby reaching to feel how tightly packed the rocks were. 'I left a drill steel below us,' he said.

'Get it,' replied Beck.

Would there be enough time? 'I'll need the light.'

Again those sounds came up to them, a grinding, a popping, a distant screeching and sighing of what must be wood on wood . . . 'I've matches and a candle stub,' said Hilary, 'but am not sure the matches will be of any use. The tin box is in the right pocket of my trousers, the candle also.' Were they all to die in an instant run to grass*, a cave-in that reached right to the surface?

Ash came near, she immediately realizing that he couldn't see a blessed thing clearly. Catching him by the hand, she let him feel the rope that bound her wrists, then guided his hand to that pocket. 'Now hold me,' she said. 'Let me feel you're really with us.'

And raising her arms, let him slip his head between them, her cheek now pressed to his, he firmly pulling her against himself, the ground below them stirring.

Parting, she looked steadily at him before whispering, '*Tu vas à gauche, je vais à droite.*'

'What was that you said?' demanded Beck.

'Only that . . .'

Deep within the mine something more gave way, Beck telling them to hurry. As timber after timber failed, the ground underfoot began to stir, and all at once the fissure above them emptied

---

* A cave-in that reached right to the surface

to reveal the light of day perhaps a good twenty to thirty feet away, but with ledges here and there that the jointing and the sheeting had caused.

Grabbing Karen, Ashby boosted her up and told her to climb out and run as fast as she could away from them. 'Don't look back. Just run, my darling. Try to tell anyone you meet that there's going to be a cave-in.'

Again and again the sounds of yielding timbers came up to them from far below as Beck lifted his gun and shone the light fully at Hilary, she darting to the right and yanking on the rope as Ashby darted to the left, the gun going off, the torch falling. Grabbing something—anything—Ashby brought it down hard, tearing Beck's left cheek open, Hilary flipping the rope over the German and yanking on it.

Falling back, blinded by blood, Beck shrieked at them, Ashby silencing him with a rock.

'Now you first,' he said, cutting the rope, 'and then myself, but do you always buy up old mines?'

'Never again.'

They climbed and ran. They had to. Hand in hand, Karen saw them getting closer and closer to herself, the land behind them suddenly falling in with a terrible roar as clouds of dust rose up.

Wetherby Cottage was perfect for writing, thought Hilary. It was now late in November and, having a new group of students to teach, Ash was as happy and busy as ever, Karen happy, too, and off at a school of her own nearby. The mine had been sealed, for Herr Beck had also died in the cave-in that had destroyed forever all evidence of that early mining. All, that is, but the bronze fibula, the cloak pin she had found on the floor of that cave.

Green with verdigris, its design was of a racing stallion whose back and hindquarters gracefully curved round and along to the hinge upon which the pin could open and close.

Holding it, feeling it, living that far deeper past yet trying hard not to, Hilary looked out of the bay window of her study. Even though overgrown and still needing heaps of attention, the garden was lovely.

Mrs. Mary Anne Livingston's body had been recovered, and

sad though it had been, the funeral attended. Ash's wife had been killed by someone as yet unknown, her body sent home to her father, and though Karen and he would always think of her, and he of Daisy Belamy, the past did seem over, except in the novel that had yet to get anywhere. 'I've too much of the truth,' she said softly to herself. 'What I now know only intrudes.'

Although the threat of war was ever close, MI6 and MI5 had gone their ways, the latter focusing far harder here at home on the German threat, though she would never be a part of either, for Ash had given Karen and herself something to think about, and in another few months her days and nights would be filled.

'It's twins,' she said to herself. 'I'm sure it is, and so is Karen.'

Taking up the fibula again, she shut her eyes as she ran a thumb over it. Cornwall was always casting up its history, and she had to wonder if in that far-distant past of Celts and quoits and standing stones, a miner hadn't come all the way from Hallstatt after the salt mines there had been buried. Viewed with suspicion, he would have had to go before each of the kings of Dumnonia. Which of them had he convinced that the tin might also be taken right from the granite? Had he proved it to a council of tribal elders, the chief Druid looking suspiciously on and scheming how best to make use of the knowledge?

When Ashby found her, she was as though a thousand miles away and he knew it would be best to leave her at it.

'Let's give our Pin a darned good walk,' he said to Karen, she to hug the golden retriever as she always did when just home from school, but when they passed the MG, she told the dog to jump in.

'Daddy, I'll drive,' she said, and though it was now quite dark and she had driven at night only once before, he handed her the keys, but said, 'Just down the lane. When we get to the bridge, we'll park and take a walk by the pub, and from the door you can say hi to Mr. Banfield and old George. They'd both like that.'

On 9–10 November, the world had awakened to *Kristallnacht*, and on 24 November, Poland had begun to mobilize. Ashby knew that war would soon happen and that he should take Hilary and Karen to the States, but with the baby coming and Karen nicely settled, he also knew that none of them would want to leave. Besides, along with the school, there were the boys, and they would need him more than ever.

About the Author

J. Robert Janes is a mystery author best known for writing histo-rical thrillers. Born in Toronto, he holds degrees in mining and geology, and worked as an engineer, university professor, and textbook author. In 1992, Janes published *Mayhem*, the first in the long-running St-Cyr and Kohler series—police procedurals set in Nazi-occupied France. The sixteenth in the series, *Clandestine*, was published in 2015.

EBOOKS BY J. ROBERT JANES

FROM MYSTERIOUSPRESS.COM
AND OPEN ROAD MEDIA

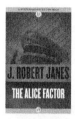

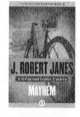
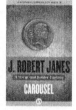
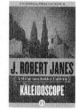

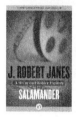

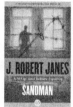
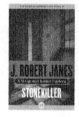
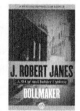

These and more available wherever ebooks are sold

MYSTERIOUSPRESS.COM

OPEN ROAD

INTEGRATED MEDIA

MYSTERIOUSPRESS.COM

Otto Penzler, owner of the Mysterious Bookshop in Manhattan, founded the Mysterious Press in 1975. Penzler quickly became known for his outstanding selection of mystery, crime, and suspense books, both from his imprint and in his store. The imprint was devoted to printing the best books in these genres, using fine paper and top dust-jacket artists, as well as offering many limited, signed editions.

Now the Mysterious Press has gone digital, publishing ebooks through **MysteriousPress.com**.

MysteriousPress.com offers readers essential noir and suspense fiction, hard-boiled crime novels, and the latest thrillers from both debut authors and mystery masters. Discover classics and new voices, all from one legendary source.

FIND OUT MORE AT
WWW.MYSTERIOUSPRESS.COM

FOLLOW US:
@emysteries and Facebook.com/MysteriousPressCom

MysteriousPress.com is one of a select group of publishing partners of Open Road Integrated Media, Inc.

THE MYSTERIOUS BOOKSHOP, founded in 1979, is located in Manhattan's Tribeca neighborhood. It is the oldest and largest mystery-specialty bookstore in America.

The shop stocks the finest selection of new mystery hardcovers, paperbacks, and periodicals. It also features a superb collection of signed modern first editions, rare and collectable works, and Sherlock Holmes titles. The bookshop issues a free monthly newsletter highlighting its book clubs, new releases, events, and recently acquired books.

58 Warren Street
info@mysteriousbookshop.com
(212) 587-1011
Monday through Saturday
11:00 a.m. to 7:00 p.m.

FIND OUT MORE AT:

www.mysteriousbookshop.com

FOLLOW US:

@TheMysterious and Facebook.com/MysteriousBookshop

OPEN ROAD
INTEGRATED MEDIA

Open Road Integrated Media is a digital publisher and multimedia content company. Open Road creates connections between authors and their audiences by marketing its ebooks through a new proprietary online platform, which uses premium video content and social media.

Videos, Archival Documents, and New Releases

Sign up for the Open Road Media newsletter and get news delivered straight to your inbox.

Sign up now at
www.openroadmedia.com/newsletters

DATE DUE

MAR 1 8 2016	
APR - 2 2016	
	PRINTED IN U.S.A.

CPSIA information can be obtained at www.ICGtesting.com
Printed in the USA
BVOW08s0356171115

426807BV00002B/2/P

9 781504 022187